Seekers of the Sacred Flame

"You know I mean to fly with you, Mr. Shea—"

"Woody, Miss Willard. I thought your father was sending you back."

"*Emma*," she went on smoothly. "I've convinced him otherwise—Woody. I'm an expert, you know, in ancient and obscure languages. And I've always been fascinated with flight."

"You're a remarkable person, Emma. I'll be delighted to have you aboard." He found himself lost in her eyes.

"There are mysteries all about us," she said, "that beg to be revealed. That is what brought me here."

"Yes," he agreed. He would have agreed with practically anything she said. He found himself reaching for her, but she had turned, pointing across the field.

"Look there!"

He squinted into the sundazzle and saw a half dozen black men in loose white robes coming out of the brush, moving swiftly and smoothly toward the biplane. Their iron-tipped spears flicked the light. . . .

JOURNEY
TO THE
FLAME

Richard Monaco

BANTAM BOOKS
TORONTO · NEW YORK · LONDON · SYDNEY · AUCKLAND

JOURNEY TO THE FLAME
A Bantam Spectra Book / December 1985

ISBN 0-553-25373-5

Published simultaneously in the United States and Canada

Bantam Books are published by Bantam Books, Inc. Its trade-
mark, consisting of the words "Bantam Books" and the por-
trayal of a rooster, is Registered in U.S. Patent and Trademark
Office and in other countries. Marca Registrada. Bantam
Books, Inc., 666 Fifth Avenue, New York, New York 10103.

PRINTED IN THE UNITED STATES OF AMERICA

O   0 9 8 7 6 5 4 3 2 1

To the memory of H. Rider Haggard and with respects to his present incarnation, if applicable. Too bad there exists no transmigratory copyright law, as yet.

To Darsi-who-must-be-obeyed

Thanks to Lou for his patience
Thanks to Adele in general
Thanks to Robin Mckinley
Special thanks to Charlene for the title of this book

JOURNEY
TO THE
FLAME

Richard Monaco

I

Beyond the softly bluishgreen lawn the morning sun was just fanning through the tops of the massive trees that bordered the grounds. The air was wet and cool and still.

Bright spring flowers, gold and blue, edged the patio where two Englishmen sat across the breakfast table. The thinner, taller one was tapping (lightly and almost soundlessly) a silver coffee spoon on the pure snowsheen of linen tablecloth. He had a long, pale, firm-lipped face with light eyes that seemed focused far away without being altogether dreamy. Like someone (though he wasn't quite the outdoor type) accustomed to staring into remoteness across steppes, icefields or sheer mountain spaces. His beard was dark and cropped around his chinline.

The other man was dapper, balding, tense and watchful. Like a detective, somehow. His glasses caught the fresh light and glittered as he sipped tea from a delicate china cup the color of old jade, then carefully dabbed mouth and mustaches with a rich, linen napkin.

The scent of April flowers hung on the easy air like wine distilled into vapor. The tense, smaller man leaned back and looked around the ample grounds with a faintly self-satisfied feeling. His eyes had a shrewd, hard glint at times.

"See here, Rider," he was just saying, "there is no such place." He interlaced his blunt-tipped fingers and blinked rapidly behind his glasses. The sun had cleared the brick three-storied mansion that was just delicate looking enough to be thought modest.

The lean man called Haggard stopped tapping the spoon on the soft cloth. He sat very straight. He was amused, vaguely gentle, very intense.

"Rudy," he said thoughtfully, "you cannot say that. You

1

cannot say, you see, that there are no gorillas in Hyde Park until you've actually looked.''

His companion partly smiled. What his eyes did was lost behind the sunglare on his glasses that seemed, for an instant, to Haggard's imagination, windows into a head full of fire.

"Well," Rudy rejoined, lifting a long, unlit cigar in one strong, tanned hand, "I shouldn't invest too much in ape cages, were I you."

Rider Haggard appreciated the remark.

"Yes," he agreed. "But, you see, there are places and powers within us that are utterly mysterious, unknown as the North Pole, yet no less real."

"If they are unknown, my dear fellow," Rudyard Kipling said, almost complacently, "then you cannot say much about them."

The sun fired the flowers, perfect lawn, the old trees with soft-looking leaves. A pair of white and yellow butterflies rose delicately and leaned and stumbled through the rich air across the terrace and seemed to fall into the flowerbeds like broken shards of sunlight.

Haggard sipped some ice water. His stout housekeeper, wearing something starched, severe and midnight blue without sheen, bustled in the background near the house. She was clearing away a serving table. Silver trays and covered dishes gleamed and mirrored the perfect green and blue morning.

He was half listening to a faint rasp, a buzzing in the background that he took for some obscure insect in the rosebushes.

He was very serious about this discussion. He poked the snowy cloth with his forefinger for emphasis, responding: "The tiny cells of our bodies were real enough, yet, until the microscope they went quite undetected." He thought that wasn't necessarily the case but didn't want to muddy the waters of his logic with speculation about occult human powers.

"Ah," said Kipling, finally lighting the cigar and puffing a blot of smoke that hung and slowly unfolded over the spotless table. "That's my point." He wasn't entirely not serious. "Science found the means to discover the cells."

"Which were already there, Rudy, that's *my* point." He waved the first coils of smoke away from his face.

"Yes?"

The buzzing rasp was noticeably louder. He was frowning slightly. Kipling seemed not to notice the sound.

"I have felt the mysteries within me," Haggard said. "They have affected my life. Yet I cannot describe them or isolate what they are. That is their very power, you see." He shrugged his hands. "Or, perhaps, there is a single mystery with many faces."

Kipling smiled around the cigar. The smoke hung like a stain between them.

"What I feel within me, generally, is no mystery," he said. "Right now it is the consequence of 'an undigested bit of beef,' I imagine."

Haggard smiled and nodded.

"Quite amusing," he said, "but I'm serious, you see."

"Look here, I'm prepared to believe in the spirit when you can put my eye to a spiritual microscope, so to speak." Then he cocked his head around toward the lawn behind him. "What the devil is that racket?"

Because the drowsy buzzing had gathered to a rasping growl.

Certainly not a damned bug, thought Haggard.

And, besides, the sound was coming from too high up. He squinted above the treetops into the sunglare. Something dark. A bird, he wondered. Not likely.

Kipling had twisted altogether around in the wrought-iron chair. Shielded his eyes with the cigar hand. The smoke unwound around his head. The housekeeper stood staring now, a silver tray in her hands.

Haggard blinked.

I'm too imaginative, he thought, *as if that were saying something, in my case. . . .*

Because he had a fleeting idea that it was a giant evil bird or bat from some strange, twilight world.

My line of work gives madness a proper home. . . .

Because it made him uneasy when dream-haunted consciousness leaked into the bright everyday, leaked from the nights when he bent over his desk into a small and lonely light and floated in dreams on a skiff of words.

He blinked away the shadows of an ominous image,

something tremendous, dark, winged, blotting over the sparkle of the rising sun.

Kipling stood up, one hand pressing the cloth, the other still shielding his eyes.

"An airplane," he said.

The double wings dipped and a trail of black smoke stained the perfect blue sky and then the craft lurched and dropped below the level of the trees.

"Lord God!" exclaimed the housekeeper. "It is falling to earth!"

It tilted, veered and then pancaked down with startling suddenness. Haggard's nerves jerked him to his feet. Buzzing and swaying, twin engines pop-popping smoke, looming abruptly over them so that he tensed for the crushing impact (too close to run), wondering distantly if the spinning blades were going to miss him. Kipling had already dived to the flagstones in a soldier's reflex.

As if time had slowed on one level, freeing his body and suspending all movement, Haggard had leisure to notice details like the sunglint on the arcing props, the flutter of the wing fabric, the pilot, long face, blank-eyed goggles, fine blond hair tugged into the windstream, thinking him a strange angel of his doom about to shock and snatch him to another world.

Then an uplurch, rush, roar, dark shadow, then bright sky and he was turned (though he never could recall moving) in time to see it flop down like some gawky, crippled bird on the pure, bluishgreen roll and dip of lawn between the trees and the house, leaving him and Kipling (who was down on one knee, cigar snapped in half) in the gust of its acrid exhaust. Kipling was already (or still) talking:

". . . but damn me if I don't admire the damned thing! There's the future of war, Rider, awkward, stinking, but real!"

He may have said more but Haggard was already, with surprising ease and lean light-footedness, for a fifty-eight-year-old man, hopping the low hedge and trotting in the dark dissipating wake of the strangely fragile yet fierce machine to where it now sat canted on the perfect lawn. He saw where the skids had ripped the loam but he knew his irritation wasn't serious or, at least, was brushed aside by curiosity and something else...yes...a sense of impending...something impending...a meaning? A message? Or was that imagination again?

Imagination, he told himself, stopping to wait while the long, young aviator unfolded himself from his cage of struts and kitelike planes and angles.

He was smiling, ashblond, hair very curly, nose long and fine, lips slightly too full for the type, Haggard decided. There was something faintly familiar about him.

"Hello," he said, long-striding as they drifted back to the patio, hands in the pockets of his shiny, worn leather outfit. "Pretty decent landing, considering," he allowed.

"Considering what?" wondered Kipling. "American, are you?" He relit his cigar, head cocked.

"I suppose so," said Haggard to the aviator, noting his cavalry boots had scuffed toes though otherwise they were highly polished. "What compelled you to descend on my property, sir?"

The American was rocking on his heels just short of the flagstones. His eyes were grayishblue and (noted Haggard) surprisingly dreamy. He seemed about to smile but didn't, quite.

"Engine difficulties?" inquired Kipling, leaning into the conversation behind a fresh jet of cigar smoke.

The housekeeper had come gradually closer, torn (as was the smallish, bony, tent-shouldered gardener) between staring at the fallen, smoking biplane and its slouching pilot.

"It is nearly among the tulips," she pointed out.

"What's that, Mrs. Higgles?" asked Haggard.

"I'm sorry for any inconvenience," said the young airman.

"That puts it right, eh?" said Kipling.

"I fear there was nothing wrong with my motor, gentlemen."

"Ah," emitted Haggard, comprehensively.

"Another few feet," put in Mrs. Higgles, "and they'd all be crushed."

"Not to bring out, you know," said the gardener, "what's been done to the loam and all."

"Look here," said Kipling, leaning closer, exhaling a

gout of bluegray smoke, "you really can't just come flopping down like that, helter-skelter. It ain't what's proper, sir."

"I'm sure there's an explanation, Rudy," Haggard said. Tilted his long, sensitive face to wait for it.

"Yes, Uncle," said the young American, rocking on his heels. "I fear I gave way to drama. My apologies. I thought you'd be excited."

"Excited? That hardly says it. Why did you call me uncle?"

"Because I'm Woody Shea, Uncle."

Haggard raised his eyebrows.

"Marla's boy?" he asked.

"Yes, Uncle."

Haggard shook his head.

"Is she well?"

"When I left she was splendid, Uncle."

"Well then," asked Kipling, amused, puffing smoke, "did you fly from America?"

"Don't be silly, Rudy," Haggard said. "That's impossible, as you well know."

Woody Shea looked back at his flying machine. He was thoughtful. And he wanted to be up in the air again. He never tired of it.

"It's perfectly possible," he told them. "Don't discount it. I've designed a craft that could cover half the distance to New York." He looked back at the two writers and the housekeeper, who was still just staring at him and then the plane, alternately, the way she might have looked at something the dog did.

"Well," said Kipling, "in this case, young man, anything less that a hundred percent is worse than nothing at all."

"The point is," Woody said, then gestured at a glass of ice water on the breakfast table. "May I?"

"Of course," said Haggard. "Are you hungry?"

"Famished. The point is," he went on, sipping the water, the cubes glinting in the rich sunlight, "it's just a matter of degree."

"Sit down," said his uncle, glancing back at the biplane. "Are you planning a long visit or will you, ah, be ascending again after lunch?" He gestured to the stolid housekeeper. "Mrs. Higgles, could you bring something more, some eggs I expect, and rolls. Mn?"

"More like birdseed would do it," said Mrs. Higgles.

Haggard glanced at his nephew for confirmation but the young man was intensely focused on Kipling, who was standing at the head of the table, cigar atilt, hands locked behind his back, golden stickpin glinting.

Jock would have been about his age just now, I expect, Haggard thought. He blinked and shifted his mind away. No good lay in thinking about his dead son. No good.

"I tell you, sir," Woody was saying, "it's more than possible that a two-engined machine with the proper fuel-to-weight ratio could accomplish the task."

Kipling grimaced around the cigar, sucking and puffing smoke. Haggard sat down across from his nephew.

"I never quite understood why your mother emigrated," he said, as if following his own train of thought.

Woody swallowed the rest of the ice water. Blinked rapidly.

"I suppose my father wanted to stay at home," the young man replied.

"He never traveled, I understand."

"Not willingly. He died within fifty miles of where he was born."

"He ought to have been an Englishman, in that case," said Kipling

Woody didn't see that.

"Englishmen," he said, "travel to all points of your empire."

"Just so," said Kipling, smiling with the pleasure of a small triumph. "The empire has put home everywhere. Were all those places still foreign not ten men a year would depart these isles."

Woody chuckled.

"Nice point, sir," he reacted. "But, Uncle, I don't believe we've met." He stood up and extended his hand, which Kipling took with vigor.

"Excuse me," said Haggard. "The circumstances were not precisely ordinary. Woodrow Shea, my nephew, Rudy Kipling, my good friend."

The housekeeper came back out. She glanced at where

the offending machine lay slightly askew like an awkward, delicate insect. Set her lips grimly and put down the tray with subtle disapproval that, while lost on Woody, hugely amused Haggard.

"Mrs. Higgles," he said gently, deadpan, "would you care for a spin in the flying apparatus? No doubt I could prevail on my nephew to—"

Kipling chuckled and gazed up at the brilliant sky above the softly tossing, feathery treetops. The bright sunlight lay broken on the grass and leaves.

"A spin?" Mrs. Higgles repeated, setting out the scrambled eggs and hot rolls, hands making slight, withdrawing motions as if (Haggard thought with delight) she were serving tea at a leper colony.

"Why yes," he encouraged, "think of the thrill of it, Mrs. H. soaring among the clouds of heaven."

"Heaven, sir?" she reacted. "I think heaven can wait a bit. When my time comes I'll not be requiring the devil's machine to raise me to my reward, thank you very much, sir."

"But that's so true," said Woody, serious, intense, poising a soft, creamy-looking roll in one nervous, strong hand. "There's nothing like it! Imagine, you're free to drift with the subtle airs above. The earth below is magnificent, all blended together, trees, rivers, roads, houses all tiny . . ." His eyes went remote as he groped for his sense. Kipling and his uncle listened respectfully. ". . . as when you see, in the precious smallness of an infant, what is wonderful in all of us. The distance, the smallness makes it pure, I think." He shrugged. "Impossible to really explain, I suppose. I'd need the powers of my uncle here." Frowned slightly. His eyes stayed remote.

"Go up in the air," said Mrs. Higgles. Her face was set like stone as she turned to her employer. "Will that be all, sir?"

He nodded.

"Excuse me," Woody said, putting something together, "Rudyard Kipling." He stood up. "An honor, sir."

"Sit down and eat your breakfast, young man," Kipling suggested.

"Yes. I was so caught up I didn't actually realize who

8

you might be." He shrugged. "My favorite obsession, I'm afraid."

"Flying, I take it you mean."

"Yes. Of course." He reseated himself and began to chew the roll and attack the eggs with (thought Haggard) the straightforwardness of an iron gut and the goads of youth.

"Well," said Kipling, "you have a right to your obsession. We all have to our own, Woody. Living as a writer is largely obsession coupled with lightness of the brain." He grinned. Nodded in self-agreement.

Woody gulped some scalding tea.

"I'll take you up, if you like," he offered.

Kipling grinned again. He squinted at the machine across the grass.

"Mrs. Higgles may have seen to the heart of the matter," he commented.

"And you, Uncle?" he asked around a mouthful, a mannerism Haggard decided might just be American. He looked at the plane. Then up at the pure, bluegreen, goldglittered perfection of the sky. Considered the idea. Didn't feel *no* automatically.

He tried to imagine the wind-washed brilliance of the upper regions of the air.

"Well, H. Rider," said Kipling, "you ought to feel the mystic call of the heavens, I imagine."

"Dare any man say no to such an offer?" he responded. "After hearing my nephew's eloquence on the subject?"

Kipling relit his cigar.

"I might just dare," he said. "And without a great deal of shame."

Haggard, now that he'd said what he'd said, found himself looking at the peculiar craft in a new way.

Amazing, he thought. *Just amazing . . .*

"Quite a morning, in any case," Kipling observed. Exhaled a gout of smoke that went suddenly bright and thin when it drifted past the roofshadow into the sunshine. "I look forward, Rider, to witnessing your first aerial adventure, with astounding pleasure and anticipation."

II

Haggard was hovering by the full-length French window in his second-story study. One strong, longfingered hand held the rich, velvety, parted drapes. The window opened onto an uncovered porch. Beyond that he could see the lawn, a grayishblue gleaming in the dimming twilight. The dense trees that enclosed the property were depthless blots of silence. The biplane was a shadow on the grass. A few stars showed above the wall of trees.

Mrs. Higgles was in the doorway, one thick hand gripping the brassy knob.

"Am I to make up two beds?" she was asking, her tone not harsh but warmthless, like, he thought, a soldier waiting for questionable orders.

"No," he said, "Mr. Kipling won't be staying."

"The"—barest hesitation—"young gentleman."

He inclined his head, slightly.

"I expect he'll be staying on a few days," he told her.

"A few days."

"Yes." He smiled faintly. She remained in the doorway, impassive, eyes like polished gray pebbles. He waited.

"I think someone should take an ax to it," she said. "That's my view, sir, and I don't care who knows it."

"Ah."

She still stood there, the hand gripping the knob pale against her dark dress.

"I don't care who knows it."

"I'm certain of that, Mrs. Higgles." He gestured vaguely in the grayishviolet, dying, smoky light. "Is there something more?"

"No, sir."

Waited.

"Well then?" he wondered, softly.

"An ax I said and an ax I mean."

"Yes."

"Don't let them lure you into nothing, sir."

"Lure, Mrs. Higgles?" And then understood. She was afraid he'd fly in it. He was pleased. "Never fear," he began to assure her except she was already gone, softly but firmly shutting the door.

Then he looked back out at the faintly luminous sky where a spatter of stars surrounded setting Venus like (he thought) jewel chips around a diamond. He vaguely recalled a wildly imaginative, clumsy, overwritten yet haunting story he'd read in some popular magazine or other about a man who'd longed so passionately to reach another world that he'd left his body and soared to the ironblood colored sphere of Mars where he'd found and fought his way through amazing adventures. The story came back to haunt him like some childhood dream.

I think I should prefer Venus, myself, he thought.

He smiled. He imagined what the sky and earth must look like from an aeroplane rushing through the hush of night.

I think this American nephew is going to be a tonic for the summer sloth . . . he doesn't really resemble Jock not really . . . His son had been slender and serious. He'd thought him hopeful, intense, questing . . . He sighed thinking how he would choose to believe that, in any case. At home the family never mentioned it. Yet neither he nor his wife ever forgot it. Not for a single day since the terrible one. Not for a single day ever. He swallowed. His eyes burned a little. Just the thought was enough to tap the unhealed grief. He took a breath and went to the new book idea that had struck him a few nights ago. He intended to feature a beautiful, imperious priestess-queen of ancient Egypt who discovered that the great pyramid had been built, not by her ancestors, but by the Atlanteans who'd escaped the destruction of their land. He considered having her reborn in the present day (and by a fluke) with full recall of that particular past life. She would know the secret power of the great pyramid and the hidden talisman sealed within. She would remember how to refashion the ancient key to the obscure doors and find the power stone of Atlantis.

11

Come to think of it that might not be such a bad title....

He paced softly and nervously on the thick shag rug. The ideas excited him though he was already questioning if it was too much like previous works.

"The fact is," he murmured, "I'd rather just speak straight out, sometimes...." *About the truth behind these creations....*

He'd been debating with Kipling just the other night:

"Rudy," he'd said, at one point, waving away the smoke that gathered in the darkpaneled study and dimmed the low, greenshaded lamps, swirling slowly and thickly around them as Kipling pressed himself back in his soft wing chair and sucked his cigar, rimless glasses full of the smoky glow. "Rudy, transmigration of souls is a fact to the adepts of every culture and popular knowledge in the East."

"I know, and, Henry, I admit it's a persuasive doctrine and not unknown in the higher degrees of Freemasonry." He'd crossed his legs where his heels dug into the rug. "But it is clearly contestable. As much so, say, as the theories of Darwin."

"Yes. I have not noticed anyone taking even a small step upward on the rungs of evolutionary progress. Quite the contrary, if anything."

"Neither have we arrested a soul in midmigration." He'd smiled. "Assuming there are such things as souls, my dear fellow."

Haggard had laughed, and blown the smoke away from his face.

"Listen," he'd said, "when you stop making so much noise thinking, you might hear your soul whisper to you."

Now he stopped at the leaded window again, leaning close, his breath faintly misting on the glass. Behind him the room was a hollow of shadows. He could barely see the outline of the biplane now.

Because, he continued the discourse in his mind, *the brain is just all one has seen and touched, heard, felt, tasted and so on...just storage...yet, at times, without a single sense operating, I learn new things even from what I know already which is the small touch of the infinite the soul swims in...no, is a ripple of...*

He pressed his forehead against the cool pane. The mist spread and diminished in the glass with each breath.

Only this dull human form strains and squeezes the infinite down to such small compass....

He sighed.

"Oh, my poor boy," he less than whispered.

III

Thinking vaguely about great things and lofty adventures, dressed for dinner in a sober pinstripe, Haggard went out the back door behind the stairs and strolled across the lawn toward one side of the house.

He liked to walk that way before sitting down to eat, unless it was raining or bitter cold. Tonight was just cool but comfortable. The stars were sharp above the depthless darkness of the trees. He smelled woodsmoke and roasted fowl. Made a right-angle turn toward the front (glancing at where the airplane was virtually invisible now) and crossed rows of flowerbeds, the scents almost tangibly thick in the utterly clean air.

His steps were silent on the deep grass. He thrust his hands into his trouser pockets. Inhaled, enjoying these few stainless moments. It resembled the feeling before a story began to quicken in him. A feeling of mystery and promise. Like love.

Love, indeed, he thought. *I'm such an ass I've had neither this world nor the other . . . or others, if it's really plural. . . .*

"Neither the stories," he murmured, "nor love are ever up to the promise."

He was thinking how they were all made of magic and did everything in their power to stifle it. *Sometimes it comes out in spite of us and we love . . .* He thought about the last time he'd seen the woman he'd loved when he was barely twenty. Lilith. *An improbably appropriate name . . .* It was at a ball in the country. She was all in white glowing ghostly beside him in the last evanescence of twilight, a murmur of voices back among the paper lanterns strung from tree to tree, strings and flutes playing a waltz, the dancers swinging gracefully together.

"I love you," he'd said.

"I love you," she'd said.

Long ago. Lost ago . . .

I don't think I ever quite forgave myself for surviving the loss, he thought.

Then he pulled his mind away and came back to the gentle evening. *If only,* he went on, *we could stay children at heart and remain where all paths led to mysteries of meaning and all forests promised enchantments, when on any warm night adventure without bounds waited across the sweet fields . . .*

He was smiling and turned his mind to flying again.

Why not?

Now he was under the massive elms that bordered the driveway. Against the pale pebbles he saw what he knew was Kipling's carriage (the horse was in the stable) and another squarish shape parked halfway to the street.

What's this? he wondered.

And then someone moved between him and the light in the hall window, he thought. *Is that Higgles? How odd . . .* Why would she be wandering around the grounds when she ought to be between kitchen and dining room?

He cleared his throat just as a man spoke behind him from the darker shadows where the hedges closed in the driveway.

"Pardon me," he said, "is this the Haggard residence?"

Haggard was astonished.

"I would say," he replied, trying to focus on the fellow, "you're certainly making an unusual approach to the door. Did you expect to find him in the underbrush?"

"I think maybe I *have* found him," was the relaxed rejoinder. "Have I not, sir?"

Something about the man irritated Haggard more than the circumstances yet warranted.

"Were you intending," he said, "to give your card to the gardener?"

"My apologies, Sir Haggard." This time the writer picked up a faint accent.

Somewhere in the middle of bloody Europe, he thought.

"Mn," he responded.

"My colleague and I merely wandered from the path. We

15

were engrossed in conversation which, I might add, will explain our presence here.''

"Ah, your colleague." *The shadow by the window?* No, because there was another taller, slim, very erect man a little behind the stocky one. He felt vaguely uneasy caught in this peculiar conversation under such circumstances. What a day! Apparently his house was not an island of security. These men seemed too cultured, he decided, to be robbers. So far, at least.

"Good evening, Sir Haggard," the slim man said. His accent was stronger.

Sounds Bavarian, the author thought.

"Delighted," Haggard said. "If you don't mind, I'm about to go in to dinner, much as I'd enjoy chatting in the bushes with you gentlemen." He bowed to their vague outlines and headed for the house. They kept pace just behind him. He sighed. "Are you hungry?" he asked without looking back, crunching along the driveway now. The light from the house was brighter there.

"How kind of you, Sir Haggard," said the stocky man. "But we could not on your hospitality impose ourselves. We wish only a moment of your time."

"Do you?" he asked, still walking but looking back now.

"We have arrived in great haste," the man's companion said, "from Europe."

"That intelligence leaves me virtually unmoved, gentlemen," he said testily. He realized he didn't like that one in particular.

"We beg your pardon," said the stocky man. The slim one had meanwhile moved up slightly in front of Haggard as if to cut him off from the house.

Nervy bastards, Haggard thought. *Must I actually remind them that they're trespassing?*

"Forgive our bad manners, sir," the slightly taller, lean man said, though not (by Haggard's lights) in a particularly penitent tone. "We are still in a great haste."

"Really?" Haggard stopped on the first step to the front entrance. "I should have imagined you were standing out here with me."

"What?" the man wondered.

"We are, in fact, about to leave on an archeological expedition," the stocky one said. Haggard noted his face was round and squared across the chin. The skin had deep creases like ruts around the eyes. The taller one had a thin, waxed mustache and a pointed chin. The way he pressed his lips together gave an impression he had an uncertain stomach. His clothes were very neat and creased sharply while the first man's Norfolk jacket barely closed across his torso. They both looked (Haggard thought) worried.

"Then I won't detain you a moment more," the author told them.

"Yes, yes," said the taller one through his slash lips, "but we need, good sir, only a few things of information from you."

"A few things of information," Haggard repeated.

The first man nodded. He seemed to be, somehow, in charge.

"We are," he offered, "as you may well suppose, Dutch."

"In point of fact, I hadn't supposed."

"Well," he went on, as if things were at last on a sensible footing, "we are Dutch. I am Professor Van Leeun and this is Dr. Helsing."

"Yes? Is that a Dutch name?"

"Not originally."

"From the university of—" began the taller one, Helsing, except Haggard cut him short.

"Look here, I'm not especially interested in ascertaining your credentials. I'm more concerned with my dinner, which is waiting for me inside." But, despite himself, he was curious. So he hung fire. "What do you actually want of me besides a rather long moment of my time?"

"You are not polite, sir," said Helsing.

"You push me too far, sir."

"We have no wish to impose," said the one calling himself Van Leeun. His eyes seemed to flash faintly amber, Haggard thought, like an animal's caught in the light. There was an insinuating quality to him, a strange confidence as if he were putting forth very little strength because he knew the situation wasn't going to extend him.

Haggard gestured in a form of reluctant acceptance. The stocky one was asking: "You recall the city of Kôr?"

Haggard smiled.

"Naturally," he replied.

"Yes. Our researches indicate that there may, in fact, exist such a place. What do you think of that, Sir Haggard?"

"About what you'd imagine," he responded. Shook his head. "Kôr," he murmured.

"Exactly so," said the thin man, rubbing his oddly pointed chin. He seemed to be trying to express intellectual enthusiasm. Haggard found it forced. "Exactly so. We, in the name of science, hope to discover this remarkable place."

"That existed in my imagination? Do you mean to safari into my brain?"

"In a sense, yes," said the stocky Van Leeun. "Where came the idea from to begin with?"

Haggard nodded.

"Good point," he admitted. He tried to remember. It was part of the story but where had the story come from? A feeling . . . an unfolding . . . discovering how images and ideas fitted together into an order that had a kind of life of itself, that was part of the mind and overlapped all other minds and things and times and places because everything in his head was part of the same thought substance as all other minds and where all minds interfaced reality and became fact was hard to say. "I don't dispute there is truth in the story I wrote but a thing may be true without being real."

"I'll the cards on the table put, Sir Henry," said the stocky man. "When you visited Africa did you not encounter evidence that such a place as Kôr existed?"

Haggard shook his head. "I wish I had," he said softly.

The man leaned closer to him. Haggard felt a strange pressure from the dark eyes that seemed pitholes in the shadowy face, as if willpower had been turned on like a firehose. His voice was intense, almost furious with conviction now.

"We believe," he said, "there is truth in Kôr. I speak frankly. I know you are aware of some of the hidden secrets of life, Sir Haggard."

"You mean spiritual powers, reincarnation and so on?"

"Exactly. Powers." The dark eyeholes looked up from

inches into his face. "You are a natural medium, I think, and were you to accompany us on our expedition perhaps interesting results would accumulate."

"You mean accrue," Haggard said automatically. He was suddenly interested again.

"Naturally," agreed the stocky man, tapping his stubby nose.

"I really have to be going," Haggard said. Now the dogs in the kennel behind the house broke into yelps. "What the devil?"

Then Mrs. Higgles's voice was shouting, shrill and incomprehensible and he was already turning, trotting back over the soft ground, swishing through the flowerbeds, thinking, *If any more happens within twenty-four hours I'll retire to the London 'Change or Bedlam as Scrooge advised. . . .* Glancing in the dining room window, seeing Kipling and Woody already heading for the hall frozen (in his glimpse) in a tableau of surprise. What would "Louise" (his wife) have thought? Or his eldest daughter? A good job they were away for the season.

As he went around the back of the building he looked behind. He clearly saw the light spilling over the white front steps but the two men were gone.

Then around the side, panting already because he was so tense, and all the lights seemed to be on, the French doors open wide and Mrs. Higgles seeming to be trying to sit on the air, going rapidly backward and finally skidding down on her backside in the light splashing across the veranda. An instant later he realized she'd been pushed even as he glimpsed a man's dark outline running across the lawn toward the darkness of the trees.

Mrs. Higgles's voice was not even raised now, just steadily saying what his shocked consciousness registered as actual swearing.

Mrs. Higgles, his mind reacted even as he wondered if she'd been hurt and periphally picked up Kipling and his nephew across the living room, noticed overturned furniture and then found himself running after the man.

Kipling yelled something lost in dog yelps, Mrs. Higgles's fluid and fluent swearing and his own puffing breath.

He saw the smallish outline up ahead aiming (he was

sure) for the road that ran along the other side of the belt of trees.

Were these all coincidence? But that was impossible. But what odd burglars.

"You!" he shouted, "you there, stop!" He felt violated and furious about it. "Stop, you bastard!" he yelled in (he distantly realized) feeble emulation of his housekeeper, whose waves of profanity had broken and left her sitting, spent, on the stones as Kipling and his nephew came out blinking and loping hesitantly.

"Where are you, Henry?" Kipling cried.

Does he mean to fly away? Haggard asked himself, because just ahead of the fleeing figure were the vaguely hinted struts and tilted angles of the biplane.

And then a blinding burst almost in his face that was more shock than sound so that he didn't realize he'd just been shot at at point-blank until after his body had tossed itself flat on the fresh-cut lawn.

Mind stunned and watching without thought in the following blot of terrific silence that seemed to rush in around the gunshot so that nightbugs, dogs, voices were instantly still as the wheeling stars and he could hear the silky swish and thud of the running feet. Now the man was a shadow joining the skeletal shadow of the flying machine and Haggard heard his breath huffing (as if the silence paused for that too) and then a single, sharp, sickening crack. Then a flimsy flutter that somehow suggested a spent moth rebounding from glass. Then complete silence. Then, first, the dogs, the bugs and the human voices filled in the night again. . . .

By the time Haggard got up and went to the biplane the groundskeeper had come bouncing across the lawn with an electric torch. He stood there swaying, catching his breath, muttering as he played the pale yellow beam over the scene in time for first Woody, then Kipling and finally Mrs. Higgles to arrive. She came clutching a hoe as if (Haggard thought, when he got over the next shock) she proposed to guard the crown jewels in the Tower of London.

"God," said Woody.

"'E was goin' through your study, sir," said Mrs.

Higgles, dropping an "h" in her agitation. "I caught the blighter red-handed, as the saying is."

Kipling was stooping over the slim little man who lay folded just under the wing, bent so that he seemed to have just toppled sideways from a kneeling position.

As if he'd been saying a prayer to the machine, Haggard thought, irrelevantly.

The electric light wavered in the gardener's bony fingers and cast spidery shadows and angles on the grass beyond the machine. But no one was looking at anything but the little man in black's folded-back head.

"I believe he struck his neck just here," Kipling said, pointing to the dented fabric and wood of the inner wingtip. "Hold that bloody light still, can't you?"

"Is he actually dead?" Haggard asked, blinking, amazed, trying to take it all in.

"It's a sure judgment on him, if he is," asserted Mrs. Higgles. "Tried to do for me, he did, the bas—" Caught herself this time. "The villain."

"He's quite dead, I believe," Kipling announced, now poking through the fellow's pockets. "I've seen a dead one or two in my time. It would seem these machines are nearly as dangerous on the ground as when fluttering overhead."

"Good God," said Woody.

"Good God indeed," suddenly screeched the house-keeper, catching up her skirts and rushing back for the house.

"What's this, Mrs. Higgles?" Haggard called after her.

"The roast," she called back.

"Look here," Woody was saying to Kipling, "oughtn't you to wait for the police before rifling his pockets?"

"Where are the other two?" Haggard suddenly wondered.

"I can rifle, as you put it, a pocket with the best of them, young man." Kipling stood up with a grunt of satisfaction. He held a dark wallet. "Why wait for professionals to bungle things? Bring that light a bit nearer, can't you?"

The gardener moved closer to Kipling. Mrs. Higgles click-clacked across the patio and into the bright house.

"Oh, aye," he intoned, "but don't nobody thank me for comin' along as I did, and quick with the light as I was."

"You're to be commended, George," Haggard assured him.

Kipling held the wallet under the wan beam. Woody was pondering the damage to the wing and trying not to look at the body.

"I say," Haggard repeated, "I wonder where those other chaps have got to."

"Others?" Kipling was peering at the man's papers. "There's nothing much here." Looked up, his glasses blanked with the light, the rest of him swallowed in shadow.

"Two men," Haggard explained, scanning the grounds. "They accosted me near the rosebushes."

The gardener looked, tilted his head. "What's this?" he wondered. "Poaching?"

"Here's his pistol," the nephew said, pointing to where it lay partly under the wing. He was thinking about how the door slammed shut just like that. Riding or flying or running and suddenly it shut. He chewed his lip. There were too many things to do, life was too urgent.

Not too soon, please, he prayed to himself. *There's so much to do....*

Kipling had the torch now and crouched over the gun.

"It's of German manufacture," he said. "Which may mean nothing much. There are Swiss francs in the wallet."

Haggard was already heading back to the house.

"Which may mean even less," he said over his shoulder. "I didn't think I had Conan Doyle for a guest."

"Doyle would abominate your sherry," Kipling said, smiling. "And he'd be seeking to interview the chap's ghost."

Ghosts, thought Haggard. "I'll ring the police," he said.

Thought about ghosts, how they were all ghosts who for a little time rode blinded in bodies and were unaware of all the ghostly overlappings and interactions going on all around them in the ghost world. The shock of death consisted in being forced to remember the ghost world. Birth was leaving it.

22

IV

Mrs. Higgles was still cleaning up by the time the constable and two other men arrived. The constable was bald with a hunter's splotchy tan, wearing tweeds and breathing around a pair of salt-and-pepper walrus mustaches.

The other two wore raincoats (Haggard observed) as if they were dress uniforms. Kipling was seated in a plush Morris chair near the unlit fireplace, drinking brandy from a balloon glass.

Woody was leaning on the mantelpiece while Haggard paced, unevenly, on the pale red and gold Indian rug.

"What did these men you spoke of, Sir Henry, what did they want with you?" The taller, older of the two in raincoats, asked this. He was broad with a face weathered by far climates and reddened and softened around the edges by drink. His hair was thick and yellowish-white with a solid, tobacco-stained brush mustache. His eyes reminded Haggard of brightly buffed blue china and with as much depth. "How did they approach you?"

The writer shrugged with his long hands.

"Absurdly," he said. "Out of the bushes."

"Yes?" The bright eyes watched him.

Kipling leaned forward, intent. Woody seemed lost and a little vague.

"Well," Haggard went on, "they seemed to think I knew a great deal more about Africa than I do."

"Africa, is it?" the young, smallish man said. He had a long, thin face with slit eyes and the eager neck movements of a ferret. Haggard felt nothing and generally reserved judgment but was inclined to try to let the fellow pass without comment, if at all possible.

"Yes," he barely said.

"What about Africa?" His lilt on the vowels wasn't

quite public school, Haggard observed without any feelings about that either.

He looked at the constable as he replied. That generally bucolic gentleman seemed content to listen.

"They had an idea that I might know something about a lost treasure," he said.

"Ah," reacted the sharp-faced man, head weaving slightly, eagerly. "Was the city of Kôr mentioned, then?"

North of England, Haggard thought, focusing on the almost smoothed-over accent.

The constable shook his head and poked blunt fingers into one splotchy cheek.

"What's the sense of all this, Major?" he asked the older man with the yellowwhite hair. Kipling's eyebrows shot up. "We've got a clear case here, I fancy. Housebreaking. The villain dead on the grounds." The fingers poked as if to test the uneven teeth under the cheekflesh. "Accomplices on the dead an' heavy."

"The what?" Woody wanted to know. As did Haggard as well.

"On the run," said Kipling quickly, watching the little man in the raincoat.

"That's it," said the constable. The big mustaches flopped as he breathed.

Haggard responded to the ferret-faced fellow who was leaning against the Oriental-motif wallpaper near a somber painting of some somber Haggard forebear.

"Yes," he said. "That was the chief absurdity."

"What's *core?*" asked Woody, suddenly focusing.

"The heart of the matter," said Kipling, "it would appear."

"What?" Woody went on wondering.

"You know," Kipling said, "that's worse than landing machines on the lawn. He'll sooner forgive that than this."

Woody shrugged.

"I don't follow you, sir," he said.

Kipling grinned and tossed off a slug of brandy. The older man with the chinabright eyes, the major, said, "A lost city of Africa. In one of your uncle's books. I've never read it myself, of course, but I'm told it has a certain merit."

"Not your dish, eh?" Kipling asked.

The major shrugged, uncomfortable.

"I'm no great reader of fiction, sir," he said.

"Nor I," put in the constable.

"Nor Woodrow here either," Kipling said, "much less Mrs. Higgles, I'm sure." Grinned over his glass. "Henry, it's a damned wonder we make a living at all."

Ferret-face never took his eyes from Haggard.

"The point is," he said, "that whether or not you find literary gentlemen and their works admirable or not, the name has come up."

"Yes," said Haggard. "And I hadn't mentioned it to anyone as yet."

The narrow face creased with what might have started out as a smile but bent, somehow, into a mere grimace that could as well have been discomfort.

"Here's a mystery then," he said, knowingly. "Let me add, that I'm an admirer of both you gentlemen's writings and I have read *She,* myself."

"I'm flattered, I'm sure," said Haggard. "The fact is, the work is entirely fictitious. Now why—"

The constable overrode him:

"There's a man dead," he said, "and you mean to discuss book writing?"

"What, precisely," queried the major, sitting down on the edge of a hardbacked chair, "did these chaps want of you, Sir Henry?"

"Directions, I suppose." He was at a loss. Shrugged his hands again. "They maintained they were mounting an African expedition. They seemed to be continental gentlemen. They said they were Dutch, but . . ." He gestured without commitment.

"Foreigners, were they?" The constable seemed oddly satisfied by this idea.

Kipling stood up. The major stood up.

"Just what are you 'major' of, sir, if I may ask?" he wanted to know. "I took you for a military man at once, naturally."

"Did you?" responded the major.

"Retired?"

"No."

"Ah." Kipling smiled. "Intelligence, I take it. And what might you have to do with a housebreaking in Norfolk?"

"Mr. Kipling," said the younger one, "you understand there's a question of discretion here."

"Naturally. What are your names, gentlemen?"

"I'm Captain Sneed. And this is Major Willard."

"And you've been on the trail, so to speak, of these foreign lads?"

The constable locked his hands behind his back and rose up and down repeatedly on his toes.

"I'm all for cooperation with the military," he said.

"Excellent, Barker," said the major. He poked his hands deep into his coat pockets.

Haggard shut his eyes.

I feel, he thought, *as if I'm already flying through the incorporeal air. . . .* The idea was starting to worry him. The more he considered it the less he could be certain. Could there be something to Kôr? In the ghostly world where dreams flowed unimpeded by gross time and place, things imagined might very well overlap the solid world. *Could I have actually tapped into some ghostly truth? Might I have imperfectly recalled something from a former state of being?*

He knew too little and too much to simply say no. He unconsciously shook his head.

"No," he voiced, "I'm sure it was sheer invention on my part." But even saying so wasn't enough.

"Who were these men?" Kipling wanted to know.

The stringy-haired Captain Sneed exchanged a telling look with the major. The constable puffed his mustaches and folded his arms.

"It's all very well, Major," he declared, "but I've a job to do."

"Quite," said the major, "and I should get on with it, were I you."

The constable moved his eyebrows and gave the major a look at once intimate (thought Haggard) and significant. Nodded. Headed for the French doors and outside to where a pair of uniformed officers waited by the body.

As he left, Kipling set down his snifter and lit a fresh cigar, for better focus. Haggard let himself sink back into the soft couch and stared absently at the landscape painting on the opposite wall. It was old, dark: a churning storm over a black land; a fleck of white above the tumult which might have been a pale bird struggling, in graceful desperation, to rise clear of the downsucking fury. Without really thinking anything he let his eyes draw him into the picture, half hearing as Kipling asked: "Well, do we just make our best guesses?"

"No harm putting you in the picture," the major said, tugging a twisted briar pipe from his breast pocket and chewing it into his mouth.

"No harm," Kipling said.

"What about the American?" Sneed wondered, head moving slightly.

"He's a blood relative," Kipling told him.

The major exhaled an acrid cloud.

"We're onto those fellows," he said. "What did the stout one call himself?" he asked Haggard, who was still watching what he believed was the pure, pale bird trying to loft itself free of the storm. "Mn?"

The writer blinked himself free of the painting.

"Van Lin, I think he said. Something like that."

"In fact," said the major, "his name is Hans Striecher. He is a member of a secret society devoted, I believe, to forms of devil worship mixed with fanatical German nationalism."

Sneed nodded.

"They're right bastards," he said. "And anything they are about would be in His Majesty's best interests to keep track of."

"Why?" wondered Kipling. "A gaggle of fanatics as you say they are."

"It is called the Thule Society," the major said. "Presided over by a man named Eckhart and they have the ear of the Kaiser and that mad rotter, Houston Chamberlain."

"The philosopher," Haggard said.

"The traitor," Sneed said.

"Who's he?" Woody asked.

"An Englishman," said Kipling, "who is essentially a German and has the ear of the Kaiser." He took out a cigar but didn't light it. "Which is preferable to the arm. He preaches a peculiar racial philosophy holding that our Teutonic brothers are chosen to bring a new civilization out of the hodgepodge and mediocrity of Europe, and so on.'' He grinned, tapping the cigar against his pursed lips.

"He's a mystic," said Haggard. "He wrote *The Foundations of the Nineteenth Century.''* He shrugged his long fingers. "He mixes absurdities with secret truths.''

Kipling lit the cigar. Tilted his head back, puffing smoke that swirled up with the pipe fumes of the major. His glasses flashed the soft lamplight.

Woody looked puzzled.

"In fine," he said, "you think these men were some sort of spies?''

"You're getting your teeth into it now," Sneed said, eyes like cold stones watching Haggard. The author fancied his mouth had a bulldog or apish look. He could imagine his gnawing a bloody bone in the brush.

"They wanted me to go with them—''

"To Africa," put in the major.

"To Africa," affirmed Haggard, "to search for an imaginary city ruled by a fanciful lady.'' His eyes strayed back to what he liked to think of as a bird in the storm painting. He never could decide whether it was winning or losing its fight to break free into the upper air.

"But why did they break into my uncle's house?'' the young American asked.

"Very likely," said the major, "they were looking for papers confirming their predispositions.''

Haggard sat forward, tapping one oxblood, gleaming shoe on the soft, pile rug.

"Papers?'' he wondered. "Perhaps my fishing license?''

"No, Sir Henry," said the major with unnatural (thought Woody) gravity, "the ironbound box, I imagine.''

Haggard smiled. Widened his eyes. Tried not to stare at the picture.

"So that's it," he said. "You're all mad together.''

The major locked his hands behind his back as if he meant to skate.

"The Germans may be on to something," he pronounced. "You cannot discount it. We had best look sharp considering the present state of Europe.''

"You think war will come?'' Woody asked.

"Do you think the sun will rise?" counterquestioned Sneed, with smooth contempt.

It's not just that I don't like him, Haggard thought. *There's something there . . . or is it something not there . . . he's like a Jesuit . . . that father, what was his name?*

He looked up and under at the two intelligence officers.

"Yes," he said, "the British and German governments had really better get busy looking for the fountain of youth, without delay."

"Yes, yes," said the major. "However, may I point out that His Majesty himself has taken an interest in the matter."

"In the fountain of youth?" wondered Woody. He didn't know whether to ponder or laugh.

The major closed one eye, heavily.

"Let's lay out the cards on the gaming table, Sir Henry," he said. "We're not precisely fools in the War Office." Rationed himself a slight smile. "Not all of us, at any rate. Certainly not Lord Kitchener, eh?" Looked around like (Haggard thought) a Muslim who'd just invoked Muhammed. *"He's* read *King Solomon's Mines,* you see, and he's been to the dark continent, as well." Rationed a single, weighty nod.

"I'm flattered to learn this, Major, er, Willard," said Haggard, "but I fail to see—"

"Treasure, my dear sir," the major explained. "There you are. The ransom of a kingdom, if need be."

"Or the costs of a war," put in Kipling.

Sneed's slit lips creased in what might have been meant as a smile.

"Quite," he said.

Haggard was going over it. There was something he'd forgotten. He'd written the book a long time ago and his stay in Africa had been when he was nineteen years old.

There were stories he'd heard, yes. And blurred things he'd seen there . . . a long time ago. . . . An image came back: the big Dutchman, sweating, red-faced, leaning into the firelight that flicked red fragments on the black river that flowed behind them, overhung by the dense, close, rotting jungle, a row of native huts melting into the humid night. An emaciated old black man talked sullenly with the Dutchman in whatever obscure and blurry dialect about what the white man later told him was a story concerning a huge city built by a vanished race of whites who could fly in the air like birds and speak over great distances by means of magic sticks and lived many lifetimes. Something more about how they were not all dead but slept in secret chambers under a great mountain. The floridfaced trader had wiped his forehead with a greasy rag, squinted, spat into the flames, swigged gin from a labelless bottle, said something about there's always a penny's worth of truth in native tales, and turned the subject to ivory hunting, leaving Haggard with a permanent basis for character study. . . .

The image came back to him now. But it had to have been, he realized, a seed of *She*. He tried to recover others.

"But I don't actually *know* anything," he told them, "that would serve any purpose."

"Ah," said Sneed, squinting one eye, "don't you, then?"

Haggard shook his head.

"I can't think what."

"There's no iron strongbox, is there?" Sneed persisted.

Haggard lifted both eyebrows.

"I have a trunk full of memorabilia," he answered, "if that's what you mean." He was leaving something out intentionally because he didn't want to reinforce their attitudes. "Lost treasures and lost cities . . ." Shook his head.

"May I point out," interjected the major, "that His Majesty himself has taken a personal interest in this matter."

Haggard looked at Kipling, who arched his eyebrows and was silent.

"Ah," he said, "I suppose that puts another light on it."

His actual connection to his country, he realized, was more habit than anything else. The King was a man, as he was himself, and Britain a piece of land with traditions like every other place on earth. The soul had no country, he reflected. But he was loyal by nature as well as habit.

"Yes, I should think so," affirmed the major. "and HM hopes for your cooperation, Sir Henry." The major sat solidly, the pipe streaming smoke across his face.

"Yes," said Haggard. "To what precise extent, if I may ask?"

Kipling cocked his head.

"As far as Africa, I expect," he suggested.

Woody leaned into this phase of the conversation.

"An expedition?" he wondered.

Sneed nodded.

"It's all been worked out, you see," he said.

"You mean those bloody Dutchmen beat you to the punch, merely?" Kipling asked.

"So it would seem," said the major. "We were on our way to you, in fact, when we learned of the sorry events of this evening."

"Extraordinary," said Haggard.

I'd like to stay here, Haggard found himself thinking, *work and dream in my study*...It seemed such a pleasant idea, to sit at his desk by the window with rich summery smells drifting up from the garden. Because he knew what was coming and that he would have to say *yes.* He'd been cornered, as things stood.

He sighed.

I don't know, he said to himself. *There may be something to it*...

Because it was hard for him to avoid thinking about the ghostworld where humans were confluences of tremendous, unseen energy that shaped all mortal destiny. So it was hard for him not to accept the possibility that he'd glimpsed images from worlds beyond time. He'd sensed things. He knew that when the five senses slept wonders stirred. Sometimes he dozed while he was awake and things came to him that were true without hope of proof. *Mother used to say I was just sensitive*...*if I go back there I might pick up something, assuming there's something to pick up*...*I know the soul survives and I might even*...But he declined to complete the thought: Contact Jock. Contact Jock.

"At my age," he said.

"You seem fit," said Sneed.

Something from some former lifetime, he thought, *some memory trickling back from ages ago*...

"Fit for what?" he asked. "Fit for aging gracefully and writing novels that almost don't matter."

"Don't matter?" questioned Kipling.

Haggard sighed. "Almost," he said. "Never mind."

Because they entertain, for the most part, and cannot open the door to the real mysteries....

"Look here"—Woody leaned in again—"I'd like to seriously discuss this expedition."

Kipling tapped his cigar ash into an elephant foot ashtray.

"Want to fly there, do you?" he asked Woody.

"Fly?" wondered the major.

"Let's discuss it, seriously," Woody suggested, with (his uncle thought) admirable sobriety.

Haggard was afraid but excited too. He had a sense that perhaps he needed the journey and that, out there again, he might be truly changed in some profound and irreversible way. The door to the real mysteries might open a crack more.

He looked around the solid room and felt the presence of his substantial house and pleasant grounds.

It is all completely irrational, he said to himself. *All of it. . . .*

V

A Few Days Later

Haggard was standing about where the biplane had rested. Woody had taken off the day after the strange events. Haggard had watched him soar fragilely into the cloudy, gray, dry morning. He'd headed to his factory in Bristol to prepare the special long-distance airplane he'd convinced them to let him take to Africa. He'd said it needed only a few minor modifications.

Haggard pondered the skid marks in the soil. The sky that afternoon was solid overcast and grayish rain was drizzling down steadily, flicking the grass (which, he noted, needed cutting again) and gradually soaking the soft earth.

I can't believe this is all really going to happen, he was thinking. Because it was one thing to be romantic about former lives and discuss mediumship but quite another to travel to the ends of the earth in the vague hope that something like a voice just might whisper to him. Well, he was packing his Ouija board and geomantic texts, and so forth, just in case. *Just in case. . . .*

He thought he saw Captain Sneed watching him from an upstairs window. They'd left that officer to keep an eye on things. But, Haggard felt, they wanted to keep an eye on him, as well. He hadn't warmed up to the narrow-headed little man. He always tried not to let prejudice warp his judgment. He didn't (as with most men) always succeed.

He frowned at the graygreen earth. Writing had always been like falling downhill, for him. But this week he'd stared more than composed.

Because he kept thinking about the trip. He'd agreed. It

was actually happening. He'd been clearing up old business in preparation. They'd be off in less than a fortnight.

Major Willard believed that the Germans would be using the same information that the British intended to rely on. So they'd all be starting from the same place. Woody insisted his machine would give them the upper hand. The major was unconvinced but liberal enough to let him at least participate.

Haggard shook his head thinking about the fact that they'd be using *She* as a first approximation. There was (Major Willard insisted) a river that emptied on the coast of Libya that answered the description in Haggard's novel even to the hill shaped like a Negro's skull at the estuary.

"It will be worth the trip," he murmured to himself, "just to see that."

He tugged the hood of his slicker up over his head.

The fact is, he thought, *if those Germans or Dutchmen are occultists then they will have little enough interest in mere buried treasure. . . .*

It also suggested they would have their own mysterious compass or psychic maps. They must have sought him out to reinforce their own indications. If, he reasoned, they'd depended on him alone, they would have come back and attempted to ransack the house again or, at least, question him further. Even Sneed lurking around the grounds should not have altogether dissuaded them.

He sighed in a deep breath of saturated air. Blinked water away that had beaded on his eyelashes.

And then someone was coming around the side of the house. With water in his eyes and the misty atmosphere he saw a golden blur like a halo above a blurred blackness.

Blinked hard and was stunned to focus on a tall, quite magnificent woman in a dark, casual long skirt and puffsleeved blouse. Her waist-long hair was unbound, brilliant ashblond, which seemed to fluff and float despite the dampness.

Like Botticelli's Venus, he thought.

She had to be nearly six feet tall. Her skin was fair, eyes large, bright, opaque blue. Looked, he thought, as she came closer, almost polished.

"My grounds," he murmured more to himself than her, "seem to have become a public park." *As well as a landing field. . . .*

Her expression was serious, concerned. "Sir Rider Haggard?" she asked.

He bowed slightly. For all her size, he considered, she was well formed and had an almost ethereal expression on her heart-shaped face.

"My dear young woman," he said, "you have, I fear, the advantage of me." *As who does not, these days?*

"I'm Lara Willard. The major's niece."

"Ah."

They stood there on the misty lawn between a wall of rosebushes and golden row of zinnias that were like wet jewels in the muted light.

She's quite striking, he thought, putting it mildly. She gave the impression that she was carefully indifferent to her effect. *She could be a queen in mufti. . . .*

"My uncle sent me round to fetch you," she said.

"I thought I was to leave in two days' time."

"That was to throw off those who might not have your best interests at heart." She stood easily, gracefully. Fair as she was, she had lips and cheekbones like an Egyptian ruler. "You are in some danger and so the feeling was that leaving with a woman might lull your enemies."

"A week ago I had no enemies apart from a critic or two, a writer or two and a publisher or two. Now I am, I fear, beset."

"So it seems. The Germans mean to carry you off."

"To Africa?"

She shrugged.

"I don't know, Sir Haggard."

"It is Henry, Miss Willard."

"Sir Henry."

"Just Henry, if you don't mind."

"As you wish."

Her eyes were so bright. It disturbed him because her resemblance to Lilith was eerie. Was this what they called karma? he wondered. No one who paid attention (he felt) could miss how each life carried its own web of fateful interactions. The test of people was how they responded to the inevitable. *The world, in fact,* he'd thought many times, *is a stage and life is a play without rehearsals and a miserably short run. . . .*

She really looked like her, he kept realizing. That fact blurred his reason and reactions to the situation.

"I suppose I should finish packing," he said, absently.

"There's no time for that, um, Henry. We'll have it brought along after."

"I suppose Mrs. Higgles could . . ."

"Quite so," she said. He thought she seemed nervous. "I have a motorcar waiting."

He followed, not quite focusing because he was inhaling her perfume, moving in her wake across the sloshy lawn, accepting it because logic had already melted away in the past few days.

They were crunching across the graveled driveway when he decided something was overodd and, by then, he could see a man in the front seat through the rain-blurred windshield. By the time he stopped trying to focus on the grayed and runny features, the girl had gracefully opened the rear door (it struck him, distantly, as rehearsed) and he heard another step behind him. He turned in time to recognize the thin spy with the waxed mustaches and a pointed chin.

He must have been in the underbrush, he thought. *There is always, it seems, someone in my underbrush. . . .*

Then he saw the revolver in his hand, big, black and steady.

"Get in, Sir Henry," he suggested, breezily.

Then he saw the soldier coming through the front door (as the car engine turned over, sputtered) and the blast of the gun that was like a club blow against the side of his head that seemed to shove him into the back seat.

I'm dead, he thought.

Except it was the soldier who spun, falling, sprawling down the steps, rolling into the driveway, the car already lurching forward as the meshed gears sang and strained and the lean German (in a reek of burnt powder) was crushing him into the woman's legs. His ears still rang in the vacuum of the shot. He hung over the seat edge of the high touring car, his face pressed into her shoe tops before he levered himself up and sat pressed between her softness and rich perfume and the man's bony hip.

"So I'm kidnapped," he asked, trying to pop his right ear with his finger. He was past shock.

The man smiled and tapped his revolver thoughtfully on his knee. Haggard looked at the girl's face as the car jerked, then crunched smoothly over the pebbles to the unpaved lane. The gaslamp at the gate flickered over the gleaming, black hood.

"Say rather, Herr Haggard," he told him, "strongly urged to come with us." Grinned, thinly. "As you English used to say: impressed."

"I'm impressed by the fact that you are very likely a murderer."

"I think not. My shot pulled to the left."

"He meant," she said in her voice that was like raw silk rubbing on itself, "impressed into service."

"Are you British?"

"What does it matter?" she returned. She was distant and vaguely (he felt) embarrassed.

Outside, lawns and massive trees and houses set well back from the road flowed past as they curved downhill.

"It doesn't," he said. Except he preferred she be foreign and wasn't sure why. Wanted her to at least be exotic, he supposed, and not a damned spy. "Where are you impressing me to?" His ear was better. He cupped it and shook his head. Definitely better.

He looked past her profile (dimly lit by the headlight backsplash) at the lights of a mansion on a hillside. He fleetingly thought that the inhabitants were probably looking forward to dinner and conversation or already eating. He felt cut off from his routine and order as much as a person who'd just been told he had a fatal disease.

He shut his eyes and for an instant, in the darkness of his head, he felt giddy and leaned into the woman as if he'd dozed for a moment. He opened his eyes with a start. It was like a fragment of dreaming: he'd seen an image, a misty river as if he were high above it, the water reflecting pale, washed-out sunlight, a dark shape, a mountain looming above with ghostly stone structures that might have been crumbled, white ruins . . . he had a sensation of terrible longing as an exile might feel dreaming of his lost homeland far away . . . couldn't tell, somehow, inexplicably, if it were his own feeling he felt or someone's cry from long, long ago . . . all this in a flash.

"It will be a good drive," the man assured him. "Sit back and rest yourself."

"Are we driving to Africa?" he asked the woman.

She didn't quite look at him, saying, "No doubt it will be a great adventure."

"You blundered," he said. "You should have taken my magic strongbox."

"Ah-ha," said the lean spy, "you think we should go back for it to get?"

"Then you might not need me?"

"You had best hope we need you, Herr Haggard," he said.

"Hans," she said, "don't tease him. We know my uncle has the box."

"Your uncle, indeed," Haggard said.

"We prefer to have you," said the man called Hans. He leaned forward and spoke to the driver. Haggard knew enough German to understand that the ship would not wait.

"This is quite absurd," said Haggard. "You'd be well advised to let me out at once. It's a senseless quest. There's no damned lost city of Kôr." Sighed in frustration.

"*Ja*," said Hans, "and with the British Army you were preparing to leave."

"They have equally ridiculous ideas."

"Oh, sure." Hans tapped the gun on his knee. "You just wanted to go on holiday." He chuckled. "You shall have your wish."

This can't be happening, Haggard thought. *Clichéd as saying so may be . . . how do I escape these madmen?*

He studied the woman's finely formed profile. She was looking out the window. He could see she was working at it. Her nose had the faintest ridge of beak which gave her an imperious quality. The perfume was like a cloud around him. He felt strangely comfortable beside her while at the same time he was tensed to somehow get away.

"You are all absurd," he muttered.

VI
In Munich

Dietrich Eckhart and two other men sat on the black, polished hardwood floor in an almost pitchdark, candlelit room. The ceiling was low. No furniture. Stone walls, windowless as in a basement or dungeon, and the door was barred.

They were naked, sweating in the humidity. There was a small pot of greenish paste in the center of the loose triangle they formed. Eckhart dipped two fingers into the gooey stuff and licked it off. His flabby body tensed and shook, suddenly. Sweat drops flew off and spattered around him.

The man on his left was short, virtually a dwarf, with a long, dried-up face that seemed all hooked nose. On his right, a thin, pale, intense man in his mid-twenties, sporting a floppy mustache. His eyes were pale and seemed strangely hollow, concentrating all the amber-red glow from the flames set in sconces around the grim walls.

"This," said Eckhart, voice hoarse with some inner strain, "will be the first of many tasks we must perform in order to create a new world."

The dwarf nodded. The thin, medium-sized, terrifically intense man with the pale, hungry, burning eyes stared at him as if he were a window to see through.

"For Germany," he said.

Eckhart shrugged.

"The nation is a tool," he said.

"The race, in that case." His voice was firm, deep and strong.

"Yes," agreed the teacher. "And to that end we must control the power, the Vril, of the inner earth beings. Since the entrances to the undercities have been sealed, except, perhaps, in Tibet—''

''Why can't we go there and search the lamaseries for the hidden tunnels?'' the thin man wanted to know.

''They would not admit us,'' Eckhart told him. ''It has been tried.''

''We should go with a battalion of *Stosstruppen*,'' he suggested, in his rumbling voice.

''You are too impatient, Ade,'' Eckhart said. ''We do better to seek the city of Kôr. The Vril power comes to the surface there. The only place on earth, as far as is known, where this is the case. It is a runoff of some kind to maintain the energy balance in the inner world.''

The dwarf nodded. Smiled with half his mouth.

''Remember, young Adolf,'' he said to the pale student, ''as you have learned, the world appears as it does because almost all humans believe in it. Our purpose is to radically alter what they believe.'' He nodded, still with the strange smile twisted into his lips. ''And so the appearance will change and things will once again be as they were in the distant past. Things from the unseen worlds will cross over into this. Even the New Race will be a tool, a means to this, and not an end.'' Nodded and the smile (if it was a smile) went away.

Eckhart's stubby fingers tapped the floor where a magical diagram had been traced with blood and wax. He was thoughtful and sincere.

''Nothing less,'' he said, ''will slow the degeneration of man. Man's godlike powers must be reawakened. The mediocre, materialistic beliefs must be destroyed.''

''Yes, yes,'' exclaimed the one called Adolf, ''the dull masses must be whipped and bled and purged!'' His voice shook the room suddenly, his bony, naked shape blown to its feet by a gust of violent, shaking energy. ''We must wake them from the sleep of the lying senses! From Germany will spring a flame to burn the earth clean!'' He clenched his fists and bit his lips with unsteady intensity. His eyes were hollow fire.

''The coming war,'' the dwarf said, clasping his long fingers over his pout of a chest, ''must and will be lost.''

Eckhart nodded. Licked more of the drug paste from his fingers. He trembled slightly as it began to affect him.

"The Kaiser is a blundering fool of no consequence," he said. His eyes were unnaturally bright now as the drug took hold. "I see the outcome." Stared. "From the ruins of the state we will create a country of magic and spiritual power not seen on this earth since the days of Atlantis."

The one called Adolf stared at a spot of candleflame across from him on the black wall. He seemed to see things in the bloodred flutter and the beat of shadow.

"I still find it hard to accept," he said, "that I will be the one." Though he never doubted an immense destiny waiting for him. Not since childhood when he'd climbed a hill behind his family's house and looked down on the town and up at the stars as twilight glimmers seemed to drain away into the darkening earth. He felt it then, like a choking power filling his chest, and saw himself with upraised sword leading a vast army into a titanic battle that shook heaven and earth with fire and fury. "At times I have felt like an absurd dreamer."

"That is natural," Eckhart said. "But the power has chosen you, regardless, Ade." His eyes were amber spots, feral. "The coming war will give you character and depth."

"I must see these things for myself," the young man responded in his resonant bass. He reached his hand for the pot with the faintly gleaming paste in it.

"You're not ready yet," the dwarf said. "But you have been chosen by the powers to return the great race to this miserable world." The half-smile was back on his slit lips.

Adolf's nervous fingers hovered without dipping into the substance.

"Is my will not fully opened yet?" he asked his teacher.

Eckhart shook his head.

"The war will confirm what I have baptized," he answered. "I don't want to lose you to seeing. The drug helps a man see but some men can be lost in seeing and lose the spur to action."

"You will have to stay close to the earth plane," said the dwarf, "and avoid the other worlds."

"Yes," agreed young Adolf, withdrawing his hand from the dish. "I am, above all, a fighter."

"And the war is hard by the door," Eckhart told him. "It will open to you and you must pass through if you are the

41

Messiah of the coming race.'' He seemed to be staring into infinite remoteness. The flames around the walls shifted in the vague eddies of that dank and draftless chamber. The creases cut into his set face seemed like cracks in stone.

The young ''Messiah'' crossed his arms. Squatted back down, brooding. Then smiled.

''Maybe I'll fool everyone and become a contemplative, after all,'' he suggested. ''Or a pork salesman, like my Uncle Gustave.''

''You enjoy indulging yourself,'' said his teacher.

Adolf sighed.

''Shall I join this expedition?'' he wondered.

''No. You cannot afford to miss the war. What is found will be shared with you later.''

''You think the Englishman will be of use? Is this lost city real?''

The dwarf had just, rather delicately, dipped his pinky in the faintly luminous paste and sucked it into his lipless slash of mouth. His eyes rolled up into his head for a moment and he shuddered. When next he spoke his voice was almost shrill and his hands quietly spasmed in his lap.

''I see it plainly,'' he shrilled. ''The broken towers and shadowed walls ... I see it ... I see the mountain of power and fountain of life....'' His eyes remained rolled back. ''I see the Great Ones as they were in the days of their might ... behold how they draw the fire up from the heart of the world....'' Then he fell backward, his head rebounding twice with a dull *thwock*. His fingers thrashed and he kept talking.

Eckhart tilted an ear toward the little man. His stare stayed fixed on his pupil now.

''Aaaah,'' mouthed the dwarf, ''you are the child of the race ... you are ... you ... the blood of the sacrifice will draw the Great Ones to unite with you and dwell in your flesh ... aaaaaaah ...''

Eckhart rested his loose fists on the floor and leaned forward, a little like an ape, the reddish light glistening on his sweaty nudity. His eyes gleamed dull amber.

''The Englishman,'' he said, ''will be opened to the power. He will lead us to the secret city.''

VII

The sea was flat, glassy, windless. The smoke from the single stack trailed behind the steamer in a straight, unruffled stain. The African coastline was a dim line across the horizon. The sun was setting at the edge, round, swollen, red, melting down into dark clouds that were, Woody thought, like ten-mile-high mountains.

He wished he were flying among those beetling immensities, struggling, soaring up and up like a frail moth. He sighed, lightly kicked the rail he was leaning into. He felt stuck in slowness like a fly in amber. The wet heat that plastered his tropical linens to his body oppressed him. The breeze from their forward motion was somehow stifling and unsatisfying.

Major Willard and Captain Sneed seemed confident that the German expedition (assuming it was already underway) would pose no problem. They were also sanguine about his uncle's disappearance. The whole thing was too bizarre to contemplate, he felt. The police were treating it as a possible abduction but (the feeling was) Haggard might have left of his own free will before the man was shot on his steps. The housekeeper hadn't actually seen him for hours prior to the shooting and she believed an overnight bag was missing.

Woody had doubts about the theories. He hoped he wasn't being narrow. He accepted that he was narrow in some respects. He'd been told it enough times. Veronice Taless had said so when (as he liked to put it) they became disengaged. She'd ridden out to the shed where he was lying on the wing fabric and thin-boned supports as delicately as on thin ice, carefully dabbing dope on a patch that sealed part of the upper wing. He wasn't even thinking that he loved it, all of it, lying there, the smell and the smooth feel and painstaking details of the work...stillness of long nights like this one...and

43

then her voice as if she'd started talking outside so that as the barnlike door slammed open he heard:

"Woodrow, I am at a loss. Truly at a loss. A gentleman ought to have sufficent respect for his intended to—" And then he'd remembered and felt like a guilty child, picturing the dinner party, the subtle looks, quiet discomfort as his seat stayed empty through the various courses until she gritted her teeth, excused herself, and headed out here in quiet fury because he'd promised, sworn.

"I'm sorry," he'd instantly cut in with, tried, but her quiet voice went on like a stream that would bend around anything he might think to say without needing even to pause.

"—keep his given word. I fear you will be lost, Woodrow, because you cannot look up from what you're doing. You will stumble to your doom, Woodrow. To your doom." This last as she was already turning and heading back out into the night without even bothering to slam the door again. . . .

He remembered, then forgot, now looked around impatiently at the passengers sprawled around the deck on loungechairs or tilted into the rail as he was himself.

The fact is, he assured himself, *we could have stolen a march on them if we'd overflown the Mediterranean.*

But no one had believed him so the disassembled plane was in the hold. He grimaced and looked around again. He didn't quite admit he was looking for the girl, hoping she'd come out on deck.

I'm surprised he allowed his own daughter to come along, he thought. Major Lord Willard K.B.E.'s dear and sole child, Emma Haws Willard. *She's clearly headstrong and no doubt a little silly though quite amiable. . . .*

He had trouble looking directly at her, though he didn't admit that either. She was darkhaired, pretty. A soft yet firm manner. Quietly confident. Perhaps the superficial confidence that wealth and pedigree generally conferred.

He leaned out over the dark, foaming water. Stared into the shadowed continent where the sun was dimming down to almost lightless color.

"It wasn't my fault," he whispered as if at the gathered shadows of the mysterious land before him.

"What wasn't?" wondered Emma Willard from close behind him where she'd just come up quietly.

Startled, he turned.

"Excuse me, Miss Willard?"

Her expression wasn't quite making fun of him. Her dark eyes gleamed in the last light. Intense. She used a little more scent than he was used to. His nose winced in a cloud of violet.

"I overheard you talking to the sea, Mr. Shea," she explained. "You said, I believe, it wasn't your fault, and, as I've nothing but a good opinion of you, I conclude that you are no doubt innocent of whatever—" She gestured vaguely. "—it is." Smiled.

It wasn't my fault that she wouldn't marry me, he thought. *I have to do what I have to do . . . there's so much to do and so little time for it. . . .*

"It's not my fault," he finally responded, "that there's so much I haven't seen or done." That, and the sense that he would not have much time. He'd always felt there was a secret in his past that would undo his life. He called it a child's fearful fancy.

"Whom do you blame?"

He came fully into the moment. Nodded and smiled himself.

"No one," he said. "Fate. Kismet, as the Arabs say, I'm told." Raised one hand and let it fall back into its grip on the rail. "I think I could have flown all the way here in my machine."

"Father feels you'll have ample time to perish once we reach Africa."

"People tend to be backward."

She shrugged, slightly.

"That may be only an appearance," she told him, "caused by excessive racing ahead." She leaned beside him watching where the sun had melted down into formless, deep-red streakings that pooled over the landscape of shadow and cloud. "God, I'm excited. Look . . . look at all this!" She gestured, embracingly. "I've never been farther than France."

He nodded, abstracted, staring.

"I'm concerned about my uncle."

"Yes," she said. "The writer. I've read some of his work."

"Ah."

in this time *frame, illiterate*

She shrugged.

"Interesting," she said. "I don't know as I'd call it great literature."

"I don't know as he would himself." Woody opened and closed his hands on the polished wood railing. "It's just unbelievable."

"Pardon?"

"About the Germans. Kidnapping him."

"Captain Sneed thinks otherwise."

"Sneed," said Woody, twisting his lips. Because the man hadn't come right out and said that Haggard had somehow defected. No. Not quite. Woody didn't like the man. Though he was, at best, a cold fish with his washed-out, blank blue eyes. A policeman's unsympathetic, distrustful scrutiny. Sneed was small and strong. Liked to rock on his heels with arms locked behind his back and just watch people. "Look here, do they really think these Germans are coming here as well?"

"Yes," she affirmed. "My father's men have been following their preparations for some time. They know the Germans are about to leave the Continent. There was, I think, a wireless message to that effect this morning. Captain Sneed expects to cross paths with them."

"Hah. Where? Where are we actually going? Look here, I have a feeling this ship is not an ordinary steamer." He'd noticed that the seamen reacted a little too smartly for the merchant service. He gestured with his head roughly behind him at where something the size of a deck gun was wrapped in canvas. "I think those things"—there was another in the rear—"are cannon."

She shrugged.

"Why don't you look and see?" she wondered. "I say, Mr. Shea, do you play whist?"

"Whist?"

"Yes. We are getting up a game after dinner."

"Ah."

He opened and closed his hands on the railing again. The passage breeze kept him in the cloud of her scent. They were close enough for him to feel the aura of her warmth and breath. He wished he knew how to play the game. Wondered vaguely if he could pretend his way through a hand or two.

46

Then thought about Kipling at the dock in London. He'd seen them off at the gangplank, smoking a pipe this time and wearing a cloth cap and a pale linen suit with a minuscule tie set in a round collar.

"Dammit, Willard," he'd said to the major, "I submit that Henry has been taken by desperate characters."

"Perhaps not," responded the major, puffing the floppy edge of his mustaches away from his lips. The passengers and crew bustled past. Cranes creaked, steam hissed, smoke blew back from the smokestacks, blotting out the ship and scene for moments at a time. Woody had been watching them lower the sections of his new plane into the hold.

"Perhaps?" Kipling pressed. "Did you not find your man dead out there? The damned housekeeper saw Henry carried off from the window." He'd shouted the last over the blare of a foghorn. The smoke had billowed, blurring the major to a shadow for an instant and left him coughing.

"She testified he'd left with a woman, in fact," the major had responded.

Woody had just begun following the conversation.

"At gunpoint," he'd put in, irritated.

The major had shrugged.

"Not a proven fact, sir," had been the reply.

"The hell you say, sir, if you'll pardon me. Are you suggesting—"

"Nothing of the kind," the major had demurred. Puffed his mustaches again. "I have an open mind on the matter."

"Perhaps the result of a wound?" Kipling had wondered, smiling faintly. "We damn well better find Henry, that's what I have to say, gentlemen."

"We will, sir. We will. In Africa or I miss my guess, and I haven't missed many."

"You've hushed this whole business up, I understand," Woody had put in. "Wouldn't it be better if—"

"We don't think so, no," the major had reacted. "Not at all. Nothing will be served by the glare of needless publicity. There are delicate aspects to the whole situation, as I'm sure you and Mr. Kipling perceive."

Kipling had nodded with an unsatisfied expression, the now unlit pipe back in his tense mouth. Another veil of smoke had drifted over them as the sun came out from a cloud so that the scene seemed to sparkle and fade into (Woody felt) billows of dark menace.

"Naturally," Kipling had agreed. "The police here will quietly follow every lead." Sighed. "I'm terribly distraught, you know. Terribly."

"Of course," the major had murmured.

"I'll do all I can on this end," Kipling concluded.

Woody blinked and came back to the present. Emma was watching him closely. Her face was a pale smoothness now in the twilight.

"I hope he is found," she said sympathetically.

"I hardly know, really. I thought I'd surprise him with the airplane." He smiled. "I suppose I did. I've always been a bit eccentric. My former intended made that point frequently."

"Ah," she murmured. Let the slight sway of the ship move her closer to him. Then she stayed where she was, leaning into his arm lightly.

He gestured, vaguely, looking across the dimming water at the smoky horizon.

"I'm afraid she never quite approved of me," he said.

"I suspect that was her loss, sir," she told him.

He missed her point. Sighed.

"I'm really very, very affected by what happened," he said.

"She meant a great deal to you."

"She? No, well, at one time, perhaps, but I meant my uncle. I barely knew him and yet I am dreadfully upset."

And then they both were already turning in time for the second flashbang that shocked the twilight and left them blinking away orange-red bursts of afterglow, with Woody, in one motion, pulling her down and shielding her with his body. A man was running toward them, others piling out of the cabin in pursuit. A whiff of cordite, outcries, yells.

The tall man, a shadow against the dim sky, paused near them, skidded, half turned, leaning into the next burst of fire as if it were spray from a hose. Woody thought he heard a sickening impact as the man sighed and jerked sideways. Then fired himself, just above them now, a woman screaming at the flash and reports. Then the tall man shouted what seemed a wordless cry. Woody was already moving, gathering his legs under him to spring for the man's gun and put an end to the nerve-shocking madness as more shots answered from across the deck (he hardly heard his own voice yelling: "Stop!") as if (he vaguely thought) the sudden night were warring with itself as in some world of dreams, gunsmoke stinging his eyes and lungs as the tall man (he glimpsed a beak nose in the next flash) was flung or dove (he couldn't be sure) over the rail into the dimly redtinted blackness of the still sea.

By the time a half-dozen passengers had crowded to the railing Sneed had elbowed in beside Woody and Emma. There was an uncertain foaming, a vague luminescence a few yards from the bow wave that might have been fish or the struggling man, or nothing.

Woody winced as Sneed fired into the water.

"Bastid!" he snarled. Straightened. Mused in the clamor around him as deck officers yelled orders and some woman across deck howled in shock and terror. "Well, report to the fish, then!"

"Whom were you murdering?" Emma wondered, shaken but poised, on her feet now, holding Woody's lean, strong arm.

"Murdering?" Sneed said. His bleak eyes flashed in the light from a lantern a sailor was now training on the dark water. "That's fine talk. He tried to do for your father."

"What's this?" she asked.

The major came out of the dimness of the deck behind them. Lights were coming on all over the ship; the yellowish splash showed him holding one hand to the side of his head.

"I see nothing, sir," the seaman wielding the lantern said to an officer who was pointing. Bells rang. The ship was already slowing.

"Man overboard," someone called from the shadowy superstructure that seemed to dissolve in the deeper darkness of smoke from the stack, blotting the sparkle of first stars.

"Father," she exclaimed, moving from Woody to the major. There was more illumination now on deck. A spotlight from the bridge sliced into the gathered night, wavering in billows of fumes as the ship lost speed and wrapped itself in its own exhalations. Woody saw a spatter of blood on the big man's cheek.

"I hit him fair," Sneed was saying, to no one in particular. "He's gone to wherever Huns go." Smiled, faintly.

"I was merely creased," the major said. Woody thought he was almost pleased or at least proud. It seemed odd.

"You're bleeding, Father," she said.

"Nothing much."

He was proud, Woody confirmed. The young American couldn't know that the major had spent too much of life behind a desk dreaming (almost like a young man) of broadstroke adventures, still thinking there was a literal substance to glory that glittered and caught in, say, the sabers of charging cavalry. Though he didn't mention it directly, this expedition was his great adventure and shining moment. He'd convinced himself it was a good gamble by simply never looking too hard at the odds. Because (though he didn't phrase this thought either) he was too old for the coming war. So he'd convinced himself.

An officer was hovering around in his deck whites, a ghostly outline against the dark coast.

"The blighter was lurking in your stateroom," he said. "He must have stowed away."

"Well," muttered Sneed, "the bastid's dead."

"See here," interjected Woody, "there are women present."

Sneed screwed his pointy, narrow face close to his. Woody smelled liquor and stale onions.

"See here, is it, Mr. Yankee?" he hissed.

"Quite so," said Woody, not giving an inch.

Then the narrow domed forehead bent toward Emma.

"Excuse me, dear Miss Emma," he said, ingratiatingly. "I was carried away by just wrath, you see."

He was not exactly insolent, Woody decided, but still vaguely odious in his familiarity. He wanted to push the man, he realized.

"It was the heat of a military moment," she said, not precisely mocking him. Woody smiled. He liked her dryness.

"Yes, Miss Emma," Sneed assured her. "Excuse me." And brushed past, close to Woody, who actually gave an inch and then hated himself for it. Whatever else he felt, he had to admit the smallish man had palpable personal force.

"He's a bit cheeky," commented Major Willard, "but a

solid man. Devoted to his job. We've quite a piece of work to accomplish out here and no assassins will put us off.''

Reminds me of a ferret, Woody thought.

"I suppose he's doing his job," he allowed.

"He's a type," she said.

"Not a schoolfellow, naturally," murmured the major.

"Personally, Father, I think competence a better measure of a person than his Eton colors." She tilted his head into the light from the deck lamps to better examine the wound. "Are you sure you're all right?"

"Fit and fine," he replied. "Just a bit of a nick, you see."

"You'd better see the ship's doctor, all the same."

"Yes," put in Woody. He watched the searchlight probe the dark sea. The glassy surface bounced the beam into the lowlying mist that seemed to be blowing out from the dark coastline now as if something there exuded a warm, clinging cloudiness.

"As far as school is concerned," the major said, a bit defensive if not actually stuffy, "there's a reliable shaping process, you see, as with certain branches of the service, that gives, well, a clue to a man's character."

"There's no chance of finding the fellow," the pale uniformed officer was saying to the major. "I imagine he's gone under. Particularly as he was hit."

The major nodded.

"Yes," he agreed.

"Had a shot at you, did he?"

"Yes."

"Was he on the hunt, do you think?"

The major shrugged.

"Perhaps," he said. "Not much of a shooter, I'd say. I was no more than five yards from the chap. Hit everything but me, really." Again Woody noted the quiet pride in his voice.

The officer stood there beside the big outline of the major, the deck lamps behind them, the thickening mist now flowing over them in soft, smooth billows so that (to Woody) they seemed to struggle to shape themselves from a general vagueness.

"German, do you think?" the officer asked quietly.

"Possible."

"Ah. The latest word is it won't be long now."

"How dreadful," Emma said. She was still at the rail beside the American. "They know there's going to be war and no one can act effectively. It's incredible."

The officer's melting shape seemed to shrug shoulders.

"You can't generally talk a fight away, miss," he said. "And, as to effectiveness, I think we British may prove somewhat capable when the whistle blows."

"Hear, hear," endorsed the major.

Woody was trying to imagine the war. He tried piecing together fragments from pictures in books and paintings he'd seen over the years: massed charges and desperate last stands with gunbutt and bayonet, even the dead and dying falling gracefully, playing their essential walk-ons in the grand drama of history. But just those gunshots and Sneed's seething face had been enough to make war clear to him. And he recalled photographs of the dead in the Civil War. He'd studied an album of them when a boy. Men stacked like potato sacks, limbs flopped; a line of killed troops behind a low stone wall somewhere in Virginia, tall, full, light-colored blossoms swaying among the dead . . .

"We'll be far from it, at least," said Emma.

The big head shook again.

"I think not, my dear," he told her. "I think we're riding to the sound of the guns, so to speak."

"Don't you see," Woody was saying, frustrated and baffled, "the fellow just went over the side and probably has drowned."

"I don't doubt it," said the major.

"It is terrible," Emma said. "All of it."

"Certainly incredible," Woody assured her.

He'd never actually seen someone done to death; knocked senseless and broken in sports, yes, a horseman spine-shattered and crippled for life . . . rips and tears, men dead in flaming wrecks of airplanes . . . the little man with his neck broken on the lawn . . . but never murder, man to man and face to face. That was the point: no matter how rationalized, war was merely murder.

He said nothing, unwilling to get into a debate on the

subject. The major would probably argue patriotism and imminent peril.

The major had said something to her.

"Rot," Woody voiced, unconsciously answering something he'd thought.

"What?" Emma wondered. Her father was already crossing the deck to where the crowd collected under the oil lamps that had been lit at dusk around the superstructure. Tints and shadows.

Woody shook his head as if to clear it. He felt strangely as if he'd been a boy up to this moment, thinking about his life as if it were a school sporting match. As if the cloudy shape of the vast, waiting, mysterious continent had revealed a terrible image, something like a nightmare tide of fire, agony and meaningless obliteration. Like the masses of cloud that had extinguished the last sunglow. Looming, and he suddenly believed that he hadn't chosen to come here, that he'd been drawn to the brink of some terrible battle where he would have no choice but to be destroyed. Because (he sensed) something more awful than even a realist's picture of combat was gathering itself and it was immense and dark and, somehow, hollow. . . .

He blinked and there was just the spattersplash of the bow wave and Emma Willard beside him at the rail and the rich smell of jungle on the offshore breeze carried on the thickening mist.

"Are you utterly a cynic, Mr. Shea?" she'd just asked him.

"What's that, Miss Willard?"

"Emma, if you please, sir," she insisted, mildly.

"Yes. Woody." He sighed. "No," he answered, "I am not a cynic."

"I think one has to let life in," she said, seriously.

"It is death," he responded, "that has my attention, at the moment."

She shrugged, tilted her head to the side.

"Perhaps it's the same thing, really. There's no light without shadow."

"Ask that fellow who went overboard which is which," he suggested.

"It is dreadful."

"They're all going to kill one another." His eyes went far away into the cloudiness again and the foreboding and tormented shapes. "Really. They are. It struck me, you see."

"All?" She took it in.

He gestured, vague and unhappy. This was not his sort of conversation. Until now he was only foggy when groping for words to express how flight felt. Now everything had become slightly unfocused. Even when he thought about soaring and drifting up above the clouds there was fuzziness in the feeling.

Just a mood, he told himself.

"Everybody," he finally said, turning and looking back across the deck at where the soft flamelight glowed on the crowd of crew and passengers.

"I assure you, Woody," she said, "I intend no mayhem."

"It will not matter what you intend, I'm afraid."

VIII

Well, Haggard was thinking, *I'm flying . . .*

He looked out the long window past puffy clouds at the sparkling sheen of the sea. The motors were a faint buzz as the huge airship floated almost silently forward.

They hadn't even bothered to lock his cabin door. Why should they, he reasoned.

The last thing he recalled was the magnificent blond woman holding the door while he got out. The lean, mustached (he thought), nasty man had stayed in the back seat of the touring car. Haggard had stood beside her on an open field where he had been assuming they'd release him. He'd felt they were close to the Dover coast. Early evening. The wind had been brisk and blew gusts of loose mist across the stony landscape.

"A charming spot," he'd said. "Do I get to walk home now?"

He'd thought her eyes were sympathetic, almost tragic. She'd almost sighed, saying, "Some things have to be."

And before he could come up with something sufficiently cutting, his head had been jerked back (he'd realized she hadn't been apologizing), and a sickening, burning wetness clamped over his nose and mouth. He'd thought of the foul paws of some nightmare beast, though it obviously was the lean, pointy-chinned man.

He'd gagged into what he understood was a saturated cloth and, as he'd sucked a frantic breath that choked and hurt, struggled for leverage to pull free. Knew it was ether. His head had seemed to shrink to a tiny speck, bounding like a balloon in a roaring, spinning wind; his last thinking (as the balloon had sailed up and lost itself in vast spaces) had been that he was going to have to die to find her because (he admitted in a remote voice that wasn't necessarily his own) he was totally hers; he wanted to fall at her feet and kiss them, seeing her nude, hair falling around her in an aura of stunning, golden fire. . . .

After that the darkness blurred away and briefly lifted a few times. And there were no golden goddesses. The first blur opened on a dim room, maybe a cellar or a chamber down in a mine tunnel and someone (he later thought) who might have done the role of Hagen, half-breed son of Alberich the evil dwarf in Wagner's *Götterdammerung*, a dead-white, bony face mixing malice, purpose, cold fury in his palely blue, luminous eyes. He was talking to someone lost in the shadows of the smoky place. Perhaps, he later thought, his dwarf father. His voice was deep and broke like thunder in that confined, echoing space. The words were only noises to Haggard, whose consciousness was mist. He didn't know that the man saying, in German with a Bavarian accent, "So this is the mystical writer of fiction. I have no use for fiction."

"Some of it is quite good, Ade," the dwarf had answered.

And then the mists thickened to solid darkness again . . . then a grayish curtain shaking, thinning, and he felt himself being lifted . . . glimpsed a gray field that seemed to swirl in soft surges. Suggested forms in a cloud and that fascinated him. Always had, since childhood. An impression of a commanding figure riding a shapeless beast . . . there was a seam he took for where the sky joined the earth . . . he was actually lying on his back staring into a drizzling overcast . . . watched the forms move in the soft grayness: a great bird opening its wings . . . then, as he somehow expected some great thing to be revealed, blackness came back and he was choking on it . . . then movement, smooth movement . . . then her face was close to his, the sheen of her hair like flaming gold . . . he believed he tried to touch her and then the choking night took him by the throat again, filled his nose and mouth and head . . .

His skull pounded for hours after he finally woke up. He understood he'd been drugged. At first he couldn't concentrate enough to care.

Now he realized he was back. He sat on the padded bench looking at the view almost, he realized, like a tourist and not a victim. That was his nature: when there was no useful action to take, he went passive and waited. But he was restless. Always. And nothing but work cured that.

Rubbed his face. He tasted bile and yet had an appetite. He felt sticky all over. Felt his pockets and poked inside his jacket: wallet, keys and so forth, but no paper, not even an address book. Nothing to write on.

Pity, he thought, *it would help* . . .

The next thing he wanted was a bath and change of at least underwear.

"I'm rumpled and disgusting," he murmured.

And a shave. . . .

He pressed his lips together and whistled tunelessly through his teeth.

This is my fate, he told himself. *And for all I know it may be a great opportunity of some kind. . . .*

He'd always been subliminally afraid that fate would somehow trap him mute, alone, with no escape but action. He'd tried to be safe from the mysteries. It was one thing to write about them.

"I'm afraid I'm going stale and starting to repeat myself," he whispered. What was fresh twenty years ago had no force now.

He went to the cabin door. Pale, smooth wood the color of smoke. He was surprised when the handle clicked and the panel slid open.

He entered a narrow passage that ran fore and aft. It was dim with diffused light.

He shrugged and went forward. He considered waiting in the cabin for whatever was going to happen. Shrugged and had a feeling that sooner or later he was going to have to hit somebody in the nose. Preferably that sneaking spy. Yes.

The river though, he suddenly thought, focused, *they may be right about the river. . . .*

IX

On the Western African Coast

The town was all heat and noise. The late July sun hit the dusty streets like a burning hammer. Woody was sure he could feel the sunpressure on his wide-brimmed, tropical hat. The white little claybrick buildings wavered in the heat as if a wind rippled a fabric backdrop.

Most of the natives seemed to be indoors, waiting out the early afternoon. A beggar slept in the palmtree shadows. Woody glanced at him; the bony, sun-leathered limbs poked out from what looked like a heap of rags. His face was long and, for an instant, the shadow effect made it seem a hollow skull. It startled him.

Emma felt him start where she walked close to him. They were heading for the river that passed behind the claybrick village. She could make out the line of palmtrees that followed the curve edged by grainfields that shimmered like golden dust in the blinding sunglare. Past that, where the river opened into a small harbor with clean white ocean beaches sheltered by lines of reef, there was the amazing rock formation that looked like a black man's head.

Only the top half lay exposed. The major stated (and was generally concurred with) that there were obvious signs of recent excavation. The dirt was loose and seemed to have been tossed back over the top of the skull in a slipshod attempt at concealment that could not have survived the first rainfall.

They all (even Sneed, who suspected everything) missed

the real point of that clue. Sneed went as far as asking a few of the locals, through their Arab interpreter, how long ago they'd dug there. They'd shaken their heads and wagged long fingers vaguely. He hadn't pressed the point because they had already denied that any white men had passed through the village for many months. If the Germans had come and gone, he reasoned within himself, it made no difference anyway. Later he was to regret his uncharacteristic inertia in the matter.

"What is it?" Emma asked him. She was wearing a white, matching jacket and skirt and a floppy bonnet that was really a hat.

"Mn?"

"You just jumped, Woody." He didn't know that she liked saying his name.

"Did I? Well, that beggar gave me a start, I suppose."

"Why? Half the population here seem to be beggars."

They'd passed the last low building and waded in a fine smoke of pale dust now. He kept brushing his hand at the small, hard-looking black flies that circled and cut around their heads. Neither of them sensed being watched. In the dark slit of window a narrow, pale, mustached face stared past them across the fields to where the biplane was parked. The face of Hans Himmel. The eyes looked past the stubby double-winged shape to the small riverboat the British were loading.

The face smiled, faintly, satisfied that they suspected nothing. Himmel sighed. Squinted and could make out part of the stone Negro head half buried in the tongue of hill that poked out into the bay. He'd kept the natives digging for three days with combinations of threats and rewards. He realized he'd risked his life, alone here, pushing savages as if he possessed some unseen power. He was pleased that he'd shown courage. Under everything, Himmel dreaded the idea of funk, of breaking down under strain and fear. He preferred the idea of death.

What a thrill, he thought, remembering when the clumsy shovels had scraped enough for him to make out the beetling brow ridges. *I'm doing quite well,* he thought. *Quite well, indeed....*

At school he'd been advised by his chief tutor that he

would do best to seek a safe but unexceptional state job. He'd never thought much about his actual postschool future until that moment. He'd found himself furious though silent. He'd nodded. He'd said to himself that they'd see what Hans Himmel did with his life and how beautiful women would fall in love with him.

Nothing much had happened to fulfill his promise. He'd managed to secure a clerkship in the bureau of military records after his mandatory army service. He hadn't shown much in the field after breaking both legs in a training accident.

Thanks to his sometime mistress, a dumpy waitress in a Munich café with a notable wart on her cheek, he met Captain Streicher at the restaurant and found himself joining the Thule Society with the promise of being part of a dynamic future involving (though he only partly understood how) politics and mysticism. Later, when he found out that the waitress had accepted gratuities to visit members of Thule after hours, he dropped the girl, naturally.

He watched the couple walking toward the plane and nodded, slightly. That was a fine-looking woman. He thought about (for some reason) kissing her bared thighs. He had a great urge to give himself over to some intense, sensual experience. He imagined the thighs. The scent. Imagined sliding his lips higher and higher while she turned and struggled with her irresistibly wakening passions....

Ah, he thought.

Woody was studying the stubby craft with a critical eye. He'd have to try a test flight that evening or tomorrow. The twin pusher engines concerned him. The problem of balancing the gas flow perfectly was a challenge. The engines sat between the wings among the reinforced struts and wiring that held the fragile wood and fabric craft together. The insides were practically all fuel tank. It was designed to lift eight passengers in a pinch. God, he couldn't wait to take it up.

Best design I've ever come up with, he told himself. He knew it was a fact but was afraid, as always, that he'd missed something—that the lift would fail, the controls stiffen in flight, the aircraft rock, yaw and buck clumsily through the eddies and pockets of the mysterious air.

"I think it will fly farther and higher than anything in the world."

She smiled. "Including the American eagle?" she asked.

"Pardon me?" He hadn't been listening.

"I notice, Mr. Shea—"

"Woody, Miss Willard."

"—Emma, sir," she went on smoothly. "I notice your attention is inclined to stray in an unflattering fashion. I presume your former intended made that point." She didn't quite smile this time, watching him archly.

"Forgive me," he said.

"If you like." She smiled now. "You know, I mean to join you."

"I thought your father was sending you back?"

They were halfway to the river, close to the flying machine which sat on perfectly flat, sandy ground facing a wall of tall trees across the field.

"I've convinced him otherwise. I'm an expert, you know, in ancient and obscure languages."

"Hm. Have you altogether convinced him or are you still dangling at third?"

"Pardon me? That's a little too obscure."

He smiled.

"I'd been thinking what a first-rate ball field this would make." He gestured.

"You are a cricketer?"

"Hm? No. American baseball, in fact. That's my game." He smiled. "I used to think what a first-rate landing spot the outfield at school would make. I love flying, you see." Shook his head. "There's nothing like it."

"I think it is evident that you love it. Your passion becomes you, sir."

"In any case, you're going in the boat with your father?" She shook her head.

"Not really," she said. They were almost to the plane now and she was studying it, sniffing. "Is that castor oil I smell?"

"Yes."

"I hate castor oil." Wrinkled her nose.

He smoothed his palm over the wing fabric.

"And gasoline and varnish and dope. Glue, to you." He

loved the smell and the new feel, the sleek wood. "If you are not going in the boat..."

"That's correct, Woody."

"I see. Interesting."

"I'm fascinated by flight, to tell the truth."

He was facing her now.

"You're a remarkable person," he told her.

"You know," she said, leaning a little against the fuselage, the violently brilliant sunlight shattering across her hat and white outfit, "you don't condescend at all. At least, I haven't caught you at it."

He was puzzled.

"Pardon me?"

"I'm used to being treated a little like a silly child. It's something men do to women."

He smiled and shook his head. He tried to see her eyes in the hatshadow.

"Not in my family," he said. His maternal grandmother was a Frimsey of the Boston branch, a clan in which men were suspect as generally weak-willed, inclined to drink, unreliable in critical matters and irreligious. He had virtually no prejudice respecting women's roles as no one living would have dared attempt to define Mrs. Frimsey's place in life.

"I think I sometimes enjoy making Father splutter," she said. She went profile to him now, sighting along the stubby body. He was thinking how many women seemed brittle in their poise compared with her. He liked her humor and frankness. He liked her altogether, he realized.

"I'll be delighted to have you aboard," he said.

She took a step and touched a propeller with a caress of curiosity. She had long, fineboned hands, he noted, again.

"Yes," she said.

"I wish your father shared your confidence in my machine." He glanced across the sun-shocked field of sawgrass at the little steamboat. The big major was strolling upriver, hands behind his back, tropical jacket a blur of brightness against the shatteringly blue water, the small, wiry, active figure of Sneed just behind him, hands gesticulating in short jerks. The stocky Arab foreman and translator seemed to be shaking a stick at a native twice his size whose dresslike white robes were a dazzle and seemed to float ghostlike, the black face and limbs blurred away by shadow and heat shimmer.

"He's really not stuffy," she was saying. "He was one of the first in Surrey to own a motorcar, for instance."

"Pardon?" He was distracted watching the squat Arab and the long native. "Your father? Really?"

"But then, he always hated horses, which may have influenced him."

Woody saw the major and Sneed stop and turn to watch the Arab. Though the wind was the wrong way he could hear shouts now. The long stick cut the air. Sneed was heading back to the scene.

"I explained," Woody said, "about the safety features I've developed." He remembered the major nodding, tamping his pipe down, applying a match and chewing rich smoke that settled around his large, leonine head. Then, still nodding in what seemed perfect understanding and empathy, he told him no, that the main party would go by water as far as possible, that they'd all follow the same map and that his function would be reconnaissance. "Like many people, he mistakes an airplane for a balloon. I can do a great deal more than just look over the country." He sighed. "I can carry eight adults plus food and equipment."

"Will you take me up with you today?" she asked.

He almost said: with your father's permission.

"Assuredly," he replied, "once I'm certain of how she handles."

"Do you dream, Woody?"

"Do you mean while sleeping or awake?"

He remembered sitting on a park bench beside his former fiancée. Her fawn-colored gloves showed no wrinkle as she delicately turned the shaft of her parasol and flicked the mellow sunbeams over them both. "You live in another world, Woodrow," she'd told him on that occasion. "Your machines are merely a symptom." "A symptom?" "Of your fatal dreaming."

Emma was close to him.

"I dream," she said simply.

He found himself lost in her eyes. They were intense.

"I understand," he said.

"There are mysteries all about us," she said, "that beg

to be revealed.'' She sighed and her focus went away from his face. He was sorry about that. ''That is what brought me here.''

''Yes,'' he agreed. He would have agreed with practically anything as he meant to kiss her.

He reached for her shoulders, stomach thrilling as if he were putting a plane into a dive, heartbeat loud in his ears. Except she had already turned and moved a step or two away so that for an instant he seemed to be embracing an invisible form before he caught himself and realized she was saying, ''Look there!'' Pointing across the field.

He squinted into the sundazzle and saw a half-dozen black men in loose white robes coming out of a screen of brush and moving quickly and smoothly toward the biplane. Their irontipped spears flicked the light.

''Hello,'' he said to himself, ''that's not looking friendly.''

He took a few steps toward them, protectively leaving her behind.

''What do you make of it?'' she asked.

''Wait there,'' he told her.

X

I have to get out of this, Haggard was thinking. *And return to England*.

Because he realized he was afraid, and not of these men or of sailing through the air either. He stood indecisively in the corridor as the airship smoothly thrummed on. He realized he was afraid of something shapeless as a child's nighttime phobia: something that tried to reach him from the wild lands of sleep and was restrained (he sometimes believed) partly by the act of writing as if the stories that poured from him kept the ultimate confrontation at bay. Because he'd had glimpses of the thing and remembered something happening. It was while he was still tortured by the girl who'd refused him. He was twenty years old then. He was half sleepless most of the time and his work had suffered. The governor-general had noticed but hadn't commented yet. He wrote fragmentary letters to her that he destroyed one after the other, each one beginning in attempts at logic as if he could, somehow, enforce himself on her because it was irrefutable; as logic dissipated in frustration the tone became passionate rhetoric as if words could net and bind her heart . . . nothing but desperate, urgent, wracking poetry in the end that was its own defeat. Always beginning: 'Dearest Lilith . . . ' So one morning found him wandering in the African predawn, in the cool, steady wind that blew out of the veldt country, too miserable and numb to crouch over a candle end and try to write anymore. He'd wandered as far as the railroad tracks that ran from —— to ——. He stood on the tracks now under a half-moon and stared across the vast, bumpy plains toward where a mountain range cut its jagged shape into the densely brilliant stars. He'd just convinced himself he didn't care about her anymore. "I don't care," he'd whispered, walking along the tracks, thinking how he would lose himself in his career, explore remote regions, bring the light of Western culture to the most backward and degenerate natives. He was bleary and unnaturally elated. He had forgotten they were at war . . . until he was wondering if he'd meant to commit suicide because the bush had gone silent around him (which he should have noticed at once) and then he realized the moonsheen on the rails ended a few steps on because there was a break there that he'd taken for a shadow. They were at war and he had no business out there alone. Boer guerrillas haunted the brush and waited to ambush trains and convoys. And it wasn't a shadow because there weren't any trees here. And he saw the figures now, dim outlines, the moon showing the slouch bush hats and the glint of rifle barrels and his whole body knew with a shock that he was about to die and his awareness instantly went remote like watching through the misty substance of a dream, moving now in strange slowed motion, turning, ducking, running for the nearest brush clumps, feeling nothing, the gunshots echoing far away, his own breath and heart bursting his chest and then two men suddenly right in front of him, coming out of the very cover he was charging into, saying something in Afrikaans. He was perhaps two steps from them, trying to stop, twist aside, suddenly floating up out of himself (fear reaction, he later concluded, though he was never really convinced one way or another) touching their weapons somehow (except he knew they were physically out of reach), the dark universe spinning and roaring like surf and they seemed feeble, shadowy things. He shut his eyes (still with an impression he was actually touching the guns) as the two barrels blasted at him point-blank. They couldn't possibly have missed. Felt nothing, and was still running when he opened his eyes again. One man had sprawled flat, the other rolling away in obvious terror (of what, his mind asked?) and then he crashed into the darkness of the undergrowth. . . .

And he came to suspect (if not totally believe) much later that an incomprehensible power had acted through him to preserve him for his work to come. At that moment he had accepted death and fought anyway. And a door in his mind had been wrenched ajar and left that way so that he always sensed the nearness of the other world that men drown out of consciousness with the noise of their thinking and desperate wanting and the rigid strenuousness of their civilizations. . . .

He was always afraid that the power would take formless form again and tear the inner gate from its hinges.

All this came in one memory without words and he thought: *I have to escape from her, she's the one who will do it to me . . . she's the one . . .*

He still paused, going over things, when a voice spoke and he turned to see a German soldier in a pillbox cap motion him ahead.

He went and was ushered onto the bridge of the control cabin. He was surprised by the large windows, front and sides. A sailor at the wheel. Standing there with an unlit cigarette in one gloved hand was a slim, medium-sized officer wearing what Haggard didn't know was a cavalry captain's uniform. He looked wiry as a coiled spring. His face was built around a long, thin nose and set off by a thin (and for the period), modest handlebar mustache. His eyes were lively, more green than blue.

Bright as buttons, Haggard thought, blinking at the brilliant dayglare. He was startled by how high they actually were. The water was a smooth sheen ending at a yellowish stretch of coastline.

Haggard recognized the stocky man with the deep eyecreases who'd called himself Van Leeun. Beside him was a nondescript man in a nondescript uniform who he never would have believed was the commander of the airship.

"Good afternoon, Sir Henry," Streicher greeted him. "You see, I have it properly this time."

"Yes," Haggard responded. "How are things in Holland these days?"

"Never mind that," Streicher said, moving his hand in a brushing gesture. "Permit me to introduce Captain Von Schnee—" The thin, fine-nosed officer tapped his heels together. His back was to a large panel of glass full of sky, water and earth. "And Commander Lustluft."

Haggard didn't respond but said, instead: "Where's the charming fellow who chloroformed me?"

While really wondering if the blond woman was on board.

"Forgive us," said Streicher, "but difficult times demand hard actions." He seemed, Haggard suspected, to be justifying himself as much to his countrymen as anyone. "We are at war, by now." Von Schnee raised an eyebrow over an eye that begged for a monocle. "Trust me, we are at war, gentlemen."

"Have you *divined* it, Captain Streicher?" Von Schnee wondered. The stresses in the comment caught the Englishman's attention.

"The wireless will soon confirm what I say," Streicher answered, in German this time. Then in English: "We cannot allow our enemies to gain a single advantage over the Fatherland. We are entering a life and death struggle. We must do battle on every front with unrelenting energy."

"Why do I doubt you?" Von Schnee commented in German.

Streicher sat down and leaned back in the seat. The commander watched him, scratching unconsciously around the edge of his dark, cultivated beard that reminded Haggard of a Russian intellectual he'd met once.

"I am totally serious," he said in German; in English: "I regret any excesses, but we will do what we must, you understand."

"Such as kidnapping civilians?" Haggard wondered, coldly.

"You were, first of all, invited, Sir Henry."

"Oh, bosh. I demand to be released."

"At once?" asked the airship commander, wryly. "Better wait until we get a little closer to ground, eh?" He smiled. The Englishman suspected he focused on his job and the machine and did his best to overlook the ugly rest of it.

"Yes, yes," said Streicher impatiently, his eyes amber, intense, too bright. "First of all, Sir Henry, I wish your cooperation." He unfolded a map and smoothed it down on the table before him. "Please be so kind as to have here a look."

"Well," Von Schnee put in, smiling without much emphasis, "I do not put a great amount of stock in all this business either."

"Be a little patient, Captain," Streicher suggested in German. "You will, I think, learn much before we are done."

"I think the Kaiser has been given—well," Von Schnee said, "exaggerated expectations regarding this reconnaissance."

"Quite otherwise, Captain," said Streicher, in German, motioning Haggard closer.

"King Solomon's Mines," said Von Schnee in English, shaking his head. "A hard one to eat."

"You mean to swallow," Haggard murmured automatically. He glanced down at the map, tight-lipped. He felt vague around the edges and his head throbbed.

"Why the devil would I help you," he wondered, "even if I had the capacity?"

He studied Streicher's eyes. Didn't care for them: hard and unmalleable facts in his mask of easy affability.

"You might want to live," he said.

"Ah," murmured Haggard, with contempt.

Von Schnee was shaking his lean head.

"This is a civilian, after all," he pointed out, in English, frosty and erect, "and even in time of war—"

"Never mind that," Streicher interrupted. "We *are* at war." His tone carried enthusiasm. "War has been declared, thank God. Our troops are on the march, at last! This will clear the air like a summer storm!"

Von Schnee pursed his lips.

"Even so," he said, "he remains a noncombatant."

"Yes, yes, to be sure. Now then, Sir Henry Haggard, aren't you curious? Look at this map."

The author finally tilted his head down. He was curious. There was a river curving like a stricken snake to end in vagueness deep in the amorphous interior. He imagined the sluggish flow rich with rot borne down from the massed fecundity of dense jungle.

He felt dizzy. Blinked hard and shook his head. The map table blurred softly as if melting into mist. Then the map leaped up at him and he knew he was falling, saw colors, sketchy mountains, the wriggle of river marked in red. . . .

Then he was floating above the gleaming water surface and dense overhanging trees were all around him; there was a mountain slope (it looked volcanic) and what seemed broken, pale white, ancient buildings. Nothing seemed to be moving.

And then he came to himself sprawled on the table as hands were already tugging him upright. He kept blinking.

His mouth felt dry. Something seemed to have ripped inside him, like a thrumming nerve in his belly.

Then a hard chair under him. A voice asked if he was all right. He felt as if the world were suddenly thin as mist that might part at any moment to reveal something vast and terrifying. . . .

He barely was conscious of the men around him. He was afraid. He'd never been so afraid.

XI

The white-robed blacks were almost to the plane by the time Woody got there.

For want of anything better, he picked up stones and stamped his foot in the dust. Shouted what he hoped would pass for a warcry. It was enough to give the warriors pause, but not necessarily for the reason he thought. They hesitated and glanced at one another.

"Shoo!" he said. They were shocked. One started to grin.

"Don't you have a pistol in the plane or something?" her voice said behind him.

Without turning, he snapped, "No. Get away from here. Run for the boat. These savages seem crazed." He gestured with the stones now. One attacker nodded his head in mock understanding as if he were dealing with a child or madman. "Scat!" Woody yelled.

That was wrong, he thought.

Because they charged. And more seemed to be coming through the underbrush behind the first four, in a spume of yellow dust, crashing through the brittle, metallically bright leaves.

A tossed spear flicked past Woody. He heard it *thunng* into the fuselage.

"Damn," he said, firing his stones in reflex. He hit one of the tall, charging warriors in the leg, more by chance than aim. Saw the rock rebound into the churned dust. The man staggered and went down on one knee. The dust puffed over him.

Then her father, panting, red-faced, flanked by two British soldiers, came pounding out behind the natives, smashing through the brush. Behind them about thirty more hostiles were coming full tilt.

The soldiers had pistols drawn and they put a few shots into the three who'd driven Woody and Emma back behind the plane. One was hit in the back of the neck and he went flat on his face in a fluff of dust. A second clutched his leg, screaming, limping sideways, robe instantly bright with blood. The third just kept sprinting past the plane, long, thin, loping legs. Woody threw another stone and missed.

The major and his two men turned near the wing to face the oncoming attackers. The wounded black was crawling toward the nearest spur of bush as if it were a long-sought goal.

"My God," Major Willard exclaimed, sucking wind, "Emma, get to the boat!" He aimed and fired beside the two soldiers. They kept shooting. The reports seemed thin and feeble to Woody and he was strangely surprised when two charging warriors went down. Another paused to stare, shocked and swaying, at his body. The rush wavered. The major produced a second pistol. Emptied it. An eight-shot Wembley.

No more hits, but the charge stopped. The natives pulled back to regather. They began shouting and bouncing in place.

"We won't 'old 'em on the next go, Major," the squat-looking corporal said. The other soldier was long and lean with dour lips under a downbent beak, a crease of blood trickling from his dark, matted hair. He knelt to the left, reloading.

"If we had our damned rifles," he kept saying, under his breath.

They were all pale with the dust that streaked on their faces like warpaint.

"Can you get into the air, young man?" the major wanted to know.

"Yes. We're fully fueled."

"I suggest you do so in that case." Because the major looked back toward the boat. The men there were also under attack. "Good God," he said. Heavy attack. A few troops and Arab workers were already running away, heading more or less for the plane. Smoke rose from the boat's deck.

"Christ," said the blocky noncom, aiming and waiting

72

for the mass of natives to charge back into good range, "we're chopped and fried."

Woody was already up on the wing, clawing into the cockpit. He could see (in glances as he moved the magneto lever down and engaged the spark) the men running from the river, blacks closing the distance behind so that they were being sandwiched by the two lines.

The soldier coming fastest had a bloody arm. The next was the short, thin, furious-looking Captain Sneed. The next man (Woody peripherally recalled) was supposed to be an anthropologist: a big, wide man in a khaki bush jacket. He kept falling back. His look was desperate. Then a gust of spears and the big man was spinning as he fled, a long stick suddenly flopping in his back.

"The props," Woody called down as the men fired again. The two-score warriors on the inland side were advancing. He leaned over and helped Emma mount up into the surprisingly wide body of the plane. The cockpit was about ten feet long with benches and storage space. The rest of the body was fuel tank. Woody never liked to consider the results of a fire.

The major was now firing two guns. He was pale. Elated and afraid and in shock all at once. He ordered the other two to turn over the propeller. Sneed was almost there. He kept snarling and firing over his shoulder without much result.

The short and tall soldiers gripped the blades and spun hard. The engines sputtered, shook. A spear clattered over the tail. Another dug in the dirt. A throwing stick rebounded off the upper wing.

"'Ere," said the stocky corporal, "what's the sense a this?"

"For God's sake," Woody yelled over the shots and mounting warcries, "again! Again!"

"Will the bloody thing go in the air, then?" the tall soldier (called Winter) wanted to learn.

"Not if you don't help," he told them.

The major looked less elated now, paler. He looked at his daughter, then at the closing lines of attackers.

"Why are they doing this?" he asked, irrelevantly.

"Spin those damned propellers!" commanded Woody.

"We paid them well," said the major.

The stocky corporal hit the lead warrior, a skinny man who staggered sideways, clutching his bowels.

"Maybe," Private Winter suggested, "this here's a strike to add wages."

"Get aboard," the major told his daughter.

Woody remembered the major rubbing his reddened, seamed face, complacently sucking at his pipe, the tobacco crackling and gusting pale, fine smoke. His eyes had been like frosty blue glass.

"In the event, Mr. Shea," he'd said, "that you outdistance us in the boat, stay near the river and we'll catch you up, in due course."

"You're assuming this lost city of my uncle's is somewhere at the head of this river?"

"Yes, I imagine so."

"Suppose you are mistaken and it is all fantasy?"

"Ah." The burning tobacco crackled and softly hissed. "Well, Mr. Shea, I can think of more than one possibility for this adventure."

Adventure, Woody thought, one layer of his concentration recalling the conversation as the right engine kicked over, popped and caught. The left tried. The major boosted fierce little Sneed into the oversized rear cockpit.

"Spin the other again!" Woody yelled over the grating roar, resetting throttle and levers.

Now the Arab who'd been arguing with the natives by the river came veering out of the brush to the left. He looked wild with terror, stocky legs driving him quite fast, white robes streaming in his wake. He was shouting.

Winter helped Emma in and was then hit by a throwing stick that he partly blocked with his forearm. The impact sound was a hollow crack that made Woody wince.

Then the second motor caught, spitting and hacking, the craft now shaking and bouncing in place.

Winter got inside next, groaning. The Arab was still plunging toward them across the fields, the natives closing fast. The stocky corporal woofed out his breath in a percussive burst that shocked Woody, even occupied as he was with easing the machine into takeoff, wishing he had more room between there and the first line of mimosalike trees. He hadn't expected to take off with a full load and would have started from at least thirty yards farther back, if possible. It wasn't.

He peripherally saw the barrel torso of the corporal rotate as his stubby arms groped for the spear that jutted and swayed from his back. He looked wildly up at his companions in the cockpit and said something in blood. The major, climbing onto the wing, looked back, for an instant seemed about to burst into tears. Shook his head.

"Father," cried Emma, reaching for his hand, "come on, Father!"

Sneed looked at the wounded corporal.

"He's finished," he said.

Throwing sticks rebounded from the fuselage. A spear ticked the upper wing and went end over end. The blocky corporal reeled backward into the propeller blades which hit him a glancing blow that took off half his face.

Woody winced and slammed up the throttles. Emma gasped. Her father clambered into the cockpit, muttering, "Had to be last..." more or less to himself. He had ideas about tradition, going down with the ship, last man to retreat and all that.

"Wait," cried Emma, "that man!"

Meaning the Arab, who was close now, ducking the missiles coming from front and rear, face all open mouth and eyewhites.

"Can't," called Woody over the motors.

They were gathering speed. Tall Winter suddenly vomited into the airstream. Stuff spattered across the tail. The major stretched an arm back for the Arab to grip. The fellow was nearly close enough. So were the blacks. The speared soldier was flopped down in the golden dust like a sack of bloody old clothes.

"Forget that," yelled Sneed, "and shoot!" He was blazing away again, this time with a rifle he'd found in the cockpit. The attackers had formed a rough semicircle around them now as the plane bounced wildly forward.

The Arab fell and just as the tail passed over him he managed to clutch it and drag himself, then struggle with panicstrength onto the stabilizier and then wrap his short arms around the narrow end of the fuselage.

Sneed's snarling ferret face was an icy slash as he aimed

point-blank and fired into the howling thick of them. The craft rolled forward, straining, bumping along. The attackers kept pace, the Arab wailed under his breath, the major looked stunned, spears and sticks arced around them. The blacks seemed to float forward on gouts of yellowish smoke that dimmed and ghosted their outlines.

"Gawd," cried Winter over the general din, "I could run this fast."

The engines sounded fine, noted Woody, leaning forward as if he were joined to the awkwardly struggling machine.

"Come on, my darling," he urged. "Come on . . ."

They were gaining a little now. A lean black with bright, sharp teeth clutched at the tail. Another clung to the outer wing struts.

Sneed fired at the one at the tail, almost hitting the Arab, who was trying to work his way up to the cockpit. He screamed as a bullet ripped past his ear.

"Don't hit the elevators!" Woody pleaded.

"The what?" Winter asked, aiming a pistol. "I'm tryin to scrag that bloody black bastid, not shoot no lift."

He shot at the man tipping the left wing. As the craft accelerated his feet dragged. Then he was hit in the leg somewhere, Emma saw, crouching behind the cockpit edge and staring with amazement. She watched him convulse and sprawl back into the retreating dust. The aircraft jerked ahead and the native on the tail, unhit, let go and vanished into the whooshing cones of dust swirled by the propellers that seemed to be continually condensing into wildly running, flapping, semisolid black figures.

Emma's lips were close to Woody's ear. In the middle of everything he still had time to feel a thrill at her breathheat.

"Will we make it?" she asked.

As he answered he realized his teeth had been clamped together like a vise.

"I think perhaps just," he said.

The wheel bounced over hummocks of mossy earth now. The trees came up like a wall. He gritted his teeth again and felt the blessed tugging as the wings finally began biting air solidly. The ground was starting to blur.

Sneed was firing shot after shot into the thickness of dust-dimmed, robed, somehow unreal shapes that were falling back now as the biplane bounced hard three times, sputtered and hung free on the slightly sagging wings.

"God, Woody," he heard Emma gasp, "we will strike those trees!"

His teeth ground as he pulled all the way back on the stick. Too soon, he knew by feel, the same way a jumper knows as his back foot leaves the ground. Too soon.

"Fifty more feet," he didn't know he said. "I need fifty more feet..."

"We shan't make it," she said.

And then the trees were leaning over them. Somebody (not Emma) screamed and Woody knew there was no hope—except they suddenly gusted up like (she thought) a moth in an updraft and while he later explained it as a "whoosh of hot air from the desert," he never believed it. They were lofted into a gap in the branches he hadn't noticed.

Sneed snarled, the major prayed to himself, Winter closed his eyes and the Arab kept inching forward into the cockpit. Sneed still fired at the vague figures in the sunshimmered dustclouds. Emma clutched Woody's waist where she crouched behind him.

They seemed to hang among the pale, fuzzy leaves that shook the terrific sunlight as the propwash kicked and thumped the branches, blades chewing green fragments.

Woody knew it was impossible. They should have gone in. It was as if a hand had lifted them clear.

He shook his head as they rose steadily and circled to line up on the curving dazzle of river. He tried to ease up and uncramp his arms and jaw.

"Incredible," he murmured.

"What happened?" she asked, still holding his body.

"Updraft," he said.

Winter leaned out over the side and vomited again.

"Take me down," he almost sobbed, "for mercy's sake..."

"Easy there," the major said, a little wild and windy (Sneed thought) himself.

Woody was following the river now, pleased by the way the ship responded, climbing smoothly. He had to beam.

"She's sweet as cane sugar," he exulted. Felt the power

swell within him as if he were actually striding on mile-long, invisible legs of pure energy.

"All those men," Emma was saying, trembling now, reacting to everything that had happened. "My God . . . how terrible . . ."

He blinked. Realized she was right. He'd been too involved surviving to fully register the impact of blood and death. Winced recalling the man hit by the prop blade; the toppling natives slammed flat by bullet hits. The images were a stain on the perfection of air and the lushness of earth.

He aimed the stubby nose toward the misty distance where the river wound away and lost itself.

The major struggled to his knees, resting one arm on the side of the cockpit. He looked down, bushy mustache fluttering in the airstream as they approached a mile a minute. He tapped his daughter's shoulder.

"I say," he called close to her ear, "are you all right?"

She nodded, sitting back on her haunches, releasing Woody. She noticed Sneed looking at her again, sidelong. Wondered, with intentional capriciousness, if he suspected her of something. The perfect policeman, she thought. She didn't care to think anything else.

A chilly-finned friend, she thought.

XII

Haggard stood on the observation deck watching the rich-looking coastline flow smoothly under the airship. Behind him the German crew was doing (as far as he was concerned) whatever Germans crews did. He chose not to care. He'd given his word of honor not to attempt to interfere with the flight.

As if I would, he thought.

So he had the run (more or less) of the ship. He didn't quite admit to himself why that pleased him. Because he didn't quite admit he was wondering about the woman.

They were moving up the coastline now. Inland, the country looked brownishgreen and barren. Lots of low, rounded-off hills, lost in distance haze.

Haggard stared, almost mesmerized by the flow of earth and the blue seasheen foaming white on reefs and beaches. He drifted . . . something flickered and he staggered into the glass as if he'd dozed for an instant: a flash of color and movement, impression of a pale, naked woman, tall, imperious . . . bright, golden energy, a domed, silvery, metallic-looking roof, the energy pulsing and seeming to penetrate her beautiful figure . . . an inexplicable sense that he could have simply reached out and touched her . . . then the cold glass against his cheek and palms.

Am I becoming an epileptic? he asked himself.

He knew he wasn't. The truth was going to be worse than that.

He turned around. The crewmen were going about their business. Von Schnee was studying the landscape through big binoculars. Streicher was gone. The commander was marking up a map with a pair of calipers. The sailor steering looked a little quizzical.

Haggard blinked and walked out of the cabin. He partly expected someone to stop him.

He had no ideas. Stood in the dim corridor listening to the engines throb steadily . . . strolled absently down the corridor past closed doors. It was hard to take in the size of the machine. Almost, he reflected, like a ship.

He vaguely thought about confronting the dapper, mustached spy who'd drugged him. Wondered if he were on board. Wondered if he could still punch someone in the nose.

The blaggard, he thought. *Blackguard . . . maybe both of them are here* . . . meaning the blond woman. He frequently thought about her. Sighed. *Unbelievable . . . all of it.* And now the dizzy spells and the visions. Was the veil thinning between his senses and the "ghost" world of hints and shadows and unthinkable intensities? For a moment he felt a deep fear such as might have been felt by the hero of a Norse epic. Thought of Eric in his own novel. *I can imagine living in those days, there is so much mist and shadow in my soul. . . .*

Events were becoming a mirror for his inner life. His soul, he sensed, was illuminating his circumstances and revealing hidden depths that fogged the surface order of his life.

We may all be players from some lost time doomed to struggle and war again and lose and love again on this present stage. . . .

So he felt what he thought might be the fear a warrior might have felt when the touch and pressure of fate was upon him, when the dim and fleshless hands that strung and unstrung mortal destiny flickered, vast and blurry, around him and he realized he was being brought (without wish or will) to face his ultimate drama and doom.

"To love or die," he murmured, having drifted to the far end of the gondola. Without thinking he opened the door and entered what he instantly took for the captain's quarters: a spacious compartment with gleaming teak floors, rugs, curtains, a fluffy bed and soft chairs.

All this one thousand feet in the air, he thought.

And then he was already withdrawing, seeing too much bare flesh even before he fully registered the strange tableau and had backed, blushing, into the corridor. He shut the door thinking how that had been no vision, filled with the opaque, brilliant blue eyes of the magnificent blond woman who'd looked up and just watched him with no expression. She'd been leaning back in a soft chair, incredibly long, bare, smooth, perfect legs a startling jut out of a rich, rose-red, silky robe. There was a small, roundish, lumpish, dead-white, naked person (he didn't yet know it was a male) squatting or kneeling at the woman's exquisite bare feet as if in perverse reverence, holding one hand as if to kiss it, soft hind flesh sagging and puckered, a bullet head on a thick neck, saying gravelly, yet shrilly, things in German.

"Well, well," he whispered, staring at the closed door, wondering why he didn't instantly move away, wondering (through a violent mix of emotions) whether she'd seen him and if he dared open the door just a crack to check if his eyes had deceived him. "What's wrong with me?" he asked himself, flustered.

"You wish something here?" someone asked, behind him, in German.

Haggard turned with a guilty start. A crewman. Young, freckled, blond hair curling around his white seaman's cap.

"Pardon me?"

"Do you wish to see the commander?"

"I don't, um, *ver-stain*."

The sailor's eyes were small and pale. He struck Haggard as capable, if incomprehensible.

"*Ach*," he said.

"Excuse me," Haggard said, starting forward. The crewman just looked at him with nothing particular in his expression.

Just as Captain Gustave Von Schnee came out of an adjoining cabin. He looked pale and frosty, yet friendly.

"Sir Henry," he said, "I want you to know, that so far as I am concerned, you shall be treated with every courtesy." He shrugged. "I am not fanatically patriotic, you see. I think that decency and manners among gentlemen transcend nationalistic bonds."

"Ah. I see. Thank you, sir."

"These others," he said, waving one hand in a loose circle, "I ask you to overlook their unfortunate background."

"I will bend my efforts in that direction." He liked this fellow. Made him feel a little better. His English, while excellent, had a strong accent. He assumed the man had not been educated in England. He was trying not to think about what he'd just seen in that cabin.

"Good. I am certain you would like to get all this over with and return home to your family."

Haggard smiled, thinly.

"To my family?" he said. "I was never more a bachelor than after my marriage, Captain."

"Ah." Von Schnee inclined his head in a distinctly worldly gesture of comprehension. "So you would like to go back to your mistress, then."

Haggard chuckled. They'd drifted up the corridor as they spoke.

"Hardly," he said. "Though, I daresay, I've been in love in my life." Why was he talking so freely to this man? He caught himself. The odd circumstances had to account for it, he concluded, as well as his natural (and for an Englishman of his class) almost excessive ease of manner.

"In any case," Von Schnee went on, resting one hand on his elegant hip, "war is one thing. But there are bonds among men that outlast the quarrels of nations."

"Are we, in fact, at war?"

Here they were, he considered, floating absurdly through the air over a land that swallowed any territorial claims in vastness and fecund, feral violence. Yes, he thought, and civilized men a trickle of pale ants, picking and creeping and scurrying and after generations would still have left almost no mark on the unending wilderness.

"Yes," the German said. He gestured, depreciatory. "Don't let that chap trouble you too much. He is a . . . how did one say, utter it at Eaton?"

"Was that your school?"

Von Schnee shrugged.

"For a bit, as you say. But that chap, Streicher, he's a bit of all wrong."

Haggard chuckled. Thought this, considering the circumstances, an amazing conversation.

"Ah-ha," he murmured.

"My English comes back to me as I speak."

Haggard felt the sinking tingle in his belly again. He found himself revisualizing the scene behind the door.

"Yes, I—"

But the intense yet languid man was still talking.

"I am actually on gloomy Julius's personal staff at OHL." He meant the commander-in-chief, Von Moltke. "He wants me to keep an eye on these things down here for the army." He went on, affable, loquacious, one hand still cocked on his hip. "I began as a cavalryman, you see." Tilted his head. "Here I am in a damned balloon, eh?" Haggard listened politely. He wished he could discuss the blond woman with this fellow. "But, you see, I am tired of Europe. Or, maybe, Europe is tired of me." He shrugged again. "I think, maybe, out here"—he gestured, comprehensively—"I can find a new place to start from. You know, to regain that whatever-it-is you have when you are quite younger."

"I make you as eight-and-twenty," Haggard said.

"I am thirty-one, sir."

"God. So old as that."

"Don't let my skin fool you about my soul, sir." Von Schnee looked almost wistful, for an instant. He leaned closer, dropping into tones of conspiratorial intimacy. "I am as much a Grailer as the old man."

Haggard was baffled.

"I don't precisely follow . . ." he said.

"The grim one. Von Moltke."

"The general?"

"Yes. yes. That's it."

"He's a Grailer as well?"

Von Schnee was delighted.

"You have right, yes, yes, indeed, old chap. And so we keep an eye on the other sort."

"What sort? You mean like Streicher?"

Von Schnee winked and nodded with pleasure.

"Without doubt."

His excitement, noted Haggard, had tangled his English somewhat. Haggard glanced back at the cabin door where the sentry now stood.

"What's a Grailer?" he wondered. He assumed it was some German word.

"*Ach*, you know. The Sangraal."

"The Holy Grail?"

"That's it, old chap." Von Schnee sighed. Touched his dry and wiry mustache with one elegant forefinger. His eyes (Haggard thought) were quite soft and sympathetic when one looked closely. "And so the Grailers dislike the paganistic . . . er . . . the racial chaps."

He says "chaps" too often, Haggard thought.

"Racial."

"Nordic superior men. All that stuffing." Shook his head. "All nonsense." He glanced over his shoulder, almost languidly. The superior men apparently made him a little careful about who might be behind him. "The General doesn't approve of them."

It seemed absurd. Here were ideas men might die over, and they spoke like conspiring schoolboys.

"Your commander believes in the Holy Grail?"

The officer shrugged.

"Something, yes. A seeking after." He moved his hands as if to clarify the point.

"And you?"

He and Von Schnee reeled slightly into the corridor wall as the airship bucked in a downgust.

"I? Ah. I wonder myself. But I am a seeker." The eyes were quite serious and somehow mitigated the absurdity. "Yes. I have to be. Or else there's not much to my life."

"And what about the blond woman?"

The officer looked vaguely puzzled.

"Woman? Is she on board?"

"You didn't know?"

"I know little about her. She works closely with the other side." He smiled. "I've seen her twice and said happy day, you know." Sighed. "Striking woman, yes?"

"Quite so," Haggard agreed. "I believe she struck me on one occasion already."

The deck tilted forward. They had to brace and lean against the slant.

"We seem to be going down," the German said. "I try not to think about this flying business."

They were already following the tilt forward toward the bridge. Haggard glanced back once or twice as if he expected the woman to emerge.

"What's her name?" he asked.

"Name?"

"The woman."

"Ah. Renate, I believe."

"Renate."

XIII

Former Detective Sergeant Hans Himmel of the Bavarian secret police stood on the flat clay roof of a white, two-story dwelling at the outskirts of the village, shielding his small, hard blue eyes against the blinding sun impact, trying to resolve details across the half-mile or so of bush country.

The charging natives had raised too much dust. He lifted his binoculars, focused into a blur of goldshimmer, flash of wet blue, figures that bounced as his hands shook and then, suddenly clear, black arms and heads, spears, white robes like thickenings of the dust . . . rocked and zagged, trying to pick up the Englishmen . . . a silvery glitter . . . held steady . . . twin propeller blades flashing sunlight as the gawky-looking craft seemed to pull itself free of the swirling dustclouds.

Himmel sucked his lips as if he'd just tasted lemon. Worked his pointed chin. Held his breath, trying to will them to plunge into the treetops.

"Damn," he muttered as, at the last instant, they lifted clear. He saw chopped leaves scatter behind them.

Lowered the glasses and watched the suddenly distant biplane curve into the sky like, he thought, an awkward bug.

"*Verdammen,*" he muttered.

He'd hired the tribe. Paid the lean chief and what he laughingly called the general, a toadlike gentleman with eyes like small, dark stones. The chief had smiled constantly (meaning nothing by it) while moving his long hands in angularly graceful gestures. The general spoke French and translated for Himmel. Himmel had sweated and paid. He'd arrived here two weeks ago, dropped off by an imperial destroyer. His job was to wait for the British party.

He thinks himself a cruel fellow, he almost said aloud, remembering when he'd said goodbye to Joachim Finoch at his apartment in Hamburg. The stocky, swarthy young man with thick, wavy dark hair and a thin, aquiline nose had leaned against the burgundy velvet wallpaper in the narrow entrance hall. He hadn't directly looked at Himmel. Not once in the conversation. Himmel thought him a perfect type for a Roman youth of the late empire. Beautiful but too refined, with only the image of the old brooding energy. In him, grace had subtly stolen force. He'd told Joachim he had to go away again. The younger man had folded his arms across his chest and not looked at him. He held his hands flat under his armpits.

"You want to smear yourself with more blood," he'd said, "like the pagan you are."

I'm really the true Roman, Himmel thought, starting now across the rooftop toward the ladder that served as outside stairs. *I do what must be done. . . .*

Except the English had escaped. No matter. The Zeppelin would follow and catch up. They'd have to land somewhere ahead—if they weren't simply lost when the stupid thing fell to pieces. He liked to think it would fall to pieces.

Wading across the dusty spaces between the crude buildings he wondered if he could recover some of the fee from the chief and general. Sighed and rejected the idea, at once. He always looked to perform well, to achieve something exceptional. Getting a refund from the natives would have had a nice effect on his superiors. Sooner or later everyone would see what an exceptional man they had in him. Sooner or later. Even this eccentric sideshow would be turned to his advantage. He'd show that fool Streicher a thing or two. What an ass to have in charge of anything. Sighed.

Bonaparte never failed to turn events in his favor, he thought.

"I do what must be done," he repeated.

A few young teen and subteen boys and girls were gathered around a cooking pit. Some kind of meat was charring on a spit. Oily black smoke spilled heavily up and billowed sluggishly around them.

None smiled. Silently watched him pass, not even sullen, just watching him stride by as if he had an immediate goal, thin, pale, alien, incomprehensible. His nervously starting shadow stretched before him about double his size as the sun swung down the far side of simmering afternoon, as if he pushed the magnified darkness of himself across the day's pure dazzle.

He was thinking about Joachim again.

He's naïve, in many ways, he said to himself. Sighed. Wiped the sweat away from his eyes. *After our troops take Paris I'll bring him to Maxim's....*

The notion pleased him. He remembered things from the last time he'd toured . . . the stone bridge over the Seine not far from his hotel where he had liked to stroll alone and lean on his stick in the thinly sunny late afternoons that autumn . . . he'd sigh in the wine-rich air and watch the slow leaves drift down in redgold bunches, collecting and sinking in the sluggish current near the shore. He'd been lonely but strangely content. *He'll have to try the new wine,* he insisted to himself, *and poached salmon at Ce Soir . . . and then the Louvre, naturally . . . dessert along the boulevard . . . any one of the cafés, practically, would do . . .*

He thought about getting fitted for a new suit; about buying several new neckties and a pair of shoes. Smiled.

Joachim can never keep a crease in his pants for half an hour at a time . . .

He reached the building where he was staying. The walls were cracked, the floor packed dirt.

He went out of the baking heat into sudden coolness. Blinked at the dim interior. The glassless windows were bright blurrings.

He sat down at a rude table on a tilted, backless stool. His leatherbound notebook was as he'd left it opened to where he'd stopped writing that morning.

He kept his back very erect as he took out his pen and uncorked the ink bottle.

It matters little, he thought, *what absurd ideas Streicher and these others have . . . like any good centurion I will help my people win the war in any way I can setting aside all superficial restraints so beloved of civilians and cowards....*

He reread the last few stanzas of the epic he was composing. He concentrated. Reached within for words to express the purity of his concept of male vigor and courage and how those qualities were the only true basis for an ideal state. Honor, courage, pride. The well-rounded man willing to sacrifice his life for his Fatherland. A band of such brothers, like Spartans, were worth a world of uninspired men.

"Yes, yes," he murmured, excited, poking his pale and pointy tongue between his thin, bloodless lips, his mind racing, flooded with words and images as the pentip scraped and tried to run forward balanced on the foaming tide of his invention. "A band of brothers," he voiced as he wrote, "their sabers bright against the falling darkness."

Joachim would see how he expressed himself. He'd submit the poem section by section to the magazines. He was confident that he would capture the spirit of the times, the spirit of purity and dedication.

The war would clean things up. Put values and masculine virtues in sharp perspective.

He paused, pen poised, reflecting. Groped in his pockets until he came up with a cigarette. Lit up and exhaled a bluish haze toward the nearest windowfull of dazzle. The smoke slowly swirled and gathered around his head while he thought about how, like antibodies in the organism, the German soldiers were being drawn to key points of the European infection of cowardice, base spirit, materialism, greed and racial decay.

He pictured, poetically, masses of relentlessly striding Teutonic men surging toward the sores that were Paris and Moscow—not the Paris he actually knew and loved, not the river scenes where the water softly reflected the almost too precious cityscape . . . not the clean café or the hotel's snowy linen or the pleasant citizens of the better classes . . . no . . . the sore was in shadow and gathered unseen on twisting, dark streets . . . the whores, he realized, were only an outward symptom, for instance . . . how to express that? The corruption was so subtle it touched almost everyone, the germ of it, a tainting . . .

He had unconsciously clenched his teeth and the strain flicked tension across his right cheek. He winced. Sucked down and slowly released a lungful of smoke.

"Come on now, mister," the naked girl in the calf-length candy-striped stockings told him, in French, "it is very simple, no?" She was curled up into a ball of shocking flesh, too-red hair flopped on the white bed. She'd faced him and spread herself. He'd stood there, undressed, stunned, heart pounding. He'd gawked at the fleshred gash. "Come, mister. Just put it inside here, is it not so?" He'd felt chilled and yet sweaty in the stuffy room. Was afraid he'd faint or choke. *I am having an attack,* his mind had shouted.

He now started on the backless stool and blinked the image away. The whore. The symbol was the point, not the mere reality.

"The poor child was a victim of degeneration," he murmured, tapping the pentip on the paper. "In the new world we will create such things will never be."

The sore would be cauterized by the war. He was concentrating so hard that at first he didn't hear the wavering hum of the motors.

"Mister,?" she'd wondered, sitting up, concerned while he'd yanked his clothes back on his narrow body.

"I have to leave," he'd said, pale and stunned. "I'm quite sorry but I have to go...."

"There's the river," Streicher said, leaning close to the glass. Von Schnee was beside him. "There's the rock formation." He was excited.

"What is that?" Von Schnee wondered, pointing at the masses of dust that were still settling in the wake of the natives' futile pursuit of the biplane.

Streicher shrugged.

"Smoke or something," he said. It was drifting on the steady wind, sifting down over the water and trees beyond the whitebrick village. "Perhaps our friend Himmel had good fortune."

Von Schnee stared at the massive rock that distinctly resembled a negroid skull.

"I, personally, do not count Herr Himmel among my intimates," he commented.

Streicher was amused and mockingly serious.

"You, my dear Captain," he said, "reflect a decadent system of aristocratic illusions. Power is the key thing, the rest, nonsense. It is precisely men like Himmel who will be useful in the coming order of things."

"You make too much of my remark," Von Schnee simply said.

"I comprehend a great deal in it."

"More than it contains, I fear." The younger captain shrugged.

Half smiling, Streicher squinted and took the measure of him with his eyes.

"Perhaps," he allowed, then looked back with satisfaction at the skull-shaped rock formation. "The dwarf was quite correct," he murmured. "We found it."

"The dwarf," Von Schnee said simply. He'd seen him come on board but not since. He'd seemed to be humpbacked, and twisted to the side with each step.

Streicher seemed very well pleased with himself as the airship gradually rode down an invisible slope toward the open fields between the whitebrick village and the writhe of river.

"We are not fools, Von Schnee," he said, smugly. "Think what you please, but this is all very serious business."

Haggard had come in just after Von Schnee and he was close enough to the window to see and be stunned by the sight of skull rock at the mouth of the river. While smaller and less impressive than the image in his mind (the terrain was different too) the fact of it was overwhelming. He didn't know what to think.

He had the feeling again, the sense that this journey was not merely to a place but into, somehow, meaning.

XIV

The sun was setting behind a wall of mountains. From just under the level of lowlying clouds the view from the cockpit was immense and breath-stopping.

Emma sat up beside Woody, who was concentrating, trying to spot a good landing site. The long shadows helped, revealing rills and breaks in the ground.

"How fast are we traveling?" she wanted to know, cupping her hands close to his ear.

"Over a mile a minute," he answered.

"God," she said.

"That's nothing. I've designed a single-seater that will reach 150 miles per hour."

Sneed was leaning close to them. His hard blue eyes watched them.

"Nonsense!" he shouted over the wind and motor noise. "Why, the wings would fall off. Farman himself said as much."

"Horsefeathers," retorted Woody. "There's virtually no limit to . . ." He broke off, dipping the wings, tilting the ship into a moderate dive, aiming for an open stretch where the river made a wide S.

The tall soldier suddenly vomited into the slipstream again.

"Try to control yourself, man," recommended the major.

Emma was absorbed in watching the glowing water rise toward them, the massed clumps of trees, the shadows across the redtinted plains. She thought it marvelous.

"God," she cried, hair fluttering loose, one hand gripping Woody's knee as he worked stick and pedals, sinking the craft into a shallow glide, the propwash kicking back the tall grasses . . . and then he cut the motors and touched down in a soft, warm rush of sweet summer air, rich earth smells, syrupy flowers and crushed green.

The landing was smooth enough. He frowned because they tilted and bounced slightly when the wheels first touched. He wondered if it was a design flaw on his part or miscalculation. He'd had to jerk the stick to compensate and that annoyed him. He hated sloppiness, especially in himself.

He sat there and let out a slow breath. Suddenly his weariness hit him. He was stress-tired. Her shoulder, arm and breast were leaning into him. He liked it. Thought about kissing her again. About running his hand improperly over the inimitable elasticity of her youthful bosom. The thing was, he'd never made love to a woman where she (or himself) was actually undressed. He'd kissed and groped at his fiancé, on occasion, to little purpose beyond making himself uncomfortable. He'd had actual intercourse at school with a rented woman, twice, in the company of two other fourth-year men, pants to knees, skirts up, on the lawn behind the old gym. After curfew. The girl, roundfaced, with a brogue, saying, "The clock's runnin', me dove. Get on with it now. Ah, there's a fine laddie."

Well, he'd done it. Both times. And then once when one of his mother's friends found him alone in the fruit cellar of their big house overlooking the Missouri River. He'd gone there to discover secret pleasures alone in the artificial dusk of dust and furnace-smoked half-windows, shelves, cobwebs, rich old wood smells and the inexpressible scents of dried peaches and apricots. He'd lain on the soft, burlap sacking, pants gathered around his thighs, staring up past the shelves into the dust shapes that hung like smoke after spuming up from the soft impact of his teenage body on the old cloth, gradually settling through the almost colorless glow. He'd been lost in imagining the girl who lived across from the Catholic church near the railroad tracks. He'd been running with other boys up from the canal, through the trees, shouting, breaking into little swirls of senseless chasing, working their way up the hill to the woodframe, sag-porched three-and four-story apartment houses called the shanties. The gray evening air had been cool and smelled of raw mud, water, cooking food and the thick effluvia from where the sewers ran open to the canal . . . fleeing in their noise (with an eye cocked for the local youths, tough, redfaced, in rough sweaters and baggy knickers) through paveless alleys until he had suddenly paused to catch his breath (after a frantic and irrelevant climb up onto a stone wall) squatting on the smooth top in his blue and white semiuniform from St. Hugh's day school (which would doom him if caught there by locals, to violence, and if by solid citizens who knew him, embarrassment and official censure) then jumping down into what he didn't realize was a churchyard until he actually saw the faded-looking stained glass and looked across a grassless plot where a cracked statue of a woman knelt facing a paintless slat fence with a paintless frame house beyond. He'd dropped down and crossed over to peer through a missing pane of stained glass (the feet of some angelic being apparently rising from a cloud) and seen, with a slight shock, the alien interior; dim pews, banked candles set mysteriously in gleaming glass cups... he'd looked with wonder and then moved on, watching the dark windows of the house behind the fencing... smoke had drifted down from the chimney and a gust stung his eyes... then he'd seen the girl in the window, her naked back to the opened sash and then the stunning impact when she'd turned and it was all there. He'd gasped. Felt a dizzying rush of heat, had an impression (before he actually ran away) that he'd brought with him to the cellar and wove there into the soft coils of his languorous daydreaming, forming and reforming the nude, epiphanic female flesh which dissolved in an instant in a sudden, damp suck of air from the opened door, a blow that jerked his whole body up, hands spasming in panicked shame for his pants, the woman already standing over him a rustle of layered garments, her face in shadow above the window line, the familiar voice (that he hadn't yet realized was amused) saying, "Don't be afraid, Woodrow, no one need know of this."

His right hand had been straining with a knot of pants material that had caught hopelessly on one hip, relenting as the silky skirts rustled and she was kneeling over him, her hands where his hand had just been and he'd nearly cried out at the amazing sensation as her head drooped down gracefully and (what he didn't yet understand was) her mouth absorbed and drew at him shockingly and he'd felt terror (only briefly) that his body might turn inside out and explode in immolative ecstasy. . . .

He shook his head as if to break a spell.

"Let me off this damned thing, by Christ," the long soldier was saying, scrambling over the side and flopping into the thick grass. "Let me kiss the bloody earth."

The major stood up. Sneed lit a cigarette and watched the pilot and the young woman.

"Are you all right, my dear?" her father asked. He was too pale. Seemed (to Sneed) a little shaky. He'd expected as much. Assumed he'd have to take charge from the (he thought) essentially deluded older man. He was too weak for the job, that was obvious.

"Yes, father," she said. "Considering the situation."

Woody stretched and winced. Sneed squatted down on his hams, resembling a gargoylish carving on some ancient temple. He ·puffed smoke thoughtfully as the last daylight drained away into the fecund stillness of the waiting jungle.

Woody felt her shudder. She hadn't moved away from him yet. He didn't want her to move. He kept thinking about how her body would feel. Her mouth . . .

"Never fear," he said, "we'll get into the air again tomorrow."

"I'm uncertain, sir," she told him, "if my fears were altogether of *not* getting back aloft."

"Please," he reiterated, "call me Woody."

He noted that Venus was already visible above lowflying clouds that had absorbed the last coals of sunset.

"Very well, Woody" she said. "And I am Emma, as you know."

"Yes."

He studied her now. Ignored Sneed watching them. Her shape was just hinted in the lost light.

"We didn't have time," the major was saying, as he lowered himself to earth, "to pack all our supplies. But, in this birdlike fashion, so to speak, we may arrive at our destination quickly enough to preclude want." He nodded, tapping the side of the stubby craft. "Remarkable thing, eh?" Looked around into the dimness. "We'll rough it here for the night." He groped in his jacket for his pipe.

95

"Obviously," Sneed said.

"Yes. Well, at least we've got the map, eh, Morris?" That was the first time Woody had heard Sneed addressed by his first name.

Morris Sneed sucked at his cigarette, finally standing up and spitting tobacco flakes from his lips.

"The jolly old map," he said. "Well, I'll do my duty, if it comes to that. Here or in any other godforsaken place in our empire."

"Our," murmured Woody. He thought it vaguely odd that he would put it just that way.

The Arab lowered himself to the soft ground and realized he had to relieve himself, seriously. The English, he recalled, had particular ideas on that subject. He headed back behind the tail assembly to look for a private spot. He was working at not thinking about what had happened. He felt a terrible foreboding of personal doom out there surrounded by what he took to be fanatical and apparently amazingly incompetent foreigners. Well, first things first. It wasn't too late to pray. The Koran made exceptions for extremities. It was merely late sunset, he told himself, night had not actually fallen.

"A lot of research and some little blood," the major was saying, standing over long, lean Winter, who was still stretched out on the weedy surface as if kissing the earth in fact or rapt in some barbaric worship, "has gone into this adventure." Got his pipe lit. "Let's get cracking here, shall we, chaps?"

"Bravo," murmured Emma. "That's the spirit, Father."

The Major complacently sucked his acrid briar and filled the windless evening with stinging fumes as Emma climbed down with Woody.

"How far inland would you say we are?" she asked, generally. Woody realized she was being brave. Present circumstances might have produced utter collapse or bratty hysteria in many women of refined background.

"Hard to be sure," he responded. "The coastline curves and the river winds steeply. We got a late start but there wasn't much headwind." He shrugged.

"A hundred miles?" suggested the major.

"Much would depend on the wind," Woody had to say.

"I feel none at the moment," she said. She was working hard, she realized, at not being afraid. There was something familiar in all this, with a dream-feeling. She felt for an instant as if the darkness closing in were somehow sentient, a misty vagueness full of perceptions and malicious intelligence.

"It changes with altitude," Sneed said.

"Quite right," Woody affirmed. "Anyway, I would estimate sixty miles or so."

"I wonder where the great swamp is, in that case," the major said.

"Swamp?" the long soldier asked uneasily.

"In Haggard's tale there are marshes like a vast moat around the mountains of Kôr."

"If such a place exists," Sneed said.

"If we make an additional sixty miles we will arrive at the latitude of Kôr tomorrow," the major concluded.

"I should think by midday," Woody said, "barring difficulties with—"

He was cut off by a shriek. He turned, strained to see into the darkness beyond the squarish tail of the plane. Faint luminescence showed where the river curved past them about a hundred yards away.

"What cry is that?" wondered the major.

The soldier, Winter, drew his pistol.

"Bleedin' natifs," he said.

"Where's old Abdul?" asked Sneed.

Woody and he were now groping forward, trying to focus. Another yell, followed by a rush of Arabic desperation.

"His name's Ayeesh," Emma said, behind them. The plane was a silhouette against the last line of deep-red sunset.

"Where are you?" Woody called ahead.

"Helping me," the Arab cried a little to the right. Woody could see nothing.

"Where's the cursed electric torch?" demanded the major. Woody could feel him trying to take command.

"There's one in the cockpit somewhere," Woody called back.

"Please . . . please," came the plea, "helping me, please! Aii . . ." Then Arabic again.

Then a reek of fumes, a flare and stuttering roar as Sneed got a kerosene lamp ignited. He'd had it in his pack. The yellowish light fanned out ahead. They were aiming for the terrified voice, Sneed now in front, the major a little behind Woody.

"Where was the poor devil going to?" Woody wondered, aloud.

"To empty his bloody bowels in bloody private," commented Sneed, holding the weak, smoky light above his head.

There he was. A shock as the light resolved him out of wavering shadows because he seemed to have been sliced in half at the waist, arms flapping and pushing at the earth.

"It's all bloody damn bog here," Sneed said, slowing down, perceptibly. It was true. Woody could smell it now.

"Oh, oh . . . of helping me, Englishmen . . . helping . . ."

"There's our swamp," the Major said, with a certain satisfaction.

Suddenly, as if released by night itself, stiff-winged insects snicked, flicked, nipped, batted at their ears and eyes.

Ayeesh pushed feebly at the muck, sinking as if the dark mass of earth were swallowing him in pulses, like a snake.

Woody slid his feet carefully closer. The slimy stuff sucked at him so that he had to stop just out of reach of the trapped Arab.

"I need a stick or something," Woody said over his shoulder at where Sneed and the others had stopped. The wavering light showed a few stunted trees, greasy-looking mud and the dull glint of the river beyond.

"Helping me . . . aiii . . . inch' Allah!" the Arab cried.

"What's that babble?" demanded Sneed, lifting the lantern so that the wan glow tossed soft shadows over the struggling half-figure.

"Illah Allah iila'ha Allah Mohammedan rasulu Allah!"

"He is praying," Emma said, from a few paces behind Sneed.

"Stay still," commanded Woody. "Grip my hand," he ordered Sneed, and once the grips were locked he inched forward, gradually going knee-deep. The major locked both arms around Sneed's waist and was in turn anchored by Winter. The major's substantial bulk did more to stabilize things than all their struggles.

"Let the bloody bastid go under," Sneed hissed in a sustained whisper.

"You're a considerate man," Woody said.

"He's baggage, anyway," Sneed said, then snarled at Ayeesh, "Shut up, damn you, and reach here!"

Woody was in range now, struggling in the warmish, porridgelike mud, stained, arching himself until he caught the slick hand and leaned into a backbreaking pull.

Emma and Corporal Winter added their efforts.

Woody's fingers and wrist burned. His back felt sprung. He saw bright flecks behind his shut eyes. Sneed cursed and yanked hard, jerky, as if he meant as much to free his hand as help.

Finally, by unbearable fractions, the stocky Arab was pulled free as if the darkness itself were trying to suck him down. And, Woody found himself thinking, swallow all of them as if they were penetrating a world where the terrors of dreams became solid, where nightmares could grow a clutching hand. . . .

And then they were gasping back where the mud was shallow, the mucky Arab facedown, arms out as if to Mecca, blowing lung-bursting breaths into the dark muck.

The major held his daughter's arm. "Are you all right, my dear?" he asked.

"Yes," she said, "considering the circumstances."

"I'm sorry you have had to endure these things."

She shrugged and squeezed his arm. He licked his lips. Squeezed his eyes together. Felt the sweat cool on his body. He thought about why he was there. Because his wife was dead and his daughter, sooner or later, would marry and leave home; because his son had died in India; because he dreaded being alive after he retired.

He sighed.

Because he hadn't done anything special and felt, as a result, a hollowness in his purpose. He seized on this (probably mad) project in a last hope of some memorable achievement. He was sorry she'd been drawn in. The fact was, he wanted her near him. He felt he'd missed so many years . . . recalled the sweet, bright-eyed, delighted child pushing her toy horse around the smooth lawns of the estate, bare toes digging into the rich earth, alive with laughter and the soft, sweet babble of childhood. . . . And then too many years abroad at the outskirts of wars and native uprisings around the empire . . . lost years . . . a master of clerks, as he thought it, while other men triumphed in the field . . . coming back to an adolescent, darkhaired (she had been a blond child) thoughtful daughter with a whole mysterious purpose in life.

"I'm glad to be with you, Father," she said. "I was intending to stow away, so to speak, as it was."

"I think we'd be well advised," Sneed was saying, "to keep close to the flying cakebox over there until daybreak. If we'd come down in this damned muck it would have been just sorry soup." The lantern showed his pale, thin-haired head, brittle eyes and pale, slash lips.

Ayeesh had rolled over. He looked like a wet clay statue. His nose hooked from a mass of slime.

"I have go to river," he muttered, "and then what? . . . *aii* . . ."

"Indeed," said Sneed. "You did a rare good job of it, too, my dusky friend."

"This place is curse . . . yes . . . very bad place . . . have of hear much . . . much . . ."

"What have you heard?" Emma wanted to know. "God," added in a murmured, "I'm terribly hungry." And she had to ease her bladder. The thought of roughing it just struck her. All these men around. And then, how to keep properly clean?

"Eh?" responded the Arab, as Sneed played the wan light over him. The flickering yellowish beams seemed to float him shapeless in a pool of shadow so that he might have seemed (to an overwrought imagination) a creature formed of mud, a blind lump made imperfectly by some earnest but not-quite-competent god.

"What have you heard?" Emma asked him.

"Bad river," he replied. Then muttered in Arabic. Spat mud and rubbed his face. "Water bad . . . sick from badness . . ."

"That's illuminating, 'n't it," remarked Sneed.

He put the uncertain light on Emma for a moment. She blinked and gestured impatiently. She looked drawn (Woody thought) but composed. Holding up very well, it seemed.

In a minute he'd get up and see to the plane. Shut down the fuel lines, check things out, oil levels and so on. . . .

She's done very well, so far, he thought. *Better have a look at the wheels and go over the wing fabric, while I'm at it. . . .*

"Let's get a fire going here," the major was saying. Rubbed his hands together. "Well, Sneed," he said, almost heartily, "a bit of adventure right from the starter's gun, eh?"

Sneed flicked the lantern light over him for a moment. Showed him mudstained and eager as a boy.

"Adventure," Sneed said, "me great arse."

"See here, Sneed," the major said, furious.

"Have a care what you say," Woody suggested.

The lantern was now under the ferretlike face, the shadows adding lean voraciousness to the expression.

"My tongue slipped," he apologized without expression. "I beg your pardon, Miss Emma."

"This is an adventure, you know," she said, diverting the subject. She sensed Woody's hostility to Sneed mounting fast.

"Call it a half-holiday, for all of me," the little man said.

Woody helped the Arab as they slogged back to the firm ground around the aircraft. Sneed sat down with the light between his legs. The almost bilious beam shifted his hollow-seeming eyesockets.

"Bear in mind," the major said, helping long, narrow Winter arrange wood for a campfire, "the War Office entrusted this business here with us."

"If that's so," Sneed said, cold, factual, "then they don't make much of it on top."

The major looked back at him with a sense of betrayal.

"His Majesty himself—" he began.

"I know that. I heard you say so before." The wide, soft beam rocked between his hands so that his hungry face seemed to melt and re-form from the empty darkness. "The general staff isn't too worried about what HM thinks."

"Whatever do you mean to suggest, Mr. Sneed?" wondered Emma.

The light twisted again and the beam lost itself wanly in the misty darkness that had closed around them. The bogreek flowed thickly around them on the freshened breeze.

Woody tried to focus on Emma's face across from where he sat. The night swallowed the fuzzy illumination like a blotter. Their outlines would go solid, then fade as the fog filled and unfilled and the lantern shifted in Sneed's small hands.

Finally the ferretlike man spoke. "No one takes this mission very seriously. They don't think much of the lot of us. These are facts."

"So, you have no confidence in me," stated the major, needlessly, thought Woody.

Sneed didn't even have to agree. He twisted the lamp and the sallow glow thinned to nothing in the shifting coils of fog that gave Woody a feeling of being pressed into himself and cut off from the time that ran the outer world. As if, he almost thought, the machine had flown not through space only but history too . . . yes, and out of history into some lost world. . . .

"I came along," Sneed was saying, "to report on whatever the Germans do. Nobody thinks they're actually looking for the lost city of spinach." Smiled too thinly to be seen.

"Is that so?" archly asked Emma.

"Yes," said Sneed, emotionless except for the underlying sense of contained fury. "It is so, miss. The Germans mean something quite military."

"Ah," said Winter, stacking the firewood carefully. "Out 'ere rippin through empty air and lost to death out in mud and muck. Ah, that's all right and military."

The light showed his long neck and small head. Woody couldn't shake the feeling that they were all just sallow sketches on the background darkness and that the darkness was somehow more substantial than themselves. . . .

XV

Haggard stood at a window staring at the dusty, whitewashed-looking village. He studied the skull-shaped formation across the wide rivermouth: empty eyeholes and parted mouth a shock of darkness in the blinding sunglare.

"Incredible," he murmured. *To find yourself in your own dream . . .*

He noticed a white man hurrying across the field, raising the fine, smoky dust. He recognized Himmel and somehow wasn't surprised.

The airship swayed slightly in the steady breeze from the sea. The crew in the field held long hawserlike lines at the front and rear to help stabilize the craft. Fortunately, the wind was steady.

I'd like to strike him in the nose, he thought.

Started and turned as the blond woman came up quietly behind him, and said, "Henry."

He just stared at her. She was wearing a dark shirt, boots, and skirt trimmed with delicate silver filigree work. Her hair was pulled back almost severely from her forehead. She waited while he thought what he thought.

"I saw you open the door," she continued.

He turned back and saw Himmel being greeted by Streicher outside. He'd just jumped down from a hatchdoor. About four feet or so. They shook hands and spoke with animation.

"Yes," he said. "It was a mistake." Remembering the long, perfectly shaped legs, aloof face framed by a golden mist of hair, the squatting dwarf at her feet. . . .

"Some people," she said, "cannot be part of the ordinary flow of life."

He didn't quite sigh. Prepared himself for some sort of

103

repulsive elitist discussion. Really wanted to ask her what the naked dwarf was all about.

"Yes?" he wondered, noncommittal, still watching out the window. He felt she was standing quite close to him now. He was within the aura of her heat and scent. The perfume he couldn't dislike. He liked the feeling. He admitted he was attracted to her. It had been a long time since he'd felt that way about anyone—all right, he'd restrained himself. He'd always restrained himself when it came to that. . . .

"It would be pleasant," she said, "if life were simple and innocent."

"Perhaps it really is, in the end." He watched, without concentration, as Streicher and Himmel moved under the gondola and he heard the hatch bang shut. Their voices were only faintly audible because the propellers hadn't stopped. She thought she heard Himmel saying something about: ". . . bombing . . . a lesson . . . black swine . . ."

"Innocent," she murmured.

He shrugged. "Despite our sophistication and attendant sophistry," he said, "yes."

Her voice had a shrug in it. She could still hear Himmel and Streicher. They were in the corridor now. Streicher was saying something about reprisals coming later.

"Sometimes," she said, "one must make extreme sacrifices."

"For one's point of view?"

The commander came back onto the bridge now and gave orders to the helmsman. The men were hauling the lines back aboard.

"Hardly, Henry. May I call you Henry?"

"You ask the prisoner his permission? I would say these are unlikely circumstances in which to concern ourselves with forms of address." He tried not to look directly at her. Felt the surprisingly gentle tug as the machine rose forward.

"I do not know what you mean by a point of view, Henry," she stated in her rich, remote voice that gave the impression she was, somehow, beyond both innocence and corruption. "I do what I must for reasons not altogether of my own choosing."

He kept picturing those magnificent legs and the squatting dwarf at her feet.

"How," he wondered, "would that differ from the general human condition?"

"I serve power. Not myself."

"German power."

She shook her head. "No," she said, "just power."

Haggard felt the conversation had a kind of dreamlike quality as if they were speaking through a blurry veil that hung between them like smoke or the dustmotes that flared into golden density as the airship turned out over the winding river heading for the interior about twenty minutes behind the biplane.

"I don't quite follow," Haggard murmured.

"I think you do, Henry. I refuse to be a slave or a plaything."

He grimaced. He would have liked (he admitted) to have touched her sleek skin, caress her legs. Blinked and grimaced.

"Ah," he said. "Powers. And I thought I was merely seeing an unclothed dwarf."

"He is a means as well," she said. "But I think you understand all this perfectly."

Frankly, it sounds sort of, well, seamy, put a certain way in broad daylight.

She moved closer while he was speaking and he unconsciously gave ground until his back was touching the window. From the edge of his vision he saw flowing green jungle and open veldtlike fields, the brightly writhing river.

"You also belong to power," she told him. "This creates, if you haven't noticed, intense fascination for others."

Her full lips parted and he saw teeth that were just slightly too long. And her scent, veiled eyes, strong, long fingers on his shoulders and then lips that were pure softness, a feathery, burning tongue that stunned him so that his knees almost sagged and he felt (it had been so long) like dry, cracked, hard soil suddenly soaked in rainwater.

His arms went up, instinctively. Then blinding pain: he cried out, struggled, pressed at her, his lower lip caught in a terrible vise, trapped, afraid to shift his head, tasting his blood, crunched flesh already swelling, leaning forward as she moved away, keeping his face pressed to hers, convinced that the hard sharpness was about to rip his lower lip off.

He sounded his pain and outrage. His hands fluttered, helpless.

"Arr," he whispered, muffled by her face. "Stop...stop ... for God's sake!" A shocked red blur in his head. He was totally disoriented by their strange, agonizing intimacy. "Stop it! Let me go!" Perfume, pain, silky softness, an image of a woman with the fanged face of a fiend, skull filled with gusts of fire, eyes like burning stones.

And then she released him and he reeled, sobbed breath, pursed his stung mouth and went to one knee, breathing steadily. Blood trickled through his fingers.

"You belong to power," she told him. Behind her the captain and a crewman were just staring.

His eyes teared so she was just a blurriness against the windowful of daybright. A melted, foggy shape.

"Oh, you bitch!" he whispered, quite beside himself. "You insane bitch." Kneeling there as if in deference or worship.

"Be calm, Henry," she was saying, soothingly. "You'll come to comprehend such exquisite experiences soon."

She looked at the sailors in the compartment. They were quite amazed. The commander shrugged and turned back to the problems of the course.

Haggard held his mouth and shut his eyes, as if a brightness had blinded him. Except for the pain, he was suddenly back under control. She was simply mad and cruel, he assured himself.

And against his dark lids he sharply saw (as if dozing in the sun at the beach) her nude, perfect limbs, exquisite feet all against a dark background where a flickering flamelight flashed, seeming to shine through surrounding masses of stone, a hot, hard fire reflected in crystal bright eyes....

XVI

Woody woke at dawn. He stared up at a misty rose sky. Blinked and shifted his body for a minute or two. Yawned. It was pleasingly warm but already getting steamy.

He tried to work something out from his last dream. Fire and smoke. He held the fading, elusive images for a few moments. Fire, smoke...massive little men coming out of the smoke waving axes and spears...himself moving on what seemed horseback... the men closing in, covered in black plate armor that seemed burned...smoke and terror all around and a desperate need to escape and save something... save...

"What?" he whispered, as the images vanished under focus like shapes at twilight.

He sat up and just stared at a wall of ground fog that enclosed them in an almost perfect circle. The air smelled wet with a sour note of decay.

He rubbed his face and scratched his back. Then scratched his cheeks. Instant blood, swelling, sweetish pain. Insect bites. He forced his fingers to stop. Shook his head.

The major was snoring. He could see the outline (in the mist) of the Arab and whoever was sleeping beside him. Emma was curled up under the lower wing, wrapped in a sheet of canvas, one delicate hand upflung near her face like (he thought) a child. She seemed lovely and peaceful. He felt a tender urge to touch her.

He started slightly when something moved, dark, out in the fog. A man. Thin and smallish. Had to be Sneed. Yes, it was. What was he up to?

The major snored, the Arab breathed heavily, troubled, and Woody found himself thinking about breath. How they were all submerged in a sea of air that flowed in and out of everyone living. How that air fed the spark of the heart, that steady, pulsing flare of life that sustained them...

He had an odd idea, suddenly, that air itself was power and that words, which, in a sense, shaped air into meaning, had power to touch everyone within themselves....

He frowned. Those weren't normal Woodrow Shea thoughts. Basically he believed that air was a problem mastered by a mechanical triumph of human logic. Except, logically, he ought to have crashed on takeoff yesterday.

Sneed had stepped out of the blurring gray and stood over him, narrow-bodied, harsh, wan-looking.

"It's all bog around us," he said, gesturing with quiet savagery. "Bloody miracle. Another fifty yards and we'd have been lost." He grimaced. "I don't fancy perishin' to no purpose."

"I don't fancy perishing at all," Woody reacted.

Miracle, he thought. *Miracle* ... The first one had been the takeoff; now the landing. *I can get off in less than one hundred yards....*

They'd have to roll the aircraft back to get a run.

"I'll do what I must," Sneed said. "Die or live, for all of that."

"For what purpose?" Woody found himself disinterested, thinking about the air again. It was astounding that this heavy weariness called the human body could float toward heaven in a cage of wires.

"For God and country," Sneed said, deadpan. "A man has to be ready to die at any moment."

God, thought Woody, looking up into the brightening, rosy haze that was a perfect dome above the round walls of mist. *What does God have to do with country?*

The air was fresh and perfect and full of the morning's life and even the richrot of the boglands was sweetish.

He took a deep breath, ignoring Sneed. Wanted to wake Emma and discuss what he'd been feeling and pondering.

It is all a miracle, his thinking went on, *all bright life and sweet air....* Because you left it all behind, it all dropped away as you soared ... all the world fused together into a single detailless blur and you were above all grit and torment and vast fields of purity opened in the hush of sky....

* * *

No one said anything as he taxied across the grassy plain that was essentially an island in the swamp. Emma shut her eyes as they bumped along and the silky, long grasses swished and the loosely machined engines (by later standards) clicked and tap-tapped. The major looked resigned, Sneed mildly annoyed. The Arab mumbled prayers and the long soldier rolled his eyes like a condemmed man.

The wall of fog was about fifty feet high and the rising sun seemed to have had no effect. It looked thick as cotton wool to Woody as he got the nose up just as they went into the cool, wet stuff that exactly demarcated the deadly bog.

For an instant it was terror: nothingness, blindness, no dimensions, so he couldn't tell if they were climbing, diving or tilting. He felt strangled. Helpless. Kept the stick pressed into his lap as if it meant something.

Over the background rush and clatter he heard Emma saying, "I feel suffocated!"

Climb, he thought, *curse you!*

He could smell it now, the fetid stink all around them boiling up on the mist as if (he thought in his new, overimaginative mode) the mud coldly burned and smoked.

"We're bloody well doomed!" cried Corporal Winter. "God save me!"

"God save the King, you mean," snarled Sneed with sudden, meaningless fury.

"Easy there," ordered the major.

If we don't break out soon, Woody thought, *we'll go in or hit a tree....*

He remembered the trees across the open space from when they'd landed yesterday. Were they actually climbing? He was afraid to touch the control as the heavy-bodied plane labored through the soupy air.

He gripped the vibrating joystick and held his breath. He kept saying to himself that they had to escape, had to overcome the blinding and blindly senseless force that dragged all life and hope and aspiration down into suffocating and relentless mire.

"Fly!" he hissed. "Fly!"

Then blinked, shocked by sunlight as they were suddenly free.

"Thank God," Emma said.

It was a fine day. Underneath, a silent sea of ghostly billows; above, brilliant gold and blue. A gull caught Woody's eye. It swooped and curved across their course in a flash of white . . . soared higher. . . .

He felt exhilarated, patted the hull of the machine.

"She's a fine lady," he said. "A fine lady."

"Lady?" wondered Emma.

"This eggcrate," he told her, proudly. "This rattling dustbin. I love the dear sweetheart."

She wiped her looseblown hair from her eyes.

"Now I understand," she said, "why your fiancée was jealous."

Before he could respond, the major, braced against the cockpit wall, was pointing behind them.

"Look there!" he cried.

Woody looked and was properly stunned to see a huge, blood-red, cigar-shaped airship following the course of the river. Even at several miles' distance he could make out black Maltese crosses on the tail planes.

Germans, he thought. Then put it together. *My uncle . . .*

On board the Zep, Streicher stood with hands on hips, round, solid-looking head cocked to one side with satisfaction. He faced the forward cabin glass.

Narrow-bodied and ready, Himmel stood beside him, gently stroking down his mustaches with his long middle finger.

"You observe, Himmel," Streicher said, "the manner in which the power of providence brings us what we desire?"

"You don't believe we have come on them by happy chance?"

The stocky man shook his close-cropped, massive head.

"That would be shallow, Himmel."

Himmel shrugged.

"If we stand so well with fate," he asked, "then why did they escape to begin with?"

The round head shook again while Streicher kept his eyes on the biplane, fragile and dark in the shimmery sky.

"Ah," he said, wearily, "and why were we not born with all we were meant to achieve in life?" He chuckled like a schoolmaster. Leaned toward the commander who had taken the helm. "Bring us in close to them, Captain, if you will."

Von Schnee was sipping coffee across the cabin, talking to a robust, stoop-shouldered, middle-aged sergeant named Müller. He looked up at the others now.

"I hope you intend to signal our intentions," he called over.

Streicher didn't turn.

"Captain Von Schnee," he said, "your duty is to attend to your men. The High Command entrusted me with deeper matters."

The fact was that Streicher's own captaincy, like a priest's or doctor's, carried little weight in the field. But his political power was another matter since it flowed from the royal family.

The bearded commander was watching Streicher and he didn't quite have to say, "Convince me before I'll act." Enough was:

"Yes?"

Streicher narrowed his eyes and gathered himself, then pushed the force of his will into the commander, thinking how later on, when things took their proper shape, these outdated officers and gentlemen would find themselves a bit humbled.

"The security of the Fatherland and the life of the all-highest," he pronounced, smoothly, "could be set in danger by our enemies were that craft there to elude us."

The commander pursed his lips. Nodded.

"You are sure of this?" he asked.

"There are enemy soldiers in that airplane, Herr Commandant."

"Even so," said Van Schnee, "they very likely don't know that yet."

Streicher set his jaw, locked his hands behind his back.

"They will soon be enlightened!" he said, ordered, "do your duty!"

"Amazing," remarked the major, watching the huge, red sausage loom up on their port beam.

"Bloody God," said Corporal Winter, drawing his pistol as if to menace the gigantic shape now blocking half the sky, the curved side seeming to lean out as if about to topple and roll over them.

Sneed sneered. Held a hunting rifle already aimed at the glassed-in gondola. He was muttering. No one heard the words over the general noise. He was saying, "Our people must prevail over the barbarians . . . these damned Huns."

Emma was impressed.

"What a remarkable construction, Father, " she said.

"Yes," he agreed.

Woody shrugged.

"It's clumsy," he pointed out. "And has additional shortcomings."

"What the devil are they doing out here?" the major wondered.

"Hah," said Sneed. "What are *we* doing out here?"

"Can it really be Streicher and those chaps?"

Then percussive, ripping sounds. Sneed instantly understood. Started answering fire. Then Woody spotted the orange-red flashes at several points on the gondola that hung under the gasbag.

"This is friendly," Woody said. In the pure silence and perfection of the air to be shooting one another seemed absurd and meaningless. Then three sudden puckers in the lower left wing and the shock instantly left him chilled and naked. "Machine guns." At any instant a slug could crash into his suddenly very fragile flesh—or hers.

He kicked the rudder pedals and slammed the stick over. The stocky craft sluggishly veered to the right and down.

More bullets ripped past. Winter was cursing and shooting beside Sneed while the Arab lay low in the cockpit and moaned to himself. Emma had clutched her father as the plane lurched into a curving dive.

"Damned if I cannot outmaneuver this fat object," he whispered.

Hauled back on the stick now, felt the structure creak with strain as the nose jerked up. He felt as if his nerves were strung into the machine's delicate braces and thudding engines.

Don't give way, he prayed.

He leveled off just above the dense ground mist.

Treeshapes, twisted limbs, seemed to reach for them, half melted in the smoky, pale billows.

He twisted around to see Sneed and Winter shooting almost straight up. The big redness still covered too much sky.

"How can they drop so fast?" he asked himself. They were too low now to veer sharply. He picked up a few feet of altitude and went into a gentle bank right.

Sneed was yelling, shaking the emptied rifle while Winter was half on the wing, vomiting again.

By the time Woody craned around again the airship was so close he could see the pale faces of the machine gunners in their open, bucketlike stations and glimpsed other men behind the cabin glass.

They're too close to miss, his mind said. *How can they lose altitude like that?* He couldn't have matched it short of a vertical dive.

They couldn't miss now, and didn't. The airframe shook as if a dozen sledgehammers pounded at once. Pieces of wing and fuselage flew off. A fragment of something rang his forehead like a bell and one eye shut down. The other swam in red mist.

"Oh, damn," he said. "Oh, damn . . ."

Tasted blood that ran down his face.

"My God!" cried Emma.

The plane bucked. The Arab screamed and rolled, clutching his arm.

"Hang on, young fellow," the major encouraged.

"Roast, you scum!" shrieked Sneed. "I've done for you, Hun bastids!"

Because (incredibly to the others who didn't understand hydrogen's intense volatility) Sneed's shots had struck a spark somewhere in the giant gasbag and the ship was ablaze. Which explained the speed of its sickening fall. the booming, hissing roar of mad fire drowned everything else out now. Emma shut her eyes as one of the machine gunners plunged past, streaming flame and smoke.

Others were jumping. The biplane curved just clear of the suddenly skeletal airship, the black bones crumbling beneath vast gobbets of smoke as it went into the mist and the swamp hissed and wild gouts of steam spewed up.

The gondola spun free and skidded to earth like a tossed canoe.

"Roast, you bastids!" yelled Sneed. "Sizzle, fry and roast!"

His delight was cut short because Woody had lost consciousness. The red mist had filled his head and then gone dark. The plane, just skimming the misty treetops, went in, miraculously flat, bounced, slewed, missed a pair of trees, scraped wings, jerked violently right and stopped, nosed over and tossed Sneed and the major clear into an open stretch of field that was relatively dry. They rolled into a puddle and skidded to a stop.

Haggard held on, shocked to see the two-engined biplane weaving through lines of tracer bullets, a smallish man standing up, braced against the upper wing, firing what (he believed) had to be an express rifle at them. It seemed a feeble blip of fire until the glass burst at the front end of the bridge.

The commander yelled. The helmsman heeled the vast vessel ponderously toward the plane, perhaps five hundred feet below. They kept firing. Haggard knew there was no way to miss but what harm could such pinpricks do?

And then he had an idea it might be Woody down there. Was it possible?

And then men were shouting wildly outside in the corridor. The door slammed open and a pale, panicked sailor was yelling and panting. Haggard recognized the word "Feuer." His heart sank. Then he heard the terrible sound, a hollow, booming roar like (he thought) a gust of ignited gas in a giant oven. Then a blast of terrific heat that hurt his face.

"Oh, my dear God," he voiced.

Leaping forward, and then already behind two others, in blind reflex pressing, tearing at an oversized window.

Suddenly they were dropping fast. It felt like a fast elevator. The man beside him kicked and the pane fluttered away. The biplane was under them, seeming to rise like a toy on a string.

They're doomed too, he thought.

The white fog made the earth uncertain. It was like falling into a soft and silent dreamscape except the heat was beating at his back as if someone had opened a furnace door. In other parts of the craft men were screaming.

I will have to jump, his mind said. *I will not be burned....*

His clothes were already smoldering. Stocky *Hauptmann* Streicher rushed out into the corridor and was driven back by a gust of flames. Stinging smoke filled the cabin.

"Dear God," Haggard prayed, "spare me great pain if I must pass over." Thought of his dead son. Even his own doom left the grief unaltered.

Shut his eyes and readied himself to go. Next he was sprawled flat on his back on the hot floor, choking, roasting, then a sickening, sudden plunge... a terrific impact... splashing, crackling, mashed by the terrific blasting of the fire.

The gondola rolled over. A hissing as the cabin filled with steam and smoke. Water thick as syrup soaked him, and he found himself scrambling, kicking, clawing out the window, other men thrashing beside him, writhing into the suffocating mire, blowing it out of his nose and mouth, wriggling, kicking, climbing over others who were climbing over him in turn like (he didn't actually think until later) primal forms on creation's first day struggling to escape to light and nourishment....

The pain in his choked lungs snapped his body into spasms and then he broke the surface. Someone's foot hit him several times.

He sucked breath. Lay flat looking up into immense, black, solid-looking coils and gouts of smoke lit dull red by the still fireblasted, melting framework of the shattered airship that lay perhaps a hundred yards off, the heat spewing steam and superheated fog into wispy shapes his stunned consciousness accepted as tormented ghosts. From deep in the tunnel of his shock he watched the pale, steaming flutter into a winglike shape that seemed to beat up into the boiling blackness then melt away....

Men were still screaming in the collapsing fire as the recondensing mist began raining back down. A few lukewarm drops spattered Haggard.

Near him someone was moaning and muttering German misery. The firewind was still shaking the trees. The screams in the fire died away. He vaguely thought about the flames of

115

hell and lost, pale souls trying to escape and rise to heaven on hopeless, tattered, fading wings.

A vast, numbing weight pressed him down into the matted, partly rotted vegetation and reeking muck. He let it. Shut his eyes. Knew he was out and dreaming now . . . seemed to see someone standing over him, barefoot, wearing a kind of pale dress. A bald man in a dress, a massive golden chain around his neck set with darkly red stones. His eyes were bright and hard like fine jewels.

There was no voice. He *felt* the figure's message . . . no, not a message, just things he knew already as if they shared the same consciousness. Something he knew . . . yes, the way to the temple, the way through the impassable mire, the single path that went the whole way to where the river could be navigated again—because it was totally overgrown for many torturous miles . . . and he was partly thinking, as the images wavered, that he had touched the actual source of fantasy, the place in himself where it fountained into the mind. . . .

"No," he whispered to himself. "This is true."

Got his eyes open. The black smoke was going up in slow, heavy folds. The heat was fading. No more screams or curses.

He was alone, as far as he could tell. The fog was regathering and big warm drops rattled on the oversized swamp leaves.

He got to his feet. Nothing hurt too badly. Some of him was scorched and torn but nothing too serious. Amazing, he realized.

A few feet away, tipped over, the shattered gondola lay like, he thought, a beached skiff. Part of it was smoldering. The crisped framework was a hundred yards beyond that, lost in the fog and its own fuming.

He and others had been tossed out on skidding impact and been cushioned by the rotting vegetation and mud.

There's a miracle, he thought. Shook his head. *Lost in a swamp . . . lost in one of my own tales . . .*

"So much for the pride of Germany," he murmured. Now that the fire had faded the humid heat was already beginning to bother him. And the bugs were coming out again. Clouds of them. *God, what a place. . . .*

He recalled glimpsing the river as they went down.

Sighed and thought about his family. How long were they going to believe Kipling's story that he'd gone to Canada?

If I can get to the river and somehow put a raft together perhaps I can get to that village....

After slogging a few hundred yards he went suddenly lightheaded. He reeled, clutching the thin, pale trees that more often than not snapped away and left him staggering.

"Something's wrong," he muttered. He leaned into an unrotted tree and vomited. Tasted bitter, burning bile. His temples throbbed.

Water, he thought. *My God, am I dying just like this?*

The dim swamp tilted as he tripped and staggered through clinging mist, insects flicking into his face. Had to sense direction and had a moment of panic suddenly knee-deep in mud. He felt doomed as in some nightmare, thrashing on like some infant while the wet, clinging earth sucked him gradually down.

His heart raced. Head pounded. Eyes hurt... and then he saw something in the mists ahead... veered, panting, desperate... thought it was a woman in a gown... closer, feeling as if he gazed down from above himself as if his neck had stretched impossibly....

He managed to follow the strangely familiar robed figure and suddenly the footing was firmer. The apparitional outline kept just ahead of him as he staggered along a twisting spine of solidness.

He kept trying to catch up. Another few steps... another ... he reached ahead for the hem of the robe where it seemed to shape itself from the soft gusts of mist... finally closed his hand on it, floating miles above himself now, the world rocking under his distant, tiny feet; then fell, glimpsing a sudden watersheen....

The trees had rushed up too fast the moment he dipped under the fog that lay like a pond surface over the swampy jungle. Emma clutched the side and shut her eyes.

She registered a crackling, swishing, and then she rocked with the impact as they went in just short of the river.

When she opened her eyes she was looking at Woody's head. She didn't register the blood at first. Then she did, and didn't cry out. Just stared and felt ill. And then someone was tugging, lifting her and she knew it was her father. He had a slashed cheek and one eye was swollen shut. Smeared with mud (as was Sneed) he'd instantly rushed back to the plane to help her. Sneed limped behind him and picked up his carbine. The plane was tilted forward but not obviously damaged.

Corporal Winter's tall body was draped over the lower wing, chopped almost in two by machine gun hits, centered in a wide slap of blood that had soaked into the fabric.

She kept staring at Woody as she was half lifted down.

"My Lord," the major was saying in a stunned voice. "My Lord God..."

The Arab was whimpering, nursing a shattered arm, crouching in the long cockpit. The major, holding his daughter close into his body, feeling trembles racking her in what seemed almost regular intervals, tried not to look at Woody. Sneed virtually sniffed with contempt studying the slumped, bloody aviator.

"He's a dead one," he said, almost scathingly. He had no comment for Winter.

Then, like a nervous terrier, he ducked around the upended fuselage and poked the rifle into the wall of fog that ended abruptly at the riverbank there.

"Hun filth," he muttered. "Well, we'll see what's what, eh? We'll sort out what's bloody what."

"There's nothing to be done for them," the major was telling his daughter. "The living must go on...the living have to go on." He was in mild shock. So was she. Nothing in her life had prepared her for this. She kept picturing the reading room at the university. An image of rows and rows of books and the feeling she had that somehow, in one of them, she'd discover something everyone else had missed, a secret, a lost truth that would answer an age of questions and open a window into uncanny and supernal meaning....

Sneed cocked his head toward the fogwall. He heard muffled shouts out in the swamp. Had to be the Germans. Some, obviously had survived.

"We cannot stay here," he said. "Work our bloody way upstream and lay a surprise for the stinking nit bastids." He sneered with unnatural confidence. "We will defeat them in detail and exact a full measure of vengeance."

He was actually thinking about his dead wife. He kept

118

remembering her sleeping, wasted arms stretched out while her insides invisibly knotted around her terrible cancer. She'd stayed sunk in drug fogs right to the end and he'd never been able to say the things he'd never said up until then. They'd stayed inside and hurt. Because she'd believed his career would raise him up and he would help others like himself since he was living proof that a man of ordinary birth could rise in life and compromise nothing of honor and decency. It hurt him to think of all he'd left unsaid, it chewed inside him, and he never found anyone later (as he hadn't before) to trust even a fraction as much as his wife. So he believed it would gnaw him forever and had accepted that because he'd been nothing remarkable and had only his singleminded focus on his duty which, in her eyes, had been a sweeping, exalted ambition. Her death (he never realized) left him cold where before he had merely been hard and indifferent to his own pain. After that, no pain mattered much. And he sought out the most difficult circumstances to do his duty in. He had to or it meant nothing since there was nothing else. He sometimes liked to believe it was for her memory, though he really knew better. He sensed his superiors distrusted him, considered him a fanatic and kept the most critical and dangerous work away from him. So, like the major, he had taken what he could get.

Neither Emma nor her father had really been paying attention to him. Ayeesh dragged himself to his feet, gripping the lower wing with his sound hand. Sneed, without a backward glance, started walking parallel to the curve of the river.

"Come," he commanded.

They followed him and went about fifty yards or so. The Arab limped along, supporting his smashed arm, greenish pale with pain. The major was staring too much, holding his daughter's hand with both of his.

Sneed spread his thin lips in a tight smile. Pointed to a mass of giant roots from a thick tree that had somehow been tilted over into the now almost stagnant, brownish river.

"We wait behind here," he said, indicating the buttresslike effect formed by the roots and packed mud. "Then we close our trap." Kept smiling. Even in her present state Emma felt he was very strange: the way he kept stressing the word "we," for instance.

My God, she thought, *that poor young man that poor young man . . . Oh, Woody . . . poor Woody . . . I . . . I . . .*

She didn't want to think about it yet. Didn't dare. Just tried to concentrate on step-by-step things: find ways to keep her father and herself safe. Find food and shelter. Find their way home. Somehow. Somehow . . .

"Yes," murmured the major, "it seems to be war. Yes . . . seems to be war, in fact . . . yes . . ." He suddenly sat down, his back resting against the massive roots. "We must fight, naturally. We are Englishmen, after all."

Emma just stood there, chewing her lower lip. She was surprised to find she had an appetite. She studied her father. He seemed suddenly so old. His cheeks seemed to have fallen in overnight and there were deeply incised lines under his eyes.

He tries so hard, poor darling, she thought. *He should never have come out here.*

"How could they do that to us?" she asked.

Sneed was pacing at the fogborder that loosely matched the bend of the river. He moved as if literally sniffing for Germans.

A tic flickered across the major's eyes. He kept swallowing hard.

"I . . ." he began. "I don't think . . . first the natives turned bad . . . then this . . . War is a terrible thing, my God, a terrible thing . . ."

"Not by half yet," Sneed said, shrilly. "Terrible is still to come!" He sniggered. "As Blücher said at Waterloo, 'Raise the black flag! Take no prisoners! I'll have any man's head who shows mercy!' " Nodded and paced, tilted his face as if to sniff. "They'll be along, those Huns, and we'll make it pleasant for them, we will." Smiled his wide, tight smile.

"War is a dreadful thing," the major said.

"A living enemy," said Sneed, not looking at anyone, "is a dreadful thing."

Then she realized she'd have to face something awful because they all had to eat and the bag of provisions was still on board the plane.

I just won't look at him . . . not his face and then I will be able to do it. . . . She told herself to be resolute and turned at once and was already heading back the way they'd come along the river bend, saying over her shoulder, "I shall be back shortly, Father, just rest and wait for me."

Because they had to survive. Somehow. And the food mattered. How had they forgotten it?

The facts were just hitting home and so she almost ran, seeing only the bright grayish blankness and gritty-looking water.

And then the tilted wings and the twisted body of the soldier became solid and as she came closer she saw Woody again except this time he was on his feet, leaning against the fuselage, one hand pressed to his hurt head. She caught her breath.

Alive, she thought. *Alive. Thank God. Thank God. . . .*

Less than twenty minutes later Major Willard came to himself, more or less. He was staring at the fogwall where the dense swamp actually began. Then he stood up. Heard Ayeesh sighing where he lay at the water's edge in great pain.

"My God," he said, "where's Emma got to?"

"Filthy Huns," cried Sneed from behind him.

He turned and saw just the man's squinting eyes and wispy-haired forehead behind the carbine he had aimed, resting the barrel on the packed earth of the uprooted tree.

"What?" the major wondered.

He jerked back around in time to see where a tall, menacing figure had just loomed up in the mists, arms outreaching, and the shocking blast as Sneed let go a shot except the man was already falling so the bullet tore into grayishblank nothingness.

Emma bathed Woody's head. The slug had ricocheted across his temple without doing more than scoring the bone and drenching him with blood. The pain, however, was like (he later said in description) having six teeth shattered with a hammer.

He could only look out of one eye at a time; both at once melted his sight into pure fire. She held the water-soaked wad of linen (ripped from her underskirt) against his forehead.

They were sitting close together when the muffled gunshot sounded upriver.

She stood up at once.

"Father," she said. "Perhaps that nasty little man..."

He was holding one hand over his left eye. It seemed to help. When he stood up the drain of blood hurt.

"Where?" he asked. Talking wasn't so good either. Listened and heard no following shot.

"Upriver," she said, distracted, wringing her hands, nervously. She was in an agony of indecision. "Not far. I have to go back..."

They paused in the silence and fog. The background sounds of the swamp had gone still and now were churning away again.

"Yes," he agreed, "we'd better have a look."

Ayeesh had rolled over onto his side, his ruined arm on top. He was trying to keep himself in a semidoze. There wasn't much else to comfort himself with.

Sneed, rifle smoking, had come out from behind his improvised parapet and stood over Haggard, who lay flat on his face on the soft ground.

The major rolled him over, with considerable effort, and was properly amazed. Looked up.

"The traitor himself," said Sneed, "has fallen."

The major wasn't so sure. Gently touched the writer's forehead.

"Sir Henry," he said. The man was coated in mud (as were they all) but there was not much blood showing. His clothes were blackened, burnt away in places.

Sneed was already, somewhat jerkily, prowling along the fog curtain again, head tilted as if sniffing.

Arm in arm, Woody and Emma made their way upstream. He was getting to be able to keep both eyes open for a few steps at a time. His head still beat in brassy agony. He had trouble taking anything seriously beyond his skull.

She recognized the spot by the uprooted tree. Woody had to rest and leaned on the trunk.

"Why would he go away?" She blinked and shook her head. Looked around. Licked her pale lips. The fog gradually pulled back as the sun culminated breaking out overhead now, spattering the dark water and treetops with flickers of hot gold. She realized that in the fog her time sense had blurred. She bit her lips, staring at the ground. "Tracks," she murmured, uncertainly, "perhaps we can follow tracks."

Woody was massaging the back of his neck as if that might help the head.

"Hmn," he sighed.

"Have you ever tracked anything?" she asked.

"No."

"I imagine they'd follow the river. That's what we did the first time."

"Yes."

She took a few vague steps that way. Visibility was about fifty feet now.

"Father . . . father," she said, quietly.

"We'd best stay close to the plane," he told her.

She nodded, abstractedly staring at the soft folds of blankness.

At that moment the major was just dabbing a strip of cloth soaked in warmish riverwater over Haggard's temples and forehead when Sneed let off another shot into the thinning fog.

He looked up as someone shot back. The bullet hit the water and bounced away with a soughing whine.

"You both missed," he said absently.

Haggard was speaking, eyes closed, head rocking unevenly from side to side.

"Ahhh," he whispered. No one was listening just then because a half-dozen Germans, mud-spattered, singed, insect-ridden, slogged out of the mists, weapons leveled. "Ahh . . . Thou art deceived, fair ones," he went on, unheard, "you seek the key . . . ahhh . . ."

Sneed stood and worked the trigger point-blank over and over. Click, click, click . . .

The stocky Streicher flanked by Hans Himmel stopped on the bank, staring at the river, more or less indifferent to Sneed, who was now covered by four long German service rifles in the hands of four soldiers. Sneed held his weapon clubbed now, in the center of a loose circle of troops.

Himmel seemed virtually unaffected. His pointy chin

was held high, chinabright eyes quick and eager. However, he'd lost most of his pants and his very thin, dead pale and knobby legs, ending in what seemed clubs of mud, made an almost comic impression. Streicher's face was black as a minstrel's. He favored his right arm, which had been seared.

"Don't kill him," he absently ordered in German. He was staring at Haggard who, all but inaudibly, was saying, "...thus will the destroyer be freed and come forth, O fair ones, and the dread eye of Anubis will fall upon Thee..." The major heard him this time but it seemed merely sounds to him. His daughter would have had an idea what tongue he spoke just as Streicher did, leaning closer while, that moment, Sneed hissed and charged the soldiers.

"We will never surrender, you rotten fish!" he cried, swinging wide and wild at the nearest, who ducked aside while the one behind him (heavy-shouldered Corporal Müller) slammed his rifle butt into the stringy Englishman's upper back behind the heart.

Sneed went to his knees, sucking air like a beached fish; then flopped and thrashed on the ground.

The troops were still too stunned and burned and beat to say much.

While Streicher stopped over Haggard, looking pleased, the whites of his eyes disconcerting the major in their absurd contrast to his sooty face.

"Yes, yes," he whispered. Cocked his ear.

"...am I not a priest forbidden to look?" babbled Haggard in a tongue that didn't even seem made of words to the major. "*Aii*...am I not forbidden the sight of the holy places?...O, the sanctum of Ra..."

"I think," said Streicher in English, "that is how it actually sounded."

"Pardon?" wondered the major. He managed to get one knee under himself. He felt drained and uncertain. Didn't quite know what he wanted to say to these men who'd attacked them, it seemed, senselessly. Nothing at all had turned out. Nothing. He'd imagined his return to England (he kept thinking about it now) smiling quietly in the ultimate vindication of success. So many of the triumphs he'd imagined for years were meant to be savored in the dark paneled rooms of the club or at country dinner parties.

He wiped his runny, bloody nose. What a disaster, really. Emma . . . he didn't want to think about Emma.

"Oh, what a bloody fool you are," he said to himself.

Streicher bent near to Haggard's listless head as if he meant to kiss his face (Corporal Müller thought) or bite his neck.

"Speak, priest," he said, in English.

The major heard just enough to react.

"Are you daft, sir?" he asked. Got to his feet, back to the river.

Hans Himmel came over and leaned on his rifle. In the background they were tying Sneed's hands behind him. Half of Himmel's mouth smiled. His mustaches were plastered flat along his cheeks. His pointed chin was blistered.

Haggard said something in no words at all this time. His sensitive hands poked and picked at his face like an infant. He believed he was talking to his son, Jock. Trying to say what he had never been able to say in a place where there was no speech.

"He's feverish," observed Himmel, in German, with faint contempt. "But you do well to speak with him, *Herr Hauptmann*. You could do little worse following his ravings than keeping to your own inspirations, I think."

Streicher grimaced at the thin spy. He was amused and tolerant, in a lofty way.

"Naturally," he said, "you have no conception, Noncommissioned Officer Himmel, that I have already succeeded in my primary aim." He nodded. "He is open to remembering now. It is necessary I direct his memories where I desire."

Himmel didn't exactly sneer.

"Would you like me to brace at attention, *Herr Hauptmann*?" he wondered.

"You make a mistake, Himmel, if you imagine your political connections place you above military discipline."

But Himmel had already turned away and was considering Sneed, who'd just managed to sit up, breathing hard, eyes like a hurt ferret's, glittering with malice. Himmel rather liked him, on balance. They had an instant kinship.

"You, *Herr Hauptmann*," Himmel said, "are using the army for your own purposes." He shrugged. Pondered the Arab, who hadn't moved, still crouching, wrapped mutely around his pain, by the fallen tree trunk. "Where do we go now?" he asked Streicher. He wondered if the woman, Renate, was dead. Amazing any of them had survived. That would be something to tell Joachim Finoch if he somehow got out of this nameless country back to civilization. Well, he'd stood up to his fate as well as possible and had nothing to reproach himself over. In the end, a man had to give everything for his nation and race, he reasoned, because the race went on while each individual melted away. A man's strength flowed from the race and his greatness was to receive as much of that power as he might bear.

He shrugged. The woman was attractive, he considered, but he preferred looking at the Italian or Greek types with their satiny, almost milky, translucent skin tones. Women, he was sure, lacked the willpower to do the work of the race and were merely breeders. A dedicated man, like himself, was excused from breeding, naturally. He was like a priest in service of the soul of the people. Intercourse with women drained the male's essential vigor into their esurient passivity. The Greeks understood that principle.

Streicher, he thought, *is a weakling or at least unfit for real command . . . true leadership is in the racial soul. . . .* These and like reflections occupied him and buffered some of the shock inherent in their situation.

"We go where he tells us, naturally," Streicher replied, indicating Haggard. "My insubordinate young fellow." He was grinning. Then fixed his stare on the prostrate Englishman. "Priest?" he asked, in English.

"Yes?" whispered Haggard.

"Look here," suddenly began the major, without much conviction

"Be still," snapped Streicher.

"He will lead us?" wondered Himmel. "I think we'd better build a raft and float downstream." He stared at the Arab again.

"Priest," repeated Streicher.

"Yes?"

"Where is the city?"

"O, fair ones . . . Thou hast stained the altars of the secret god and will let loose the terror from under the mountain of Hell . . ."

Streicher bent his round, stolid face to within inches of the Englishman's. He might have been the dark tempter leaning over a starving ascetic in the wilderness, his creased face blackened by the fires of Hell.

"Where is Kôr, priest?" He demanded.

"Ahhh..." was the lucid response. Himmel grinned but said nothing.

"Follow the river?" Streicher prompted.

"Yes...river..."

Himmel nodded, mockingly, to himself.

And next Haggard's eyes opened, glassy, bright, remote. His fingers plucked at his beard.

"Obviously," said Streicher, straightening up.

The writer's stare was on the sky above the thinning mist. A gull, having drifted far inland, was circling there, a shock spot of whiteness in the hazy blue. As his eyes tracked the long, slow, curving swoop, he seemed to come back to himself somewhat.

"Well," he got out, licking dry lips, "so I seem to be alive." Blinked.

"Sir Henry," said the major.

"Hello." He strained a moment, partly sitting up, then falling limply back. "Sorry...I don't seem to be able... just now..."

Streicher was still over him.

"What do you recall, priest?" he demanded, blinking his small, hard, dark eyes.

"Eh?" Haggard stared at him, then looked over at the major, who looked vague and stunned. "Have I been rescued?"

"Rescued?" he wondered. "Were you kidnapped by these German chaps?"

"Rather," said Haggard.

The major looked nervous. Himmel was sort of sneering behind him. The soldiers were watching, dour and uninterested. Sneed was sitting cross-legged, arms bound behind him, smiling as if it meant something. Ayeesh, Haggard noted, looking weakly around, was lying on the riverbank staring away across the brownish, clogged water.

"I seem to have lost track of my daughter," the major was saying. He puffed his cheeks and let them collapse. "This whole business has been...most...unfortunate."

"For you British, yes," said Himmel. "We Germans love the swamp. No doubt it recalls the delights of Bavaria to the captain here." He grinned. He had picked up Streicher's southern accent almost at once. He, himself, was a Berliner and quite a snob about it.

"How are you, Sir Henry?" asked the major, almost clutching at this moment of normality.

The author stirred and looked away. Felt the fever rekindling.

"Ah," he whispered.

"You have fever," said Streicher.

"Very shrewdly comprehended," Haggard muttered, loud enough to draw a smile from Himmel. Haggard caught it. "You damned little spy," he said

"Forgive me," the pointy-faced fellow responded, "but I had to do my duty."

"Duty, yes."

Himmel shrugged.

"War had to come," he said.

"Yes," said Haggard. "War had to come."

The mist seemed to have gotten into his eyes. Sometimes things loomed up...boiled into shapes...sounds went strangely muffled. He wanted to say some more on the subject but his energy seemed to melt into the earth.

Suddenly he recognized the man bending over him: the sensual face a coppery mask that he knew concealed the inhuman countenance of a guardian of the underworld.

"You would grip Osiris," he told the face, "and keep him in the shadows." Streicher knew the tongue again though it was no Egyptian guessed at by scholars. Yet he knew it. "I cry out against Thee, O Ptah, lord of chaos." Whoever named Ptah lord of chaos? wondered Streicher, later.

"Show Osiris the way out of here," requested Streicher. Then to the men behind him: "Prepare a litter." Two had set down a heavy case they'd borne on their shoulders. "Lash the gun under it. The priest here doesn't weigh much." Müller, the corporal, heavy-shouldered and stooping, shirt hanging in sooty strips, looked displeased.

"That weighs—" he began.

"Do as I say," ordered Streicher.

Himmel sneered impatiently.

"Victory will soon be ours," he said, sarcastically. "All we need to do is find a sufficient source of sick Englishmen to carry."

"So," said the major, as if he'd just realized it, "we are prisoners?"

"Unless we decide to shoot you," Himmel said. "Though I think we will only have to make you sick and then you will be more valuable than gold or guns." He was cynically amused. Streicher ignored him, more or less.

"Huns," said Sneed, getting to his feet, rolling his shoulders, hands tight behind him, obviously in great pain from the backblow. "Huns . . . we will drive you back to the stinking bogs you crawled out of," he assured them.

"We seem to be there already," Himmel pointed out.

"What did he say, sir?" wondered Corporal Müller, in German, naturally.

"Wants to drive us back where we came from," Himmel explained.

"He's the man for me," Müller said. "What's he waiting for, sir?"

And then the Arab spoke, having managed to sit up and stare at the proceedings.

"No one," he said, "no one get away of here . . . no one, I am saying this . . ." His pain-drawn face grimaced. "I am saying, all lost here . . . all lost here . . ."

XVII

Von Schnee was supporting blond Renate under the arm.

"We must keep moving," he was saying in German.

They staggered from hummock to mossy hummock over a stretch of relatively shallow slime. He was limping. Something had cracked in his left leg when he'd leaped from the gondola just before it actually broke loose from the blazing gasbag. Blood had dried òn his chest where he'd been ripped by something.

He'd found her wandering in the fog, tattered but amazingly unmarked. He'd given her his bloody uniform jacket. It came just below her backside where her skirt was raggedly slit. In a way, he thought, it made matters worse. He was surprised at how, even under these conditions, he was having sexual thoughts. He'd had no sex since leaving Bremen, where his mistress was visiting her parents while her husband was abroad. They'd made love in a skiff under a tree at dusk. He recalled the steady lapping of the river as the long craft bumped to their steady, subdued motions. They were low in the boat under her parasol and quite isolated. He remembered how her thighs had excited him when he raised the frilly dress and parted them. . . .

My God, he chided himself, *I am an animal.* . . .

He wasn't sure why this Renate had been on board. He gathered she had to do with the intelligence service and that unpleasant little Himmel fellow. Well, what did it matter now? They were finished, one way or another. The thing was not to give up until the last breath was spent.

They groped blindly toward where he hoped the river was.

"Very strange," she said.

"Strange?"

The slimy mulch was warmish under her bare feet. She'd

been knocked out of her shoes on impact. She tried not to think about what must be under the swamp surface. The insects were just starting to work on them; the mud and soot on their skin helped somewhat.

"As I fell," she went on, then caught herself. There was no point in getting into her secrets.

As she'd fallen, just above the fogbank, she'd had an impression it would be like hitting soft sea billows. It wasn't, but, for an instant, before smacking flat into the reeking ground, time had stopped, nothing moved, and something filled her with a sense of ineffable strength and meaning. As if she were suspended above a world she could shape as she pleased, a world waiting for her commands where the forces of nature would bend to her needs . . . nations would bow . . . all men would kneel and kiss her perfect feet in humble adoration . . . endless glory and majesty suffused her . . . and then the world moved again and the soft stinking earth slammed into her.

"We must, in any case, reach the river," he was saying, leaning into her, partly lifting her through a sudden deep place. Her body was soft, fluid, strong. He imagined a yielding yet inescapable embrace. "Our best chance."

She was about to say they were quite hopelessly lost and that was that except that she suddenly didn't believe it. How could she be lost? It was her world. Her servants would discover her and defend her. She blinked. Had no notion what these ideas meant or why she had them. Perhaps shock was affecting her mind. But some of that unlimited strength seemed to well up within her again.

"Come ahead," she said, taking the lead. "We will come out of this mess."

Elsewhere the Germans and their captives were following a great bend in the wide, sluggish, grayishbrown river. The fog continued to roll back until they had better than fifty yards visibility.

A wall of dense trees and swampy, heavy-leafed, dull greens hemmed them close to the water. The sun was hot and blunt now. Steam rose from the river. Flying bugs nipped and nicked and cut close to ears. Sweat beaded and stayed. All garments were soaked. Most of the soot on the Germans had been washed away.

"My God," said one of the troops, a wide-shouldered, hard-jawed young man, "this place is worse than Hamburg."

"Easy, Gustave," rejoined the stoop-shouldered Corporal Müller, who was taking a turn on the back end of the litter. "This is the army, after all."

Himmel overheard and sniggered. He was looking at Sneed and the major. He'd strung them together on a short length of rope.

Streicher and the other two soldiers flanked them. The stocky captain would cock an ear toward Haggard whenever the author's delirium shook words from him.

Back by the plane Woody lay down on the fairly dry moss while Emma got some food out of a case in the cockpit. She went with a tin of sardines and fruit.

He kept saying he'd get up in a minute or so . . . but the sunheat soothed and enervated him so he kept dropping off.

After a couple of hours he sat up and ate a little. The pain had receded. He felt stronger. Stared at the aircraft while saying, "We'll follow them. They obviously are moving upriver."

She stared across the open, fairly dry field revealed when the fog thinned and drifted back into the actual swamp. They had come down on a high jut of land. When he thought about it he had to accept, if not another miracle, then, at least, a profoundly strange coincidence.

"Do you think," she wondered, "any of the Germans survived?"

He shrugged, getting to his feet and walking around the plane.

"God knows," he said. Then: "I think it might just be possible."

"That they lived?"

"What?" He'd gone to another track. "I don't know. I meant I think I might be able to salvage the old girl here." Leaned up to peer at one of the engines. "The prop shafts are all right and nothing seems to have burned. We've a good chance."

Von Schnee and Renate actually went straight to the river where it happened to bend in steeply toward them while Streicher and the rest were following the shoreline and so walked several miles farther in order to arrive at the same place.

It was Hans Himmel who first noticed movement back in the gradually increasing density of brush and rotted-looking trees.

"Look there," he said, pointing at shadowy outlines at the edge of the dankness that was pressing them closer and closer to the riverbank.

The Germans paused. Sneed smiled as if he possessed some secret knowledge that these events tended to confirm.

"Their dark plans will be confuted," he muttered under his breath. He was strung to the rope in front of the major and felt him yaw wildly as they struggled along.

The major had never quite recovered from the shock of the natives attacking them back at the coast. He kept trying to focus on what to do, how to get away, find his daughter, bring off some dashing coup and capture all the Germans and return in triumph and vindication to England . . . he would suddenly see it all before him in vivid images and he'd find himself doing the things he saw, lurching wildly back and forth on the rope that bound his hands to Sneed's.

"There," the young soldier supporting the front of Haggard's litter shouted, pointing with one hand at what he first took for a black, naked child who seemed to have been exhaled into solidity by some vaporous, fecund whorl of decaying swampjungle.

Sneed set his slash lips in what wasn't actually a smile. He instantly realized it was (as he put it to himself): *Some dwarfed subspecies of nigger. . . .*

Streicher felt the intense fury as if he'd been physically touched. He raised his rifle at once to approximately quarter-arms.

Himmel was already aiming.

"Wait," said Streicher.

"I bet I can knock him over," said Himmel. For some irrational reason (he realized) he was angry. All his good, patient, intelligent work had been undone, he felt, by the incomprehensible caprices of Streicher. His occult ideas had led to disaster. Probably they would all die out here to no purpose. He wouldn't have hesitated much, he realized, to turn his gun on the captain. The man (he sensed) sought a dark, chaotic existence where values melted away and he and his kind could triumph because all standards and aspirations had been leveled. Greatness and order built on glories of the past were needed, Himmel had reflected many times. Man had the power to bring order and win a magnificent world through courage and sacrifice. Heroes were needed, not magicians, not men who believed in nothing real or essential but their own petty desires! He was angry. He was just understanding that he had always been angry because men did so little with what nature filled them with. Mankind had to be weeded out until only the best were left. Yes...

I must get back to Berlin, he told himself. *I will be needed in the coming world... I will be needed... I have the power in me as much as any historical figure... as Napoleon told Culaincourt... yes...*

"He won't be alone," Streicher was saying. "No sense stirring anything up."

"Hm," vocalized Himmel. He hated to admit the captain was probably right.

"Let's keep moving," Streicher ordered.

As they passed the diminutive but strangely menacing figure about fifty yards inland from them, the pygmy didn't seem to move.

"Ah," said a short, thin soldier to Müller, "I got a feeling that swine has got brothers and his brothers has got the fire under the cooking pots."

Müller grunted. His arms ached from the weight of Haggard and the packing case.

"Take over this end, Stoss," he said. "You'll be so stringy from sweating not even a nigger will try to make sausage of you."

Less than one half-mile up the long, slow curve, the river disappeared, overspilled its banks so that there was a huge, shallow lake that Streicher knew at once would be infinitely treacherous. Trees poked out of the stagnant, greenishbrown, scumflecked surface that resembled dirty glass. He realized they were going to be forced inland to grope for firmer ground.

* * *

Von Schnee and his blond companion had just paused to catch their breath and take stock. They sat on a mossy hummock they'd reached on a huge fallen treetrunk that lay tilted athwart the massed creepers, crumbly trees and sluggishly moving water.

The forest roof was dense and left them in perpetual, steamy twilight.

She sat with her magnificent legs drawn up under her. He stretched out, feeling lightheaded and bone-weary. Hungry and thirsty too. He was afraid to drink that sludgy water. He had a feeling the unseen creatures teeming there would drain him into a bubbling pool of flux in short order.

"Are you satisfactory?" he asked her, shutting his eyes to test how near he might be to sleep. He was close but too tense to cross over.

She seemed self-contained, neutral. The sense of force had submerged though she sensed it was still within her, waiting.

"I am satisfactory, Captain," she replied.

He watched her for a few moments. Swatted at a few bugs that flicked around his face. They didn't seem to bother her much. Decided she seemed cool enough to have ice in her veins and what insect wanted a cold drink?

"How did you get mixed up with those men?" he wondered.

"Am I mixed up with men?"

She seemed incredibly at ease for someone sitting, filthy, cut, bruised and miserable in a godforsaken swamp lost in the dark continent. He continued to be impressed.

"Streicher and Himmel, yes?" he said. He grimaced, scornfully.

"They are not gentlemen, hm?" she responded, expressionless.

Von Schnee made a dismissive gesture.

"I am not a class-strangled snob, you know," she said.

"How fortunate for me, in that case," she said, almost smiling, "since my father was a postal worker in Prague."

"I take you for German, *Fräulein*."

She shrugged. Her brilliant eyes weren't watching him. She'd wiped her face almost clean with the sleeve of his jacket dipped in the murky water. The skin was streaked and pale.

"You take me," she said. "How nice."

"Are you German?"

"Does it matter?"

He shrugged.

"No," he said. "A point of curiosity, merely."

"I am somewhat German."

"Anyway," he said, leaning up a little, "I am not a snob. My objections to those gentlemen have altogether another basis."

Now she looked at him.

"Himmel," she said, "is a patriot." He couldn't tell what she thought of that. "Streicher is . . ." Pause. "A philosopher-in-action, I suppose."

"Indeed?" Smacked a bug that was grating like clashed steel at his ear. Crushed it. It felt too big and hard to be natural. He shuddered. The damned jungle. "A philosopher. By no means a greedy, power-hungry fellow but a man who plumbs the abstract depths."

Her face showed nothing but the strain one would expect with the soot and mud smeared like (he almost thought) wild Indian warpaint.

"Another sort of philosopher," she told him. She was watching a long, pale snake slowly unwind itself from a drooping, soft-looking treelimb.

"Ah."

"He has some remarkable gifts."

"We seem, *Fräulein*, to be suffering from their application."

"I do not claim to admire him." She shrugged, looking away from the torpid snake into the webbed denseness over the grayish subtleties of the water.

"And what of you?" he asked.

"I am neither a patriot nor a philosopher, *Herr Hauptmann.*"

"My name is Gustave," he said.

"How gracious of you." He couldn't tell if she mocked him.

He was amused. The idea of their conversational point and counterpoint while lost out here was absurd, somehow. It said something about the persistence of civilized inanity.

"So you're a radical," he decided. "You hope to bring down the aristocracy and the Kaiser." He smiled. "As if any outside help were needed."

"I am not the least concerned with politics, *Freiherr Von Schnee*."

"You still insist on titles? Here?" He gestured at the dank, rank landscape.

She looked at him, this time.

"It seems you are attracted to me," she said. "Titles suit us better here than courtship." She smiled. "Would you like me to excite you with my mouth?"

He wrinkled his brow and shook his head.

"Delightful conception," he said.

She looked at him (he felt) from remote heights.

"Be grateful, *Freiherr*," she told him, "that this adventuress, as you must by now think me, chooses not to enslave your soul."

"Adventuress. That says it all, *Fräulein*."

In fact, the thought of her mouth on his (much less applied anywhere else on his body) had a softly stunning effect.

Enslave, he thought. *Enslave* ... To hold her wanton attention, to keep it, to grasp a sunbeam or the breeze ...

He shook his head.

"You have a good opinion of your charms," he suggested.

She didn't have to reply. He realized, after contemplating it, that he hadn't really found out a thing about her.

Normally he respected anyone's privacy but she irritated and attracted him in equal proportion.

"*Fräulein*," he said, "what *is* your name?"

She was just smiling this time. She locked her hands around her wonderful legs and looked very entertained. In context, it had a strange effect.

"*Herr Hauptmann*," she told him, "are these circumstances where such informality is endurable?"

He shook his head, chuckling, liking her.

"You are correct," he said. "Better call me Your Majesty, I think."

XVIII

Stripped to the waist, Woody was working on the engine. The sun was low in the west. The air was steamy hot. The sweat clung to him.

"Hand me the wrench," he said over his shoulder. She stood behind him, holding the greasy tool. She pushed it into his backreaching hand. He held something she couldn't see up inside the cowling. He struggled a few moments. Muttered. Lean muscles tensed as he leaned into the wrench handle. Finished. Let out his breath. Sucked two ripped knuckles.

"Well?" she wondered. It was all quite mysterious to her.

"This is the next in sequence."

"Next what?"

"Intolerable coincidence."

He cocked his head to look at the body and wings again. They'd already tilted the machine back level. He'd walked the ground and was sure they could take off.

"Which one?" she wondered. She was trying to be brave and was surprised at her calm. She trusted Woody more than was logical. Somehow, they'd find her father again and escape.

"That we happen to have landed just where we happen to be able to take off again." He grimaced. "How much longer can our luck hold?"

"If it is luck," she said, not quite knowing what she meant by the remark.

"What then? Divine providence?"

She shrugged.

"I don't know," she said.

"I used to think life an infinitely complex machine that might be perfected someday if the means and method could be discovered. Fixed. Controlled by man's mind."

"And now?"

He shook his head.

"I was silly," he said. "It is all beyond comprehension."

"I could have told you that."

"I had to come to it by my own path. There's really no coincidence at all, you see. Perhaps that is why I came to this place, to find that out."

She sighed. She didn't want to think about having come there.

"What next?" she asked, to keep her mind on what was at hand.

He touched his hurt head. It throbbed dully now. He was trying to recall something he'd seen or dreamed or imagined after the bullet glanced off his skull. As they'd fallen he'd seen vivid images of some other world or time or life. A voice seemed to have been trying to speak to him. He couldn't brush it aside, somehow. He realized he wanted to hear it.

"Tomorrow morning we'll fly upriver," he said. "Circle until we locate the others."

It's our best chance, he thought.

"Do you think," she began. Stopped.

He smiled at her and nodded.

"I can set her down virtually anywhere," he assured her. "If they're visible from the air we'll find them."

He taxied to the end of the stretch of relatively dry, almost grassless ground. Then back. Estimated the wind by watching the treetops where the swamp closed in.

Suppose I'm out of miracles? he asked himself. *Even if we take off what are the chances of finding another safe place to land?* He shrugged. Gunned the motors. Looked over at where he knew the airship had gone down. There was no smolder visible now. Shook his head. Leaned around to call to her, wishing he could devise a way to properly baffle the popping exhaust. There was nothing to equal silent gliding when you were up there. The grinding of the motors reminded the flyer he was an earthbound lump clawing his way into the unforgiving sky.

He didn't see her. Stooped up and peered over the top of the wing as the engines shook to a stop.

Call of nature? he wondered, scanning the nearest brush bordering the riverbank.

"Woody," she called.

He twisted around, stared. Started to say something, then sighed with resignation.

God, there's no end to it....

Because he'd started to feel light and ready to ascend and now sagged back inwardly toward the earth again which was the tug of death, the slow, relentless gathering of gravity and he only had, against it, a wordless sense that one could finally float free of that dull grip and above oblivion's pull....

There she was where the fog was starting to creep back, coldly steaming, across the open space by the swamp's denseness. There she was under twisted trees where the mist was softly ripped by bare branches.

A dozen or so reddish-black pygmies stood around her as if exhaled by the shadows in the fog.

"Now this," he muttered.

Haggard opened his eyes. The dense, dripping branches moved unevenly above him. He had no idea he was being carried. His memories were mist. He blinked at the strange men in the blurry range of his vision. he believed he was in Hades, lost in gray forgetfulness.

He moved his lips that the fever had dried and cracked.

"Ah...I must have...drunk of...Lethe's dark waters..."

His breath burned his mouth. He heard voices speaking what he assumed was the nameless tongue of the underworld.

"He spoke, *Herr Hauptmann*," announced the youngest soldier, Stoss, who was taking his turn at the back of the litter.

Streicher was poking a long stick through the shallow water to test the bog beneath. At this rate he knew they were doomed even if the dwarfish natives left them alone. The power of destiny, the predictions of the Thule inner circle seemed insubstantial as the uncoiling knots of smoke.

Himmel was just backing out of a sudden pit, rotating his arms for balance, cursing in fear and fury.

"We'd better go back the other way," he said, standing there, puffing.

The major and Sneed were still looped together by ropes

from their wrists. The major was staring, the little policeman grinding his jaws and contemplating ways of turning the tables on the hated Huns.

"What did he say?" demanded Streicher, moving closer to bend over the semiconscious author.

"I don't know," said the soldier.

"Priest," commanded Streicher, "speak!"

Haggard looked at the blocky, sooty, sweaty face with the small hard eyes and stubby, beaked nose. He saw (through the lens of fever) it was a disguise, a crudely human mask covering the beast face.

"May my soul be cleansed of the stains of human existence," he told the face.

"Priest," he improvised, slogging along with the two weary bearers who moved mechanically, largely sustained by the habit of being soldiers, "priest . . . guide our steps through this grim land."

Haggard was racked by sudden chills. His teeth clicked together.

"Nay, deceive me not," he whispered, "with Thy false face . . . this is Thine world. . . ."

Streicher concentrated. Remembered what Eckhart and later the dwarf, Lange, had told him, insisting that they (in some mysterious way that he accepted from past evidence of their methods) knew that Haggard was the key to finding the lost city. Streicher had various imprecise ideas about what this might mean to him, personally. He pictured himself going back to Europe clothed in intangible power, a giant striding into a world of little men.

"You must find your way, priest," he said, "to the place where Ra escapes the eternal night to be reborn in heaven."

The pale eyes went wide and hollow. Tracked the graygreen, humid canopy above them.

"Ah," he said, one thin hand struggling on his chest as if groping for a lost chain or talisman, "ahhh . . . you seek to trap my Ka for eternity, yet . . . I shall be free . . ."

They'd all stopped. Himmel leaned into a tree, staring with despairing scorn at the tableau by the stretcher.

"A man who from the fever has a rotting brain," he said, "ask him the way."

141

"Point," whispered Streicher, in Egyptian, "and my servants will carry you."

"O Ra," Haggard muttered, "save me from these snares." He sat up all at once, stiff, violent, forefinger clawed, pointing. "There is the way and I must follow it!"

Hope lit Streicher's dulled eyes.

"Yes, yes," he whispered, "you see the way!"

Haggard saw a thin, perfect sunbeam, reaching down through the massed obscurity above. It moved and left a trail of sparkle on the boggy surface. A trail like golden music.

The priest who was stirring blurrily within him sighed in unaffected rapture and gazed with compassion on the trapped shades around him lost here in dread obscurity.

"There," he told them, pointing, then falling back, his hand like a compass needle, aimed across the swamp.

"Forward then," commanded Streicher. "Forward."

Himmel leaned on the moss-slimed tree and barely didn't giggle.

"By all means," he said. "We might as well follow a raving madman as a bald one."

Streicher reacted. His blocky face was harsh.

"You happen to be speaking to a superior officer," he pointed out.

"I cannot imagine what you could be superior to, *Hauptmann Streicher*." Almost giggled again. Because none of them understood who he really was. Fools. They'd learn, to their abundant sorrow, and feel the impact of his genius. He felt a rush of warm strength flowing up into him as if from the murky earth itself. He sensed great triumphs ahead, immense battles with himself on a hilltop, mounted, directing his troops in brilliant charges and encirclements. It didn't disturb him that the men he pictured carried muskets or that the cannon shot balls or that he wore a cocked hat.

"You'll regret those remarks, I think," Streicher said. He was preoccupied with sighting along Haggard's rigidly pointing arm.

He led the way. Felt a little thrill of satisfaction when he found himself on suddenly firmer ground.

"Come on," he called back, now on a straight spine of slightly raised earth. He noticed that as the litter shifted with its bulky crate underneath the arm of the again unconscious Englishman rotated to keep pointing at the underwater ridge.

Meditating on his coming victories, Himmel followed last. He gave Sneed a kick in the backside just to relieve his tension.

Sneed snarled, then smiled, staggering forward into the major, who wandered vaguely along behind the litter, flanked by Müller.

"You Hun bastid," he said, "enjoy it while you may."

The old fellow's melting under it, Himmel thought, watching the permanently stunned-looking major stagger in tandem with Sneed, who was, himself, thinking how fortunate he was that none of them had recognized him yet. He couldn't quite repress a smile of secret power.

Soon they'll all know who I am, he thought. *Soon . . ."*

XIX

"It will be dark soon," she said to Von Schnee as they worked their way, sometimes hand in hand, across a treacherous stretch of knee-deep stagnant water. He leaned into a stout pole in the worst places and managed to keep pushing along.

"We have to find high ground," he said, panting a little. He was stripped to just his tattered pants. Only his hair had really burned because he'd jumped early and had been lucky enough to land in a deep pool. His face was crusted with dried mud and swollen with insect bites. They seemed to leave her more or less alone. As they waded along he tried not to think about the leeches that had to be there.

She seemed unmoved. He found himself admiring her composure, except that it might have been tainted with suppressed hysteria, particularly when she said, too calmly, "My children will find us, even in the dark."

"You are a mother?"

She blinked. Looked up thoughtfully at the rotted forest roof. Refocused herself. For a moment she'd gone giddy and wasn't sure what she'd said.

She found herself thinking about her own nature, which was decidedly not like her. She had always found self-contemplation morbid. She disliked dwelling on the motives for her acts. She had desires and tried to fulfill them. She believed herself simple-hearted. She'd been poor and ill-used by men in her childhood. She now had power over men. She'd involved herself in the Thule Society and become the mistress of Eckhart. And enslaved a few others along the way. She didn't altogether believe in their magical ideas and ceremonies but went along the way she went along with most of what men did: to humor them while she profited herself. In that sense she remained a peasant, shrewd, suspicious, calculating and often, through a kind of stubborn reticence, getting the best of her betters. If she had any weakness, it was for dominating powerful men. She was likely to go out of her way to do it, if she could. Biting Haggard had been an extreme example. It was part of her witchcraft.

"Excuse me?" she wondered.

"What did you say about your children?"

"I have none. I was never married."

"Isn't that why you came on this expedition?"

"What? To find a husband?" She was smiling.

"Of course."

We might as well keep up our spirits, he thought.

"You are a sarcastic fellow," she said.

She braced him this time as he struggled sideways, one foot in a sickening hole. The stick was wrenched from his grip and was left standing in the muck as if to mark something. The fog was returning, silently filling in the askew and twisted treetrunks. He was impressed by her strength.

Even if she is somewhat mad, he thought.

"Thanks," he said as they waded into the gradually dimming, ghostly twilight.

"Aristocrats are supposed to be cynical," she said.

"I deny being cynical. I have high hopes."

She almost smiled again.

"Of getting out of this mess?" she asked him.

"Yes. Your children will find us."

And then her face changed, went aloof, icy cold. She seemed more beautiful, despite knotted hair and stained face, but terribly cold.

"They are near," she assured him, looking across a stretch of deeper, darker water at a wall of trees that now seemed to be melting into vaporous gray. "My poor and foolish—"

"Poor which?"

She gave a little, lilting cry, almost a song. Stopped. They were both just standing there. He could have sworn her sounds were echoed across the swamp followed by something like (it had to be some strange, windy beast, he was sure) a sighing moan of awe and despair as if the fecund darkness itself answered her.

"Poor?" she wondered. She was herself again. Instantly.

A slight giddiness passed over her. Her aunt used to faint, frequently. She'd despised her for it.

"What was that sound?"

"Which?"

"You just cried out and then there was a sound . . . out there."

"I felt faint."

"Hark," he said.

Because he heard something ahead. Voices.

My God, he thought, *are the odds improving?*

He tugged her along now.

"Look out!" she warned.

A snake, grayishgreen, the color of the water, went thrashing past like a sprung spring, eyes like wet stone chips.

"I heard voices, I think," Von Schnee said.

They went on. For the first time (perhaps since childhood) he thought about not wanting to die. He used to feel there was so much he had to do and see. Since he never had to work he became an officer. Why not start with adventure? There had been talk of war. That was ten years ago. He had been an efficient officer. Was promoted twice. Had been offered a staff post but declined in favor of foreign service; but no longer in the hope of adventure. Now he just wanted to keep away from too much civilization. She was close, he thought, but had missed it: he was weary, not cynical. He was tired of sophistication, empty affairs, politics, parties, aborted passions . . . inner indifference had subtly grown until last year, on his thirtieth birthday, he'd drunk a bottle of brandy, put his pistol on the table and asked why not? Had no answer. Brooded. Put the barrel to his skull and felt nothing either way. Put the pistol back on the table.

"I will go somewhere far away," he had said.

She felt the giddiness again. This time she didn't quite black out. Darkness welled up in her head, swirled like smoke, but there was something this time like fire in her mind and she felt very sharp and clear and an image floated there, a female face with large eyes full of what seemed flame, behind it something like broken columns, arches, towers melting away like clouds in a twist of wind. . . .

"No," she voiced, unconsciously.

"What?" He was supporting her now as they went slowly through the gathering night.

And then he distinguished what had to be a line of men passing slowly across their direction just at the limit where the steaminess was becoming opaque. He recognized the two soldiers carrying the stretcher. One of Haggard's thin arms hung down and swung with their lurching steps.

"You," he called out, "*Gefriede*." Which was to say, corporal. "Müller! Stoss!"

Then he saw the long form of what had to be Tjaden as the men turned.

Renate was looking at Streicher.

"So he lived," she said, as if it meant something. It was strange enough to get Von Schnee to look up. Her expression was intent as if someone were talking to her except, he thought, someone was not.

She'd just fractionally blacked out again. It was hitting her more often. She was almost getting accustomed to these spells. Her sense now was that, mysteriously, these events had been designed to (somehow) destroy Streicher—no, rather, to block what he somehow carried with him or which carried him along, unseen . . . the ideas made no sense . . . she tried to blink them away . . . who could have designed, she reasoned, blind chance?

"He is not the only one," Von Schnee was saying, unheard.

"*Hauptmann*," called Müller. "Greetings, sir."

She felt she was hallucinating. She was really no mystic. This assignment had meant a substantial fee and a chance to work her way directly to the Kaiser's court. She'd had enough of rich businessmen and ranking officers. She aimed to end as the wife or at least principal mistress of a nobleman or some unseen lord of international finance. She had a picture at home of a chateau. She'd painted it one summer as a teenage girl. It showed a certain talent. An imaginary chateau where the sunlight was honey thick, the edifice old gold, the trees bright, bluegreen shapes on a vast lawn where it was always summer and overrich gardens were sunk in a languorous calm.

"Well, well," Streicher was saying while Himmel, just behind him, tapped his long middle finger against his pointy jaw. "Welcome. I salute you both. As you see, we too have overcome our difficulties."

Von Schnee was dragging himself and the woman the last few yards onto the relatively firm strip Haggard's pointing had apparently led them along.

Von Schnee was panting. Renate held onto a twisted treetrunk and gathered herself. The mist curled and thickened around their calves as the twilight sourcelessly blurred the landscape into a single, smoky grayness.

"A wonderful victory," Von Schnee commented, looking at Haggard's bony, overstrained features where he shifted listlessly on the litter. "Imagine if the whole war went as well."

Himmel stood a little apart, leaning on the butt of his rifle. He still fingered his pointy chin. His mustaches were plastered insanely athwart his cheeks.

"Naturally," he agreed. "And now, with the aid of this delirious foreigner, total success will shortly be ours." He chuckled through a meaningless smile.

"Close up your face, Himmel," suggested Streicher. "Save your breath for going forward."

"Into the swamp."

Von Schnee was looking at Haggard as he asked, "Do you have any water?"

"Here, sir," said young trooper Stoss, fishing out a canteen.

"What is wrong with this man?" asked Von Schnee.

"The fever," said squat-shouldered Müller.

"We'll all have it, soon enough," added Himmel, still smiling. "Then we'll all be prophets."

Von Schnee was getting back into his job now, which helped a little. Glanced at the major and Sneed. Noted that the older man's eyes were vacant and his lips kept moving.

"Untie him, Tjaden," Von Schnee ordered the lanky soldier who had been on a break from carrying Haggard and the crate.

Streicher shook his head.

"No," he said. "Are you in command here?"

"Of my own men." He touched the major's wide, dead-pale forehead and wiped the soot and mud away with his palm. "Are you ill?"

"I have seen all things under the sun pass away," the older man said, hoarsely. "There is nothing to mortal power. It is all hollow."

Von Schnee glanced at Renate, who was watching and waiting, one hand working out knots in her long, blond, smeared and tangled hair.

"You may be right," he said.

"I will not survive the next battle," the major said. "My crown will roll in the dust."

"He is normal," said Himmel, scratching mud from his mustache.

The major looked hard and sideways at the thin German spy.

"I will die fighting the dark enemy whose name you all know," he said. "He is among us, even here, in this fellowship of true warriors." He leaned closer to Von Schnee. His breath was hot and smelled decayed.

Sneed, tethered to him by the ropelength, grimaced.

"He's round the bloody bend," he said. His slash lips flickered in fluid tics. He crouched there, small, ferretlike, defiant, hands pressed together as if in enforced prayer by the rope lashed around the child-sized wrists.

Von Schnee thought he resembled a furious child, in fact. A nasty child who'd just been frustrated.

Müller looked uncertain.

"Maybe, sir," he suggested to his captain, "these madmen are better kept restrained."

Von Schnee nodded, absently.

"Very well," he agreed.

The major's lips were moving but no one was listening now. It didn't matter. He was whispering as if to the thickening vapors of the evening, his shrilled and breathy voice lost in the underroar of jungle and swamp sounds, insects, birds, obscure animals . . .

"Yes, yes," he was whispering, "I will follow to the end because I saw the secret light . . . I had to see it . . . we are made new by the light . . ." The shining in a dark and reeking world. He'd knelt in the cave when the lovely young priestess had lifted the cup of brilliance and flooded the assembled warriors with golden ecstasy. ". . . I tried . . . I tried to help . . . I tried . . . I was too weak . . . too weak . . ."

They'd come to a relatively dry, mossy hummock.

"We'll camp here for the night," Von Schnee announced. Stoss and Tjaden set down the litter that rested on the long crate beneath it. Müller stretched out and sat down near where Ayeesh the Arab lay flat. His arm was swollen. He was in constant pain and said very little. Seemed numbed. Stared dully before him.

Himmel stood beside Streicher, who looked as if he might dispute the younger captain's decision. Renate squatted and worked at opening a tin of sardines. She seemed more detached than usual.

"A cosy spot," said Himmel.

Streicher turned his attention to the wounded Arab. Said nothing. He looked thoughtfully at Renate, then leaned over Haggard again, who was breathing in flurries and was completely out.

Streicher was thinking how the Englishman had to be drained of all he knew before it was too late. He looked like he might be dying. He studied Ayeesh again and came to a decision. A sudden decision to do something that, in fact, he'd never done before. He should have wondered how the idea sprung full-formed in his brain. He didn't. The ritual he contemplated seemed familiar to him. Seemed logical and natural.

Pondered Renate. Her smooth legs pushed out from under the officer's jacket and the tatters of her clothes. A racial beauty of the highest type, was his next thought. A fit mate for him, for greatness.

XX

Woody kept shifting his legs and back, trying to get comfortable. Moved his stiff, swollen fingers as much as possible where his hands were tied together behind him.

The night was like a solid wall around the campfire where the little men with a reddishblack tinge to their skins sat in silence. The mist swirled around them in heat eddies.

Emma had a wide hide rope knotted around her neck with the leashlike end tied to a stake driven into the semisoggy turf. At full extension she was about a yard from Woody. She was picking uselessly at the knot. Her fingers were raw from the effort.

"I cannot loose these cords," she said, quietly.

"They wet the knots. The leather then shrinks." His hands were already swollen. "They seem to be waiting for something," he observed.

"Will they eat us, do you think?"

"I see no pot," he said, wryly.

She shifted, miserably, on the damp earth.

"My poor father," she said.

"Yes."

"He was always so...disappointed...in everything... even, I fear, in me."

"In you?"

She stared and felt so dulled. There was so much to do and she had done little. She shrugged.

"I should have been a boy," she said.

"No," he responded, watching her pale, serious, unhappy face. "Never."

She was feeling the pressure now and asking herself how was she going to do it? Because she had to very badly now. There were no bushes within reach of her tether.

She nearly wept. It was all so hopeless and she was so

151

small and futile. What were they in the face of all this desolation and decay? They had wandered into darkness and were doomed, lost forever. . . .

And there were no bushes and it hurt now.

"I'm sorry," he said, generally. He wondered what the natives were waiting for. A chief, perhaps. He hadn't thought much about natives when he came out here. He'd imagined flying, soaring over a blurred greenness, landing on rolling fields among antelope, zebra and astonished birds. . . .

"Oh, this is dreadful," she said, in a tense flutter of fear and anger. "Oh . . ."

"I'm sorry, Emma," he said, as if it were his fault.

"Oh, do stop sniveling," she said, then covered her face with her hands. Sighed a deep breath. How much longer could she hold it in, she asked herself.

"I suppose you're right," he said, gritting his teeth. But this was all real and not schoolboy fantasy where he might simply break the bonds and overcome the savages with graceful, irresistible energy.

"I cannot stand it," she exclaimed. She tried to think of how to ask those horrid little brutes to let her go into the bushes. "This is a nightmare . . ."

"Yes," he agreed, unsure of what to say, on the edge of snarling himself. "We must escape."

"Ha-ha," she said, bitterly. "You are really hitting the bull's-eye, are you not?" she sat up, pressing her legs together. Now that she was overconscious of it, the pressure in her bladder was becoming unbearable.

"Command yourself, Emma," he said, firmly. "These outbursts, however understandable, will accomplish little."

The pygmies, squatting around their fire, sat in moveless silence, watching.

She nodded into her hands. Sighed a kind of sob.

"Forgive me," he said. "You are not to blame for these misfortunes." It was dark, she reasoned, almost desperately, probably dark enough. Probably . . . what choice? So she just sat there, finally, and let it happen under her. She was crying now, silently.

"We will find a way," he said. He meant it. He was coldly determined. The plane was ready. These savages would have little understanding of the mechanics so they couldn't know what to prevent. If he could get his hands in front the knots might be chewed loose.

And then they were stirring, standing in the firecircle where the mist seemed to pulse in the reddish glow.

A shape that seemed a giant (partly by contrast) suddenly loomed over them. It had a deep, rumbling voice. Male. The words were gibberish to Woody. Though he knew it was nonsense, he had trouble not imagining the newcomer was a spirit exhaled by the condensing darkness of the miasmic swamp.

The figure was pointing at them.

"My God," she said, "what's that?"

Woody shrugged, calculating how, once everyone was asleep, he would draw up his feet and force them through the loop of his arms.

"The chief, perhaps," he said. *But why would he be so much bigger than the rest?*

All the pygmies suddenly sighed in virtual unison, all looking at the captives. Woody found it unnerving.

They'd made camp on a fairly dry hummock and Corporal Müller had managed to start a fire using gunpowder collected from a few shells.

The major had fallen asleep beside Sneed, whom Streicher had tied to the moss-eaten trunk of a tree. Sneed's intent eyes watched the Germans with unwavering enmity and scorn. His look had convinced Von Schnee to leave him bound.

Von Schnee sat down and watched Stoss and Tjaden cook the rations. He kept glancing at where Streicher was in close conversation with Renate, who seemed to be agreeing with something proposed. That bothered him. What were they up to?

He knew he was going to sink into sleep soon. The weight of the day was dragging his eyelids down. What secrets did they have? Were they lovers? He scoffed at the idea but still had it.

Hours later, near midnight, most of them were asleep. The fire guttered. Slow, thick smoke rose and sank sluggishly.

Streicher and Renate were awake, sitting up outside the dim, tossed firelight. She wasn't looking at him. She had no intention of involving herself in what she considered his "mystical tricks." There was little more to be gained from the Thule people, as far as she could see—assuming she somehow escaped from this hideous place, she would move more directly toward her goals. This whole adventure had been a mistake. There would be no King Solomon's gold at the end of it. She sighed. Seemed to be listening as he explained the meaning of the ritual he meant to perform that night.

". . . so we will bring the Arab along with us, you see. He will serve."

She saw the eyes first. Just close enough to the perimeter of dull light to show. Amber glow . . . an animal? He caught her stare, loosened and drew his pistol. A dark form moved toward them, silently on four legs. Seemed big as a leopard. He wondered if the bullets would turn it aside if it charged.

"Don't shoot," she said.

Because it was human.

"A pygmy," he said, as a thin, misshapen man crawled into the clearing. What he took for black skin was crusted, filthy muck. The fellow was virtually naked. Hairless. Squatted up on his haunches like (he thought) a monkey. He kept the gun pointed at the longish face.

"No," she said.

Which was correct because the new arrival spoke in German: "Are you not exceeding your authority, *Herr Hauptmann?*"

"What's this? Some creature crawls out of the swamp and criticizes me?"

Renate was amused.

"You don't look yourself, you know, Lange," she said to the little man, who was stretching his long, thin lips into a smile. Then, to Streicher: "He was on board but you never met."

"Lange?" Streicher was amazed.

The dwarf nodded.

"How did I survive out there?" he asked, rhetorically. Raised his skinny arms. "My dear," he said, in the same low tones they all were using, additionally muffled by the dank fog, "it was your loveliness that drew me irresistibly through the terrors around us." He seemed amused by that. "I prefer the blank snowfields of the Himalayas where I was trained to live on air and snow." Despite his abominable appearance, he seemed perfectly at ease.

"You are Lange." Streicher hadn't expected one of the inner masters of the society to turn up out here. He obviously had been on board from the beginning. Had something to do with the woman. Interesting. "Why do you say I am overstepping my—"

"The ritual you have in mind is quite correct," Lange said, squatting, almost gleeful-looking. "But you could never have performed it without me. So, you see, I have come at just the right moment." He slitted his eyes and stared at the dim outline of the officer's face as if it were bright daylight. Streicher squirmed slightly. He felt as if the dwarf were, somehow, invisibly touching him.

"I do not really understand," he said.

"I am sure you do not." Lange tilted his head. "They are already taking you over, you know. Your mind and soul are not altogether your own."

Streicher was uneasy. Was this really the Thule master? What mysterious game was he playing? Was he not, perhaps, mad?

"Herr Lange," he tried, "you have not eaten, perhaps. No doubt you require sleep and—"

"You and these others are too weak to resist. That is why I came out here in the first place. The closer we come to the power the more danger you are in. The ceremony would open you completely to *them* and you would be lost." He stood up, stooped, thin but unhumanly intense. Streicher was now sweating from more than the humid heat.

I am strong, he said to himself. *What does this misshapen fellow know about that?*

Renate was half-listening. The conversation did not yet concern her. Then, without finding it strange, she found herself looking forward to the ritual they were discussing though she knew nothing about it. She felt there would be pleasure in it. She needed pleasure or else she tended to get nervous and bitter.

Lange had said that all of them were subject to whatever it was. But certainly, she told herself, that did not include her.

"We must hurry," Lange said, pointing to Haggard.

"Bring them and follow me. There's an excellent spot not far ahead." He smiled his slit smile again.

Streicher blinked.

Let him think he's in charge, he thought. *When the hour comes I will assert myself. . . .*

The place was roughly round and surrounded with dense trees. They reached it, burdened as they were by the litter and the surly, injured Arab, who muttered as he went. His wound was festering, throbbed. He was lightheaded and kept saying, in his own language, that he was Allah's prophet and that soon he would be instructed to destroy all the infidels. Images of their doom comforted him.

They were about one hundred muffled yards from the campsite. Streicher and Renate had carried Haggard's stretcher. The Englishman moaned and tossed languidly the whole distance; struggled as if in invisible bonds.

Streicher had produced a can of oil and soon they had a very hot fire hissing and popping, lit by the single torch they'd brought when they'd slipped out of camp unobserved. The heat blast billowed the fog into wild swirls.

Renate was strangely excited by the preparations. She kept looking at the Arab, who'd fallen from weakness but was still talking to himself.

"I am the Mahdi," he was saying, in Arabic. "I have the space between my teeth . . . I have . . ."

The dwarf had already stripped off the last of his crusted rags. His voice was a scraping hoarseness:

"Prepare him," he commanded, prancing around the fire with stiff, strong steps, reminding the woman of American Indians she'd seen in a Hamburg circus.

Renate felt herself on the verge of something thrilling, forbidden. At the same time, as if she were resisting a voice at her ear, she wanted to go back to the camp and throw in her lot with Gustave Von Schnee. Something about this business was beginning to disgust her. Lange had tried to do something "magical" to her on board the airship. She had thought it rather silly, but he was an important man and so . . . but here in this jungle swamp it seemed altogether madness. So she reasoned. But it meant no more than the temporizing thoughts of a lover about to sin and betray, the ecstasy burning aside all other considerations.

"In for a penny," she murmured, too softly to be heard.

Streicher took his own clothes off and stood there, stocky, thick-armed, oily-looking.

"Well?" he asked the dwarf.

That worthy squatted as if to evacuate. Waved one skinny arm around at the shifting, red tinted mist.

"Scorpio is the very essence of swamp, decay, death and the darkness beyond the veil," he said. "All is well here. All is as it should be."

"Scorpio?" wondered Streicher. "This is August."

"Were you taught nothing useful?" Lange inquired. "We are not here to chart someone's birthday. The spirit of the scorpion is focused through the unseen moon tonight. It is she we are approaching."

"The moon?" Renate asked, as the dwarf began his strangely stiff movements again, circling closer to the Arab, who'd rolled away, facing the dark wall of trees and fog.

"The spirit of the dark moon," Lange corrected. "Do not pretend you have no acquaintance with her, woman."

Ayeesh was sighing in fear and pleasure because he saw them coming now to his rescue with flaming scimitars and pitiless, steel-bright eyes . . . he saw the angels of Allah slashing his enemies to shreds . . . saw them riding in on lightning bolts to smite all pale unbelievers. . . .

Haggard had an impression that he was lying under still water, in perfect silence. Above and outside he saw the woman and the men moving, meaninglessly. His impression was of the pathetic triviality of their interests and desires. They had entered the world with energy and power and had used it to serve themselves and to fulfill tawdry little dreams. Each flowed into the whole of life and everything one did affected all others. That was the simple fact they hated to face. The only justification for existence was to make the whole better, to move in general harmony, to let the light of compassion shine a little brighter in the brooding gloom that was man's world.

Fools, he thought, *they have learned nothing in a thousand centuries . . . they still want to extinguish the glory, cover the precious jewel of unending light. . . .*

Renate told herself that if they expected her to parade naked for the sake of their absurd ritual they had better think again.

She stared into the flames. the tossed shadows hollowed their faces and Haggard seemed to twitch as the gleaming shifted.

And then the fire was in her head, a burst of silent, heatless burning and she thought, with sudden slyness:

While they do one thing I shall do another. . . .

Because this was the ritual of finding and she already knew the way. But while they were looking she would use the released energy for her own ends. She smiled, remotely, as she shed her tattered garments.

Ayeesh was amazed that the angels of doom had held back this long because the sight of nude Streicher, squat, glossy, muscular, resembling a primitive carving, was too much to bear as he took the Arab by his rent and mucky djellabah and lifted him to his feet, then slammed him effortlessly against a tree while the dwarf sort of capered, half hopping, and quickly looped a length of thin rope around the Arab's wrists. The pull on the swollen arm was bad. The man sighed and shuddered with agony. Made no other move because everything was clearly hopeless and he could only wait now for his avengers as he cried out, over and over: "Bright ones, strike them down! Smite! Smite! Smite!"

Streicher's eyes seemed red and hollow in the flame reflection. Still in his stiff, tranced dance, Lange circled the tree with the slack until the thin, unhappy, maddened man was firmly bound.

Streicher clapped one thick hand over the Arab's mouth, saying, "Not yet, my goat. Save your cries. You will have better use for them soon enough."

Renate stood in front of the victim now, tall, naked, breathtakingly curved, a faint breath of smile touching her lips. Her eyes seemed (more than Streicher's) to be all flame, like a window on a furnace. Ayeesh sucked breath around the heavy hand and thrashed in panic, puffing stifled grunts. His lips were being crushed so hard into his teeth that blood now welled around the stubby fingers.

These petty fools, she was thinking, *soon you will all know me. . . .*

She saw, in a single inner glance, the tangled strands of so many tangled lives and the threads of her own plans, laid ages and ages ago, to bear cumulative fruit in various incarnations.

The veil would be rent by the soulburst of this sacrificial death and she would absorb and direct the subtle energies that these gross fools could not hope to detect, much less utilize. . . .

Emma and Woody looked up at the tall, skinny black man. His face was edged like an ax blade, nose a long, hooked beak in angular silhouette to the fireglow. He wore a jet black, tentlike garment that covered his arms and ended at the ankles. The pygmies (about half his height) stood respectfully back.

Emma was too miserable to comment at this point. She felt degraded and hopeless.

The ogres and the shapeless ones are winning, her mind said. Where did those words come from, she wondered, a moment later.

"Shapeless ones?" she murmured.

Woody stared at the long, sharp, glossy black face.

"God," he said, "I wish I could talk to one of you benighted devils." He thought of just grunting inanely and at first missed it, then was saying, "What? What?" Because the man had said something that he was afraid he'd just imagined was French. Then: *"Comment?"*

"Ell deisr vot prencu," repeated the long man.

Woody blinked.

"She?" he wondered. "Desires . . . *vot*?"

"Votre," she said, looking up.

"Desires your presence," he concluded. "Who is she?"

The black came closer. Was looking at the flying machine. His teeth seemed sharp. Woody imagined they'd been filed.

"Nus?" he asked, indicating Emma.

The robed man nodded. Shrugged almost delicately.

"Ee," he agreed. Pointed to Woody. *"Un."* Then he said something in native to the others. They came at once and loosened Emma and Woody's bonds.

The American stood up, stiff, aching. Carefully worked

the numbing tingles from his arms. His fingers were dead sausages.

She didn't want to rise because if she did she'd want to get to water and wash herself. She just wanted to sleep now. Suddenly she was leaden.

The grayness was brightening generally in the east. Emma felt like just flopping down now.

Dawn . . . God, dawn . . .

She eased back. She was out almost before her head touched the loamy earth and she was instantly in a dream. She was looking down from a tall tower. There was a shadow around her and she understood that she'd fled to the slit, glassless window that looked down on an empty, grayishgreen, strangely lifeless landscape. There was no sun. She knew she was imprisoned by the harsh ones. They were fearless, powerful but pitiless. They had been her people until she was . . . what? Changed . . . something bright, something that had set fire to the subtle glow surrounding all living beings. Her people could all see that glow, to some degree. She and some others had gathered in a secret cave . . . that was it . . . and the white brightness was, somehow, there . . . a cup of overflowing light . . . they'd all been changed . . . they'd wanted to be changed because the world they knew was dull, cruel . . . something . . . she no longer gloried in the men's perfect violence or was moved to song by their astounding feats of power . . . and so she'd been taken to that prison and questioned by soldiers of the great leader because too many were seeking the change, the place of the hidden light. . . .

She saw, below, on the bleak fields, a single armored rider, trying to cross the misty barrier that the wills of the warriors had created from the thick, vital atmosphere. He loved her. He wanted her alone. That was forbidden too. And he was coming to his doom. . . .

She saw him draw his sword because a wave of tall warriors on strangely supple horses came out of a fold in the ground and charged him. She tried to cry out, to leap from the embrasure; his name, which was more images than words, welled up within her as she strained to throw herself down and felt the unseen grip holding her . . . and then she burst free and was falling . . .

* * *

She woke in the biplane, Woody strapping her to one of the benches that ran front to back in the elongated cockpit. The fog was shredding as brilliantly hot sun broke through. The swamp was steaming in the background.

"I love thee," she was saying.

He paused, not looking back at the tall, lean black man who was standing with four pygmies just behind him. The ax-faced man leaned down and looped a thong around her neck and inserted the handle of a dagger in the knot.

"See here," said Woody, furious except there were four short spears aimed at him, *"Chien, couchon!"* he cried.

"Silncur," said the black. *"Faar en creaton apport!"*

The sun was climbing. The fog faded to a general haziness. Straight above the sky was soft, bright blue.

"Not on your life, nigger," snarled Woody.

The long, black, dusty-looking hand twisted the dagger handle in the knot until Emma began to wheeze.

"Bin," said the native. *"Trebin."*

"My lord," she gasped, "these foul beings...they mean to..." She began to convulse slightly. Then the grip relented a little. She coughed, choked, spoke: "My lord, they mean...to steal the...cup of light..."

Woody was frantic, sweating. He feared his reason would break.

"Compose yourself, Emma," he cried. He'd pressed forward into the steady speartips until four points of blood trickled down his body. "For God's sake!"

The black man in black gestured with one long, bony hand at the sky.

"Apportu," he said, indicating Emma, *"ou l'el so't mor, compru?"*

"Do not harm her," Woody said. *"N'elle blessez-vous pas!"* He hoped that was correct.

"Apportu." Twisted the handle again and Emma gagged.

"Oui! Oui!" Woody exclaimed.

One of the small men leaned forward, gravely intent on her protruding tongue. He said something in his rasping language. The razor-faced leader eased his grip as Woody went and sat in his seat, then tried to explain, mainly with gestures, how the propellers must be spun. Four of the pygmies standing on the ground were instructed.

Emma had blacked out for a few moments when the blood was cut off and then suddenly restored. This time she saw (as from a great height) the armies of shadow flowing over the earth like almost liquid-thick smoke, closing in on the golden mountain that was the refuge and hope of the new race, the mountain where the ineffable fire blazed unseen and yet whose leaping reflections sparked in human hearts and minds. . . .

"They are closing in!" she cried, facedown, cramped into the bench. "O, sir knight, we must fight, we must not soar on these enchanted wings and lead the cruel ones who cannot feel the colors . . . not to the place . . . not to the glory . . ." Her breath held out but the effort left her panting.

The vision persisted. Shapes hidden in the curds of smoke. Coal-eyed steeds ridden by lean, long men in jet armor. Armor filled with seething, astral flame and malice . . .

"Emma," he called over his shoulder.

"They are evil," she went on. "They have denied the new light." Then she spoke in what he realized was Latin (he remembered a smattering from school) and it seemed the black leader understood it. "They," she was saying, "want to make this world like the old world. It is too late for them."

"Ehh," put in the black man, switching to a harsh Latin that she followed well enough, "so you speak speech of the little men, white whore. Well, I will tell you this, I, Go'ebb, will your heart eat when we come where we must come." He grinned. His teeth were bright and pointed. He pondered Woody as the pygmies now bound him into his seat. "Rise us into air, base fellow. I know these machines brought from cities by Great Ones."

"Whom do you serve, black dog?" Emma demanded. There was unstudied contempt in her tone which Woody didn't miss, though the Latin was hard for him to follow. He thought she sounded like a queen.

"Don't provoke him, for God's sake," he called back. He set the spark as the pygmies spun the propellers and the back-kick tossed one end over end to general amusement.

The black dog leaned his narrow face close to hers where it lay twisted and pressed to the bench.

"Soft-fleshed bitch-goat," he whispered. "We are not as

162

thee. We serve ruler of all. I shall eat thy heart and liver, whore. Go-ebb promises.''

"The ruler of Hell," she responded, "rules only Hell and the dogs of Hell, vile one.''

"I think no, whore-goat," he assured her, driving a vicious, bony fist into her cheek and spattering blood from her lips.

Woody snarled and went pale.

"Hurt her," he yelled in English, "and I do nothing!''

Go-ebb understood well enough. He straightened up. The ax face was cut by a grin.

The right motor caught and they respun the left. The engine hacked, kicked, then both were roaring. The pygmies on board looked uneasy. Go-ebb looked self-satisfied. He stood up, one hand holding the upper wing as they jounced away from the rest of the watching tribesmen.

"Speed toward where sun sets," Go-ebb said in Latin. "Keep river on right hand."

XXI

Von Schnee was wandering in a wilderness of skeletal, pale gray trees. The sourceless light was without color. He was running, desperately. There was a spear in his hand. Light, silvery armor tinkled faintly with each step.

The brittle branches snapped in his wake. He reached a bald hill where a cliff on the far side dropped to a smoky, churning river of darkness in a deep ravine.

The major was beside him in battered, bloody armor, supporting himself on a broken spear. He wore a helmet worked into a golden crown. The vizor was torn away. His face was netted with rills of dark blood. he felt his despair touch him with voiceless eloquence.

"We are lost," the major who was a king there said. Pointed with the shattered haft at the sky where (Von Schnee hadn't noticed until then) a vast swirling of black clouds formed a tornadolike funnel that reached down to touch the top of a huge mountain shaped like an exaggerated volcanic cone, across the canyon.

There seemed to be a shape in the smoke, something miles long, thin, with clawed limbs reaching out of the dark whirlwind into the heart of the mountain where a speck of golden brightness gleamed intense and hopeless against the dark torrents. He somehow understood that the shape was the dread power that possessed and amplified their enemy, the lord of earthly lords whose men had nearly killed them in the mistland.

As they watched he knew he was in two places at once and that he had to escape from there where the battle was lost. He had to escape as a long, knife-thin hand and arm reached across miles from the torn, blackened sky, and jet fingers the size of tall trees clutched at them.

He fought to escape to the other place, braced his futile

spear as his master roared with the voice of the winds in revenge and triumph (because the young captain had been one of his prize warriors before defecting with the hated woman who poisoned his realm) and Von Schnee (though it was not Von Schnee anymore) cried out: "She is lost! O let me die! She is lost!"

And then woke up, sweating, choking, thrashing on the clammy ground. He sat up, staring across the glowing ashes at the sooty-looking fog that had closed in while he slept.

He blinked and rubbed his face. The major was lying facedown, arms outspread, mumbling into the earth.

"Where are the others?" he said, half to himself. Heard something, a screaming, muffled. Out there. Another. "What terrible agony," he murmured.

Or some wild swamp creature . . .

The major shouted in something that sounded a cross between German and English: "The kingdom is lost . . . lost . . . the light goes out . . . *aiiii* . . ."

Haggard came to himself for a moment. He believed he was caught in a nightmare. He was sure he was asleep. He saw things in places where he was not. He saw things that would not have been visible were he not dreaming. In the hot light of an intense bonfire he watched a fantastic scene.

The blond woman was nude, hair almost to her waist, standing, wide-legged beside the naked dwarf. There were other shapes around them, redtinted but not reflections of the flames; vaguely formed, but not fogstuff . . . and then spinning like a dervish, blocky, glossy, sweaty, naked Streicher, the fogshapes seeming to swirl around him as if (to his dreamish perception) they controlled his movements and above him, like a shadow within shadows, reaching down like a cyclone's cone, a power and fury that (he felt) meant to twist the whole earth into its image and shape . . . he saw (without recognizing) Ayeesh the Arab where he was bound to a wrenched-around tree . . . and the blood, almost a glitter in the firelight, the bayonet in Streicher's hand suddenly whirling down and a splash of intestines following the glinting stroke, unwinding in front of the gutted victim who thrashed against the trunk . . . the dwarf squatted before the still-shocked-looking, dying Arab and reached one thin arm up into the ripped body cavity and strained and twisted his fist free (in a spew of strange, reddish color that was not fireglow) filled with what had to be the still pulsing heart . . . the scene shuddered and Haggard perceived another age where pyramid-shaped structures cracked and crumbled in an immense earthquake; a great city, wind-racked seacoast crumbling, swarms of doomed inhabitants going under in a series of seething tidal waves . . . on a tall spire of dark rock stood a lean, white-bearded man (he somehow felt the man was himself) in a silvery cloak raising his arms as if in benediction over the cataclysmic scene . . . felt the man (or himself) emptying out, a luminous, fluidic energy (that he knew was the soul) flowed out, arced like an electric spark across time and space and re-formed itself, pouring into a teenage boy walking in a spring green landscape, leading a cow by a tether toward a collection of clumsy thatch and claybrick huts, the boy's slack, drooling mouth, stripped and blasted idiot's eyes suddenly alive with will and purpose. . . .

And again, leaping centuries as from stone to stone to cross a stream and slamming into H. Rider Haggard this time, the impact too much for his consciousness so he was already failing, falling back, aware that the death energy of the tortured sacrificed Arab had released terrific pyschic forces and opened a way for the ancient being to reach him while the shapes and shadows seethed around the terrible scene which was, to him, an abstraction of flameflashes, nude bodies, pressing smoky fog, the eviscerated victim, the dwarf holding the bloody lump torn from the chest, stocky Streicher gripping himself between his legs . . . wild shadows . . . the magnificent female standing over him now as he fell away into dreams . . . she placed one perfect, bare foot on his chest and smiled, saying something in some strange language that the new force or intelligence or memory was translating: "We will have the secrets now."

And his own remote, somehow amplified voice answering in the same noises that were words he didn't know he knew:

"Fools, you have freed the beast from the abyss and he will devour you! You have drawn me to you and I am the fang and the bane!"

And next, consciousness was gone and he floated away on a hot river of fevered dreaming. The intelligence (that was himself now too) took subtle form in the dreamscapes, a glow of many hues, explaining, wordlessly, that they would rest and wait and then strike those who had been warned. It was required that they be warned just as it was known they would not heed. This was a battle in the war for forever and these ego-twisted wizards had stirred a deep terror that would pour all its power and intent into the human form of a terrible Messiah who would himself spill oceans of blood and turn the world to ashes, to no real purpose, and leave behind a smokiness that would cloud the human mind for ages and stain the heart's innocent eternity...the dreams flowed on and showed him lost worlds and the hope, a cup of dazzle filled at a fountain of eternal fire for men of the New Race to drink deep...the light and cup that must be secured and defended until time was finally stopped and the unending dawn awakened for the last earth of all earths where the sun and moon would be one thing and death itself would die....

For an instant his eyes opened and he saw the flames and smoke and pressing darkness; the stocky, redly gleaming demon-man forced his clenched hand over his virile member while the dwarf-creature squeezed blood from the heart into his slash mouth like a fruit, the hot red spattering him, the blond and lost goddess towering over him, tilting back into the fog and fire, her foot still pressing him down as if he were fallen game, feeling her saying or thinking:

You will all obey me....

And then dimmer dreams washing over him, sinking him down past touching....

In camp, Von Schnee was on his feet, leaning, listening to the wall of darkness that was the swamp. The major was still raving, mumbling into the earth. Corporal Müller suddenly sat upright.

"God," he exclaimed, "what dreaming!"

"Silence," commanded Von Schnee. "Listen..."

They listened. Insects droning, muffled wails and coughs of night creatures...a predator's shrilling...snores in the camp.

"To what, Captain?" Müller wondered. Beside him Private Stoss was twisting and rubbing his hands over his face, muttering, then sinking back to deeper levels and snores.

"In the distance. Outcries."

Müller shrugged.

"I dreamed the damned blacks were roasting my liver and feeding it to the dogs," he said, shaking his head as if to clear away the images.

"Where are the others?" the captain suddenly asked, looking around in the dimness. He saw Sneed's eyes glittering in the last shreds of firelight, his back to a tree, watching as if he hadn't slept at all. Von Schnee addressed him in English: "What do you know about this?"

Sneed smiled without mirth, eyes bright, wide, malicious. He said nothing.

"They're all mad, Captain," Müller said. "And I think, pretty soon, this place does it to me too."

XXII

"I don't care for what I must do," Woody said in English to the uncomprehending black who spoke a sort of Latin and perverted French. He stood upright in the airstream, holding onto the upper wing, exulting as he gazed down over the brightening landscape, rolling fields of mist, gleaming river, sawtooth mountains on the horizon.

"As it was," he said in some other language altogether that the pygmies understood where they crouched and clutched the sides of the oversized cockpit and stared fearfully around, "as it was, I say, my children, in the great days of the glory, so it must be once again. Ah, when the masters coursed through the air in birds made of cloth like this, whose great magic kept them safe."

Woody tried once more to make rational contact in his crude Latin: "What do you . . . what to do with us?"

The black shrugged.

"The ruler say. Who knows? The womanflesh we eat." He grinned. "Her fate more easy."

"God, forgive me," Woody said, in English, wondering if the plane would stand it. He'd done loops and rolls in lighter craft but they were still serious, dangerous maneuvers. A wing could tear away, tail section split. Aircraft were still kites with small motors better for gliding than powering through the uncertain atmosphere.

Hit the stick left—except his hands froze. Was it a spell? Did this native possess some strange power to control him, make him fly to certain doom?

But he realized it was himself, he couldn't simply kill these men. Not like this. And yet there was no real choice.

His heart was thumping erratically from stress, throat dry. He felt giddy.

"I have to do it," he murmured. "To save her. To save her..."

He believed he was going to faint. Uncanny that the tall black should be so confident. He should know nothing of flying machines. And where did he expect to fly them?

He spoke just to postpone acting now, over the motor noise: "Where are you taking us?" he tried in Latin again. "To Kôr?"

The sharp face leaned close to his.

"Who wait there for you?" he asked Woody.

"Is this..." He wanted to say riddle but had no idea how. Then he tried something else, absurd as it seemed: "She. She."

"She-who-must-be-obeyed," said the black's slash lips. Eventually, reflecting on that feature, Woody was to conclude that the man had been crossbred with Arabs. "She who will eat you heart, white fool."

"You mean to kill?"

The black grinned, though Woody couldn't see the grimace as he was facing front.

"Woman is meat, yes," the man said. "You belong She-who-must-be-obeyed."

Woody's hands tensed on the stick again.

Fantastic, he was thinking, finally more or less translating what the Latin expression meant. *Fantastic... have we not entered a world of dreams and madmen altogether?*

He reeled in his seat. Felt himself fainting, heart leaping in terror because he believed he was having an attack of something like cardiac failure or epilepsy....

He gave a shrill cry, felt the stick jar hard left, tilting up the wings into a sudden roll and didn't really hear himself, in a firm, new voice, saying, "Die, black dog!"

The pygmies fell like toys, shrill, starfishing in a flailing clump until vanishing into the ground fog. Woody tilted back his head and watched. He felt grim satisfaction. Death to the enemies of the hidden light, he more or less thought without having to worry about what that meant.

Emma was saying something, suspended upside down by the ropes that trussed her to the bench. He wasn't paying attention because he realized that the black man was hanging by his hands from what was now (because they were flying upside down) the lower wing. His long body swayed like a pendulum. Ground was sky, sky ground. Woody (or whoever he seemed to be) saw a shadowy outline, red-tipped talons ripping into the wing fabric, a snarling face full of fangs.

"Devil beast!" he cried. "Back to thy Hell!"

He groped as if to draw a dagger and was furious to find none at his hip. Slammed the controls around, shaking the upsidedown ship, then felt the lift when the weight suddenly was gone and the figure soared (from his reversed perspective) toward the wildly angled and careening world.

It is sure wizardry that gives me command over this magical device, he reasoned, as his hands and feet made the moves to right the machine.

He worked at his bonds next. Wondered where his weapons were. Freed legs and torso. They'd doomed themselves by lashing him and the girl down. The girl.

He twisted around.

"Have courage, woman," he called back.

She was herself again, for now.

"Woody," she said. "What has happened? I must have fainted." Her face was sore from banging against the boards. "How did we come to be here?"

"The enemy sought to enmesh us," he explained. "They were overthrown by holy power. But, lady, how came we to be in this magical craft of the air?"

"What? Woody, I—"

"What is *woody?*"

"Are you injured?"

"I am whole."

She twisted her head until she could see him, at right angles from her position. She kept trying to remember what happened when she'd blacked out.

"Why are you speaking so oddly?" she asked.

He was staring ahead now toward the fanglike line of mountains that walled off the swampy low country. He aimed specifically for the central peak where dark, solid-looking smoke billowed up and sank into the lowlands where it blended into the pervasive groundfog that made it seem the landscape was dissolving.

"This will bear us to the holy place," he said.

171

"Holy place?"

He smiled, wryly.

"My lady," he reacted, "were you not yourself versed in the secret knowledge you would never have been, with the help of the perfect power, preserved this far on our quest."

He seemed quite certain on that point.

"He must have fever," she murmured. *How will he be able to control this thing?* she asked herself, nervously. Her body was cramped and sore. "Woodrow," she said, a little desperate, "please . . . try to bring us to the ground again."

"Fear not, lady," he replied. He was stretching his freed legs and torso. He was feeling calm and ready. He'd find a weapon along the way. He was trying to fill in the gaps. There was much he didn't remember. He'd been fighting . . . yes . . . the enemy was overwhelming them . . . yes . . . a sloping field, a blazing fortress low and massive across the crest of a hill, billows of acrid, black smoke backdrafting down the slope over the clashing armies, himself on a tower parapet with two other men in silvery, cloaklike, soft-looking armor, the heat from the burning place blasting up into them.

"We are lost," one had said.

"No," he said. "No."

"It is truth, Lord," the other had put in.

"No," he'd repeated, without expression, staring down at the hordes smashing the last thin line of silver troops back into the ruined, flaming castle. "This war is not finished." He'd leaned on the stones. The heat had beat wildly through his opened helmet. One arm had hung limp and he'd felt the slow leaking away of his blood down his side. In the boiling smoke and flameflare the dark armored enemy seemed exuded by the shadows. "Not finished until the great fool is freed from his own darkness. Until his armies are smashed and broken. I swear this! The fight will never end!"

Sworn with all his dedicated and unending fury. Swore it in blood and fire. And, at least, the girl and the thing they sought to destroy had not been there. The girl who had been the living-map of the way to the hidden light. Because she was dead. Slashed nearly in half. And it was good that he was about to die because he would not have to think about her that way.

"Fear not," he told her now, "I have escaped from Hell's teeth to find you again, in this new life, and finish the battle."

"My God," she said, "he's mad."

He didn't hear her over the windrush and motorsound. He felt exhilarated, confident. Had no sense of passing time. Accepted this present as an answer to his last prayer, as a dream where time and place are both one thing.

So he accepted the strangeness and only hoped that a few of his old companions had been called here with him. That would be interesting. In his epoch, transmigrative principles had been taught in their equivalent of the classroom.

Exhausted and worn into numbness by the unrelenting stress, under the steady whooshing and drone, she drifted in and out of thin dozes where she met strangely vivid images of Woody and herself together on a rainy day under a canvaslike covering stretched between tree branches, fresh scents of water and earth somehow clear as in childhood's purest memory. There were horses tethered a few yards away in the misty downpour. They were undressed. The air was muggy. She felt excited, afraid, forbidden...alone lost in the watersound as they embraced and kissed on a sort of rug thrown over the damp grasses and prickles... drifting with engines and the air hissing through the wing struts and stays....

I am feverish too, she thought, drifting.

Giving herself up to him, wearing just a silver neck chain with a small moon pendant, his naked body on top of her, the rain hitting one outspread leg now, feeling an overwhelming sense of sin and joy...

"Ah," she murmured, amazed by the vivid images, struggling a little on the hard bench as the biplane tipped and gently bounced through the bright air.

And she suddenly felt that her life had been strangely incomplete. A terrifying thought because it was also an incomprehensible pressure to do something beyond her experience and understanding, a sense that the myths were more real than the rest of life and that she would have to give herself, somehow, to the myths, let them enter and fill her... a mysterious sense that the great actions and symbolic wars, the imperishable loves and dreadful dooms from beyond

173

eternal mists, heros and demons all-burned with an intensity that thinned and grayed-out all waking human life . . .

She felt the clear edges of her life dissolving around her. She was frightened too because she almost recognised him. Knew it wasn't just Woody, that Woody was incomplete as she'd known him, that he was also a living myth.

Haggard was unconscious and saw only reflections of what was happening around him in wild, burning, tortured dreams.

So he saw a strange beast with many mouths devouring pale, lovely women, black taloned feet searing the fair earth and myriad devils rising from a soiled, boiling sea, sweeping over the land like filthy whirlwinds of dull fire and poison, saw black angels quivering in dark descent holding the kings and masters of the world in their subtle webs and wings, whispering tales of blind gods of promise and power, of machines that could seem to think and men of flesh that ran as if with gears, visions of terrible greatness, of weapons that could shatter and disease the whole earth, whispering and playing lightless beams over their brains from the black lamp that was the sponge of glory and hope and help . . . he saw the beast with many mouths lapping blood from fang and lip, bearing the chill nothingness on one harsh palm and moving toward the volcanic peak where the hidden brightness still gleamed in a world of gathering, entropic fumes, moving to finally cap the source where the soul's secret sunlight entered reality while men dreamed of great machines and dreary triumphs. . . .

Had he been awake in his senses he would have seen Streicher fall on his belly and wriggle to the blond woman's naked feet as the hot fire began to hiss and squeak in a sudden downpour that beat and foamed the mud around them as his surprisingly long tongue lashed out and over her rounded, smooth, perfect toes while his left hand stayed reached under and between his legs and moved rhythmically.

And Haggard would have heard him cry out, swamped in pleasure and strange, inner imagery, devouring the foot she planted on his turned-up face while her own fingers parted the crease that opened her to spasms of fire and dark joy that no rain could extinguish.

Would have seen the dwarf leaping, squatting up and down like an obscene, bouncing baby:

"I am we are me we all power and all glory! Me! Me! We me!"

He then howled and rolled into the now steaming fire and, still howling words that had run just to sounds now, spasmed on the sticky ground downslope and on into the undergrowth until he was only a voice from the dark mist, voice and soggy sounds:

"We . . . come . . . eat . . . flesh . . . me . . . we . . . me . . . me . . . we . . . me . . . drink . . . blood . . ."

And her head turned, watching where he now wasn't, smiling, secret and pleased as if viewing her finest handiwork.

The rain was steady and hard. It gradually swallowed all other sound and beat the last sparks into mush while washing the ruined body of Ayeesh the Arab, blurred the blood away in ripples and night.

The dwarf thrashed off in the marshes. Only Haggard, in his fevered dreaming, glimpsed him wearing something like a shadow fifty feet tall, eyes unearthly flame, a force and terror that had just entered the waking world through the ripped open soul of the dwarf. The woman didn't see this, but she seemed to understand and be amused. Streicher saw little now, lying on his back spent as she walked away a step or two, the rain pouring over his muscular squatness.

So it was no wonder that Haggard wrung his pale hands and cried out from his stretcher: "Help! Help! Help!"

Then was aware of an old man in silvery robes and long beard, the only stable shape in a madness of tilting black and flame where the great beast moved in a spume of chaos. "Please help me!"

He was still unconscious at leaden dawn when Streicher and Renate, redressed in their saturated clothes, carried him back through a light drizzle to the camp.

The others were awake. Then Stoss and Tjaden had rifles leveled their way as they came out of the morning's dank mists.

Von Schnee squinted, bloodshot, at them. It was already getting hot. The day shift of insects was gathering in thick masses. He felt trapped and was afraid to fully admit it to himself.

"Where were you?" he demanded. He was asking himself which way they would go. Were they really going to continue to follow the pointings of the delirious Englishman? If he even yet lived. He looked ready to bury.

Streicher was pleased with himself. He felt vigorous and restless to push on. A recharged battery.

These weaklings, he was thinking, *I can dominate them whenever I wish...I shall keep the woman and get rid of these dregs after their usefulness is over...only the truly hard can hope to exist in the coming world or even today...the time is coming...*

He believed the whole situation out there was a test stagemanaged by fate and the hidden powers, intelligences, which shaped history on this world for the sake of secret wars for unseen kingdoms.

His brain was racing as it drank dark beams from the chaos churning within what seemed only fog. He knew now that history was the will of nations focused through the will of each individual genius. A spirit, a throne, a dominion...the whole white race (he thought) would be the expression of his own brain...he could speak and act for millions and when he moved his arm millions would move and when his ideas stirred millions would echo them. His body would be the body of nations....

He was sweating with the impact of these revelations. All his acts would have eternal significance. This swamp here was a symbol, the attainment of Kôr a metaphor and his final possession of the secret flame of life would become a drama for the new bible that they would have to write. The swamp was how low the world had sunk, this search for the lost city was the search for what would purify and transform the race...yes...it was all perfectly clear....

"You ask where we were," he said to Von Schnee, smiling.

"We've seen natives out there," Von Schnee said.

"Afraid of the niggers, Captain?" Streicher retorted. He was amused by this weakling. He would subjugate the blacks whenever he wished. Destroy them except for a few slaves. Perhaps their bodies could be converted chemically into useful products. Interesting idea. His brain seethed with ideas.

"It is not a question of that," Von Schnee said. He was looking at Renate, again. She seemed quite indifferent, wrapped in her secrets, looking down at Haggard, who struggled slightly on his litter.

"It is dawn," Streicher said. "We go on now."

"Exactly to where, Streicher?" Himmel asked. He now trusted neither English nor German. There was nothing left but mire. No great achievements. Without the hope of glory he could see no point to life and there was only death in endless fog and mud. They were all hopeless and crazy, he thought.

Dumbheads all, he said to himself.

He stood up, leaning on his rifle. He'd made up his mind to survive. A Roman had to survive. He was part of a general greatness. He would live and drag himself from this muck. Yes.

These men, he assured himself, *are fools. I will lead this rabble and teach them what it is to be part of a legion . . . teach these dogs and barbarians to be men. . . .*

Haggard's eyes popped open. Blurred, tall, pale, the woman seemed to float above him, her form subtly secured in the changing mist.

"Yes?" she asked him.

"The nearer you come to Kôr," he told her in a rasping, breathy voice.

"Ah, yes?"

"The closer the more *it* will hollow you." His cracked lips worked.

"Hollow."

"Ancient things will fill all of you."

"Ah," she said.

His voice was a whisper: "You will be empty, yet full."

"Peace, O Holly," she said, smiling. "I will be all I was again. The others may perish or not."

"It is too late already." Whispered, rasped, eyes shut again. "You mistake me, woman, I am not Holly."

"Who then?" She bent closer.

"At the hour does the bell strike," he told her and fell back into the depths of the fever.

"What does he tell you?" Streicher demanded.

She shrugged. Her eyes veiled something.

"Ravings," she said.

Sneed watched from across the still snoring major. Sneed's breath hissed softly. His eyes were too bright. He hissed and watched.

Then there was a terrible screech back in the mists. Not pain but (it seemed to Von Schnee) pure malice. A gibber of fury. Was it human?

"That's a sweet noise," Müller commented.

"I heard little monkeys . . ." Tjaden began and broke off.

"You heard what?" Müller demanded with disgust.

"Little monkeys out here can sound off like lions."

"That didn't sound like a lion," Stoss put in, rubbing his eyes and panting slightly from the strain of waking consciousness.

"Your nerves are not good," Streicher commented to his fellow captain.

"Never mind my nerves. Where is the Arab prisoner?"

"Do you miss him awfully much?" Renate wondered, gently mocking as they prepared to break camp. The strange knowledge was gone from her eyes again.

"We will eat as we move," Streicher said.

Young Stoss was already strapping the pack of rations to his back. Enough still (if supplemented by game) to last them all a week or more. No reason to panic on that score.

"He must have escaped," Tjaden said thoughtfully.

"The monkey?" asked Müller.

"No, Corporal. I mean the Arab."

"So," said Müller. "Then he's dead and that's his spirit howling."

"Yes, yes," said Von Schnee, unconvinced but realizing there was no point in pursuing the matter. "I will learn to live without him."

Hours later the invisible sun was a whitish blur of bright heat above the mist-saturated swamp.

Von Schnee was beat. The mosquitoes were maddening. Sticky sweat clung to him.

They were following another narrow ridge of fairly solid ground that Streicher claimed Haggard had indicated from his trance. Von Schnee was too tired to debate anything.

Corporal Müller was leading the litter while Tjaden struggled along back by the Englishman's head.

"If his damn fever would waste him quicker," he said to Müller, "my cursed arms wouldn't be pulling off my body."

"Haven't you listened to the Kaiser?" Müller remarked. "We Germans are superhuman."

He half tripped over a slick root. Cursed. They all stooped along in single file passing under a lane of netted branches. The smoky fog went thick and thin but never really opened out.

A slight, whispery ripping sound and an arrowshaft was suddenly shaking in a tree an inch or two from Streicher's neck.

To Von Schnee it seemed utterly incongruous, almost dreamlike in effect and fragile.

Then another out of the same silent mists that had just pulled back a few yards under some stagnant halation of vague breeze.

"Attack!" he suddenly yelled as if shaking himself awake. "Down and return fire!"

"At what?" asked Müller, upslanting his rifle and dropping behind the litter beside Private Stoss.

Streicher crouched. Himmel shoved the mumbling major flat on his face and knelt behind his weapon while Sneed and Renate stayed standing, she with a kind of cool detachment, he with cold, intractable fury as if arrows were shadowy straws. The Germans were shooting blindly, sporadically. The shots were muffled pops.

"It were better ye died now," Haggard suddenly said, "than endured hereafter."

No one was listening.

"There's a nigger," snarled Streicher. He emptied his pistol into the grayed blurs of trees and fog curds. To Von Schnee it suddenly seemed absurd, as if he were firing a popgun into unending, unformed emptiness. He felt a strange near-sadness. They were all lost, he felt, and these gestures were hopeless vanity.

Then a shock when a shrill voice out there howled in German: "We shall suck out your souls!" Then simply screamed, long, high, tearing.

"I've killed one," Streicher insisted, "I know it!"

Himmel lay low and waited. No more arrows. No more sound. Cocked an eye at Renate, who was still upright beside the thin, vicious-looking British prisoner, wrists bound, sneering into the fog, eyes like bright stones.

Next a gush of shafts hissing in from two sides.

Enfilading fire, noted Von Schnee. *Trouble, yes . . .*

None went near the woman. Squatting Streicher blinked at a near miss that was quivering in a tree near his head.

The strange, wild, cracked, harsh, dry, insane screech sounded again out there. Dozens of the dwarfed natives inched closer and were visible now as if shadows had thickened the vapors into distorted, semihuman shapes.

"Who taught those bastards German?" Stoss wondered.

Before anyone fired again, Renate, blond, imperious (Von Schnee had a fleeting impression that they'd slipped forward just to get a better look at her) raised one arm as if in Roman salute or barbaric benediction and called into the muffling mists (too loud, Von Schnee thought, for a female throat or maybe just too deep), commanded with words that were just sounds to the Europeans, a roar and a purr:

"Naaagaanurrrnaaaanaaanurrra," was what he made of it.

The natives, apparently, did better. They emitted a sighing noise, a cross between a rising and falling wind and sheer despair.

Himmel and Müller let off a volley but the little men blurred away and left only slow-stirring folds of vacant gray. No more arrows, no more shots.

Von Schnee stared at her. Almost shook his head. He was as sophisticated as the next man but it was a shock that seemed to hit harder than most of the preceding violence and terror. Müller and Tjaden were gaping past their riflestocks; Stoss was facing the wrong way; Streicher barely noticed; British Sneed looked amused and scornful; the major stared madly at nothing, while Himmel appeared disgusted, stayed low behind his gun and scanned the periphery of whitish gray smokiness.

Because she'd peeled off all her tattered and mucky clothes and stood there, quite nude and magnificent and remote (Von Schnee thought) as the frosty pole.

"She is off her senses," Müller said.

"The fever," grunted Tjaden.

Stoss reserved judgment, looking with wan lechery at the long limbs, the muddy puff of golden hair at the thighs' twin setting.

"We are all for it," Müller said bleakly, glancing at Haggard, who lay almost motionless now. "*He* wouldn't much care if there was ten of them naked," he muttered.

"She's for the damned officers anyway," said Tjaden, philosophically.

XXIII

I will have to devise a self-steering mechanism, Woody told himself as he looped some of the rope he'd been bound with to rig the joystick more or less in place.

Then watching the improvised automatic pilot over his shoulder he crawled back to where Emma was bound to the bench and freed her. Helped her sit up. The airstream fluttered her hair. She held him by the shoulders.

"Keep this strap across your lap," he told her, buckling the belt.

"Woody?" she asked.

He smiled.

"To the best of my recollection," he replied. Kissed her forehead.

"You are restored to your senses," she said.

He looked puzzled.

"I suppose so. I seem to have blacked out. I very vividly dreamt that I was in some strange country." He glanced at the steering, then down at the river.

Somehow, he reasoned, *we rid ourselves of those stubby savages . . . she looks weary . . .*

"Do you recall what happened?" she asked.

He shook his head. Glanced back and forth at the engines. Stood up, supporting himself on the upper wing. The foggy swamp drifted past below. The hot, bright sky domed over the landmarkless scene.

"I was fighting," he said, over the motor and air noise. "Armies were dying around me." He stared, saw the swords and axes. The black armor, lean warriors pouring out of banks of choking smoke, sweeping around silvery knots of battling defenders. The images were so vivid they still shocked him. More like memory than dream. He felt dazed and a little vague.

"I meant here," she called up to him.

"What, then?" he wondered.

The sun was hot pressure on her face. She vaguely thought she was going to have to relieve herself again soon. How was that done in a flying craft? She supposed, normally, no one flew this long.

"You recall none of it?" she asked. She was hoping it would all, somehow, be all right, that he would explain everything, take charge, find her father, then fly them home . . . somehow . . . she kept remembering home and the university, reading in the paneled library with the rich sun timing the slow afternoon through the leaded casement windows, glowing on the polished mahogany tables. She used to like to imagine (as an undergraduate and the third woman student at the college since it opened its door under Henry the Eighth) how she would discover a lost language on some exotic fragment of long-buried stone and that the lost culture that produced the language would be the repository of amazing secrets that would clarify all the Cabalism of the Jewish Bible and reconcile all ancient religion with Christianity . . . the memory came back just then with considerable force as if the peaceful image of the reading room were essentially a message, a clue to something, and not just the exaggerated ambitions of a woman never quite taken seriously enough. . . .

"I told you," he was saying, "I appear to have blacked out for a time." He blinked. His skull throbbed a little. "The last I recall is we were taking off at the mercy of those savages."

"Yes," she said. "You made the machine fly upsidedown."

"Ah."

"The chief one hung from the wing for a time."

"Ah."

"Yes."

"Upsidedown," he said. Tilted his face into the wind hoping to clear his thoughts. Nothing there but the dream, the night, smoke and blood. He winced with his lips. "Poor devil."

She was looking at the distant mountain range where the volcanic peak spilled ropy coils of dark smoke into the lowlands where the river seemed to finally unwind into amorphous blackness.

She felt it again, melting her, her life into some mythic energy as the twilight seemed to gather and seep up from the very earth itself. She understood there was no way to turn aside. They were doomed to this. She sensed that the myth possessing her would reduce her life in a cold, pure flame and strand her on the far side of hope and ordinary joys. She wished she could go back, instantly, to England, back to the school grounds flooded by rich old evening sungold under thick, mellowleaved trees... back to the library to think long thoughts over old books....

"Woody," she said, almost desperate because the chilling power and intelligence was there again, a vast energy pushing at her, neither male nor female, inhumanly pure, a power without virtue because it had never known vice. A terrible simplicity. "Woody," she almost cried, feeling it taking her even as he turned and it closed over him too, "Woody, I love you." Except she'd meant to use another name. No name she actually knew. A strange sound she didn't quite get out.

"Emma," he said. Then sat up straight and looked suddenly austere and calm. "You live. I thank the God of light." He looked thoughtful. Moved his body as if he expected it to be smaller, lighter. "Amee," he called her, smiling faintly. "Here you are. I thank the God."

"I..." she began. She was trying to think as the myths closed in while they droned forward as if striding on unseen legs across the mysterious, shrouded continent that was gradually going dark ahead from the dense volcanic fumes. "Who?" Trying to remember the name that wasn't a word yet. Just realizing that she really wanted the feeling back, the strange force that was clean, clear, complete... and then aware it was already there, gentle this time, giving her a chance to understand and brush the irrelevant details of her personality aside, the neurotic fears and silly ambitions, automatic desires.

"Yes, dear lady, Amee," he said. "I am Celo't."

She had nothing to say to that. She nodded vaguely.

It is really very serious, she thought, *it is really getting very serious....*

"Yes," she murmured. "Mustn't we, don't you think, set down for the night?"

"To what purpose?"

"Will we not crash in the dark?"

He shrugged, sitting down on the bench across from her as much, she considered, at ease as if he were in a drawing room.

"We are upheld by magic past my understanding," he reflected. "We are in the hidden god's hands. This craft will take us to the stronghold that was once the fortress of fear which became a place of hope." He shrugged. "I am still strong."

"I don't understand, you see."

He looked puzzled.

"Amee," he said, as if that were enough explanation.

"I don't..."

"The Lucifers," he thought aloud, using the ancient name, "hid themselves in the world's darkness."

She felt his power and was amazed because while Woody was fine and grave and adventurous, he was not really like this version. Was it merely the personal force of madness? There was such a thing. Yet he seemed so archaic, religious, deadly in a way no modern sensibility could be quite prepared for which better comprehended viciousness and desperation rather than this total commitment to purity and violence.

How beautiful his gaze is, she thought. She found herself impressed and attracted, but cooly, without real desire, just admiration and tenderness.

Behind him the sun now was dropping behind the wall of black smoke that seethed above the mountain range, a molten line like (she thought) burning, portentous blood. Like her first sight of the African coastline.

He was calm, she kept noting. Oblivious to the height, the steady sputtery engines, the unutterable alienness of it all...

"Why aren't you afraid?" she asked, suddenly.

"Your Lady speaks to you," he said. "My Lord to me. I am here, as you are, Amee, caught in these enchantments to complete what we began long ago. We fought for a good cause." He smiled, cool, remote, yet passionate. Shrugged. "The power that brought us here together again will bear us up a little longer, I think."

"What cause? Who are you? You are not Woody any longer."

He smiled again, looking at her this time.

"Woody? I was never dense as wood, was I?"

"What cause?"

"You truly have forgotten," he said. "Perhaps it is not my place to recall all things to you."

The force was subtle, took her like wine, intimate. The force was the myth itself, inescapable.

The wind was cool and the mountains slowly floated toward them as in a dream. She tried not to look directly at the volcano silhouetted by the sky of burning blood.

"Who are you?" she asked again.

"Celo't," he told her, simply. "A warrior of the hidden light." He reached across and touched her hand. "It is good to find you. The 'Voice' has returned too, I think, to try and drag us back once more."

"What voice?"

"He. The King of Luce, Lord of Will." Shrugged and withdrew his touch. "He who wants to drag us all back to the mist world." Sighed. "I came to hate fighting, yet the spear was ever in my hands."

She somehow understood him though she could not have expressed it in words. Words were thinning, for her. She sensed that the closer they came to that jut of smoking stone ahead, the more ancient, mute powers would stir and manifest.

He was suddenly too close, kneeling before her in the gently rocking cockpit where a following wind reduced the airstream to almost soft gustings. Like lying outdoors in March, at home, she said to herself.

He pressed his lips to the back of her hand.

"Wo—Celo't," she found herself saying. Was she enchanted? Hypnotized?

"Think you I had forgotten?"

She sank back into the gathering mythforce that washed around her like the sourceless twilight itself.

She let him move over her and it seemed a thousand voices and faces (similar yet altered) danced in her memory as their lips sealed together, hot and wet into a kiss that left her aching, desperate, feeling boneless, drawing him over herself, going under altogether in a wave of recognition and sweet fear.

"O my God," she cried as the plane bumped and

swayed almost lazily along above the ghostly fog sea. "O
. . . God...No-o-o...o...Wood...oooh...Cel... Cel..."
Opening herself in every way to that remorseless joy...

XXIV

The German party sloshed and struggled on, led now by nude Renate, who (through instinct or magic, thought Von Schnee) managed to thread a way through the dense, sucking, intolerable swamp.

He managed not to think about the fact that she had nothing on. Almost managed. He felt he was running a little fever now himself. Müller was still all right despite his regular predictions to the contrary. Tjaden believed he was going to be devoured by some swamp beast long before anything as mundane as sickness took him. Himmel and Sneed seemed impervious to the reeking, steamy, decaying environment.

No one had much to say just then. Haggard writhed occasionally on his moving pallet and Streicher would slog nearer to cup an ear over the delirious man.

They'd just struggled through a wall of brush and come out on the riverbank, some distance upstream. The water there was almost black and choked with weeds. A dead creature that might have been a lion was caught, rotting into the general decay. Part of the bare skull showed, fangs half closed on a thick, greenishblack curd of current.

A nice effort, Von Schnee commented to himself. *Not much more futile than the rest of us trying to feast on worthless nonsense as we die without meaning.* . . .

Following the curve of the river on slick but firmer muck, Von Schnee noticed that the pale mist was darkening though the sun was still high in the hazy sky.

And the hot, clammy air bit his throat a little now. The faint scent of burning.

"Perhaps we're near some village," he said to Müller, who was laboring stolidly behind the litter. Though he could have pulled rank and had Stoss and Tjaden on permanent porter duty. A good man, Von Schnee had noted in the past. The Englishman's weight would have been inconsequential but for the weapons case strapped under the stretcher.

Müller's stare had gradually gone glassy and bloodshot. He was, like everyone else, soaked with sweat and greasy with mud. He shivered in the oppressive heat, which was not a good sign.

"What we are near, sir," he responded, "if you ask me, is the great beyond."

Lanky Tjaden, who had stoically marched with his massive peat digger's hands locked around the poles, suddenly stopped in his tracks, looking at the sluggish, brownishgreen waterflow. He twisted his small head around on his turkey's neck. His face looked chapped and vaguely outraged.

"I'll go no more," he sullenly said.

"What's this?" Müller wondered. "Mutiny?"

Tjaden set down his end, jackknifing Haggard somewhat.

"No more," he repeated. His eyes were glassy.

"We're German soldiers in all weathers," Müller said. The tall private wasn't looking at anything.

"I'm going back home. I don't owe no more service."

"You're to serve for the duration of hostilities, Private Tjaden," put in Von Schnee. Shrugged. "Sad for us all."

"Never in this stinking place led by loonymen and undressed whores like from the French Follyberg." He kept blinking. "A lord ain't entitled to more than three months' service."

"What?" wondered Von Schnee. "What?"

That was a feudal custom, he thought.

Streicher had stopped up ahead. Himmel gaped because a face without a body was confronting them where the mist had partly drawn back almost like a parted fabric. The dwarf was leering at them from much higher than his body length could have lifted him.

Von Schnee moved up the line until the face was looking at him eye to eye. There were glittering green flies in the mouth. The gaze had no more focus than grayish glass marbles.

The domed head seemed to ride the curdles of fog. Himmel, looking disgusted, poked the thin spear shaft (which supported it like a trophy) with his rifle barrel. The face swayed.

"God," said Von Schnee.

The major blinked at it rapidly. Said nothing above a whisper. Sneed cocked his head as if in significant, unvoiced communication with what Von Schnee was imaginatively thinking of as a signpost or a warning that they were about to cross some mysterious frontier.

The head got Müller's, Stoss's and Tjaden's attention.

"There's something," Müller said. His eyes hurt.

Tjaden grunted, clenching his knobby fists.

"There's where we'll all be soon enough," Stoss felt. He was sure he had fever. Imagined he felt a finger of chill probing under his ribs and moving in a shudder up into his head.

"I've served my time, I say," repeated Tjaden, "and I've got my rights to go back to my village. The King himself can't say different. Much less no petty baron who fancies himself a black wizard."

He went on, mumbling. Müller really didn't pay attention except he was starting to think it had gotten to the private. Streicher seemed unmoved. He peered into the now constantly darkening mists.

We are getting closer, he decided. *The force is gathering. It wants to be free ... to be free ...* He believed he could feel its immensity and coldness and world-girdling power.

He shuddered. His eyes briefly rolled up as if he were having a mild fit.

And I shall free it and destroy the rebels and the degenerated races. ...

He stepped forward, reached one stubby hand and caressed the dead dwarf's stringy cheek.

Himmel and Von Schnee looked at him.

"This is a sign of victory," Streicher said, almost ecstatic. "I will free you."

"Hah," said Himmel, "I'll save you the work." Reversed his riflebutt and smacked the head from the pole.

The meaty *thwock* nauseated Von Schnee, who looked away as the thing rolled into the wet brush. And, looking away, he was the first to realize that Renate was gone. ...

190

XXV

They were wrapped around one another. She felt vaguely octopodal . . . hard to tell his limbs from her own even now as she dropped back into herself. A few moments ago it would have been impossible to know where his flesh began and hers ended or his breath, heartbeat, rhythms . . .

At last, she was thinking, *after ten thousand eternities I have found you again O my soul O my lost love. . . .*

Remembered the sacrifice, giving him up, giving all worldly existence up in the shadow of the doomed city that had been the last fortress of brightness before darkness overran it.

Stepping into the place of the light, feeling it stream into her being and change her, purify and clean and transmute confusion and agony into simple comprehension.

Leaving him to go out and try to touch the enemy with the secret that shone within her. Because all of them, the rebels, the New People, were doomed otherwise by the Lord of Will whose deadly warriors sought them everywhere and whom she (and others like her) uncorrupted, fled to meet. . . .

"But I am Emma Willard," she suddenly said, fully self-conscious again in the softly bucking biplane.

"So I understood," he said, twisting around and freeing himself from their embrace. "I must have blacked out again." He was frowning. "Damn it." He adjusted his clothes. "My God, I seem to have just missed something. What an understatement!"

Before the situation really sank in he realized the aircraft was tilting down into black billows of choking smoke from the volcanic cone.

His eyes burned. He blinked and squinted and then nearly went up and out as the wings groaned and sprung and they were sucked into a terrific downdraft.

One hand stayed gripped around the stick as he slammed into the upper wing—which saved him. Emma was held by the strap that still was looped around her waist.

"Christ on high!" he cried, his head banging off a template.

They were dropping faster. Nothing but burning blackness. He dragged himself down into the cockpit and managed to belt himself in. He shook the stick, trod the pedals, but without result. He was cut off from her and everything else as if falling into a pit.

As they spun the engines backed and choked, wires sang shrill and popped. Fabric peeled from the wings and body.

Anymore and she'll come all to pieces...

Dropping...twisting...dropping...blinded, he couldn't tell if they were falling or wrenching sidewise or rising again as he was tossed back and forth, over and under.

And then they fell out of the choking, hot cloud and he saw the earth covered by sooty billows looping overhead from the mouth of the black volcanic mountain by some freak of convection, leaving the slope and part of the valley clear and, upside down, then banking into a glide, he saw (eyes tearing enough to clear the soot) he made out a ghostly white city, walls, broken towers, built into the jagged mountainside in a semicircle with a megalithic structure that suggested a half-mile long altar, marking the most elevated point in the wedge of city.

Slanting through erratic crosswinds, grateful for the extra strength he'd built into the airframe, he aimed for the city hoping the flat-topped structure was as smooth as it looked.

He glanced back and saw Emma sitting up, hair sucked back in the wind, face, in that bilious dimness, like (he thought) someone in a minstrel show, stained jetblack with eyes and teeth a shock of white.

Suddenly the air was full of whizzings and soft pings.

"Down!" yelled Von Schnee.

The slim Bavarian private clutched himself, yelled, danced in agony, crashing into trees, snapping branches, blood jetting over his rather delicate hands. Von Schnee saw the thin shaft transfixing his neck as he finally went over backward in a dark puddle.

"Stoss," cried out Müller with instant grief and anger. "*Ach!...Ach!*"

Streicher was down flat, cursing, firing without aiming at the small, vague figures in the darkening mist.

Müller was leaning over the litter, long rifle tracking the little ghostly warriors who were loosing arrow after arrow at the party almost cued (he didn't quite think) to Renate's disappearance as if there might have been some inexplicable collusion.

Von Schnee covered a shadowy figure with his pistol and shot at the glint of teeth. The figure drew back and he couldn't tell if he'd hit anything. An arrow dug into the root beside him. The blackening, stinking, biting fog swirled.

Tjaden was firing now too. The natives flitted, darted phantasmically through the undergrowth.

Sneed was crouched, amused by the thought he could not be slain by mortal means. God had just explained to him that he had divine protection so that all these ungodly, miserable traitors to righteousness could be destroyed and their altar of black art and idolatry overthrown. God told him that the enemy was evil itself and that once they led him to their temple he would reach lightnings and thunders into his hands to smite them with. He did not doubt that the voice in his head was God's. The voice was like muted thunder and commanded most of his attention.

The major stood, dully, staring, saying, "The New Race is lost...O my daughter, forgive me...I have fallen into the toils of the enemy...I have failed you...I have failed my people...the slayers will eat our flesh..." An arrow hit his chest. He yiped like a hurt dog but didn't do more than flinch. Stood there with uncanny, mad dignity like some heroic statue cast in ancient times. "We must prepare the souls for the new bodies..." Zip, thock, another shaft quivered in his chest. He doubled up. "I am slain..." Staggered forward dragging Sneed to his knees. Something was stirring in Sneed's consciousness, a feeling that he was not a part of any of them, that he was playing a role and waiting for his chance because they were all his enemies. All alien. As another arrow hit higher the major's words became blood and sound. "...the new bodies..." He finally fell. Bubbles of blood popped in the murky surface.

Sneed snarled, dragged to his belly by the rope that tethered him to the dead major.

The arrows whizzed, gunshots flashed. The ghostly dwarfs ducked, faded, seemed to all but dance at the periphery of stinging mistsmoke.

Sneed stared at the major's bloodstain spreading over the dark water. The pattern formed shapes, faces, familiar scenes of agony and terror and he found himself remembering and enjoying and hating, feeling a great power pushing up from the stinking swamp earth into his body, overspreading his mind and soul like the bloodstain on the foul surface . . . hate and wild freedom, a growl in his throat as limbs crunched under his attack and his teeth ground bones and ripped muscle and split flesh . . .

"Yesss," he whispered.

He remembered himself, now. Knew who he was, the hunger and fury of who he was. The outcast who would save his people, the most cunning of the strong ones. He remembered and knew who he hated. Looked around at them. All of them. Hated all of them. Murderers of his family.

At the same time Himmel had a revelation. His memory, he reasoned, must have been blurred over. He felt like a man struggling to see through gouts of smoke when a shift of wind frees him. Somehow he'd been lost here among these outlandish barbarians but the Legions would rescue him and he would continue his march against the city of enemies. These fools knew him not, it seemed. Soon it would be too late for them.

He smiled thinly. The master of Rome would master these savages. Beyond these mists and bogs lay the stronghold whose fall would lay this land at his feet. And then it wasn't Rome either . . .

Revenge on those who'd slain him. A vivid memory that seemed so old, somehow. A dully shadowed wall, gusts of hot wind through the marble pillars, steep steps behind him overlooking the obsidian, glossy city laced with lush gardens and fern-like trees. City of mists. Going in the massive temple door with a few others, black robes fluttering, feeling satisfaction because he'd won the war. Even that moment the rebels were bleeding, impaled on polished stone stakes. Very good. And Lord Relti himself had given him unprecedented honors ... the trees hissed in the stifling wind and he felt uneasy ... movements inside as he blinked to adjust his eyes to the dimness ... shadows moving ... steel flashing, screams ... scraping, blinding pain as a blade ripped across his ribs ... flashes ... redmist ... blows that weren't even pain yet ... thinking wildly that they'd drenched him in water until he knew it was blood and tried to cry out and drowned in his own voice ... spinning around and around, blurred faces rushing past, windows full of hazy brightness ... suddenly steps hitting him and darkness bleeding into his mind ... and a terrible feeling that he had been cheated and was going to have revenge as his protesting voice (or was it another's?) choked liquidly into silence ... the scene melting like a dream as if he just woke up, shuddering in the jungle swamp, muttering under his breath:

"I am returned they could not slay me I am returned to do what I must do."

He blinked. The barbarians were still firing their strange, explosive weapons at the shadowy dwarfs. Very strange, but he'd deal with those things when the time came. If they were useful he'd use them.

Sneed was gnawing the ropes to free himself from the major's body. His thick jaws and grating teeth soon parted them. Next he began wriggling flat on his belly through the wet brush and dank leaves.

"I will slay these soft ones," he muttered in hisses and *ooks* that no one there would have taken for any language at all.

Haggard watched from within the blurriness that was now himself. He had no sense of body or name. Just a vagueness watching other vaguenesses, waiting for something he didn't understand yet.

He actually perceived the whirlwind of dark energy and intelligence that the ferretlike little man had felt screwing into him. It was cyclonic, churning. A vortex where smoky shapes of consciousness swirled in a whirlpool of souls centered on the steadily fuming volcano, pouring in and out of the cone in a steady pulsation suggesting the slow beating of some immeasurable heart.

He perceived the beings, souls pouring like stormspun clouds over the dimming landscape, pouring into all of them in waves of fever, the occult wind gaining intensity the nearer they came to Kôr itself.

He perceived that the dark, unseen smokiness had almost completely filled some of them, dimming their natural soul light.

And the flame too, the fire of the world's heart, the ineffable spark left in the dense darkness when sun and earth were pulled apart to circle in holy harmony. The fire. And he perceived where the fire touched some humans (where there were already flickers of light within) and broke up, burned away the dark clottings.

That light had touched him where he lay wrapped in fever and strangeness. That light was now a sword sheathed within him. He understood that the time would come when the blade would be drawn.

"They will all be full of demons and oppressed spirits," he said, "by the time we come to the edge of the pit."

XXVI

They sat in the cockpit, the motors off, staring up at the black, surging dome of soot and smoke that curled immensely over the spectral, ruined city before spilling down into the swampland. The effect was something like being inside a waterfall.

He unstrapped her and helped her down from the plane. They stood on the flat, gargantuan, granite roof. The redtinted glow from the quietly fuming volcano created a sunset quality.

"Now what must we do?" she asked. She felt incomplete again. She partly rebelled against the idea of that tremendous otherness taking her over again, yet she longed for it. She felt shivery as if with fever. "How can we hope to find Father?"

Woody was about to say that they could only hope he would come all the way upriver and that they'd find a way to fly him back out.

Instead of speaking he thought he saw a flash, a spark of soothing, intense golden fire that was somehow within his mind and felt an instant strength and calm.

For a moment he was conscious of two worlds and personalities: he was both and yet more. There was a force behind them and he felt it, clear, austere, not human but the best of the human heart, a stainless flame of compassion and sternness that was pitying in its fierceness. Both personalities were sustained by the power. For an instant he saw both worlds and he knew the other one was no less real than the very stone he stood on under that brooding sky of smoke and ash. He understood that the war was being fought forever in a barren, craggy landscape among boiling, lavic lakes and broken hills, burnt-out civilizations, shattered cities, wasted farms, a wasteland where twisted, uncouth monsters prowled, starving, savage men and cannibal women wandered, furtive, hiding in caves in the depths of dim, stunted forests . . . a land of ashes, dead, dying, straggling peoples mutilated by disease and the aftermath of endless fighting . . . he was aware that there were a few, scattered outposts where sane, whole men and women held out against the twisted hordes of dwarfed and savage races that had (he understood) sprung from the depths of the earth: rapers, torturers, perverters who sowed no crop but misery and fed off the flesh of all that lived . . . degenerated killers in black and silver armor, some with ears like bats; some deaf with fox's sight, a mad mélange of furious beings swarming, destroying because there was still a single fortress that had never fallen where the light was kept. The last hope for the darkening universe that was now entering Woody's world, swirling around all of them . . .

Emma saw the flash too. She understood. Felt a bitter-sweet sympathy for all the unhappiness and pain closing around them.

"Come," he said to her. "The enemy is near and I would meet him again."

His face was set, eyes cold with old anger.

"Yes, my lord," she said, following him across the gigantic, ghostly pale slabs.

Renate's blond hair streamed behind her as she fled along a subtle track of firmness through the black swamp and stinging smoke.

"Come, my children!" she called into the choking billows in a voice more resonant than normal, using words she would not have recognized before.

The pygmies seemed to know the words because a half dozen of them were suddenly around her, kneeling, holding their weapons over their heads as if asking for benediction. They sighed moaning, wordless ululations.

She stood tall, imperious, swirling energy rising through her like a whirlwind, pulling her toward Kôr itself because, in a thinning roll of mist and smoke, the gate was suddenly, dimly visible—a pale arch of half-shattered stone at least fifty feet high.

"Follow me," she cried out. "I am returned to you across the abyss itself from Hell's Gate, O my children!" She rose on her toes, naked, magnificent. "The doorway to my temple stands ajar!'' She ran lightly forward, the little people falling in behind like dogs.

Behind them, in the muffling clouds, long, clattering, stuttering reports sounded. Then a series of dull, percussive blasts.

She went through the arch and suddenly was under the black dome of smoke that enclosed the dead city. It poured down into the surrounding swamp in a turbulent wall sucked outward by some freakish convection.

She started across a perfectly straight, level causeway that ran over the buildings and ended at the steps leading into the gigantic, flat-topped temple where Woody and Emma had just landed.

Streicher saw her as he came out of the wall of smoke and passed through the archway. Müller and Tjaden were at his heels. The heavy-shouldered corporal had a shaft in the thigh which he'd hardly registered yet. Tjaden was puffing, cradling the Maxim water-cooled machine gun, the barrel smoking.

Von Schnee had paused to cut Sneed loose from the dead major.

"Come on," he'd told her. "You have no hope here."

Sneed had growled and snapped at his fingers. Von Schnee had stared, nonplussed. Let it go.

Turned and ordered the enlisted men to follow Streicher and the woman. Tjaden had let off a last burst, then lifted the weapon from the tripod mount. Müller took the tripod.

The natives had blurred back into the shrouds of smoke under the ripping, spanging fusillade.

Sneed watched them with sullen contempt, his ferret face a pale slash.

"O new men," he said, "you will not save your lives this way."

He stood up, fluidly, eyes like dark blue pebbles.

"What is?" Müller asked him, distracted, trying now to work the arrow loose from his flesh.

"I'll not spare any of you," he said in what seemed growls and barks.

"He's mad too," Von Schnee said. Felt rushes of fever himself. "Come, men!"

And Sneed stayed there, watching them go. Von Schnee glanced back as the smoke closed around him. He and Müller and Tjaden passed through the arch onto the bridge, the two enlisted men automatically picking up Haggard and resting the machine gun on the litter.

Von Schnee was in the lead and, as he came out into the suddenly smokeless air (as if passing through a wall) he saw Streicher seeming to take aim at Renate's naked back though she was really out of pistol range.

The dwarf blacks with her (which seemed a pack of guard dogs) turned and were ready to charge back toward the Germans.

Von Schnee didn't hesitate. He rushed forward feeling suddenly lost, feeling it was far too late for him, feeling strange, dark pressure swirling around him, pressing at him, smothering, chill, alien . . . and it was too late even to be afraid, sensing something was blocking whatever fell fingers were reaching for his soul . . . nothing had ever meant enough to him and he realized he was going to die there, lost without understanding why or how . . . because he was a fighter, in the end, and she was beautiful, as if that were really enough, standing out on the bridge to the smoldering mountain, pale and perfect, glowing among the mud-colored savages in the flickering, dull red flamelight above that ancient, ruined, empty place at the end of all human maps and desperate desires. . . .

Streicher was actually trying to grip her with his will, unconscious of the gun in his hand, for the moment. He felt the old power reaching out through him to touch her.

He was startled by the impact that lifted and tossed him aside and never felt the gun fire, snarling, "Coward!"

Meaning a nameless, shapeless demonic creature that had not seen the surface of the earth since before men were formed. The great power possessing him believed for that instant an ancient enemy had attacked.

It wasn't until he slammed on the stone that the blocky man knew it was Von Schnee who'd tackled him and was clutching his neck.

"You hound!" Von Schnee was raging. "You filthy hound!"

Von Schnee thought him strong as an ape as they rolled

200

to the edge where the ancient guardrail shattered. He kicked and thrashed but his own windpipe was now in Streicher's thick hands and was starting to crack. His face felt swollen enough to burst. The blows he now levered at the hard, round head meant next to nothing. His twisting kicks into the dense stockiness were futile as kneeing thick rubber.

"Swine!" hissed Streicher. "Spawn of Jews!"

Even as he knew he was dying, Von Schnee was shocked. *Jews?* he asked himself. *What has it to do with Jews?*

And then the thick weight went away, leaving him gasping in a flood of images as if waking from dreaming. The silent scenes were eloquent and he wordlessly comprehended that somehow, in some lost world, he had been what he saw: an armored warrior riding with eleven others through a misty landscape where giant, fernlike, supple trees bent over wide, rolling plains spotted with almost crystal bright blue flowers while in the background jagged chains of volcanic mountains walled off the horizon, rising above the mists where strange, lean animals moved with the ungainly grace of giraffes. He understood that the scene was unthinkably ancient. He and the other warriors (tall, strong, fluid-looking men, riding horses whose muzzles were a little long and curved forward), bracing spearheaded lances in one hand, rode easily without stirrups, saddle or reins. The animals were keyed to the rider's nervous system. The two were raised together and were paired from foaling until death. They moved fast and easily through rolls and rips of the soft, warmish fog in a world where things were softer and lighter than at present. Somehow he was comprehending (as if he were outside himself in a totally generalized consciousness whose precise judgments were more terrible than any rage or agony could have been). He comprehended that man (in that time) was changing from one racial type to another. The (then) dominant race was ruthlessly hunting down the new peoples who were developing new abilities to reason and organize and fight with purely physical means. The older race (sometimes called Lemurians in later mythic history) had totally developed imagination, resistance to pain and pity, possessing willpower that could literally seize living beings, move them, shape them and (if they lacked strength to resist magically) kill them. The Lemurians had begun in perfect dreaming harmony with nature but time had corrupted them and a few had subjugated all the others and were finally ruled by a harsh, fanatical, magician-king, Relti III, intent on extirpating every trace of what his race considered weakness so as to leave only polished, intrepid, pain- and pity-immune males and perfect breeder females who would rule all other creatures.

Relti preached these things in thunderous speeches. The males of the great race, he liked to tell them, had to live only from combat to combat, like carnivores, hunting or perishing. Perfect fighters following nature. Devouring the weak. Their women were intended for dreaming, prophetic song and sensing subtle, psychic forces—except that the New People, the rebels, were undermining the work of ages, making, as the King put it, "men into half-women, mixed together, degenerate weaklings." His fury on the subject was boundless. He would storm around the immense stone fortress that had been carved from the living rock of a mountain peak, gazing, sometimes, from the topmost tower at the lake of lava in the valley. He loved the glow and shifting patterns of the molten stone. When he spoke, his words created images that actually lingered in the atmosphere that would have reminded a modern human of being underwater. The gist of all he claimed was: "Like the worms that eat the heart of the mightiest Shaiya tree reaching in fluid perfection for the sky, the maggot-peoples will kill off our race, yes, even ourselves, the true descendants of the Thoramm!" He would bring his fist down on the stone parapet and, backed by his incredible willforce, the blow actually shook the foundations of the fortress itself. His men, in their black, woman-woven armor that seemed almost silken, were awed by his strength. "If a single enemy escapes," he insisted, "be it man, woman or child, the poison will spread. Each maggot must be destroyed. A perfect stone must have every facet polished. One single imperfection spoils the whole, just as a single coward ruins a battleline." No one disagreed. The compelling sounds and images were ecstasy to them.

So, in Von Schnee's secret vision or memory, he knew what they fled from because they were still no match for the magical warriors chasing them across those smooth plains through the warm, dense air . . . not without proper weapons.

The New Peoples were physically stronger than the

Lemurians but they could only counter their auric force (what moderns would call psychic powers) by means of symbolic weapons in that environment where symbols (shaped into swords or spears) thickened the still dreamy fabric of reality and were as deadly as the purely material (or apparently material) means of later ages. But what Relti III, Lord of Lemuria, feared was the hidden light, the subtlety that heatlessly burned into men's souls and opened their receptive, feminine inner nature that ten thousand years of rigid training had locked deep and dormant. Von Schnee sensed another consciousness, old, sure, ungentle yet tender, enclosing him, explaining. So that he somehow knew the Lemurian males transmigrated (he had never thought twice about reincarnation) into later ages and kept their old powers locked in their souls and the ancient training could still be tapped by their reborn masters of old, like Relti, who ceaselessly strove, in ever later age he appeared in, to revive his people's glory and strength—except the forms of the later, denser world increasingly resisted magic's full working. Von Schnee remembered, in the timeless flash, that the hidden light had been caught in a crystal cup. Eternity's brightness rushing up from the untainted core of the world had filled it. The harmonious shape of the cup (molded by bright beings not made of flesh) held the vibrant brilliance for a time.

He understood that as they all neared Kôr, they were being reborn into legend because there the world was more like the ancient days where myths could take substance and the unseen could manifest with unbearable lucidity.

For ages after the fall of Lemuria, Kôr remained capital of the world. Even through the days of Atlantis.

In their satiny armor they rode up the long slope rich with oversized, manyhued, delicate flowers toward the low, grass-covered mountain. Von Schnee (in that infinitely suspended moment) felt himself riding in the lead. They were racing to reach the mountain peak where the source of the holy light poured up through the well that was bottomless and (even then) as old as the rocks themselves. The cup had to be recharged before King Relti's Red Claw riders caught them. He could sense them back in the mists, could feel their concentrated intent reaching out.

The woman actually held the cup of light, in folds of

white, metallic cloth. Only a woman was permitted to hold it. She was dressed as a warrior. The deception was weak, of course. Well, they were all doomed, even if they succeeded in reaching the hidden chamber in the mountain. He understood and accepted that. He just thought about how he loved her. Trusted her with his heart and life.

He who had been bred to trust nothing but his own powers and the yieldless will of his leader. He trusted her. She was so lovely; her hair soft gold. She was all he knew to trust now because he'd been bred a Lemurian guardsman and yet had followed her and let the strange light shine on him in the ceremony. A year ago he might have been riding in pursuit . . . except he loved her and before had only desired pleasure and the joy and terror of combat . . . love had surprised him like that subtly soft light he'd drunk like a silvery fluid from the holy cup that had tingled without actual taste and melted away before he could swallow. . . .

They'd mated when she was a songspeaker in the capital and he still a captain in the leader's guards. He'd found out she was part of the hidden light movement and it was his duty to arrest or kill her outright. By doing neither he'd doomed himself. So he'd fled and joined the rebels in the hills.

All this came back to him while lying on the stone bridge as if Müller had been suspended forever in the act of lifting blocky, raging Streicher half into the air and tossing him aside. His massive shoulders cracked with the strain.

"They're coming fast," Von Schnee said, wildly. His eyes were staring at nothing. "We must protect her!"

"The niggers, sir?" Müller said. He felt chills and flushes of fever. He waited for the madness to sink him under. Knew it was about his turn now. Felt remote as if he were not altogether himself. Though it was life and death, there was something almost trivial about what was happening to them. They were such small pieces of eternity. How vast and unmoved eternity was by their fractions of grief, joy and pain.

"What?" asked Von Schnee. "What? The damned Claw Riders, fool! Relti's master cutters. They'll have your guts for stew meat."

She ran, nude, lightfooted, as if the air bore her forward toward the gigantic stone temple that gleamed ghostly white under the dome of churning volcanic smoke. Here and there, where the black clouds were rent, slivers of a full moon flashed briefly like a longlost image.

She easily outdistanced the little men, the ancient, glass-smooth stones of the immense bridge a joy under her rapid feet. Her hair streamed back. She kept repeating to herself that she was home . . . home.

There were no words in her thoughts, just vivid pictures now. Rich, muted colors like dreams of undersea landscapes. Home was there, deep in the images, home was waiting beyond the temple gate, the doorway to the secret flame that had once burned in the whole substance of the earth. Now it was concentrated there because the rich magic and exquisite softnesses of the old time had been burned away by the violent sun.

And then the world split: a line of terrific brightness divided sky and ground and skull too, a soundless pressure and she fell out of herself, fell through images of lost worlds without number . . . fell out of time . . . saw herself, innumerable times, crowned in glory . . . saw the images unfolding to nothingness like uncoiling smoke.

Something hard smacked her. Blackness crashed down. . . .

Emma and Woody were descending a long flight of carven steps that curved down into the temple from the roof like a borehole. There were glowing patches along the walls that cast a palely green luminescence.

They came out in a vast hall. He led her unhesitatingly. She followed without question. He *felt* the way, as he'd been taught in the free lands beyond the shielding mountains where his people lived tribally in the incredibly rugged slash rock and intercut cliffs and foaming rivers that created a natural defense system against the troops of Relti the Destroyer. Relti III. The last supreme Lemurian King. The worst. For generations, he'd been trying to exterminate the Free Peoples, as they called themselves. The isolated groups had survived and struck back when they could. They were superior in calculation to the more instinctive Lemurians. The personality that now manifested in Woody was a recall of that particular period in the age of war that had lasted until the central continent was actually submerged under the sea.

The New People retained some of the suprasensible skills of the older race. Woody was using one now. For the moment his name was again Celo't. The New People had denser bodies because they lived less and less in magical worlds. But he still retained subtle powers almost totally atrophied in modern man.

So Celo't felt his way down and around through the semigloom, following a kind of psychic scent past pillars fat as redwood trees.

"Hark," he said, quietly, pausing. He felt enmity close by. Then heard muffled, echoing cries and sounds he didn't know were gunshots.

He realized he was partly remembering now. He'd been there, ages ago.

"What is it, Celo't?" she asked, touching him.

He took her hand. "The way to the fire is near," he said. "There's a gate set in one of the pillars of the world." That was what they called the vast supports. "One must penetrate the formless fog." The fourth pillar, the pillar of the fog, fire and wind, the tunnel maze that ran deep into the bones of the mountain until the seeker came to the place where the sun would trace the way across the abyss once a year when he entered the Virgin in heaven. He remembered the lore. "Come," he said. "If we win this race we can block the way for a thousand years."

Because the voices and what he didn't know were gunshots echoed in the immense hall itself now.

"Yes, my lord," she said.

Renate was wiping blood from the side of her head. The bullet crease throbbed. She found herself lifted to her feet by Von Schnee.

Müller and Tjaden were facing back the way they'd just come. They were halfway across the mile-long bridge.

Von Schnee (or was it Awan of the Lemurian guard) stared at her, feeling pleased and bitter because he knew he was going to have to die again and lose her again—no, not lose because he'd already lost long ago—just watch her swept away.

"Ayess," he addressed her, watching the pain-touched, remote eyes where the fire and smoke flicked and wisped.

"Ah, Ayess." And kissed her with more hopeless tenderness than passion.

She just waited, not looking at him. Absently touched the hurt streak on her skull.

"A bad time for romance, I think, Lord Awan," the guardsman who had been Müller said. He was mounting the Maxim machine gun on its tripod. The overlap of personalities created no contradictions to him so the weapon seemed normal. He broke the shaft, strained and pushed the thin arrow through the edge of thigh. Winced, then grinned, thinly.

Tjaden was sullen. He plucked a short arrow from his baggy shirtfront. It hadn't struck flesh.

"I go home," he muttered, "directly."

"Come here and feed the belt," Müller commanded him.

Because the little men were coming out on the bridge, fast this time. Hundreds, massed shoulder to shoulder on the broad span.

While Awan still held the unresponding, nude woman. Who no longer could have known him.

"Captain," she said, "what are you saying?"

She looked around and was surprised. Made no effort to unwind from his embrace. Kept blinking. Decided she'd blacked out from jungle fever. She'd expected Von Schnee to succumb to her charms and she imagined there would be some advantage to it. The strange fogginess seemed to have passed away from her consciousness. But what was he talking about and why was she naked in front of the other men? That seemed a poor road to satisfactory intimacy.

"Ah, Ayess," he murmured again, "even in the eye of this death too I stand entranced by you."

"How interesting," she said. "Where are my clothes?"

"Lord, look sharp!" cried Müller.

"The not-men," he sneered. "Magic-made with beasts' souls."

He spoke German without realizing it. Tjaden looked up from where he was feeding the belt into the firing mechanism. They'd all forgotten Streicher, who was slipping away across the bridge, thinking he would set a trap for them later.

The force that possessed them was capricious and inconsistent. It mixed past and present personalities, language and logic.

Suddenly Tjaden was himself again, in some inexplicable lull in the soul-storm that whirled invisibly around them. Müller, still a warrior of long ago, squatted behind the handles of the not anomalous machine gun waiting fire as the dark mass of natives charging them seemed to pull itself into shadowy substance from the seething wall of smoke.

"Sir," Tjaden wondered. "we were taught that even niggers have souls."

Awan frowned. Looked around for a weapon feeling more naked than the woman he was prepared to die defending though he expected her to betray and destroy him. It was her nature, he reflected, just as it was his to love her. Although he never trusted her, he made no effort to defend himself.

He eased her behind him and snatched up a pair of spears. Said to the two men he knew as members of his old battle group, "We fall back abreast." He looked sternly at them. "Arm yourselves, fools."

Müller looked up too this time to blink at his commander. A lull in the psychic gale released him. To him it was a break in the fever. The heat burned in his eyes. His thinking was cottony, distant.

Renate had backed away a few steps. She'd turned and was watching Streicher's outline where he'd almost reached the foot of the massive steps. In scale, against the temple structure, he was a scurrying dwarf.

"Now the captain is mad," Müller was saying.

Awan crouched, the spears held in a X before him. He glanced back at the woman he knew as Ayess. She was stunned yet already calculating chances. She'd survived much within her shell of softness. The plum's pit, the stone heart, some had called her. She was thinking that Streicher might be a better play than casting her lot with a madman. She weighed it and gently touched the bullet crease. It still burned but there was little bleeding. She wondered what had happened.

This attractive captain, she thought, *is ill and cannot last to the end of the course.* . . . In the reddishtinted, swirling dome of darkness, she held hard within herself, as she always had. For an instant her control wavered and she seemed to float above herself and saw them all, natives and whites and self alike, as deluded shades fighting phantom battles. Lost in greedy dreams while the world whirled into endless night. *I must get back to Europe, that is the chief thing....* And then the current of lost times took her again and she thought: *The sweet light has failed and I must endure ... there is nothing more precious than life ... the Great Lord Relti can save me ... the Great Lord ...*

The charging pygmies were a low wall of spears topped by a gust of arrows that spattered over the Germans. Several hit Haggard's litter. One tip sliced across his thigh; another clipped Awan's left ear.

Then Awan raised both eyebrows because the Maxim stutterchattered and the massed pygmy ranks were ripped to tatters in midcharge. Warriors toppled, staggered wildly, some actually roughly cut in half.

"Good work," he said grudgingly. No one heard him. He assumed these were symbol-weapons forged by the New People. The soulwind showed him the true forms of the pygmies: Lemurian Claw Riders under the blood banner. "Now we fall back," he ordered. The natives who weren't flopping and screaming in their gore had fled back into the wall of smoke. Müller looked up at his captain. The gunbarrel smoked.

"Sir," he said, "they cannot stand against us."

"Where do we go, base-born fellow? Into the swamp again?" He half grinned. "Come!"

Müller slung the gun over his shoulder while Tjaden took the tripod. They looked down at Haggard.

"Poor bastard," muttered Tjaden.

"Maybe he had a father," said Müller. "Anyway, there's no bastard under God's eye."

"What?" Tjaden wondered. "How comes that to be?"

"He's the father of all."

"Here's a sermon from *Gefriede* Müller," Tjaden said, grinning.

Müller was blinking, lightly and rapidly, at the heaps of shredded dead and dying.

"It's true," he said, as if surprised.

"Come, fools," ordered Awan.

With both hands supporting the massive gun, he wiped his sweaty face with his shoulder sleeve.

"I'm burning up," he said. "I am a sinner and have wasted my life. I should have cherished all things. I . . ."

Tjaden stared and then the smokiness was in his eyes again.

"Come along, flatlander," he said. "This Brynman will teach the art of slaying to you, free of levy."

Blinking, stepping back, nearly tripping over the litter, the corporal tried to focus his blurry sight upward because he thought he'd glimpsed a rent in the seething cloud fabric that gusted steadily from the heart of the earth and domed away the sky. A flash of muted yellowwhite that had to have been the sun.

Nothing now but the reddened black billows. His head pounded and what he believed was fever took the memories of Müller away.

"The masters will not be far behind this herd," he said, indicating the fallen pygmies.

"Correct," agreed Awan. "Leave the wounded."

"Why not drag him the rest of the way?" the Brynman wondered.

"No," said Awan. "We don't need to meet the masters one step sooner than need be."

Because he would have to die then. Though she would betray him again he would still have to die for her.

Haggard was aware of everything now.

His body would lie tranced while his dreamform went to war, sustained by the vast intelligence that had chosen him. His enemy would not be the lost Lemurians but the unseen, implacable, furious being who played them all like pawns. Relti III. Relti the Great.

He perceived the Germans falling back past him and saw the shadows of lost men and times fluttering around them, possessing them. Noted Streicher climbing the great steps. Renate moving quickly as if following him. It was cloudy but his vision even penetrated the massive granite blocks of the temple and glimpsed the edgeless outlines of Emma and Woody moving inside; and other movement, shadowy, tall, too thin, yet man-shaped figures drawn to confront the intruders like dark ants. . . .

Himmel had handed Sneed a pistol from the brace at his belt. He'd come up from behind a fallen tree after Von Schnee moved off and the natives had temporarily fallen back into the blackened fog.

He stood there, relaxed, watchful, cradling his rifle.

"I like your looks, *Englischer*," he said as if they were meeting formally during an interview for a position with the firm. Sneed made no reply. Pondered the pistol in his cramped and swollen hand. "I think you're a man as I am." He shrugged. "Let us have a truce until these blacks are subdued" His slash mouth split into a grin.

Sneed responded with his own smile that was nine-tenths wince. He felt sly. These *men* had surprises coming, he told himself. Surprises...

Himmel's eyes were suddenly full of smoke. And when they cleared he was someone else. Someone from ages ago. And he understood his purpose with the supple wit of a madman.

Streicher stopped on the top step in the shadow of the great entrance arch. Panting hard. He watched Renate coming ahead of the others. Her long hair was a shimmer on the hot winds gusting up from the city, lighted by the intermittent fire from the smoldering volcano that flashed on the swirling canopy of smoke.

I should have used my powers, he told himself.

He squinted to watch the soldiers coming behind her, red gleaming on the machine gun in Müller's massive arms. Beyond them he dimly made out Haggard on the stretcher. He couldn't tell if the little savages were coming back out of the boiling wall of darkness at the other end of the bridge.

When the right moment comes I will strike ... no point in being premature ... He didn't think directly about the machine gun. *Traitors and fools ...*

"Traitors and fools," he voiced.

The wordless speaking spoke in his mind and seemed to say: You will triumph over all things if you can bear my power within you without bursting asunder, if you would be the chosen one. Be patient for now and all will be added to you and more than your dreams.

211

He was excited. Cocked his head as if listening. Though there was no voice or words, his mind made speech.

"Yes," he replied, "we will dispense with all the weaklings."

In the new world, the unvoice responded.

"The new world."

He jerked out his sidearm and stared thoughtfully at the thin barrel. Blinked. Almost thought about the machine gun. Frowned.

Later we strike . . . He felt the comfort of the great power that spoke to him.

He backed into the shadows and moved through the great arch into the dim, vast interior. Heard a shuffling, dry sound that he didn't realize were hundreds of feet coming up inner chamber steps that led from the city level.

He moved across the immense place past the supporting pillars that plunged up into obscurity.

Not far ahead, Woody-Celo't and Emma-Amee, hand in hand, went through the opening in the pillar into a hot gust of steamy fog and their feet lost all traction as if the floor were an inclined plane of ice.

They fell, skidded, rolled into the heat. He wondered, vaguely, about the light source because the steaminess was blinding white.

His head cracked against a side wall as they spun almost frictionlessly down.

In the ringing impact he became just Woody again. Since the last he knew he was in the air, his brain instantly tried to explain by thinking they were spinning down through a stormcloud. His hands groped for the controls.

The ship's been destroyed, he thought.

Slammed into her, clutched an arm, as they accelerated madly and then he realized they were on a twisting, solid incline of some sort. Another shock.

The fog was getting chilly. The unseen illumination went leaden.

Lord, he thought, *how can this be?*

He groped. Wet syrupy mud. He could only see when he brought his hands up to his face. Lead-colored mud.

"Emma," he called. His voice was totally deadened. Scary.

Where is this place? Why do I keep blacking out?

He felt utterly deserted.

"Emma!"

The dead-sounding voice was mockery. The syrupy goo clung to his feet. Each step was a slog that turned his limbs into lead. The cold fog seemed almost as resistant as the ooze.

His heart pounded.

Am I dead? Is this the end?

Emma—Amee was groping too. She had confidence that Celo't would extricate them. She struggled forward like (she didn't exactly think) some antediluvian creature trapped in deadly resin. . . .

She sensed obscure, incompletely formed intelligences all around her, caught here, aware, yet lost, incomplete beings that had been unable to advance beyond a wormlike consciousness where no ray of clarity stirred the gloom or dried the unending muck.

We must pass beyond here, she told herself, calmly. Because she felt the pull of dreary dullness and it would have been so soothing and easy simply to sink down . . . rest . . . doze for a timeless time in soft, warm mud. . . .

"No," Woody—Celo't muttered to himself, "I cannot pause. I must escape from here . . . Emma must be here as well . . . she must . . ."

Streicher jumped nervously as he crossed the immense temple floor. He kept poking the pistol around at the shadows, convinced he heard shuffling steps padding just out of range. Kept telling himself he would reveal his magical powers of will at any time now . . . any time . . .

Renate was just entering the gigantic doorway, looking back across the dim bridge where the shapeless ranks of pygmies crowded behind the three retreating Germans.

Haggard lay motionless on the litter. Eyes shut, he, nevertheless, saw everything around him. Heard voices as if he were underwater. He just waited as if he'd known that

Himmel would be saying to the pygmy leader, in some nameless tongue that resembled Sanskrit: "Bring the sick man."

Because Himmel believed he was Go'b Ingor, lord general of the armies of Relti III. When the pygmies surrounded them he'd nodded with satisfaction. He felt it was about time they joined him openly.

Sneed clicked his teeth together, the muscles around his too-thick jaws knotting. He was waiting to strike. He could already taste the blood and feel the small bones splintering under his teeth.

In the wan, amber-colored light Go'b admired his troops. He saw supple, catlike Lemurians moving in perfect formation, their wills like shields, ready, this time, to turn the magic fire missiles of the weaklings.

"To the attack," he told them.

As they stepped off, he blinked and the scene blurred. This is a dream of Hell, he believed, looking around at the fantastic landscape, the dim demons around him.

And then, as if a sudden swirl of fog blew through his mind, the outlines and meanings shifted and without missing a step he knew he was Go'b Ingor and had finally trapped the fugitive rebels in the broken fortress. All later wars (he somehow sensed) would be but shadows of this one until the memories melted into hints and troubled dreams and men fought without knowing why.

Felt rich pride watching his dark warriors in black armor as light and fine-meshed as woven silk bearing spears tipped with blood crystal that focused soul-energy that, backed by a strong warrior's aura, could pierce into solid stone. Who could defeat them, trained to endure flaying without a wince, to drink blood for water and wine when need be, to fight totally without a single thought or hesitation? He recalled heroes who, weaponless, had struck hard blows with a sliced-off arm or leg . . . great Kau'ts who'd been literally shredded in a battle and who, as he finally fell, threw his own liver into an enemy's face . . . Kau'ts . . .

He frowned. The rebels, the weaklings would undo that perfection of manly courage developed over ages. Shook his head. No mercy for them. None. He imagined their fates. The maggot poisoners of the perfect blood. What he would have done to them. He already wore a cape of tanned rebel skin. When they were stripped raw he liked to make them dance until they died. Not even the leader himself was as cruel as Go'b Ingor. Relti had kissed him on the cheek and told him so. How sweet that had been. "You are the cruelest of all men," he'd said.

"Bring him," he repeated, indicating Haggard, who lay like a waxen corpse showing no sign that he was watching from a suprasensible plane of existence. Go'b Ingor grinned at Sneed, who he thought was called Waf'n, a great, independent assassin, respected by all Lemuria. "You see," he said, "you have joined the winning side this time. Here is the sage Renmil in a trance and when we wake him we'll unravel his traitor's wisdom."

Sneed understood. He had used the name Waf'n while passing among men. He looked Lemurian. But his mother was not. Many would pay for what his mother was not. The wave of blurring had wakened all his memories, he believed. His thoughts were slow and sly. He was suddenly stooping and shuffling slightly. He'd left his people, the beast-people. The men had slaughtered too many and driven them deeper and deeper into the arid lands and cold hills. His parents had been roasted alive and eaten by Relti's men and he had become a hired killer (a respected profession) for the joy of killing any Lemurians. He was Grat-lag the Great, and he would eat many of their hearts before his course was run. The hairless filth. He hated the fact that he resembled his father and had little pelt. He shaved it while among humans. He had listened, slow and sure, and made new plans. He hoped to steal the power the humans had hidden in the fire mountain. He was the hope of his people. This man-chief trusted him and admired his prowess. Well and good. While they battled the despised ones would slip in and possess the power (whatever it was) and slay them all.

Suddenly there was a dim but definite glowing overhead and the footing was firmer. Too dense still to see, but he heard a voice he didn't yet know was Emma's. He felt he was just a vagueness in the steamy obscurity where time had been clouded out of reckoning. He felt as if he had no name yet . . . no purpose but to wander . . . no history. Woody's life was remote and didn't really touch him. He felt crude and incomplete. He felt he had to keep moving or sink back to chaos and the endless lead. So he followed the voice he didn't know was a voice, much less a person. Things were shifting again and he knew he had to hurry or be reabsorbed into the primal, colorless muck . . . he was hungry for the voice and moved on in a swirl of vagueness. . . .

Streicher fled as the tumultuous yet whispery footfalls came rushing out of the dark recesses of the gigantic place.

He crouched behind a pillar and tried to spot Renate. Backed steadily away from the entrance and suddenly realized he was surrounded by smallish menacing shapes.

"Aaah," he snarled, whirling. Dozens. More . . .

Backed aside hitting one, turning into a womanshape in the lost stirs of dull red lavalight seeping in the arched windows high above.

She, he thought.

Except, even as he clutched at the slim limbs, the cold, hard figure (he next took for a statue) toppled flat backward and thumped dully on the granite flooring.

He stooped. Touched the dead thing . . . yet it had been flesh, he realized. Rows on rows stood around him, silent, unthinkable ancient, swallowed by the immense obscurity of the hall.

He recalled a passage in Haggard's book: the ancient inhabitants of Kôr (a noble white race that he didn't realize were the last Atlanteans) had their bodies perfectly preserved by the infusion of some amazing balsamic oil no doubt related to the vital energy of the hidden fountain of light in the mountain. Yes. And the natives supposedly used pieces of the limbs for ceremonial torchlight because the preservative burned bright and hot.

"Ahhh," he whispered, crouching among the dead, peering out to where he'd heard the feet, thinking how he'd been chosen over all the others in Berlin, how he (and not that neurotic, loudmouthed bully they all touted) would be the German Messiah and the savior of the Aryan race. The iron Christ. He could see Von Schnee and his men just entering the great door, limned against the reddish glowing outside that shifted and darkened with swells of cloud.

As he moved among the preserved people he thought how his power would be sufficient to shape the world: stern troops would march, beautiful women sing and bear unblemished children and live in massive buildings of glossy, dark stone and metal in cities lined with immense statues . . . himself on a raised dais with the blond beauty seated at his feet.

But where was she? He frowned. Peered through the forest of standing dead. Nothing moved. The shuffling, myriad footsteps had stopped.

"I'll find her," he muttered. "I will put forth my power."

She would service his needs, which was a female's duty and joy. And bear the heir who would embody the magnificence of the great race, the fighters and shapers of the earth.

Chewing these and other large conceptions, he moved on, now and then blundering into a body, rocking it stiffly . . . until something, a faint golden gleam, showed near the closest wall that had to be her hair in the lurid, redshot gloom and he exulted, believing his will had kept an unbreakable grip on her soul.

He passed out from among the mummified inhabitants of Kôr and followed where she turned into a passage that cut into the mountain rock itself. He felt the slight trembling as the molten furies far below shuddered in their inconceivable pressures.

He crouched as he ran, imagining nations crushed, millions of subhumans immolated or chopped to shreds, her pale limbs, supple flesh and knowing eyes, himself in a chained collar, bound and lashed at her bare feet, sucking the perfect toes in ecstasy while legions of remorseless warriors spread over the earth, reshaping the stones, the very continents themselves. . . .

"Ahhh," he sighed. "Ah."

Tjaden, Müller and Von Schnee ran into the lean, dark natives who'd moved on whispery feet across the half-mile-wide floor. They had long swords, not spears. One spoke a command and Von Schnee (suddenly recognizing the language) became Awan again.

Awan knew they were caught between the little men and

217

these new foes. He knew who they were and expected no mercy.

They were too close for the two soldiers to unship the Maxim so they both went for hand weapons while Von Schnee brought the rifle he'd picked up to the ready.

"Don't shoot yet," he ordered. "We don't know their numbers."

But there could be no mercy. He knew that. These were the killers of the shadow-race, the ones before Lemuria who could only exist there in the energy field of the flame that sustained all epochs and all beings; there, where time bent into a whirling circle.

The thin, part-faced shadow-people who saw without eyes and earless, heard. They sensed the auric dream substance of all things and their swords, he remembered, were not physical in any real sense. They were mankind in dream bodies, premankind in a way, hermaphroditic with genitalia more plant than animal in structure. And deadly. Filled with strange rage and hopelessness because they had been left behind as the earth thickened and changed form.

"The lost ones," he whispered. His head was pounding again. Von Schnee almost resurfaced half thinking that the fever was melting his mind. He knew words were pointless but he tried anyway: "Peace, friends."

And the response was a feeling that formed a picture in his brain. What he didn't realize was an image of himself seen from their subtle world, a thick, heavy, chunk of ugly flesh moving in muddy colors, a thing that crushed and trampled the sweet, graceful softnesses, a thing to destroy.

"Fall back," he commanded Tjaden and Müller. There were too many, and, semisolid as they were, bullets would shatter their delicate structure but the touch of their weapons he knew was like death by poison. One lost control of nerves, heart, brain, and fell to babbling pieces.

As they retreated their enemies moved in lithe whispers to cut around and enclose them.

"Black dogs," said Müller, who'd briefly dropped out of his ancient persona as the winds of whim curdled and shifted around them. He staggered, holding his head as the fever drummed and then was gone again.

Von Schnee kept seeing the image language of the new

attackers. A Lemurian nervous system was sensitive enough for that. The pictures were distracting: the three of them as lumps of alien ugliness staining the sacredness, the three of them blasted, rotting, dying . . .

Then among the dead Tjaden flailed his gunbutt sending preserved bodies crashing down like dominoes.

"Statues," said Müller.

Tjaden was spitting dry, foamy flecks, muttering: "Brought here . . . far from the lands . . . into the teeth of the wizard's mouth . . . no right . . . no right to make me come here . . . I am a Bryn of the crags . . ."

Backing away from the tall, lean, rapacious black shapes who flitted around them; tripping into and over the naked dead, the muzzleflashes when they shot tossing wild shadows around them so that the standing bodies, shadowy attackers and the darkness itself seemed one melting and re-forming, smoky substance.

"Filth!" snarled Müller, trying to aim, snapping a shot. Missing. "Lord Awan," he said, "we should have stayed with the leader, I think."

"Too late for that, fellow," his captain replied, firing the rifle and feeling the image-impact as the bullet tore through and disrupted the loosely physical etheric shape that had darted too close, stabbing with its greenishpale glowing needle sword. "The dream-shades will have us soon enough."

Flitting, ducking, spinning around them, among the stiff mummified peoples, with uncanny grace that fascinated Awan.

"Conscript me," Tjaden was saying, "Suck my arsehole as well."

The dreams of hate and dreadful loneliness and despair. The dreams of the forever lost, locked out of time and a world too bright and thick for them. Dreams defending dreams. Ghosts at war with ghosts, their spirits haunting solid men on blazing battlefields far away, fighting for secret causes a million years lost and gone.

"Relti looks prettier to me now," Müller said, shrugging.

"Don't you want a glorious Lemurian death?" Awan asked. He fired again and missed. It was the nature of the forces there that he accepted the weapon above his natural spear. It was the nature of Von Schnee's training that he shot well. He leaned against a stiff woman. Through the gunflashes

219

and shadows he could see she was very beautiful. He was first to realize they were not statues. He marveled. Fired at another black outline. A hit. The shade disrupted in chill, hollow, hopeless images. He found himself sweating with cold horror and pity for the things.

"Come near and die," said Tjaden in a flat, harsh, almost hysterical voice.

There seemed no end to the upright bodies as they retreated into dim lengths. The movements around them were hypnotic. Müller (though he no more than Tjaden would have recognized his name just then) drifted for a moment and a needle blade pricked his arm before he could jump back. His body shuddered. He seemed to rock within his flesh which felt like a stiff, hollow shell. He nearly fell. Just a scraping wound and yet his heart puffed and bumped and nearly stopped. He felt he was falling into fragments: hearing here, seeing there, feeling miles away . . .

Was in the present again for an instant. His skull was a furnace. The redness of blind fury was burning away his brain, he believed.

"Yesss," he hissed. "We will be avenged!"

He thought how he would die that night beside men who had been his enemies once: a Brynman hill clod and a traitorous captain of the Red Claw guard. The Hidden Light had united them. Well and good. He would die for the light. At least he would have that. Lost in the dark, he would die for the light.

A shadowy blur, a pale flicker of sword at the captain's back. Müller fired in time but more were pressing close. Silent things. Neither he nor Tjaden was sensitized enough to pick up the image language. They had not drunk from the crystal cup as Awan had.

Something solid cracked the back of Awan's head and he turned, snarling, rifle clubbed, before realizing it was the far wall. By the time he twisted back around front the dream-beings had closed in.

Tjaden cursed and fired and swept his bayonet in vicious cuts. Müller freed his entrenching shovel from his belt and slashed savagely, the steel tracing glitterarcs. Shadows. Glowing needles of death.

Awan clubbed and poked the rifle at them sliding along

the smooth, chilly wall. He was deadly as if his body saw clearly with no help from his head and acted freely.

Back across the chamber where the masses of standing dead began there was sudden commotion. Awan—Von Schnee assumed the pygmies (whom he knew as Claw Riders) had made contact with the shadow-people.

Sneed stayed Grat-lag and didn't shoot the pistol Himmel had handed him. As the pygmies (or Claw Riders) engaged the elusive needleswords of the protohumans he growled in his chest and ducked and clubbed his fists at them, moving in a rolling, bouncing squat, knuckles scraping the flooring. He suddenly lashed out and caught a thin, flimsy leg, unsurprised when he whirled the almost weightless body over his head and shattered it on the stones. He expected to rip mere men limb from limb. He assumed these enemies were the same solidity as himself. A hot killing fever filled him now. He trampled on the shell-like form and enjoyed things popping and snapping.

Himmel (or Go'b Ingor) had been talking with the pygmy leader whom he believed was his old subaltern, M'odr, of the inner guard. A caprice of the occult wind (which had become a cyclone as the whites came close to Kôr) had them all speaking a babel of languages and yet understanding each other perfectly—except it was Haggard who first grasped that it was not translation but rather that each heard what made sense to him or her and fitted whatever they presumed was taking place. Because it was a war of ghosts and (he later wondered) which war wasn't . . . ?

The pygmy, M'odr, believed he was talking to a white god-warrior as per the legends. He was pleased that the calling techniques had won these powerful beings over to their side. M'odr (as G'ob knew him) believed his people were the true descendants of the old rulers and had been waiting for a sign from the lost gods before attempting to reclaim the temple. The voice-in-the-fire had said that the white goddess and her serving gods would return to guide them into the secret mountain.

He believed the tall, terrifically thin blacks were bad men. He kept repeating this to G'ob, who interpreted the words into his own half-imagined world.

"They bad men," the pygmy said. "Very bad men."

*   *   *

Things were grim against the wall. Awan had just taken a stab in the forehead, the icy point ripping an inch from his eyebrow, filling his sight with blood. His body seemed to fly apart, rise and twist. He heard sounds from far away, outside, where the distant sun was shining on fields of smoke and death and he whirled above and watched millions of men swarming through poison smoke, chewed to pieces by flailing steel and bursting fire...whirled back down into himself...was Von Schnee again, trying to take in what was happening, realizing, vaguely, as the deadly figures closed in on him, that he had just witnessed the war in Europe and that great horror was echoed in the temple chamber in ghostly terrors.

He was about to die, back to wall, shocked by the aftereffects of the needleblade that left blood dripping as if he wept from a single eye. Then Müller (thinking he was hurling a power symbol that would paralyze wills with unseen energy) ripped a grenade from his belt and tossed it into the thick of them among the ancient, preserved dead.

They were all surprised by the gout and impact of sudden fire that ripped the nearest fighting swirl of skeletal black fighters apart, followed by a lightning series of flares, without concussion this time, unbearably bright in that gloom.

Himmel—Go'b Ingor shielded his face. He tripped sideways over Haggard's stretcher and as his eyes adjusted to the violent brilliance he realized it was empty.

He crouched there, then retreated and circled the mounting heatpressure as the terrific burst of flame spread from the blast center and sucked the flames inward as the preserved bodies exploded and hissed, bubbling away like wax. The dead seemed to leap and shudder and rush together as the blaze mounted to the high roof into a furious blue-red pillar.

As Awan and his men were running along the wall, the shaking light revealed a narrow passageway. They raced and dove inside to save their lives from the mounting heat. Their clothes were already scorched.

They kept running up sheer stairs cut into the mountain rock, climbing in darkness and, after a few minutes, panting and staggering, slowing...

When Awan looked back down the doorway was a faint coal below and the roar of the mad blaze a whisper.

Go'b Ingor saw them enter the mountain wall.

Traitors, he thought, *all unwitting you will lead me to your stronghold and your dreadful, poisonous work will be at an end. . . .*

He circled toward the wall. Grat-lag stayed close. The heat seemed to push them away like a gale, then actual wind began to suck them toward the roaring tower of fire. Their shredded clothing and most of their hair had been singed off.

About a dozen pygmies (including M'odr, the chief) survived to follow them. There was no sign of their tall, skeletal opponents as if (Go'b registered without actually thinking about it) their substances had been like tinder and puffed to ashes at once.

"Soon we will have them all," Go'b said over the hissing thunder of the blaze.

"Soon, yes, soon," echoed Grat-lag, meaning something else.

"The fire of the gods," the pygmy chief exclaimed to himself with awe as they began to mount the carven steps that tunneled almost straight up into cool blackness, "is our friend. All is well. We walk with gods. Our enemies are thrown down. We will have all that belongs to our enemies, women and cattle and their strong huts of stone. Thanks be to the gods."

Woody—Celo't was climbing . . . climbing forever up and up until the mist cooled and thinned and there was a point of intense brightness far above him. . . .

Climbed . . . remembered the things far below only very dimly now . . . they were things from long ago; images of strange lives he'd somehow left in the hot mists and leaden dimness.

Climbed a twisting path of rock that the streams of golden, growing brightness brought into full color: tiny violet flowers like spatters of morning sky; green mosses; graceful grasses shaking the light, and then he came out into bright day, the sun high, the sky brilliant violetblue, air cool, clear, and he stopped on a soft flat ledge that was almost like a lawn on the slope of the volcano.

He looked down into the valley and could see the roof of the temple far below, the ghostly city gleaming in reddish tints because the smoke parted in a narrow strip just above where he stood before massing down almost solidly around the lost city. It must have received just enough sun every day to sustain that strange, natural garden. All around the rocks were black, dead, bare.

He felt comfortable, untroubled. He made out the shape of the biplane down there and knew it had something to do with him. He felt no pressure. He looked around with a kind of innocent curiosity at the dramatic view and then back at the sharp sweetness around him. Knelt where a spatter of icy clear water worked down the mossy wall. He drank and bathed his face. Felt good. Thought he was getting a little hungry. Recalled both Celo't and Woody Shea of America. Found it interesting because it left him almost peacefully detached from both. He had been others too, he reflected. What of it? All those struggles had ended and here he was again, renewed. He didn't want to be drawn back into that madness, terror, obsession and violence.

Shook his head and leaned back against the rock staring at where the dome of cloud formed and boiled down over the valley, solid except for where it parted overhead there, curled back on itself in consistent freakishness and left a space for sunlight in all that smoky dimness.

Above him on the slope, dull reddish beams broke now and then from the fuming cone. He realized the tiny strip of brightness might only be visible for a few moments a day down below, depending on the angle. Though he didn't know it, Müller had had a glimpse on the bridge.

"I want no more," he said to himself. Felt reborn— except the memories haunted him and he didn't want to think about what he would do after he got back down.

He stripped off the rest of his chewed-up clothing including his shoes. It felt good to be naked there. Before he left he'd make a loincloth or something, he thought vaguely. The sun was an indescribable joy on his body. He was tired but felt well and strong.

He sat down with his back against the mossy stone. It

suddenly hit him: he'd been following her and then had climbed for the light. He'd somehow (in his distant, dreamy state) assumed she would be here, waiting, that she'd always be waiting. He frowned. That was silly. Blinked. He wasn't a child, he was supposed to take charge of things. At which point he realized he was very like a child. And always had been, in other ways, in either of the two lives he was able to recall and probably a few others as well.

He'd have to go back and look for her. He couldn't just drift along or hope to fly away this time. He realized Veronice had been right about him. Strange to remember her now. . . .

"I have to find . . ." he said, standing up, thinking: *Emma-Amee* . . .

A new life, not like either of the memories of Woody Shea or Celo't. New. Rebirth. Because he finally understood life had no machinery but only ebb and flow forever and man swam in a sea of time and mystery that was itself alive and he was its song and whisper. The mystery was everywhere and he had to devote himself to it because it was holy. And if she would stay he would keep her with him.

She was already climbing out of the same hole he'd come through and he realized they'd been near one another all the time.

She crossed the strange splash of rich brightness and sharp, mountain perfume, naked herself. Well, those who had crossed ages to be together, he reflected, had little need for modesty or immodesty.

He didn't know what name to call her so he said none. Embraced her. Then he asked: "Was it the same for you? Do you understand this?"

She smiled and kissed him.

"I understand everything," she told him.

"And then . . ."

"I love you, dear one." She held him very close, yet tentative.

"By any name."

"Yes."

"We don't need any past."

"No," she demurred softly, and he felt the first twinge of what he realized he'd expected, like the bad news behind the doctor's diffidence when he told you the bad thing and

225

you stared out the window at the hopelessly remote sunshine and breeze-swayed trees and wished you could run out and lose yourself and his terrible words in the long fields of youth . . . a memory from late childhood, the man's gentle but firm mouth as he told Woody Shea he was sick and the cure would take time and Woody Shea wanted to race across the gently dipping unfenced horse pasture he could just see from where he sat beside his mother in the stiffbacked waiting-room seat . . . wanting to race and leap up over the fence and imagined himself suspended in air, riding the wind down the green valley and soaring up into the paling evening. . . .

"Yes," he insisted to her.

"No," she said again. "We have to finish. We're ordinary, but we have to finish."

He shook his head and partly pulled away.

"I'm going back in the plane," he said. "Are you afraid to just be ordinary, Emma?"

She nodded.

"I suppose so," she admitted. "But I am. But we have to finish it. We owe it. We were brought here to help. We didn't just come. The myths are real and so are the terrors. But we owe it."

"I owe nothing, Emma."

"Woody doesn't and Emma Haws Willard doesn't," she said, quietly, not letting go of his hands. "But we do."

She dreaded being ordinary, she'd admitted, climbing through the hot mists and gray muck up from blind dimness to this improbable ledge on a fantastic mountain of fire and mystery. She longed for great achievements and now understood that human beings invented size. There was no size, only life, the few flowers and scatter of grasses and thread of water where they now stood as entire and perfect as vast forests and mile-high waterfalls. She understood and was grateful for the peace of understanding. She understood she'd been brought to that place by ghosts from long ago. She had always been part of a great myth and her life and death had been drama. Long, long ago. And she'd have to see it through again. He too. She sighed. He too . . .

"No," he said, without meaning it, looking up past her head across the smoke-sealed valley at where something had caught his eyes. One of the lost gulls again? A speck of soaring white moving (he thought) toward the rent in the cloud where the sun spilled through though it had slid down nearly to the turbulent bottom of the opened seam of cloud.

"Don't be afraid, Celo't." She kissed him. "I want to see it again." The hidden light.

He sighed. Lost sight of the bird as the sunbeams began to dim and spread around the cloudedge.

"That," he said. "I have to perish for that again." The sudden dimming paled the tones of grass and flowers but without dulling their loveliness, he realized. Yet it depressed him slightly. He tried to turn away from her. She held his hands looking from his troubled face to the scrawl of water streaking down the mossy wall, a lavender and violet burst of flowers where it touched the turf and spread away to nothing. "You insist on it."

"I love you, Woody Shea," she said. Because they had to do what they could to keep it from being totally covered. She had never known that as Amee but knew it now. The light had to be freed altogether to shine in everything. She shut her eyes and had an image of a globe of utter brightness rising from the broken mountain sinking into its lava and stinking billows of choking smoke . . . the brightness rising until the sky blazed and the whole world burned with it and there was no more night on earth. "My love."

He was looking at the temple roof where the fragile plane waited and wondered if he could escape through the opening as perhaps the gull just had. . . . There seemed to be a fire in the building because he saw thick gouts of smoke rolling sluggishly out to billow and spill along the bridge and buildings below.

She knelt and kissed him intimately and he tenderly, with surprise and sadness and instant passion, took her head in his hands.

"Ah," he voiced.

"I love you forever," she said into his body.

XXVII

Haggard–Remnil ascended the third way, not far behind Renate and Streicher. He'd passed around the flaming tower carried by four pygmy warriors. He was quite limp and his beard had gone white. His dream body commanded them.

He sensed his enemy was near now, waiting for its moment. Its moment was close. They hadn't met in ages on ages.

This way was a curving series of ramps, a longer but easier climb than where Von Schnee–Awan and the others went up. The pygmies hardly felt the burden of the partly wasted Englishman who gazed out psychically at the world through the personality of Remnil, wizard-master, and the only being Relti the Great truly feared. They had been pupils in the same mystery school and had developed their powers side-by-side. Relti had slain their mentor for a power object and was surprised by Remnil. He failed to overcome him and fled. Later he made himself emperor and had a thousand men searching for his brother wizard for a decade with no results. Remnil had retired to the remote mountains to perfect his spirit. Relti eventually learned that the other master had helped originate the rebel race by exposing a young Lemurian couple to the secret flame. A long-vanished poet had filled a volume with that tale. . . .

Well, Remnil–Haggard concluded as the little men bore him smoothly along the now level corridor that led directly to the chamber of the flame, another canto was in progress.

He will come here because he must, his mind said. *He must* (image of a brooding darkness with a thousand faces watching, waiting for a chance to break through the immaterial barriers that blocked it from touching the earth and fill itself into flesh because it ached to be in a body shape again and the strange forces at Kôr could make it possible). *He*

*must come here to incarnate and then close the mountain and
seal the light in blackness for another age* (image of massed,
molten rock pouring into the well of fire and smothering it).
He hopes to fully enter the foolish man (image of Streicher)
*and use his flesh and physical brain to win a foothold in this
time while dimness lies on the face of the earth* (image of
dimmed days, great fogs rising, of steadily swelling swamp-
lands covering more and more green land, great, ancient
beasts rising and rebreeding in thick humidity, volcanoes
opening everywhere until a pall gathered and ordinary humans fled and perished by the millions). *Well, we will see
what can be done. . . .*

Renate and Streicher reached the chamber one behind
the other. The opening she found and he followed her through
(which she took for the street door of her parents' house in a
Berlin suburb and imagined—without questioning—she was
going out for an early evening walk) was the most direct
passage to the secret chamber. She'd actually been walking
toward a blank wall and Streicher, a few yards back, had
stopped and looked nervously around, afraid the whispery
feet were following him across the gloomy space, thinking
himself trapped. She'd seen no wall, just the hallway, flower-
pots, mirror in an ornate darkwood frame, the darkwood
door, vague light (the lamps not on yet) filtering from the
other rooms. Then an explosion behind them, a burst of flame
and the shadows leaped and showed a crack in the wall and
Renate's pale, nude, graceful body going through—except she
was actually wrapping herself in a torn, silky hanging that
had draped the wall there, knotting the red and black material
across her chest thinking she was putting on a light coat for
the warm summery evening in the city. . . .

They'd climbed shallow stairs lit by patches of greenish
phosphorescence. It was the most direct of the three routes to
the hidden chamber. There were inches of dust on the stairs
and her feet made the first prints in centuries.

A straight, triangular-shaped passage led to the triangular entrance, six feet on a side. The air was different there.
Subtly vibrant. Like warm, soft, early spring days. She'd
paused. She hadn't noticed he was several steps behind her
all the way, gloating a little that he'd followed her so cleverly,

convinced that the ceremony they'd performed with the dwarf and the poor Arab in the swamp had drawn her on in a spell of finding. The fire and splashed blood and the taste of the still pulsing heart . . .

Master of Thule, he told himself, *master of Germany . . . master of the coming race . . .*

He didn't realize that the more or less accidental wound his bullet had creased across her temple had displaced her obsession that she was a goddess. Like him and Haggard she was now shielded from the direct effects of the psychic whirlwind whose center was this very point within the mountain. Nothing possessed her but an illusion, a blur between dream and memory.

"Wait," he said, in German. She couldn't perceive the dark cloud gathered around him, shielding him. That cloud was the first touch of Relti's spirit. The German captain didn't realize that his senses were being dimmed, gradually and irreversibly, by that power.

She turned, surprised because she believed she was outside the house. His presence tore the illusion. She'd been walking on the sidewalk past the iron fence at dusk. The colors drained from the flowergardens as the atmosphere sank into grayishviolet, smoky blurring. She'd been sure of the sounds and smells and had actually been watching a young boy and girl (perhaps seven or eight) playing on a garden wall. She'd wanted to get down and he'd offered to help.

"Hold my hand," Renate heard him saying.

"You'll drop me."

"No, I won't."

"I don't believe you. You'll let me fall."

Renate had no idea that she, herself, was the little girl. She blinked rapidly, nervous, reaching to explain the strange tunnel and door, the stocky, ham-handed Captain Streicher.

I must be ill, she thought. *I must have fever . . . God, but I'm still lost among these madmen . . . God in heaven . . .*

Because she took no comfort in his saying:

"We have been guided here by the world-spirit." He stepped raptly past her into the pyramid-shaped interior, gripping her arm in passing with his hard, thick fingers. "Come. I am the chosen one of the world-spirit. You shall be my consort."

"Encouraging," she murmured, not bothering to resist.

"We shall rule in its name," he told her. "I shall be harsh to the wicked and the weak."

She was enough herself to say, wryly, "I am relieved to learn that."

I have to escape, she thought. *My head hurts and I'm sick....* Touched her head and felt the scab and a sharp biting edge of pain. *My God, a wound...no wonder I am hallucinating...I have to be free of these madmen....*

The air in there tingled and quickened her senses. She felt lighter and stronger, suddenly. He seemed to slouch down and his squatness repelled her. The floor and sides were all pure white marble and a subtle golden-tinted light flickered and she realized it came from a hole in the apex almost directly overhead.

He'd stopped tugging her and was staring down at a hole in the floor which lined up precisely with the opening sixty feet above. The hole was dark and he released her to stoop and peer into it.

The opening above pulsed with muted, golden light, fascinating her. When she looked around the room a golden afterglow lingered in her eyes and Streicher seemed misshapen with an aura of unpleasant dimness around him like smoke caught in a jar.

"Can the flame be dead?" he asked. He squatted and tilted his head as if to sniff the well-like opening that was about three feet across.

In the strange, hinting illumination Renate saw a steady, circular movement in the air centered on the axis of the two holes. Vague shapes changing, coalescing like oil in water. She sensed the shapes were somehow alive though phantasmic. She watched them pass right through her body and felt nothing.

I should run away from here, she told herself. Because one of the soft roilings formed a cloudy scene for an instant. She had a shock of terror because she saw herself in it. Herself lost, a wailing ghost drawn away to eternal emptiness...

Streicher leaned his head into the opening.

"Flame come forth!" he shouted. The sound was dull, echoless. "Goddamn it! Come forth!"

Haggard was just being brought into the pyramidal chamber. The four natives simply stood still facing the center with his thinned body supported on their small shoulders. Renate stared at them. Blinked.

Haggard was high above his body now, riding on the invisible wings of Remnil. Felt Streicher's lust for the magic fire and Renate's sudden fear. Knew he could do nothing about what happened in that place. He was already rising above the temple up to the borders of the smokedome. Soared there and to ordinary eyes tinged with suprasensible vision he might have seemed to be a pale wide-winged bird sitting on the shoulder of the wind.

Because his ancient opponent was coming, was close, was gathering himself in the fuming clouds that rained steady soot over the ruined city. Was preparing to reach into the chamber with his full might and seize the blocky German who had been anointed with his fogs already, who breathed darkened air and saw through smoke. Without the human flesh to ground his energy (Haggard knew through Remnil) Relti the Destroyer could never penetrate to the flame and the light. The light that glowed in the spherical chamber above the pyramid with that single entrance from below where Renate saw hints of golden gleaming.

Fools, he understood, *seek only the flame which is the spine of the world and full of power but the light is the mind of all things.*

Weary, wary and shaky, Awan and his two men groped alone through a lightless corridor at the top of the steep steps that went up the shaft from the main hall that was now full of smoke from the smoldering, ancient corpses. The shaft created a chimney effect for the oily fumes and they were coughing and tearing in total darkness before they reached the top and they were barely ahead now as they groped through a series of tight S twists.

"What a death of disgrace," complained the one who had been Tjaden and now knew himself as Armire the Brynman.

"What disgrace do the dead feel?" wondered the former Müller, now R'oemc the Lemurian rebel.

"Much," Armire said, bitterly, "in the ghost world." He spat. "Choked in darkness. *Ai!*"

"Better than burning," thought R'oemc, aloud. He scraped his sore arm against the passageside. Winced.

"I don't swear to that," his fellow warrior said.

Awan led the way because with his altered senses he saw dimly. They went up a short, steep ramp and came out at the luminous walled triangular tunnel that led straight to the flame.

Awan paused and the battered, half-burned, hungry, thirsty, miserable men came up beside him.

"What doom now?" Armire asked.

Awan blinked at the (to him) slightly bright, greenish luminescence.

"I have heard the telling that describes this holy place," he said. "We are close to the light."

"So, so, so," said Armire, the lanky Brynman, "like, I have little doubt, the glow that flickers around a dungpile at night." He spat again. "Show me food and drink that I may choke to death properly. What care I for your wizard's fire?"

"That's only part of it," his captain said, trying to remember something more, something she had told him while they were alone in the copper hills, hiding from the Claw Riders. They'd been naked together in the steamy night air, lying on a soft coverlet. The huge moon (it was nearer earth in those days) showed vaguely but very bright through the ever-present mists. Her body was a breath of pale perfection and he kept reminding himself that she was mortal and that they'd just made love. His hand, almost wonderingly, stroked her sleek belly just above the breath of fuzz that centuries later, on their descendants, would be actual hair.

"Above the wizard's fire," she'd said, "is the hidden light. In the arrowhead chamber."

"You have persuaded me to follow you and give up my life," he'd said, kissing her shoulder, relishing the smoothness, the faint musky scent. He didn't say I love you because Lemurians didn't. But it was unnecessary in any case and she knew that too. "I need no further convincing."

"I realize that," she'd replied, "but I like to tell you things I know. My mother handed me the cup. She thought I was silly, I think. But I wanted to please her."

"Where is she now?"

"Killed."

He'd kissed her long, fine hands then.

"And you must renew the cup at the flame?" He'd wanted it confirmed, just to prolong the moment.

"At the light above the flame," she'd corrected. "That's what I have been taught, Awan. They say the flame is true power and tempts whoever bathes in its vitality with immortality and command of all beings. They say dread Relti once drank from the flame." He hadn't quite noticed how the idea excited her. "The light is what must pour into the holy cup." She sighed. "I sometimes think we will be caught and slain like Mother. I am not very brave."

He'd kissed her and said, "I'll be brave enough for us both then."

R'oemc was talking: "The sole light I care to see is the blessed sun, Lord Captain."

They followed Awan into the six-by-six-by-six tunnel.

"She will be here," Awan said, to no one. "And it will be hopeless again. She was so weak . . . so weak . . . and yet I love her."

We have all died and come back, he thought, *yet nothing will be different . . . is that a memory too? How do I know that? . . . I do not know it, yet it chills me with truth . . . If I have come back, where in time am I? . . . How many empty years have rolled away?* He shrugged. Better for a warrior not to ponder overmuch.

He licked his dry lips and headed into the dimly goldenglowing chamber where he could already see shadowy outlines. He knew hers at once. And now, so close to the heart of the world, all the old memories flooded over him. He remembered his death.

Her weeping, pale, lovely face looking down at him from among the black armored Claw Riders who stood there among billows of warm mist and tall ferns. His head was at a crazy angle and he felt nothing. One of the warriors (the leader) was casually fondling her bared breasts (he distantly recognized Go'b Ingor) while her voice reached for him with remote and fading words while the earth drank away his last blood and strength, the spear that pinned him down swaying at the edge of his unmoving, dimming vision, not even connected to him any longer because there was no body, just lingering grief and humiliation and, yes, pity . . . and the fading, hopeless words:

"I am so sorry, my lover, I am so sorry . . . forgive me in peace, O my poor one! . . . I will grasp the power of the flame, I will avenge everything . . . everything . . ."

"Have I not forgiven?" he muttered, walking through the triangular arch.

"What?" wondered R'oemc.

Awan looked at her, pale, tall, blond and (he had to think) weak, still so weak. Wearing a loose robe that left most of her legs bare. She looked at him with little in her eyes but curiosity and fear. And he sighed.

There was less this time, he thought.

He barely glanced at Haggard, who was held on the shoulders of the dwarfed, stocky black men whom he took for Lemurian slaves. He sneered slightly at the sight of Streicher, still bent over the well as if, he thought vaguely, vomiting into a toilet hole.

Then he felt it: the deep, distant rumbling tremble that she'd described to him, so long ago. He could see she recalled nothing. She obviously took it for the volcano and was terrified. He understood it was the flame's regular, eternal pulsation: it would pour up for a time, and then withdraw. As with all things on earth.

"*Arii!*" he heard behind him down the corridor. "Doom!" He turned to see Go'b Ingor coming in full cry. Remembered the long, thin-lipped face kissing and fondling her, his weak and treacherous love. Made out thick-jawed Sneed beside him and the last little, degenerate Claw Riders. "*Arii!*" The old warcry.

"We are all here," Awan said. "We are all back."

Which was true because now Celo't and Amee had come in from outside to let the whirlpool of fate spin them all together at last. They came behind the rush of pygmies through the thickening smoke that was filling the corridor. Amee pointed at Streicher, who was just straightening up, his pistol leveling at once, snarling, his back to the sudden uprush of brilliant, heatless energy that sprung in a spout of pure fire, whirling tight around itself, and poured into the chamber above. A shock of golden light streamed down in response through the upper opening as if the sun itself were trapped in there.

The charging pygmy–Lemurians hesitated. Their leader shouted, in joy, "We are among the gods!"

Renate threw herself on her face in terror. Amee looked up in joy and drank in the radiance. It pressed at her eyes and left a golden singing in her mind.

"Ahhhh," she sighed, softly stunned.

Sneed–Waf'n hid himself behind the motionless pygmies supporting Haggard's body. Streicher crouched and fired into the little warriors, shrieking curses at Himmel for treachery. As his senses dimmed the voices seemed far-off, movements shadowy. The smoke was curling into the radiant pyramid now dimming the golden beams and the thickness seemed (to Amee) to be concentrating around Streicher as if drawn to him like something living.

Müller–R'oemc and Tjaden–Armire, closer to the charge, emptied their pistols and closed in a struggling knot with bayonets flashing. The lanky soldier, blinded by a gust of smoke, fell first with a spear through his throat. He spun across the room, blowing breath and blood while in the center the flame throbbed and roared and the inflooding fumes twisted and circled around the flame pillar and gathered over Streicher like a thunderhead, a shape, face seeming (to Celo't and Amee) to form in the coils and puffs.

"It is the Destroyer!" she cried.

As Tjaden saw his farm in Germany, the sun on the wheatfields, the wind blowing the wheat, just seeing that, the ripples of gold . . . blowing away . . . away . . . and then himself too on the wind . . . gone . . .

Müller, two spears clattering in his body, swung two pygmies by their feet and slammed them into a wall, their heads splitting like melons. Then he stood there, panting and wobbling, while Streicher cried, "I am he who will purge the blood of Jewish filth! I am the Messiah of the sword! My chosen ones will be immortal!"

He'd reloaded and kept shooting. Because he was farther back no spear had hit him. The pygmies were all down now. Sneed–Waf'n was creeping carefully around the walls as the smoke swirled.

Awan had rushed to protect Renate, who stayed flat on her face. Müller–R'oemc had finally toppled, looking grim and unbent. And was just Müller again. And thought how this was all he'd ever expected. Was surprised at how little pain there was . . . refused to remember anything . . . looked up at the golden gleaming above the flame . . . thought it was the sun . . . tried to smile . . . saw only the brightness, then saw nothing . . .

The flame roared on, half obscured now. Emma–Amee moved behind Celo't, who charged when he saw Streicher was backing closer to the flame, obviously intending to bathe in the spiraling power. The boiling cloud around and above him had formed into a face, hollow-eyed, long, like a knife blade with eyes like coals. Relti. And he knew what he meant to do: to enter the fire in Streicher's flesh and live and rule in this world, immortal. Like the priestess-queen had attempted, long before. He knew the story of Ayesha, She-who-must-be-obeyed. This has been her sanctuary before the hidden light was found above the flame.

At the same moment, Von Schnee–Awan, kneeling beside Renate (who he thought was wounded) took dead aim at the blocky captain, through the stinging, thickening fumes that were about to be sucked up into the chamber above as they swirled closer and closer around the flame.

Except Himmel–Go'b Ingor, snarling with fury and triumph, leaped from a curd of smoke and tossed a spear along the deadly, invisible rod of his will and struck the doomed lover in the chest, knocking him across Renate.

"Traitor," he said. "Death to you."

Above the city Haggard–Ramnil's dreambody floated just under the boiling black clouds. Waiting. His perceptions reached everywhere at once in a perfect globe. What he saw was not exactly what the eye would have seen. Everything was color, dull to very bright (as where the clouds were rent and pure sky showed) but all blended together, the energy forms of beings, plants, rocks overspilling one another.

And then the hard, icy greenishblack outline of the enemy was forming in the clouds. He saw a long, thin hand and arm suddenly reaching down into the mountain, reaching for the blocky man in the pyramidal chamber who appeared as a swirl of turbulent, sour colors, reaching to join his flesh and soul to itself. When the human stepped into the flame the fusion, Remnil perceived, would be irreversibly complete.

So Haggard–Remnil struck. A white bird with golden eyes and a beak of astral steel, dove, flashed in a whirl of brightness and ripped into the hand just as it touched the mountainside.

In order to act in the world they had to become partly physical and so could feel, be ripped and suffer destruction.

The beak bit deep and tore cold, hard stringiness. The arm recoiled and something like a shrill cry rang in the clouds from which Relti was forming his substance. The billows were instantly beaten into fury as the great wings that bore the overswollen shade convulsed in agony. The arm thrashed and lifted the bird (shaped from the bright air and vapors where the smoke dome was rent) toward redfanged jaws.

The bird (that was Remnil and Haggard because Remnil had needed his sensitive flesh to focus himself into the solid world) pulled free with a strip of the strange flesh still gripped in its beak just as the jaws clamped shut in red fury. The eyes were coals.

The great, dark form in the smoke was stronger than Remnil had anticipated. Relti's power had grown across the ages. His brother wizard had spent too long, maybe, in pure contemplation. The beast could be hurt but not destroyed. And his jaw or grip would be fatal.

So, Haggard understood through Remnil's cool consciousness, *they will have to win on earth themselves because we can only distract this depraved, ignorant, power-gorged beast, pitied in heaven and cursed on earth* (image almost incomprehensible of great radiances like exploding suns colliding and sadness like an organ tone that would burst the world with resonance could it have been sounded) *and they must overcome it alone* (image of Relti joined to Streicher stretching out his arms to raise vast armies from the earth, cities in flames, millions heaped in vast graves . . . astride his capital, mountain-sized buildings of black, glossy stone in a new world of swamps, smoke, hot mists, lost beasts and lavic fire . . .).

The bird veered aside as the other hand clawed from the

ashy fumes and ripped at it. Veered again and cut in tight
toward the long, harsh face.

These are the days of dooms, Remnil's consciousness
expressed, as the bird shape ripped at one dull red eye in a
whirl of white and gold. A flash of heat as the socket burst. A
terrible cry and then claws slashed down as the bird tried to
bank away and was caught. One wing was torn away. A wing
for an eye. And then spinning down over the wildly tilting
mountainside, tumbling into the smoke, a terrible darkness
(Haggard screamed in the flame chamber below as in a
fiendish nightmare) and then into the burning cone itself
carrying just a glimpse of a long, wiry, monkeylike arm
reaching into the mountain again and Remnil released Haggard and winked out of that time and space, giving him last
images and his outrage to keep if he survived, winking out
not in defeat, not after so many ages of protecting the light
and the children of the light . . . above them the dome of
clouds (partly shaped by supernormal forces) collapsed under
Relti's frenzy and the masses of smoke and ash poured down
onto the pale, ruined city. . . .

On the shoulders of the tranced pygmies, Haggard twisted
and moaned. The spell snapped and the little men dropped
him and staggered in the whirlwind of choking fumes and fled
into the tunnel, coughing, gasping; then two struggled back
again because the smoke was everywhere, searing eyes and
lungs. Only around the flame of life was there still breathing
space. The other two pygmies were already dying in the
tunnel.

Von Schnee–Awan lay beside Renate, who kept her
face hidden in her hands. Himmel–Go'b Ingor was standing
over them, holding a second spear. He was (like the others)
blackened with soot, mainly nude, sweaty and lost in a ghost
world of ghostly hates and enterprises and loves and despairs.

He grinned at Streicher, who had backed almost to the
flame, the swirling cloudiness all around him and spinning
around his head as if in mirror of the way the fumes that
entered the room circled the fountain of fire. It was so dense
near the apex roof opening that the golden light was almost

totally blocked from shining into the tumult below. To Amee it was like the sun swallowed by grim clouds. The one clear flash she'd had still glowed within her mind.

All this in moments while the dark hand was still pushing through the dense rocks, slowed in its grip by being semisolid and by the distraction of its pain, dull red still dribbling from the ruined eye.

"All the rebels are dead, my lord," Himmel–Go'b Ingor was telling Streicher in whom he recognized his master, Relti. He didn't see Celo't–Woody charging out of a swirl of smoke or the beastman Grat-lag. "I have done your will."

The clouds (in anticipation of the great hand) thickened around Streicher. He was pleased. Victory was his. He was the Messiah. The Jews had been unable to stop him and now they would pay for trying. That evil race who'd helped drag down the Great Ones. Spawn of slaves and weaklings. He confused the rebels his master meant with Jews. He had learned to confuse practically everything with Jews. He was not alone in that.

Woody–Celo't was coming in on an angle and had almost reached Streicher, a pygmy's spear in his grip, when Go'b Ingor saw him break out of the smoke. Emma–Amee was moving on hands and knees behind him down where the air was clearer. Renate had partly sat up and was staring in shock at Von Schnee, who had just lifted one bloodied hand to touch her stained, frazzled, yet still luminous hair. His fingers fell short and just creased her naked side where the improvised tunic had torn away leaving her essentially naked again. The fingertip left a streak of blood on the pale skin. His eyes tried to speak. His lips couldn't.

It was always too late for us, he tried to say. *I forgave you long ago . . . may there be light in your heart. . . .*

Go'b Ingor was supple and fast. He uncoiled himself and sprang low, intercepting Celo't's desperate charge with his spearpoint, piercing both thighs and dropping him on his face almost at Streicher's feet. Go'b, in the same motion, bowed low to his master.

"Death to all maggot-peoples, Lord," he said.

The fumes around the blocky German were thickening. The outline of his face resembled the lean, rapacious features of Relti, partly shaped now by the smoke, the bulk of which

240

still spun around and around the chamber, the pale pillar of flame the only light. The smoke thickened as the thin, black arm forced its way (Relti had miscalculated slightly, himself) slowly through the molasses-like thickness of mountain and lavic stone. It was taking more time than he'd expected to reach there in his quasi-physical state. He was not used to such a condition.

Emma–Amee now crouched over her hurt love. Sneed–Grat-lag still circled around the flame straining his somewhat dim brain to come up with a plan. He sensed there was some way to use that terrible fire (which he had a beast's instinctive fear of approaching though the smoke forced him gradually forward) but nothing came to him. He was behind Streicher on the other side of the roaring, throbbing fountain of heatless brilliance and eternal life. None of the others could see him.

Haggard, shuddering, had come to his senses. He was weak but the feverish feeling had left him. He was thirsty and sore but knew he'd be all right now. His memories seemed madness and he ignored them for the moment. He'd just rolled over on his side to look at the flame, in wonder.

So it was true. What would "Louie" have said? Pictured his wife as she might be just then at Ditchingham, perhaps in the garden or sipping tea under the old trees, maybe talking to Kipling. Good old Kipling. Raising his bushy eyebrows and worrying about poor Rider H. And the children. How were the children . . .

All in a flash as Streicher was saying, out of his aura of fumes: "Bring me the women." Stepping closer to the flame, basking in the tingling vibrance it radiated, he stripped off his ragged pants and kicked away his shoes, holding just the pistol which he rubbed over his belly, unconsciously. "Bring me both."

Renate stared, looking stunned and fearful, one hand wiping at the bloodmark on her body that Awan had left, as if it were sore.

Go'b Ingor moved fluidly to Emma and dragged her by the hair to his master, kicking the spearshaft that transfixed Woody's legs, to stir him.

Woody, still Celo't too, sighed in pain and tried to drag himself forward but his arms skidded on the smooth surface and his legs shrieked with whitehot pain. One hand clutched

something dry and loose that tangled in his fingers. He didn
look to see if it was ancient but unrotted human hair. Pal
possibly blond. The forces in that chamber could have pr
served even untreated flesh for ages. His fingers as
struggled (and the smoke darkened above him and the le
grip of Relti strained closer to final closure with his creatur
brushed parchmentlike stuff he didn't notice was shrivel
white skin and then clutched a femur he took for an Afric
throwing club.

Haggard remembered what had just happened to him a
saw the images Remnil had left in his mind and cried ou
"Stop! Don't let him touch the flame!"

His voice a whispery croaking.

Renate half crawled to Streicher while he said, "I sha
bathe myself and give eternal life to those who are loyal." 1
her: "You shall be my queen or my slave, as you choose
love me or resist."

Her eyes on him with fear and calculation, licking h
lips, Renate, kneeling under the smoke that was almost sol
above them (the terrible clawed fingers just pushing throug
the roof into the violent chamber), she pressed her face to o
of his widespread feet.

"Let the slave adore," the blurred, shifting shape
Streicher commanded, and Himmel, as in ritual, forced Emm
Amee's face into his master's pouchy sexual organs, smilin
thinking how he would soon have his own pleasure with th
slave as a reward and maybe fry the hearts of the slain in o
to break his fast.

"No!" croaked Haggard, trying to stand, the whirlin
smoke tipping him over again.

Woody–Celo't, sobbing with agony, forced himself
his knees with the spearshaft locking his legs together, bloo
gushing, muscles ripping. He screamed as he tossed the bon
he thought a club point-blank into the blocky German's face

It glanced off the side of his bald dome and spun into th
upspiraling magical fire. It silently exploded. The flare wa
dazzling. The smoke reeled back for an instant. The grea
black, shadowy hand was outlined, fingers spread about
close over Streicher.

Where the bone had disintegrated now hung a brigh
shimmering womanshape of pure energy which seemed t

twist and revel in the whirling vitality, then poured itself from the flame in a silent lightning bolt that struck groveling Renate on the back of her head. She rolled over and over, screaming and beating at the smooth, white stone marble flooring, bouncing into Von Schnee's body, then rising suddenly, fluidly to her feet facing Streicher and Himmel, who'd released Emma, who'd recoiled back to embrace Woody, who'd fallen over again, fainting from the pain.

"My God, what's this?" screamed Himmel in shock, all his ordinary memories flooding back. Go'b Ingor whirled away to nothing the instant the blazing energy flew from the flame pillar. The last he remembered he'd been in the noxious, foggy swamp.

Grat-lag had scuttled back into the smoke as he became Sneed again. Haggard was the first to actually grasp what was happening and only the feeling that he would be able to say it was a fever dream if he lived or some out-of-the-body state, allowed him to accept it. Because SHE had come out of the flame and there was no SHE except in his imagination so that maybe it was some reflected madness that had blazed into the blond German spy (as he thought of her) because she was saying, in a level, resonant voice, speaking what he took for Greek: "Stop!"

The smoke seemed to shrug back and press farther from the flame. Her right hand went up, palm outward, as if to salute the claws closing around the smoky shape of Streicher. A white bolt blazed from her fingers and the hand recoiled. A shock that hurt human bones reverberated around the chamber. Sneed, on his belly, staring wildly, hair gone white with shock, covered his face with his hands and began to mutter rapidly and unintelligibly, words that were no words at all, pressing his head down very hard into the yieldless stone.

Haggard, accepting everything so as to stay sane, crawled a little closer.

"SHE," he said to himself. "Great God. Great God."
What would Rudy say? I wonder. I wonder . . .

"Dogs," SHE said, in something like Arabic this time because Himmel understood as he wrung his hands in panic. "Dare you pollute my secret place?"

"No, no," Himmel protested in what broken words he knew. "Not . . . we go, yes? Yes?" And then he glanced up to follow her gaze and saw the huge dark hand, recovering, reaching down again and he screamed and ran into the smooth wall of smoke heading for the utterly choked corridor, then virtually bounced back out, coughing and blinded like the two surviving pygmies who were crouching on their bellies, worshiping her, groveling in awe and grim satisfaction because their legend was truth, in the end.

Now in some other tongue, raising both her arms this time, SHE spoke to the hand: "What smoky magic."

And blasted it with twin bolts of more than lightning and it withdrew into the stone above their heads, hurt but undestroyed. Far away, unheard by ordinary ears, there was a shrill cry of frustration and pain. The grip that squeezes men to dullness blasted by a woman from the heart of dreaming.

The smoke had withdrawn to the triangular entrance now and boiled there as if behind a wall of glass. The power radiance filled the chamber again. The golden light showed above but the goddesslike woman, glowing herself with electric force, kept her eyes on the floor or level.

Emma was holding Woody, who moaned and opened his eyes again when the golden rays touched him. She cradled his head, tenderly. SHE noted this, coming closer.

It is madness, indeed, thought Haggard, *yet I must speak into madness and bargain with phantoms while I am here because the war must be won in dreams before there's any hope for waking. . . .*

"Ayesha." He tried her name as he imagined he'd invented it for sound.

"Peace, priest," she said in Greek. "I know you. But I have little time. And little patience, which was ever my failing." She smiled, faintly. "But I try, my priest." She was looking only at Woody now, his agonized, drawn, handsome face. "I try. I have slain no one here yet so do not chide me, old friend, though I think you think you are asleep now." She stood over Woody. "Outside all is smoke and evil and I can only keep it back a short distance. The beast up there is very powerful but it has few places to be strong in left on this world. I have no time to discuss deep matters with you, old friend. But witness, I have slain no one yet."

"I pray you do not," Haggard said. He stayed on his knees from weakness only.

Streicher was talking, his back to the pulsing, whirling, geyser of energy. Haggard kept looking up at the golden, subtle brilliance above the flame.

"Be still," she said, in Arabic, taking him for an Arab.

"You will be my queen. We will share all power together. I am the Messiah and will smite the Jews who have poisoned our race." And on.

Across the floor, face down, what had been Sneed muttered and raved continually into his hands.

She pointed a finger and twisted her wrist and Streicher's mouth locked shut. His eyes bulged. He was sweating. Couldn't make a sound.

Himmel crouched, still coughing and wincing his eyes.

"Just let me get home," he whispered. "Just let me please get home." He refused to look around or up. He didn't want to see anymore.

"Who did this thing?" SHE asked Emma, indicating Woody. "Nay, I know."

Emma understood Greek, of course, and could follow the strange diction.

SHE looked at Himmel.

"Ask me, priest," she said, not turning. "Ask me why I care who hurt this man."

Haggard shrugged, finally getting his feet under himself.

"I don't really know," he admitted, standing.

Trapped in my own book I had better humor her. . . .

"He recalls someone else. Someone I loved."

Haggard wobbled, staring at the flame now and Streicher strained to speak, pulling at his mouth with his fingers. He was backing toward the geyser. The smokiness was forming around him again. The hand of dread Relti was back but SHE had bent and broken off the spear close to the wounds. Woody gasped.

"Peace, my love," she told him.

Plucked the piece of shaft tree. He cried out and fainted again.

"Don't hurt him," Emma said. Couldn't help it. Her double memory kept her calm though she was very afraid. She and Woody had come expecting death so it would not be too bad, she kept telling herself.

Emma had spoken English but Ayesha grasped her tone.

"Shall I wither you?" Ayesha asked. "How dare—"

But Haggard was shouting: "The damned hand is back! Look out!"

SHE turned as Streicher leaped into the flame of life, the clawed hand finally closing around its joyful puppet—except Ayesha was smiling because she alone knew and could feel every change and pulsation of that eternal energy. The uprush was just collapsing back to regather in the mysterious heart of the world. The golden glow above faded.

So there was nothing to support Streicher and he fell from the vacant grip, with sealed mouth, down into emptiness to a fate past human knowing.

The dark grip, with no purpose there, faded, went to smoke and wisped away. The psychic whirlpool that had possessed the various members of the party had dissipated the moment SHE took form and concentrated herself into Renate.

"This body pleases me," Ayesha said to Haggard. "I shall heal this man." She looked at Emma. "You may live." To Haggard. "Not him. I am not grown so pitiful as that." Raised a palm at Himmel who ran shrieking through the strange silence that had followed the cessation of the firespout. Bolted into the smoke-choked corridor, his voice going to a rasp and dying out though they still heard his foot impacts going on to the end of the passageway. "A fitting doom. He has paid some of his ancient debt."

Haggard sat down. He was too weak though the sickness had left him. He could hear Sneed's babbling across the pit. The glow in the air was fading slowly, and at the hole above where (he later noted) Ayesha never looked.

He shut his eyes and instantly opened them. Because he'd seen the last image Remnil had left in his brain and he didn't want to see it. Not now. Not yet.

SHE carried Woody in her arms as if he were a babe and stood near the well's edge. He'd lost too much blood, Emma kept thinking. Too much.

"I deserve something," Ayesha said. "You two will sleep for a time here and the smoke will withdraw enough to let you find the upper way out." She shrugged. "I spare her for your sake, old priest. But I have little and deserve love again. He brought me back and he is mine. This place is lost to me now. The fire would unmake me again. I will bathe him

246

in its glory and he will heal and remember nothing but what I teach him. He will be content and never die.''

"Content," Emma said.

"Could you promise that much?" Ayesha was amused. "Happiness is past even a goddess to promise."

"I don't think you are a goddess."

SHE smiled again. "Only by contrast," she told her.

"Leave him alone," Emma said.

"Can you heal him?"

Emma bit her lip. Even her double memory could not restrain her grief. Even knowing the ancient lifetime and the secret meanings.

"I love him," she whispered.

Haggard sighed, trying to keep his eyes open so the image wouldn't return.

Oh, child, he thought.

"Then you will grieve, as I have learned to grieve," Ayesha said. "This place is dead for me. The smoke will cover it for centuries, I think. There is nothing here." She nodded. "I will go out into the world I have not seen for a very long time. Perhaps we will rule it together." Shrugged. "It is senseless to grieve when your life is so small," she told Emma, who just looked at her in silence because she wanted Woody to live.

I am so weary, Haggard thought.

"There is no way, I think," he whispered, "to touch you."

"Poor priest. Sleep now."

"I will find him again no matter what," Emma vowed.

Ayesha turned to face where the flame would be rising. She felt the first tremors in the earth and her strange soul.

"You will perish, I think, in the swamps and smoke," SHE said, not turning. "Now sleep," she commanded, and as Emma followed Haggard, who had already toppled forward, she glimpsed the rising roar of energy and SHE lifted Woody as if he were a child's toy, to suspend him within the vibrant flame. Just a blurring and outlines like an ancient frieze and the roar. As she hit the stone floor, arms in front, something hurt her left hand. But she felt nothing by the time her face touched.

"What of the light?" she thought she said and thought she heard answered:

"There is no light. It is stifled forever. There is no more light."

And her mind cried into the numb blankness:

No! No! No!

Epilogue

When they awakened they said almost nothing to each other. Sneed was gone and the triangular tunnel was clear. Haggard was strong enough to walk. He imagined it was the aftereffect of being so near the flame. It was dormant when they woke and neither even had to say we will not touch it.

When Emma's eyes opened she sat up found her left hand had locked itself clenched. It didn't hurt, didn't even seem stiff. She decided it was shock, nerves. She'd read that such things happened in war and under other great stress. Or was it some prank of that supernatural woman? It felt like there was something in her palm. Felt warm in the center. She tried to pry the fingers open as they walked and climbed out the way she had come in with Woody, reaching the little plateau of grass and flowers—except it had been leveled over with soot and hot ash. The trickle of water was muck. The whole slope had been covered when the clouds fell in and their footsteps raised puffs of black dust. Down below the whole valley was like a black lake.

She helped him as they worked their way down the harsh slick slope, toward the temple roof which was cut into the mountainside and lay under the upper layers of the smoke that kept boiling sluggishly out of the cone. The clouds were shifting, reshaping and draining away to fill the river valley.

The sky was sunless, leaden gray but with no promise of rain. The air was stifling hot. Halfway down, their mouths were painfully dry from the fine choking dust.

"There's water and food in the flying machine," she said, at one point.

"Ah," he murmured.

He definitely felt recovered from the fever. He kept his mind on somehow, getting home. The idea had never seemed so sweet. And it kept his thoughts from the other things. He found himself recalling when he'd actually considered (hard to believe now) buying a farm down in Boer country and emigrating. Youth, youth, he had to think. What days they were though, nineteen or maybe twenty (hard to remember precisely) being schemed against by Dutchmen and ambushed by natives.

He'd had the almost timeless plans of youth. Dreamt great things and done small ones badly . . . and the great hurt because of that devastating girl named after the occult moon or was it Adam's first lover? How fitting. The girl he'd loved in large dreamings while he'd left her in England imagining that his pure affections and the sheer scope of his plans and hopes would keep her pressed to the upstairs hall window watching for his glorious return like some Penelope. He smiled, wryly, recalling. Why, he now knew, to her he had been a foolish young man who'd offered marriage, a lifetime, then immediately rushed to the ends of the earth.

Youth is a matter of miscalculations, he thought, *which might still be recovered from . . . and rarely are. . . .*

He looked at the sluggish clouds that covered the lost city. Except for the outline of the temple there might have been nothing there, after all. A river of darkness flowing toward the sea.

His foot slipped and they both nearly fell. His leg hurt. It must have been banged, he believed, while he was unconscious in those amazing fever dreams.

"Are you all right, Sir Henry?" she asked.

"Yes," he said, softly. She was quite strong, which surprised him. And seemed calm and sure, unlike his first impression of her.

"We're almost there."

"Yes. Where?"

But "Louise," made the difference, he decided. The compromise.

The woman after the broken heart that like . . . how does it go? . . . like a broken mirror that now shows, no . . . "as broken glasses show a hundred lesser faces, so my ragges of heart can like, wish, and adore, but after one such love, can love, no more . . ." magnificently put, Dr. Donne . . . youth is the time for imaginary love that can be perfect but a flower

250

never to be plucked because, like so much else, it rarely survives marriage....

They were just entering the clouds that swept steadily in lightless waves across the immense rooftop where he could distinguish no hint of the biplane.

Let all of it have been just insanity and fever or some gas in the damned smoke, he thought, *and let the dream die and the visions and all the mysteries I longed for in my unhappy, adolescent heart...let there have been no tortured demigoddess clutching desperately at long-lost and cursed love...no ancient souls warring for hopeless and faded victories...O God!...*

He sighed. They were on the level roof now, just over their heads in the thinner fumes, the harsh mountain at their backs. His eyes teared.

"I know it is straight on from here," she said. "I know it."

Let it just be that they were merely people who drowned in their illusions as we are both likely to do, shortly...Ah, but I should love to see home again....If my poor boy had lived....Some of the tears were wept now. Had that been the case I should never have come here....

Level with their eyes now, just the sea of hot, black smoke as if their bodies had melted into arid, formless substance.

"Straight on," he said, not wanting to tell her they were going to die there, breathing fumes of blackness. "Yes."

"You must keep trying, Sir Henry."

"Yes. Of course."

There was no question of that. That was all he wanted now and he forced his mind to hold just to the task at hand, keeping his awkward, wasted body moving from one job to the next without elaboration until it finally failed him into oblivion.

Let her believe what she must...

So that even when they'd actually stumbled into the wing it made no difference because, after swallowing some water and gnawing a strip of jerky, it merely meant they were going to perish in slightly improved circumstances. He accepted it and let her help him up into the cockpit. The gases didn't sting quite so much at that level and it was almost comfortable to sit with his head back and stare across the endless black current at where the mountains met the dull sky.

"I suppose it's an English sky, anyway," he said, almost smiling.

She was at the controls.

"Can you fly it?" he wondered. Her head and shoulders were fairly clear where she worked the spark and gas levers. He thought that might make a better end.

"I don't know," she said. "I watched him. And I can try."

"Of course."

"I have to climb down and spin the propellers. Once it is moving I shall jump back aboard. I am going to find him, you know, Sir Henry. That is all I think about now."

"I understand."

She was lowering herself over the side. It was a little difficult with one hand frozen into a fist but the hardships and outdoor life had toughened her more than she realized. She still felt as if she clutched some mildly hot stone.

"Something has to be done," she said.

He shut his eyes because they burned but blinked them open again when the image was still there, as if waiting for him. He wondered if he should ever be able to sleep again before dying.

"I agree," he responded, to be supportive.

"We can follow the river back to the sea. The smoke won't make any difference once we're in the air."

"No. Naturally not."

And then the plane trembled as she snapped down the blades on the first engine. It popped and hissed. Spat oil. Again. A pair of sputters. Finally it turned over and the plane began to shake itself forward, turning left. She ducked around and got the other motor going. He knelt over and got a grip on her knotted hand as the aircraft started to slip past her into the dense billows. She had to run alongside now, coughing and gasping.

"Come on," he cried. "Jump!"

Because if she fell she'd simply vanish into the smoke and it seemed horrible for her to be left for last while he went over the edge to smash into the valley.

So he kept hold even when she slipped and dragged and

his yawing hand went numb from the side of the cockpit cutting into the armpit. He strained and gasped sooty air and put his whole strength into it and more than strength as if everything depended on never letting her go. Until his sight was torn by blackness and red pain, the aircraft bouncing and veering in a wide circle (from the drag of her weight) the blades spilling churned blackness, her face vanishing at times under the dark stream until he believed his arm was about to be pulled from its socket and he gritted his teeth and thought that was fine because he would never let her go.

"Never!" he yelled, waiting (almost hoping for) the end of the roof and the plunge, not realizing they were circling just under the choking surface and that the motor would fail from clogging long before they'd spiral incrementally far enough to fall.

His hand slipped from her wrist to fist but no further. He believed it a kind of hell but that too was fine because he would never let go.

And then, somehow, her other hand caught his forearm and she levered high enough to swing one leg up and over. Moments later, black with ash, she lay gasping inside. Haggard fell back, his hand still gripping the fist she couldn't open as the plane plunged straight ahead now, churning through the blinding stuff.

"I hope that was my last act," he whispered, the sound lost in the rush of choking air and the motor rasp. "I am not up to another."

And then he felt her hand go and knew (because he couldn't have seen that far even if he looked down) that she was trying to the end, crawling to the controls she only partly understood. At least his part was over and he could stare up where the fumes were thinnest. The gray overcast was opening in long rents now. His eyes automatically tracked the brighter streaks.

Just as the plane suddenly tilted and dropped off the edge into space and suffocating blackness he saw a few soft sprays of sunlight and a flicker of blue. He had been close to fainting from the strain so the sudden rush of blood did it and he tried to keep just the sunlight and shard of sky in his mind to hold away the image he dreaded as he finally went out. . . .

The next thing he knew there was warmth and brightness everywhere. And a sound he took for soaring, chorused voices. He felt soft and comfortable and it was a long time (he believed) before he opened his eyes. And there was wind and sunlight and cloudless sky in shimmering, blinding brilliance.

It took moments before he understood that the sound was the rattling buzz of the engines and that he was staring at a perfect sky past a wing stained jet black (as was everything else on board) by the volcanic ash. The plane was sluggish and the motors uneven but they staggered along.

He blinked and breathed and smiled, a little.

"It is a miracle, I suppose," he said, not loud enough for her to hear up there.

Therefore, it is possible we will descend intact . . . I must have slept . . .

She sat with the stick in her hands and her feet on the wooden pedals just as she'd seen Woody do. She'd learned fast, pushing which did what. And he'd made a point of how much fuel they had and so on, and, in any case, there was no sense worrying about that. She simply aimed along the curve of the river with the mountains of Kôr at her back. The blackness was slowly spreading over the whole swamp where they'd come as if to blot it out from all the bright world around. The river had gradually gone to brown and, far ahead, she could see it glinted bright blue in the terrific sunlight.

She knew she was a different woman though she wasn't really thinking about herself now. But she knew it. She was calm and ready and determined, in a less brittle way than before. Because she'd been to the end of dreams she was safe from that now too.

She realized her father was no doubt dead but she wasn't going to grieve yet or consider all he'd meant to her. She remembered him as he once was when she was small: a lean man always smelling of stale pipesmoke and (she'd believed) dust, rarely at home, leaning back at an angle, her mother (who was still small and round-faced and quiet) listening from her favorite chair in the parlor while he paced by the French windows that opened into the little yard where the plants seemed always half-brown and some leaves dry even in summer ... while he paced and talked fluently, waving one arm as if to embrace so much ... so much ...

She bit her lower lip and adjusted the course. The wings dipped too far but she caught it and corrected. Tried not to think about getting back on the ground. She kept her clenched left hand in her lap. The heat she felt in it seemed to pulse, slightly, like a slow and steady heartbeat.

"I shall find him," she said.

Haggard was leaning against the side of the cockpit looking down at the bright river in the afternoon sunslant. In a few hours they passed over weeks of agony. That amazed him. The land spread out green and mistless here and he could see the glitter of the ocean.

She was trying to ease the plane down incrementally. It bounced and dipped alarmingly. She bit her lip and struggled. Overcorrected. They pitched and then hit an air pocket dropped them so hard Haggard's teeth clacked together.

"Are you all right?" he called over, leaning forward, one hand holding the upper wing.

"I don't know, really," she managed to say as she lost too much speed and skidded into a stall. The craft reared up like a balked horse and fell off on a wing, starting to spin. They were nearly over the bay now and he glimpsed (as he braced against the twisting drop) the shimmer of white beach and the white buildings where the natives had attacked them. Then the sea, the promontory with the skull-shaped rock that should have been warning enough. Then the same again ... again ...

She kicked the pedals and thrashed the stick around but (in those days) very few master pilots knew how to free those delicate aircraft from the forces of a spin, much less an accidental amateur.

It took a long time for them to spiral down the few hundred feet and Haggard kept thinking how beautiful the sky was and no wonder poor Woody loved it so ... and what glories there were in the wind-washed landscape, scents of growing green, sheen of sunlight on water ... like strength and understanding, tenderness and love ... there was love there, in that moment, riding doomed wings down, a benediction in the kiss of color, whisper of wind, the rich earth itself . . .

His mind was flooded by the brilliance around them as they spun almost delicately and Emma kept trying though there was no point in it at that altitude. And then they hit, almost perfectly flat.

The shock drove him down into his seat and, after a brilliant flash as his head jerked violently past the sun's blaze, there was a dull impact and darkness (he nearly thought) struck him over the head.

To Emma the blow was a splintering crash, stun and shatter of foamy spray rising over her and then a blast of soundlessness as she was driven through the floor of the cockpit into a strange, dim, greenish glow and she saw the woman Haggard had called Ayesha lifting Woody's bleeding, broken-looking body into the lightning-colored geyser of fire, and her mind said:

Even from here even from death I shall come to you, my love. . . .

Her senses spun. She was suspended beyond time. Her clenched fist seemed to burst into golden brightness as if she'd crushed some of the sun's substance into her palm. She felt strange joy and wonder, spinning slowly upward now, feet above her head, breaking the surface into blinding daylight, lungs bursting for air. Broke into a steady roar she didn't yet know was low surf and shouting voices that a moment later she realized were English.

Brown uniformed men wading out to her where she now trod water . . . and then her bare feet (she was naked) found sand as she drifted into shore and she began to bounce and stand, wiping the sting of salt from her eyes.

Hands had her. Soldiers. British. She twisted her head around and saw the wreckage floating into the beach, the steady onshore wind crackling the fabric of the bent wings and driving them like a sail with Haggard in his seat as it slowly sank and turned, grinding on the sand, spreading the soot around it as the waves washed away the smoke of Kôr. Half a dozen soldiers were in the sea. Others lined the shore. A wiry-looking man in a white suit and pith helmet was wading to the cockpit.

"Hello, miss," the red mustached sergeant holding her

arm, said, as she staggered out of the waves with him. He kept his eyes averted with a twinkle. "Quite a rum descent, eh?"

"Yes," she responded, absently. Someone wrapped a light tropical sheet over her shoulders. She was watching them lift Haggard from the broken cockpit. He raised one hand to her, weary but not feeble. "Poor Woody loved that machine," she whispered.

"What, miss?" the sergeant asked.

"It was a fine lady," she told him. "It saved us."

"Did it, miss?"

She sat down on the hot, white sand which felt good on her bare bottom under the sheet. The sergeant squatted beside her while the others kept a slight distance.

She looked back upriver past the negroid skull set in frozen ferocity or maybe simple fear because it was too blurred by time to tell. She stared at where the water curved away into a wall of heat-shimmered green and blue.

She was wondering where she would start looking for the two of them. Well, that could wait a little. It might take her whole life. Her father might have understood, she decided. Yes, he might very well have understood.

She sat there and felt the sun begin to steam the wet from the sheet and dry her hair. It felt so good.

"Are you hurt, miss?"

She glanced at him and then back upriver.

"Not really," she responded. He had a friendly face. Strange to think his profession involved murder.

She understood so much. She would find Woody Shea (or whatever he might be called now) and there was more than looking because wherever she went a precious drop of the light would go with her now. Yes. The light.

Raised her closed left hand and opened it effortlessly this time. A piece of broken crystal had pierced her palm when she'd fallen in the chamber of the flame. Slow drops of blood oozed around it. One, she noted, then another. But there was no pain. It caught the sun in a flare of dazzle.

"What's that then, miss?" Red mustaches bent closer.

"Look at it, Sergeant," she told him, holding her hand out to him while still looking upriver at the misty shimmer of horizon, feeling *déjà vu,* that she'd said these words before, long before. "Look and learn." The refraction spattered his face with rainbowed gold. As he squinted and blinked.

"That's something," he said.

As Haggard went unconscious he was falling through churning, furious smokerush, his white wings trailing, shattered golden eyes full of stern pity, seeing an image formed of fumes, a gloating, angry face because the bird fell above a battlefield where two endless lines of men crushed together in searing flame and shock and boiling smoke into torn, bleeding, broken heaps (he knew it was the war in Europe) the green countryside, farms, villages leveled, flaming while shells shrieked and rent the tense air and churned the earth and armies into poisoned muck and bloody mush. . . .

The bird fell and saw (what Haggard had tried not to see) how the destroyer spirit, thwarted at Kôr, had found another door into the world. There, on fields of unmatched agony it had regathered in smoke and reached down to pour itself into its chosen vessel because the light had been sunk in black clouds and there was so much death and pain that the law keeping it out, the wholesome bindings of nature, flesh and earth, had recoiled and it had poured in. Saw the chosen face down there, pale, avid, brooding, ecstatic all at once while the shells smashed around him and his fellows. They were all charging wildly toward a line of trees through choking billows while sparks flickered among the shattered trunks, bullets ripping, spattering, scything, chewing the ranks to shreds, the chosen one charging, sprayed with the blood of his comrades, racing in fierce joy into the jaws of doom as men were knocked flat or flew to pieces on every side. Cloudiness whirled around him, lit by inner, lurid red flashes of power and fury, the face filling Haggard's mind now (the bird vanished) the burning, hollow, glaring grayish eyes, beaked jut of nose, bony forehead, drooping mustache, an ordinary soldier in *feldgrau* uniform, spiked helmet; ordinary with a titanic, cloudy, winged darkness riding on his back and twisting down into his soul, lit by the fitful flamelight awakened by shock and terror, shells and blood and pain . . .

And then Haggard was fully conscious again. The sunbright

made him wince and he looked, without recognition, at a face close to his in a white tropical helmet, rimless glasses reflecting the vibrance of sea and sky.

The mustaches freed his memory while he was still talking within the vision or dream:

"What horror . . . what horror . . . our world . . ."

"Rider," Kipling said, bending near as they laid him down on the hot sand and covered him with a blanket. Kipling's tropical linen suit was sopping wet. "Good God, he's all skin and bone."

"Rudy," Haggard said, blinking, voice raw. Kipling took his hand firmly.

"You're fine now, Rider. Thank God I came here." He smiled faintly. "Did you practice that landing maneuver much?"

"Ah," murmured his friend. "It went rather well, now that you mention it." Smiled.

"One or two more would suit, eh?" Kipling said, straightening up, putting his pipe between his teeth. "I didn't tell 'Louie,' naturally." He slapped at his wet pants. A young lieutenant handed him a tin of matches. "Thanks." Lit one into his cupped hands but never got it past the breeze to the pipe.

"Want a smoke, sir?" the slim officer asked.

Haggard widened his eyes and shook his head.

"God, no," he said. "A smoke? My God, not at all."

"I see, sir." Then: "The medical officer is on his way, Mr. Kipling."

"Excellent. We'll have him right in short order, I think." Squatted beside Haggard. "What were you saying earlier?"

"Saying?"

"Something to do with 'horror,' I think."

"Ah," Haggard sighed, turning his head away and looking toward Emma, who was still sitting under the pale sheet like (he thought) some young priestess from some ancient land off on a pilgrimage. He checked his reflex of imagination. The soldier who'd just bent over her hand, straightened up again. He looked (at the distance) thoughtful and uneasy, Haggard felt.

"A dream," he told Kipling.

"Yes?" Kipling tried another match but the light failed and he realized the tobacco was wet. "Damn."

"A horrible dream."

"The thing is to save the story until you're fit again, Rider." Kipling stood up. "And I have located some dry mixture."

"Yes," agreed his friend, still watching her sitting there down the beach, the reach of river melding her into the haze and shimmer of distance where the river flowed down out of the smoke and mystery into the unending, untainted renewal of the sea. "We'll have to talk," he said.

Like some priestess, he couldn't help thinking again, *at the beginning of some eternal quest....*

From the beginning of his college days—Columbia University 1966–1969, where he studied English and Musical Composition—Richard Monaco has published and edited poetry; composed musical works which were performed and broadcast; and been commissioned to write screenplays by Universal, MGM, and Columbia Pictures. His novel, *Parsival or a Knight's Tale*, published in 1977, was a main selection of the Quality Paperback Book Club, nominated for the Pulitzer prize—and was a bestseller. Since then he has had over half a dozen books published, including *The Final Quest*, another Pulitzer prize nominee, *Runes, Broken Stone, Blood and Dreams* and *Journey to the Flame*. He is currently at work on a novel, *Shadowgold*, which Bantam Spectra will publish in late 1986.

Special Offer
Buy a Bantam Book
for only 50¢.

Now you can have an up-to-date listing of Bantam's hundreds of titles plus take advantage of our unique and exciting bonus book offer. A special offer which gives you the opportunity to purchase a Bantam book for only 50¢. Here's how!

By ordering any five books at the regular price per order, you can also choose any other single book listed (up to a $4.95 value) for just 50¢. Some restrictions do apply, but for further details why not send for Bantam's listing of titles today!

Just send us your name and address and we will send you a catalog!

FANTASY AND SCIENCE FICTION
FAVORITES

Bantam Spectra brings you the recognized classics as well as the current favorites in fantasy and science fiction. Here you will find the most recent titles by the most respected authors in the genre.

R. A. MacAvoy

☐	23575-3	DAMIANO	$2.75
☐	24102-8	DAMIANO'S LUTE	$2.75
☐	24370-5	RAPHAEL	$2.75
☐	23205-3	TEA WITH THE BLACK DRAGON	$2.75
☐	25260-7	THE BOOK OF KELLS	$3.50

Robert Silverberg

☐	25097-3	LORD VALENTINE'S CASTLE	$3.95
☐	22928-1	MAJIPOOR CHRONICLES	$3.50
☐	24502-3	TO OPEN THE SKY	$2.75
☐	24494-9	VALENTINE PONTIFEX	$3.95

Harry Harrison

☐	22647-9	HOMEWORLD	$2.50
☐	20780-6	STARWORLD	$2.50
☐	20774-1	WHEELWORLD	$2.50
☐	22759-9	STAINLESS STEEL RAT FOR PRESIDENT	$2.75
☐	25395-6	STAINLESS STEEL RAT WANTS YOU!	$2.95

Prices and availability subject to change without notice.

Buy them at your local bookstore or use this handy coupon for ordering:

Bantam Books, Inc., Dept. SF2A, 414 East Golf Road, Des Plaines, Ill. 60016

Please send me the books I have checked above. I am enclosing $_____ (please add $1.25 to cover postage and handling. Send check or money order—no cash or C.O.D.'s please).

Mr/Ms _____

Address _____

City/State _____ Zip _____

SF2A—9/85

Please allow four to six weeks for delivery. This offer expires 3/86.

Read the powerful novels of award-winning author

ROBERT SILVERBERG

One of the most brilliant and beloved science fiction authors of our time, Robert Silverberg has been honored with two Hugo awards and four Nebula awards. His stirring combination of vivid imagery, evocative prose, and rousing storytelling promise his audience a reading experience like no other.

- ☐ THE CONGLOMEROID COCKTAIL PARTY (25077 • $2.95)
- ☐ VALENTINE PONTIFEX (24494 • $3.95)
- ☐ LORD OF DARKNESS (24362 • $3.95)
- ☐ LORD VALENTINE'S CASTLE (25097 • $3.95)
- ☐ MAJIPOOR CHRONICLES (25530 • $3.95)

Prices and availability subject to change without notice.

Read these fine works by Robert Silverberg, on sale now wherever Bantam paperbacks are sold or use the handy coupon below for ordering.